INCAS

Book Three

The Light of
Machu Picchu

INCAS

The Puma's Shadow
(Book One)

The Gold of Cuzco
(Book Two)

INCAS

The Light of
Machu Picchu

A. B. Daniel

Translated by Alex Gilly

**POCKET
BOOKS**

LONDON · SYDNEY · NEW YORK · TOKYO · SINGAPORE · TORONTO

First published in Great Britain by Simon & Schuster UK Ltd, 2003
This edition first published by Pocket Books, 2003
An imprint of Simon and Schuster UK Ltd
A Viacom company

Original title
Inca
La Lumière du Machu Picchu

International rights management for XO Editions:
Susanna Lea Associates
© XO Editions, 2001. All rights reserved.

English translation copyright © Alex Gilly, 2003

1 3 5 7 9 10 8 6 4 2

Simon & Schuster UK Ltd
Africa House
64–78 Kingsway
London WC2B 6AH

www.simonsays.co.uk

Simon & Schuster Australia
Sydney

A CIP catalogue record for this book is available
from the British Library

ISBN 0-7434-1606-6

Typeset by Palimpsest Book Production Limited,
Polmont, Stirlingshire
Printed and bound in Great Britain by
Cox & Wyman Ltd, Reading, Berks

PART 1

CHAPTER 1

Cuzco, 1 May 1536

N O ONE TOOK ANY NOTICE OF GABRIEL MONTELUCAR
y Flores squatting at the corner of Gonzalo Pizarro's
cancha. It was approaching noon.

The tunic he had been wearing for weeks was grimy enough
not to draw attention, and he had rubbed clay into his cheeks to
camouflage his blond stubble. To the Spaniards, he looked like any
other squalid Indian in rags, one of the many who now thronged
Cuzco's alleys. And with his square hat with its odd, pointed angles
pulled low over his face, he looked, to the Cuzco Indians, like yet
another peasant from Titicaca. A small bronze club hung from a
leather strap under his *unku*: and in this humble weapon he had
invested all his hope.

Gabriel had arrived in town at daybreak, having traveled by night
to avoid the endless stream of warriors called to arms by Manco
and Villa Oma. He had walked from Calca without halting. He
had become lost once or twice in the darkness, and his journey had
taken longer than it should have. But his rage and suffering had
driven him on, denying him any rest.

Only now, as he squatted at the base of the vast, sun-warmed
wall, did Gabriel become aware of the hunger and fatigue that
was making his limbs stiffen. Yet the thought of heading off
in search of a meal and a rest never once crossed his mind.
His eyes remained fixed on the *cancha*'s door. He would have

time enough later to eat and sleep – if those needs still had any meaning by then.

He was here to kill Gonzalo. It was his sole remaining mission.

For the better part of two hours, he saw only servants and a few courtesans coming and going from the Governor's brother's house. For Gabriel, they were for the most part new faces, men whose demeanor and dress were still redolent of Spain: they stamped their heels hard on the dusty ground with all the manifest arrogance of recently arrived masters.

Gabriel was extremely tired: he could barely keep his eyes open. Sometimes he trembled from thirst and hunger. Yet nothing on earth would have convinced him to give up his vigil so that he could find food and water. He fantasized about the moment when he would strike Gonzalo, at last ridding the world of the man's wickedness. He took a few coca leaves from the cloth pouch slung round his neck, next to his skin under his tunic, and chewed them deliberately until his hunger faded.

The dwarf's terrible tale still lingered in his mind: 'Gonzalo entered Anamaya's room while she slept. She only woke when he already had his hands on her. She cried out. They fought. Manco wanted to kill him on the spot, but Anamaya feared that the Strangers would seek their vengeance against the Emperor. So instead, we fled Cuzco before dawn . . .'

Gabriel had been turning these abhorrent words over and over in his mind for days. The words had become images that inspired an icy hatred in him, a fury that fired his nerves more than physical hunger or thirst. With each breath he took, he savored his vengeful plan as though it was nectar. His eyes remained wide open, his swollen fingers tight around the hilt of his bludgeon.

Gabriel sweated in the afternoon heat. The light and the warmth of the sun befuddled him, and eventually he fell asleep, his mouth full of dust, before Gonzalo had come out of the house. He sank into a nightmare: he saw Anamaya, cold, distant from him, her face hardened with determination. She wrapped her arms around her gold husband and said to Gabriel:

'We must take up arms against the Strangers – against you – because only our love and courage will keep the Mountains and our Ancestors from slipping into the void. I shall be at my gold husband's side when he fights, for that is my right and proper place. You must distance yourself from me, my love . . .'

He wanted to protest, to explain to her that they couldn't confront one another as though they were enemies. But although his lips moved, no words came out. He made a heroic effort to be heard. He begged, imploring Anamaya to soften her hard gaze. Nothing. No sound, no cry emerged from his mouth. He woke so suddenly that he heard his own sob. Haunted as he was by the vision of Anamaya, he didn't immediately recognize his surroundings.

The feeling of helplessness that Gabriel had experienced in his nightmare followed him from sleep into wakefulness. And then, as though driving a dagger deeper into his own chest, he recalled the answer he had given Anamaya after their passionate night together at Calca:

'So, we must fight one another. If during the battle your place is at Manco's side rather than mine, Anamaya, then it means that I have become a "Stranger" in your eyes. And if that's the case, then my place is with the Strangers.'

Anamaya's lips had trembled with hurt. Stroking his cheek, she had murmured:

'You are the puma, my beloved. You are the only man who can reach me, whether here in this world or in the next. You are the only one who can touch my heart and show me the joy of the world.'

Gabriel smiled, not realizing that tears were running down through the cracked clay that covered his cheeks.

Yes – there was no doubt that she loved him as much as he loved her.

And yet, it was impossible between them. The distance was too great: the sad, alienating realities standing between the sorceress wife of an Inca lord dead for many years past and a Stranger who was nothing, even among his old brothers-in-arms, were too many and too strong.

All that remained for him to do was to kill Gonzalo.

And it would be a welcome gift from his destiny if he were to die at the same time as his enemy.

What Gabriel had been waiting for finally happened shortly before night enveloped Cuzco.

A great hullabaloo woke him from his reverie. Terrible cries rang out through the alleyways. Gabriel sat up, his knees cracking, his thighs painfully stiff. A huge pig emerged from a nearby street, its mouth wide open – an enormous, hairy swine as black as night, a true Andalusian *cerrano*, weighing fifty pounds at least. It bared its canines, fearsome as those of a wild bear and sharp enough to gut a horse.

From behind it burst a herd of other hogs – at least thirty of them, running with their heads down, squealing as though their throats were being slit. The males stormed straight ahead, crashing their heads into the *cancha*'s wall, while the big-bellied sows dragged their udders through the dust. A dozen terrified piglets added their shrill cries from behind and scurried between the legs of the inept, yelling Indians who were trying as best they could to herd the foul-smelling pack.

These mud-splattered peasants – recently promoted to swine-herds – thrashed their long sticks through the air; yet they did not dare use them to strike the pigs' rumps. Rather, they seemed ready to bolt in terror each time a piglet bumped into them. A crowd of locals, gathered at a judicious distance, looked on, laughing at this strange cavalcade.

Gabriel let out a roar as he bounded into the middle of the alleyway. He kicked a few plump pig buttocks, grabbed a young male by its ears, and so halted the chaotic flow of pork. The pigs stopped dead in their tracks, instantly ceased their squealing, raised their snouts, and gazed around complacently.

The swineherds, flabbergasted, gazed suspiciously at the new-comer. Gabriel greeted them in Quechua to reassure them. But when he asked where the animals were bound, he met with silence. He realized that his accent must have bewildered the Indians as much as his attire, the dried mud flaking off his face, and the green coca juice dribbling from his lips. Eventually, one of them pointed at Gonzalo's house.

'They're for the Stranger. They're his animals. He had them brought from Cajamarca. He plans to eat them.'

The man seemed amazed by the idea, though his tone remained deferential. In a flash, Gabriel understood that chance was smiling upon him.

'I shall help you,' he said, 'I know how to manage these beasts.'

It still took unusual effort to get the entire herd through the *cancha*'s narrow trapezoid door.

And once in, the pigs continued to cause quite a commotion: the excited animals alarmed the Indian servant girls, bolted around the courtyard, knocked over and broke several jars, and startled the horses that were being groomed.

Gonzalo's house hadn't changed much in the two years since Gabriel had last visited it. Solid doors now divided the rooms, doors finely worked by Spanish carpenters, and a bridle rail had been set up in the courtyard.

Gabriel abandoned the pigs and stood in the centre of the yard. He had only been there a short while when he heard shouts and laughter approaching. He recognized that hated voice.

A small group of Spaniards appeared, among them Gonzalo who was wearing a ruffled shirt, velvet breeches, and shining boots. The other men were a couple of his courtiers. They took no notice of Gabriel, mistaking him for an Indian, and continued their frivolous play. One of them grabbed a young servant-girl by the waist, upended her, and brought her face to face with the fiercest piglet, 'introducing' them. Before the young hog had a chance to charge her, however, Gabriel whipped out his studded club and brought it down hard on the idiot's arm, forcing him to release the young girl.

'By the blood of Christ!' cried the fop. 'You damned monkey, you almost broke my wrist!'

Gonzalo and his mates were furious. They made to strike the stranger, but when Gabriel threw back his hood, they stopped dead in their tracks. He rubbed away some of the mud from his cheeks with the back of his hands, revealing who he really was.

After the initial shock, however, Gonzalo quickly recovered his old sarcastic aplomb.

'Now isn't this a pleasant surprise! My friends, allow me to present to you Gabriel Montelucar y Flores, who has come with the swine. Well, my dear fellow, it seems that you have found your proper place at last!'

The others had already unsheathed their swords. Gabriel ignored them.

'Rumor had it that you had disappeared, run away or even died,' continued Gonzalo, hitting his rhetorical stride. 'But no, here you are, as alive as can be – and as filthy as ever, I find. Am I to understand that my dear brother Francisco has at last decided to be done with you?'

Gabriel's eyes shone with violent rage. Gonzalo and his side-kicks instinctively took a couple of steps back.

'Hell awaits you, Gonzalo,' snarled Gabriel, swinging his club. 'The day has come for you to take your place there.'

'Holà! If you think that you're going to frighten me with that . . . implement!' guffawed Gonzalo.

'I'm going to crush your balls with this *implement*, Gonzalo. You're out of luck. I'm not one of those who waits for God to punish scum of your sort. I shall have the pleasure of doing it myself.'

Gonzalo's companions tried to disguise their fear, frowning fiercely. Gabriel lunged forward. His bronze club clashed against their swords, and he thrust them aside with a fierce back-handed swipe. Gonzalo jumped back and pulled a dagger from his breeches. He made a short, awkward stab at Gabriel's arm. But his weapon sliced through thin air and, meeting no resistance, he lost his balance. Gabriel ducked to avoid the other blades slashing down at him and he simultaneously dealt Gonzalo a severe blow to the thigh.

Gonzalo crumpled in a heap, screaming in pain. Gabriel made to continue his attack, but a sword cut through his *unku* and hissed past his ribs. He rolled to the ground as the two Spaniards still standing whipped their swords back and forth through the air above him. He held them off with his club, but its handle, repeatedly gashed by their blades, was weakening.

Gabriel thought of the horrible powerlessness that he had seen so many times when Inca warriors had had their weapons smashed by Spanish steel. Like them, he would soon have nothing with which to defend himself. But suddenly an idea came to him.

He let out an enraged cry and windmilled his club like a sling before flinging it at his nearest enemy's face. The Spaniard didn't have time to dodge and the bronze bludgeon slammed into the side of his head, smashing his jaw and splintering his bones with a loud cracking sound. The man collapsed, unconscious before he hit the ground. The other man froze in terror. Making the most of his adversary's temporary immobility, Gabriel dove onto one of the piglets that had been panicked by the fight, picked it up, and brandished it at arm's length, like some strange, wriggling shield – just as his assailant recovered his senses and lunged forward to run Gabriel through. The sword plunged through the animal as though its flesh was butter, and became embedded so deeply that the weapon stuck fast. Heaving with all his might, Gabriel flung the piglet across the courtyard. The sword twisted deeper into the young hog, tearing the poor animal's guts out, and the beast squealed in agony as it landed with a thud. Gabriel kicked the now disarmed coxcomb in the gut, disabling him instantly.

He threw himself at Gonzalo and grabbed him by the throat like some demented demon.

'It's over, Gonzalo,' Gabriel growled. 'It's all over for you – the world has no use for your kind!'

Hypnotized as he was by the sight of the eyes popping out of Gonzalo's all but asphyxiated head, Gabriel didn't hear the voices nor the footsteps approaching from behind. A steel-capped boot slammed into his ribs, and it was surprise as much as pain that made him lose his breath.

He let go of Gonzalo's neck and fell across his enemy's legs. Another blow, this one to his head, almost knocked him out before he had a chance to pick himself up. He was hardly conscious of someone holding his hands behind his back. His rage and frustration gave him one last burst of energy. Gathering all his remaining strength, Gabriel tried to stand, hoping that whoever was pinioning him would finish him off for good.

But then the back of his neck exploded in pain, and he fell into blackness.

The liquid dark became first of all a confused red before slowly brightening into a lucid agony. Gabriel's head felt as though someone was hammering nails into it. He was surprised to discover that he could feel his hands, and that they obeyed him. He ran his fingers over his face and opened his eyes, letting them adjust to the now blinding light. He took stock of his surroundings.

He was lying on a beaten-earth floor. He recognized the room: it was the same one that he had stayed in a long time ago now, before Don Francisco had ordered him to leave Cuzco.

Still groggy, Gabriel sat up.

A man as round and large as a barrel was carefully hammering closed a shackle around Gabriel's right ankle, its chain fixed to the wall. He worked with astonishing precision, despite his size. Gabriel noticed that his black eyes displayed neither cruelty nor pleasure, merely weariness. Four others surrounded him and gazed upon their prisoner with grim, menacing stares.

'What's your name?' asked Gabriel.

'Enrique Hermoso, Don Gabriel. But my friends call me Kikeh.'

'Well then, Kikeh, do what you must do, and don't worry too much.'

Kikeh sighed and continued with his task. Gabriel gritted his teeth. He tried to distract himself by examining the others, whom he did not know. They wore thick new leather cuirasses emblazoned with the Pizarro coat of arms: a pine cone and apples flanked by a pair of upright bears. Also new were their halberds with sickle-shaped blades, which they held carelessly against their shoulders. And it was with no real surprise that Gabriel saw them make way for a large man sporting a well-groomed beard and wearing a spotless starched lace ruff: Don Hernando Pizarro.

'I shall be finished this instant, my lord,' said the fat man.

He brought the hammer down onto the shackle one last time. But the tool slipped and came down on Gabriel's ankle instead, bruising it horribly and provoking a cry of pain. The jailer chortled awkwardly as he said:

'Well, with this chain on his paw, Don Hernando, he's not about to cause any trouble, much less dance a saraband!'

'Just so, Enrique,' said Hernando, amused. 'Rather, we shall invite *señor* Montelucar y Flores to a dance of our own devising.'

As the fat man rose to his feet, breathing heavily, Gabriel got up too, gritting his teeth again to smother any hint of the dizziness gripping him. His ankle was so painful that he could barely stand.

Hernando shook his head.

'The passing of time has seen little change in you, Don Gabriel. I leave you hot under the collar, and I find you exactly the same some thirty months later! Although, looking at your clothes, I see that you have changed somewhat after all. Now you are even lower, even closer to the manure that is your proper abode!'

Gabriel spat blood.

'Very well,' Hernando said. 'That explains the stench floating about since your arrival.'

One of the men in the leather cuirasses made to move forward, but Hernando held up his hand.

'This time, Montelucar, you won't be able to count on Don Francisco to save your skin. I am master here now. My good brother the Governor was so happy to see me back from Spain that he very officially nominated me Lieutenant Governor. What's more, the scales have at last fallen from his eyes concerning you. He has learned how you abandoned the mission with which he had entrusted you.'

'It won't help you,' said Gabriel, leaning against the wall.

'A grandiose title can never hide the true mediocrity of its bearer. Pig's shit you are, and pig's shit you will remain, Don Hernando.'

Hernando slapped Gabriel hard in the face with his gloved hand, splitting his prisoner's upper lip and knocking him back to the ground.

'You're in no position to be insolent, you whoreson dog!' spat Hernando. 'I could crush you like the insect that you are this very instant. I could leave your fate in the hands of Gonzalo, whose most fervent wish is to gut you with a spoon! But that would be too good for you. In Toledo they were particularly insistent on the importance of trials. Well then, I'll give you a trial, my friend, in due and proper form! That way all of Spain shall know why we hung the bastard excrement of the Montelucar y Flores family. All of Spain shall learn the name of the Crown's first traitor in the New World!'

An odd snigger came from Gabriel's bloody mouth.

'You'll have to hold your trial quickly, Hernando. Your charming brothers treated Manco and his people with such considerate courtesy that the Incas are now baying for blood. Manco and his generals have amassed tens of thousands of men in the valleys north of Cuzco. I saw them with my very own eyes. There are more than a hundred thousand of them! Tomorrow or the day after, they'll number twice that, and then they'll be here.'

His words had the desired effect on Hernando's men. They looked intently at one another, their stares hard and grave. And Hernando uttered a laugh a little too disdainful, too obviously defiant, as he said:

'Well, that's what I call news! If those wretches imagine that they're going to take back their city with their sticks and stones, then they shall be cut to pieces once again. If I were you, Don Gabriel, I wouldn't place too much faith in them. And since those savages can't save you from your inevitable fate, I suggest you turn to prayer!'

CHAPTER 2

Cuzco, 3 May 1536

GABRIEL'S CELL LACKED EVEN A STRAW MATTRESS. THE jailer had left him a jug of water and three ears of boiled corn in a corner. But he hardly touched them in two days. He opened his eyes slowly and saw a fat man coming to check if he was still alive.

'Don Gabriel?'

'I'm here, Kikeh. At least, what remains of me is here . . .'

'I'm so sorry about . . .'

Kikeh mimed the motion of a hammer missing its mark. Gabriel raised his hand languidly and gave a choked-sounding laugh.

'I thought you were more dexterous than that. So, I assume you didn't do it deliberately, then.'

'Of course not, Don Gabriel, I promise you! I even went so far as to disobey Don Hernando's orders by leaving you your . . .'

The jailer pointed at Gabriel's *chuspa*. Gabriel had chewed all the coca leaves it had contained to alleviate the pain radiating through his muscles. He had chewed so many leaves, in fact, that the bland paste they had formed in his mouth had swollen to the size of an egg.

'Thank you, Kikeh,' he said quietly. 'Now please let me be.'

But instead the fat man cradled Gabriel's neck in his hand and poured water into his mouth. Gabriel could smell the tart stench of the jailer's sweat and, in his extremely weakened state, this human closeness seemed so miraculous to him that tears welled up in his eyes.

Then he was alone once more.

His fatigue had diminished somewhat, but it had given way to a nausea that he couldn't shake off, not even when he stretched out flat on the floor. Sudden bouts of fever left him shivering and curled up on himself at the foot of the wall, his fingers clenched around the links of his chain as though he was holding on to keep from falling into the void.

He was frightened of falling asleep. Yet he nodded off frequently into dreadful nightmares. He witnessed a series of images so startlingly real that he could hardly believe they were only dreams.

Gabriel had a lucid vision of himself on his horse, traveling across a salt pan whiter than bleached linen. He saw his bay's legs snap as they broke through the salt crust into a hole. He had forgotten the name of the desert. Water gurgled between his horse's hoofs and its broken legs. The animal looked at him imploringly with its big round eyes. He saw himself staying completely immobile for a long time, his arms wrapped around his animal's head, the sun scorching them both. Then he saw his dagger suddenly piercing the horse's throat.

A deluge of blood – far more than the animal could have actually contained – streamed from it without coagulating in the sun, a flood of boiling gore engulfing everything.

Now the sun was immense, so big that it seemed to swallow up the entire horizon of the earth so that no shadow remained. Gabriel wanted to protect himself from it by climbing into his horse's carcass. But when he pared back its skin – like peeling a fruit – and opened its gut, he metamorphosed into an animal himself, into a powerful wildcat able to dodge death.

The madness of Gabriel's dream brought him intense pleasure. What he was now experiencing was no longer shackled to reality. The sun was once again distant and gentle. The desert had disappeared.

Each time he made another catlike leap, he was overcome by the kind of extreme joy usually felt only by children. He looked at his own shadow, his own fabulous feline silhouette slinking along over the fields and dusty roads. His body was covered in a thick pelt, and he felt its fur brush past the leaves on the highest branches. Rocks felt soft and padded beneath his claws. He was carried like a bird by the breeze and the passion of his beloved.

Gabriel glided above the endless blue of Lake Titicaca. He lay on his side on its shore and listened to the Master of the Stone's lesson. He watched him play with a sling stone and fling it high into the air. He was astonished to see it remain suspended there, as though it was as light as a feather. The Master of the Stone grinned at him. It was a warm but sad smile, a smile in which Gabriel could discern a wish never uttered aloud.

Then he heard a laugh.

Anamaya appeared, clad entirely in white. She was clasping a gold statue that seemed alive, almost human. She extended her hand toward him and called to him.

'Gabriel!'

Her voice was gentle, musical, and he couldn't resist it. The ferocious feline that Gabriel had become went to her.

As he lay down beside her, he realized that the golden man had disappeared. Now Anamaya was naked, fragile and beautiful. She offered herself to him, and he burned with desire for her. She showed no sign of fear. She wrapped herself around his feline body and kissed his muzzle. He could have destroyed her with his fangs. She didn't feel his claws when he put his paws on her body.

For a while they were lost in a soothing happiness. Then Gabriel saw, over Anamaya's shoulder, the golden man watching them from the shadows. He was shimmering like a star in the night.

The statue spoke to Anamaya without moving his lips. She left Gabriel without a moment's hesitation. She didn't even turn around when he let out a raucous growl – the cry of a savage and fatally wounded animal – that echoed over the mountains.

The violence of his own howl sundered his soul. Gabriel opened his eyes.

His tattered clothes were stuck to his chest with his own sweat. He had a bitter, pasty taste in his mouth. The pain that had been throbbing in his head ever since he had been beaten and kicked in Gonzalo's courtyard returned with a vengeance.

Later, benumbed, he couldn't tell if he had dreamed all this or if insanity was possessing him. Had he had the strength, he would have prayed to God to let him sleep until the end of time.

A bitterly cold dawn brought a strong wind that woke Gabriel. The narrow dormer window was covered in frost, the harbinger of winter.

By the frail light that preceded sunrise, Gabriel discovered what a wretched state he was in. His filthy tunic was torn to shreds, barely covering him. His body ached from head to toe. He felt his face with his fingertips. It was still swollen from all the blows he had taken. The skin around his ankle under the iron shackle was chafed raw. His nausea had faded, but his head felt as though a host of drummers had taken up residence in it and were beating a call to arms.

He carefully brought the rim of a jug to his swollen lips and at last slaked his thirst. The ears of corn brought by the jailer two days before were shriveled now. But the hunger gripping him was too strong, and he devoured them feverishly.

Only then did Gabriel realize that the pounding he could hear wasn't coming from his own battered head or from his pain-racked body. Real drums were beating, their tempo increasing as the sound drew closer and closer.

He swiftly recovered all his lucidity and strained to hear what was going on. He pulled his chain toward the window as far as it would reach and heard the first cries in Spanish from outside his cell:

'The Incas! The Incas!'

The narrowness of the dormer window limited Gabriel's range of vision. At first he saw nothing. He could hear only an increasing number of panicked cries rising from the pre-dawn shadows around the town:

'The Incas! The Incas!'

Then a riotous cacophony of trumpets and human cries drew his attention to the eastern hills overlooking the town. What he saw chilled him more than the freezing wind whipping at his face.

It looked like a forest of bushes or hedgerows being shaken by the wind. But in fact he could make out arms, spears and banners rising from its mass: he was looking at thousands of warriors silhouetted against the lightening sky.

The vast Inca army had completely surrounded Cuzco, covering the crests of all the hills around the town like some giant, monstrous snake. It was as though the wind had whisked away the greenery from the hilltops during the night and had replaced it with this massive, multicolored crowd, now howling like madmen.

The beating drums and the deep wail of horns and conch shells grew louder. Panicked Spaniards emerged onto the streets.

After his initial shock had worn off, Gabriel found himself admiring this extraordinary spectacle. So: Anamaya and Manco had gone ahead with their plan. The bitter prospect of the Incas' revenge warmed his heart. At first, he completely overlooked the fact that the army on the hill represented as grave a danger for him as it did for the few hundred other Spaniards in Cuzco.

And, in fact, when he did eventually realize his situation, he knew that it mattered little to him if he perished during the attack – the *justified* attack. He actually preferred to die at the hands of warriors commanded by Anamaya than be butchered by Hernando and Gonzalo's henchmen.

He remained standing by his window for hours, waiting nervously for the attack to begin. He underestimated neither the Incas' overwhelming force nor the power of their rage.

To Gabriel's surprise, the great Inca army still hadn't attacked the town by midday.

By then, the ranks of warriors had swollen to the point where he could no longer differentiate one brightly coloured tunic from the next – the Indians looked like a single compact mass. They hadn't eased up on their deafening din. But Gabriel could no longer hear any cries from immediately around his jail – or, indeed, any movement at all. Cuzco seemed abandoned.

Then he heard the bolt being drawn back on the other side of his cell door. He stood absolutely still, holding his chain in his hand.

His pot-bellied jailer appeared, holding a large gourd in one hand and a *manta* containing cornbread and boiled potatoes in the other.

'Kikeh!'

'Don't welcome me so warmly, Don Gabriel. I don't deserve your gratitude.'

'I would welcome the devil himself in these circumstances, my dear Kikeh. Never before have I understood so clearly how one's own existence is affirmed by the presence of another.'

'Please, no philosophizing, Don Gabriel. I never understand it at moments like these. Or at any other time, for that matter.'

Gabriel noticed the fear distorting his jailer's expression. Kikeh examined each corner of the room as though he expected to find an army of Indians there. He threw his load at Gabriel's feet.

'You'll have to make do with this for the moment,' he mumbled, 'I'm sorry to say that it's all I could lay my hands on.'

'Ho!' protested Gabriel. 'I'm meant to be tried, not starved to death!'

But his jailer's laugh was joyless.

'You must have heard them. Those savages out there, I mean. You should be grateful that I thought of you at all before I made myself scarce!'

'You're fleeing? Are the Spaniards abandoning Cuzco?'

'Oh no! No one's fleeing. It's too late. But I've found myself somewhere to hole up in before those Indians cut me to pieces.'

He approached the window and glanced at the hills.

'You can't see anything from here. They're everywhere. They cover the southern mesa like ants. They've already captured two cavalrymen trying to get through. They cut off the horses' feet and their riders' heads.'

So, thought Gabriel, *Hernando's pride and his disdain for the Incas has rebounded against him.*

'What's odd,' said the fat man sadly, 'is that they haven't attacked yet. I guess they have a reason. I don't want to be around when they decide to reveal it.'

'Something odd happened to me too, Kikeh.'

'What?'

'Suddenly I don't feel like dying anymore.'

The jailer stared at him with a look of boundless surprise.

'What do you expect me to do? I've given you all I have. But don't worry: it'll last you until they fall upon us. And when that happens, then being hungry will be the least of your worries.'

'In that case, I thank you, Kikeh.'

Gabriel's calm resignation surprised the fat man once again, and his small black eyes grew wider.

'Stop thanking me the whole time. It bothers me more than if you were haranguing me. Here, take this.'

He drew a packet from his filthy doublet and handed it to Gabriel.

It contained a thick slice of ham wrapped in pork rind. The smell of the fat stoked Gabriel's hunger. He looked up at the jailer's back as Kikeh headed toward the cell door.

'You're going to thank me again, aren't you?' the fat man grumbled.

'No. I'm only going to pray that your life is spared.'

Kikeh stopped short, still with his back to Gabriel.

'I was told that you don't believe in God, Don Gabriel.'

'I believe in Him enough to pray for you, friend.'

The door closed. Gabriel stayed still, transfixed.

He felt the chill of fear pervading his limbs as he held the slice of ham between his hands and murmured something under his breath.

Perhaps it was a prayer.

CHAPTER 3

Cuzco, 6 May 1536

THE JAILER HAD GOT IT WRONG.

The Inca warriors didn't attack after all. Not that day, nor the next, nor the day after that.

They remained on the slopes and hilltops. Their numbers swelled continually until they covered the entire plain to the south of the city. At night, the thousands of fires they lit ringed Cuzco like jewels in the night. But they had stopped their shouting, and their drums had fallen silent. And this silence, this waiting weighed perhaps even more heavily on the Spaniards than the cacophony that had preceded it. Every now and then Gabriel heard a demented shout from one of them who could no longer stand the tension.

Indeed, after two days of this silence, he himself started to grow impatient for battle. But at least the pause had permitted him to recuperate and gather his strength a little, despite the minimal amount of food that he cautiously allowed himself each day.

Because he was worried that Gonzalo's henchmen might profit from the general confusion and come and cut his throat on the sly, Gabriel slept only in short spells. He spent his time fashioning himself a crude weapon: he carefully broke the water jug, making sure to preserve a long, thick shard still attached to the handle. He spent hours mechanically sharpening it against the stone wall. But this repetitive, mechanical activity left his spirit empty, and his thoughts wandered constantly to Anamaya.

He was no longer haunted by nightmares, but he still dreamed of his beloved's face, of the unique scent of her skin. Anamaya's musical laugh echoed around his mind like a song he couldn't stop humming. He closed his eyes every now and then as he polished the increasingly sharp shard and imagined that he was in fact caressing the nape of his beloved's neck, or else stroking the small of her back.

How happy they might have been at this very moment, Gabriel thought, had she fled with him away from this chaos to the shores of Lake Titicaca.

But, alas, as soon as he opened his eyes again his dream was chased away by the reality around him, by the irons bruising his leg, by the straw mattress rotting in the corner beneath the cold shaft of light passing through the window set in the thick walls of his prison.

Anamaya was far away in the mountains. She was the living hope of a people among whom he, Gabriel Montelucar y Flores, a Stranger come from afar to steal their peace and their destiny, could never belong. The Incas' very survival depended on their taking Cuzco, on their destroying all the Spaniards without exception and regaining the power that they had given away. Gabriel would have to die along with the rest of his compatriots. Soon he would be nothing more than a memory to her, one that Manco and the influential priest Villa Oma would gradually succeed in erasing from her mind.

How had he ever been able to believe even for a moment that he could have done differently, that he could simply have held her hand as one does with an ordinary woman and, thus joined to her, pursued happiness?

If God existed, then He was punishing Gabriel for his delusion, and if He didn't, then Gabriel was simply paying the price of his own naivety.

Gabriel scratched his skin until he drew blood to prevent himself sinking into the useless mire of his doubts.

The shard that he had been painstakingly polishing for the last two days now appeared to him as the most ridiculous, grotesque piece of work ever undertaken. Being thrown into this forgotten hole was a far worse fate than having his throat cut. What use had he for a weapon? The Pizarros wouldn't even bother to stick him with a blade. All they had to do was forget about him totally, let him succumb to hunger and thirst, abandon him to the fury of the Indian warriors, and their aim would be accomplished.

Enraged, Gabriel hurled the shard against the cell wall. It shattered, and became dust once again.

He stood stock-still for a moment, shocked by his own action. Then he rolled himself up into a ball, wrapped his chain around himself like a blanket, and sought the oblivion of sleep, his final refuge.

A soft noise woke Gabriel. He recognized the creaking: someone was trying to lift the heavy wooden block that barred his cell door as surreptitiously as possible.

He instinctively propped himself up on his arms, silently picked up the links of his chain and held them in his fist like a flail. His earlier resignation had evaporated during his slumber, and he felt the urge to fight energizing his body. His pride dictated that he should defend himself with enough fury to destroy his attackers.

It was so dark that he couldn't see the door open, but he did feel a slight movement in the air. He couldn't know how many they were. He crouched with his back flush against the wall. He forced himself to breath slowly, deliberately, and tried not to think about the fact that he was living his last moments.

Suddenly Gabriel heard a squeak as someone opened the shutter of a dark lantern. The yellow light of a tallow candle swept across the cell's walls before settling on him. When its beam fell on him, the light jerked, as though the person holding the lantern had started with shock.

'Gabriel!' exclaimed the lamp's custodian in a low, hushed voice, a voice that Gabriel nevertheless recognized even before he made out in the dim light the fringe of the long cowl. 'Gabriel, don't be frightened. It's only me.'

'Bartholomew! Brother Bartholomew!'

'Dear friend,' whispered Bartholomew, his smile evident in his voice.

The monk, to banish any lingering doubt, thrust his strange, fused fingers into the faint beam of the dark lantern.

'God's blood!' exclaimed Gabriel. 'You are the last person whom I expected to see here tonight!'

'Which is why I take care to show myself in the light before you can attack me.'

Gabriel laughed and let go of his chain.

'A wise move!'

But when the monk offered him a fraternal hug, Gabriel pushed him away and said:

'It pains me to forgo your embrace, but I think it's best that we don't.'

Bartholomew slowly ran the light over Gabriel, examining him from head to toe.

'My poor, poor friend. What a state they have left you in.'

'Yes. No doubt I foul the air even twenty leagues from here!'

'Here, take the lamp. Shine it on me,' whispered Bartholomew. 'I've something outside that will make you human again.'

He returned a moment later, carrying a large basket.

'Some things with which to eat your fill, Gabriel,' said the monk, setting the basket at Gabriel's feet. 'Water too, enough to wash yourself with, as well as drink, and a few salves to treat your cuts and bruises.'

'Why, there's enough here to wait out a siege . . .'

'You've never spoken a truer word! But we'll talk about that later. First, eat until your hunger is assuaged.'

Gabriel shook his head with feeling.

'Last night, I had resigned myself to dying alone, like a dog, with no one to prevent the vermin picking my bones clean. I thought that the last human face I would see in this vile world would be the pot-bellied jailer's – who isn't the worst of men, by the way, although he's a long way from Erasmus and Socrates. And then, here you are! Now I feel strong enough to pull this chain from the wall with my bare hands!'

'God indulges us in His own ways, Gabriel, even if you choose not to notice,' quipped Bartholomew, offering him a water skin full to bursting. 'And now it seems to me that it would be in both our interests if you were to wash yourself a little. But I regret that I am so indifferent to clothes that I didn't think to bring you something to replace those rags!'

'Don Hernando came to tell me about your return and subsequent arrest,' explained Bartholomew while Gabriel tore roasted llama meat from the bone with his teeth.

'"Brother," he said to me in the sweetest voice, "that man deserves nothing less than death. And I'm sure that death is what he will shortly receive. Nonetheless, we know that a hasty verdict offends Christian charity. So we're going to give that bastard a trial. And you're the only person here that I can think of who is morally irreproachable enough to conduct it," he said. And that is how he made me your judge.'

Bartholomew chortled quietly as Gabriel gulped down water and slaked his thirst. The monk went on:

'Don Hernando returned from Spain more conniving than ever. He found himself in an extremely uncomfortable position in Toledo. The Pizarros' methods have shocked a great number of people at court. The queen and her suite in particular were especially moved by the story of Atahualpa's end.'

'I should hope so!'

'Oh, you know, it didn't result in much: Hernando was still awarded the Order of Santiago even though the two of us would have preferred to see him sent to rot in the prison where you and I first met.'

They both smiled at the memory.

'So I asked to interrogate you immediately,' continued Bartholomew. 'They tried to dissuade me, using the pretext that you had to be given some time alone to repent. That told me that they had no doubt caused you dreadful harm.'

'And what exactly do I stand accused of?'

'The attempted assassination of Gonzalo. But also of treason, for having disobeyed the Governor's order to follow de Almagro's expedition to the south.'

'Oh yes, that fine mission! It consisted of helplessly watching Almagro wreak horror everywhere he went. You cannot imagine what I witnessed in the south, Bartholomew. You say that the court in Spain was distressed by Atahualpa's execution? They would have vomited like sick dogs if they could have seen what my eyes saw week after week! Those gallows birds following de Almagro tortured and massacred the Indians as though they were nothing more than rats. Children, the old, women – who were raped as well as butchered – the sick . . . those bastards spared no one. I watched them decapitate corpses, so great was their blood lust. For hundreds of leagues, they burned and pillaged every village they came across.'

'Yes, I've heard about it.'

'I was *there*. And there was nothing I could do. When I tried to protest, de Almagro simply pointed a crossbow at me. Try to imagine what it's like to spend day after day amid all that horror, without being able to stop it or even ease the burden of suffering. Imagine the shame of being taken for a murderer, to be seen to be cut from the same cloth as those dregs of humanity now sweeping through the south, rabid in their hunger for gold!'

'Why are you saying that? You did nothing.'

'Exactly. I didn't help spread the horror, but I didn't stop it either, which is just as bad. Henceforth, the peoples of this land will see Spaniards as all the same.'

Gabriel pointed vehemently at the red glow of the Inca fires through the dormer window and said:

'For the thousands of warriors surrounding us, howling at the tops of those hills, there are no longer any good Strangers or bad Strangers. In their eyes, we all deserve to be annihilated. This is what Hernando's diplomacy has brought upon us; this is what giving free rein to de Almagro and hellhounds like Gonzalo has brought about.'

'Well, I see that at least you omit the Governor from your list,' said Bartholomew, making an appeasing gesture.

Gabriel uttered a harsh growl and rose to his feet. He walked over to the dormer window to breathe in a little fresh air, pulling his chain behind him.

'Don Francisco is no brute,' he conceded. 'But he knows how to turn a blind eye when it suits him. Which it often does.'

The first light of dawn was emerging on the eastern horizon, although barely discernible because of all the Inca fires lighting up the sky. Thousands of fires set the surrounding hills aglow, as they did every night, and their light reached right up to the walls of Cuzco. Gabriel caught glimpses of silhouettes moving about here and there.

'I think that your trial will be forgotten,' remarked Bartholomew, joining Gabriel at the window. 'I'm going to help you escape, Gabriel. I'm going now to find some tool to break your chain with. In all the confusion presently gripping the city, no one will notice your escape.'

'Thank you, Brother Bartholomew. But please don't harbor any illusions. Whether locked up in here or free in the city, we're all doomed to the same fate now. Our hour of judgement is upon us.'

Both men stood in silence for a moment, spellbound by the river of flames linking the hills together.

'There're maybe two hundred thousand of them,' murmured Bartholomew suddenly. 'You have to wonder why they're waiting to storm us.'

'They're simply waiting until we have no chance of resisting them.'

'Or until we all starve to death. There is less and less food. I had to steal what I brought you tonight, and you won't see a basket as full as that again. Today, a *caballero* called Mejia was absolutely determined to charge out of here and cut himself a passage through to the plain. He was immediately unhorsed. They decapitated him, then sliced clean through his horse's hocks.'

'What defences has Hernando ordered?'

'He plans to assemble the cavalrymen and charge the enemy, to try to breach the human wall of Incas and fetch reinforcements.'

'How many horses does he have?'

'There are about sixty in the city.'

'What madness.'

Bartholomew gave him a piercing look. Since Gabriel said nothing further, he asked:

'Why do you say that?'

'Oh, one only has to give it some thought. But milord Hernando Pizarro is too convinced that he faces mere savages, and so he doesn't bother to think of proper tactics, let alone strategy. I know a little of their war chiefs. They are very well aware of how we fight, and they know our weaknesses. They're waiting for exactly what Hernando's planning: a grouped charge – still, to this day, our one and only military ploy against the Incas.'

'Perhaps that's because it has always succeeded before.'

'It won't this time. The Incas will let the cavalry pass by them without really trying to stop them. At the most, they'll offer some feigned combat. And what will happen in the meantime? Two or at most three hundred Spaniards will be left in Cuzco to face a hundred thousand Indians. And those Spaniards will have nothing better to defend themselves with than their swords and their wits. The battle won't last a day, Bartholomew. Manco's men are formidable in hand-to-hand combat. Their sling stones pierce the thickest armour and shatter the blades of our swords. I tell you: the miracle that was Cajamarca will not happen again!'

'What other solution is there?'

'To make peace! To restore to Manco all his royal rights, and to return all the gold stolen from him. But that will never happen, and in any case it's too late. The Incas won't want to parley. Why should they, when they can crush us like ants?'

Bartholomew nodded in agreement. But his voice changed in tone slightly when he said:

'Don Hernando pretends to believe that you have become Manco's agent, his spy, and that you helped him escape, and helped organize this siege . . .'

'. . . And that I've hidden away an enormous statue made of solid gold, not to mention an Inca princess said to be the gold statue's wife,' interrupted Gabriel with a bitter snarl.

'It's true that the oddest rumors about you are starting to spread,' sighed Bartholomew. 'But then, considering your return here

disguised as an Indian peasant, as well as your violent attack . . .
Gonzalo has had a nasty limp ever since, and you well and truly
shattered the skull of one of his best friends. Why were you so
savage?'

Bartholomew's demeanor grew suddenly distant, and the monk
displayed the detached curiosity that so often in the past Gabriel
had suspected hid dark intentions.

'Is this the beginning of the judge's interrogation?'

'Gabriel!'

'At this late hour, I can confess everything to you with total
candor, Bartholomew: my greatest regret is having missed my
mark. My club should have crushed Gonzalo's head, not his
companion's. For that, I will gladly accept my punishment.'

'I fear I still cannot fathom the reasons for your hatred,
dear friend.'

Gabriel hesitated. Outside, above the hills, the sky grew paler
and paler. The Inca warriors seemed more active than usual.

'More than a year ago now, while I was far away, Gonzalo tried to
rape Anamaya,' he said in a muted voice. 'That was the infamy that
caused Manco to flee. He realized that neither of them were safe
in Cuzco. Gonzalo, of course, didn't boast about this particular
exploit of his. You couldn't have known.'

'Dear God!'

'Gonzalo, unfortunately, caught Manco and flung him in irons.
As for Anamaya, she managed to escape with her friend the dwarf.
She hid in the mountains and organized the rebellion. Her first aim
was to free Manco, who was suffering the worst humiliations here.
I knew none of this until later. Then, when I learned that Manco
was being kept prisoner by that madman Gonzalo, I assumed that
Anamaya was also in his hands. The mere thought was unbearable.
I immediately left de Almagro's expedition, where in any case I had
had my fill of atrocities . . .'

'I understand, I understand,' said Bartholomew, placing his
hand on Gabriel's shoulder. His voice was warm and friendly
once again.

Gabriel moved away from the dormer window and, in a few
succinct words, described to the monk how he had tried to cross

the salt pan to reach Cuzco as quickly as possible, how his horse had died, and how he himself had only been saved at the final hour by Katari, the Master of the Stone.

'I was dead, and he brought me back to life. Literally.'

'Katari . . .' murmured Bartholomew, moved. 'Ever since I met him, I have always believed that that man would be consecrated as a saint, were he one of us. It is as though he has some prevision into our mysteries. He taught me my first words in Quechua, and I taught him his first in Spanish. Merely gazing upon him, I realized that he was that rare thing, a pure soul. I will gladly meet with him again, if it's God's will.'

'Ah!' exclaimed Gabriel, hardly listening to the monk at all. 'I came to in the most beautiful place in the world! An enormous lake, almost a sea, which the locals call Titicaca. The surrounding mountains are the highest that one can imagine. They wear a permanent blanket of snow and, on certain days, their peaks reflect on the surface of the lake, as still and pure as a mirror. And yet, the climate is as mild as that of Cadiz! The people there are peaceful and kind. I daydreamed of returning there to live with Anamaya. I dreamed of fleeing there with her . . .'

He fell silent. The nightmare that he had lived over the past few days returned to the forefront of his mind like a punch to his gut. He wished that he could speak frankly to Bartholomew about it, but something held him back. Perhaps his pride wouldn't allow him to admit that he dreamed of being an animal. So he confined himself to describing his arrival in Calca, and how Manco's warriors had already been gathering from the furthest reaches of the Empire of the Four Cardinal Directions.

'It was there that she declared her love for me, but also told me that it was impossible for us to remain together, for a war was about to erupt. To tell the truth, Bartholomew, what she told me with her kind words and kisses was that, in her eyes, I was different from the other Strangers, and that—'

'Gabriel!' exclaimed Bartholomew. 'God's blood, Gabriel, look! Almighty God . . .'

Gabriel stopped short, then bounded to the window, his chain clinking loudly behind him. He unwittingly uttered a cry of amazement.

In the pale glow of dawn, he saw that the fires had come down from the hills, as though the Indian warriors' river of fire had broken its banks. Suddenly the piercing sound of horns erupted, causing the air to shiver, and immediately after that horrendous cries rose up into the sky.

'They're attacking,' murmured Bartholomew blankly.

'Look up!' said Gabriel. 'Look at the sky!'

A thick cloud of arrows streaked across the sky, so densely packed that it seemed like a giant blanket had been lifted from the ground. The two men heard terrified cries in Spanish rise up from the alleys nearby, and then they saw the thousands of arrows whistle down towards the ground. Bartholomew instinctively retreated from the window. But the archers were too far away and the *cancha* in which the prison was located was still out of their range. Gabriel was now oblivious to the cries. He watched in a daze as the blanket of death came down from the sky, covering the roofs. The thousands of arrows making impact made a dull, drawn out, tearing sound, clearly audible despite the panicked Spanish cries. Drums began rolling, their noise replacing the jarring sound of horns.

'I must go and join Hernando,' said Bartholomew.

Gabriel caught him by the arm and said:

'Wait a moment. It's too dangerous. Something is about to happen . . .'

He had barely finished his sentence when an odd, throbbing sound thickened the air, echoing even into their chest cavities, as though some god was trying to drown out the cries and agonized moans of those wounded by arrows. Yet they could see nothing.

'Stones.'

Indeed, a downpour of sling stones now succeeded the shower of arrows. They were flung not from the distant hills but from the great fortress of Sacsayhuaman overlooking Cuzco, in the immediate vicinity of the city's houses and alleys. The stones flew much further than the arrows. Gabriel and Bartholomew listened silently to the dull thudding as the missiles came hurtling down against the roofs and walls. The sound increased in volume, indicating that a greater quantity of stones was being launched. There were so many now that some crashed into one another in mid-air. The storm lasted for what seemed an eternity. The Spaniards' terrified cries grew far louder, and the war cries from the hills increased as though in response. Another salvo of arrows came whistling down, mixing now with the stones, creating a deadly storm. It felt as though the sky itself was crashing down on Cuzco, as though the firmament was at last acting to exterminate everything living, engulfing life with a wicked determination that would only end when nothing remained but motionless piles of corpses.

'I must go!' cried Bartholomew.

'Then put this over you,' exclaimed Gabriel, shaking all the contents out of the basket and placing it, upside down, on the monk's head. 'It will give you some protection.'

Bartholomew opened the door, then froze.

'Dear God,' he murmured, making the sign of the cross.

Smoke was already rising from a dozen of Cuzco's thatched roofs. Flames began bursting upwards here and there, as though some invisible hand was stoking them.

'The sling stones must be wrapped in burning cloth or grass,' explained Gabriel. 'That's what they were for. The sling stones are setting the thatch alight.'

'They're going to burn the entire city,' cried Bartholomew.

Gabriel yanked on his chain, enraged.

'Find someone to release me from this damned chain!'

'Don't worry, I won't leave you here to burn alive.'

The monk quickly embraced him.

'Do you promise me that?'

Despite the quick nod from the monk before he disappeared into the smoke, Gabriel doubted that he would ever see him again.

The wind fanned the flames well into the night. The entire city had become an enormous pyre. Only a few of the houses around

the great square were spared, either because they were out of
the fire's reach or else because of the courage of the Spaniards'
Indian allies who doused the fires with water at the risk of their
own lives.

At dawn, the smoke had become so thick that at times it was
impossible for anyone to see a wall or alley directly in front of
them. The acrid smoke penetrated lungs like poison. Men fell
to their knees, unable even to cry out in pain, so little breath
did they have left. All the horses were terrified. They snorted
furiously, shuddering at their withers, rolling their bloodshot eyes,
their nostrils quivering and their chops trembling. A few bit their
masters, others neighed shrilly with terror.

The storm of arrows and stones never diminished, whistling
through the smoke. They crashed into walls or thudded into the
flesh of the abandoned wounded whose suffering didn't last long
after they'd been struck.

Inca warriors, their mouths masked with moistened cotton and
using the thick smoke as cover, slipped silently along the narrow
roads on the edges of the city. There, they erected barricades,
laying down tree trunks and setting up palisades that they had built
in advance. They blocked all the exits from the city one by one,
making sure that the barriers were too high for horses to clear.

At Villa Oma's order, small groups of infiltrators penetrated
even further into the city. They finished off any wounded they
came across, then scaled the walls of the *canchas* that had been
burnt to cinders. Canary Indian women and children, the whites
of their terrified eyes stark in their blackened faces, begged them
for mercy. But Manco's men spared no one.

For the first time, the Incas were fighting with the taste of
victory in their mouths.

'I've waited a long time to see this,' gloated Villa Oma, giving
Anamaya and Manco a smile, a very rare thing from him. 'Emperor,
it is truly a great joy for me to be able to at last present this battle
to you. I hope that your father the Sun and all your ancestors are
celebrating as we are.'

They were sitting on the highest tower of the Sun Fortress, Sacsayhuaman. Cuzco, one massive pyre, revealed itself before them in the gathering light of dawn. Warriors whipped their slingshots around unflaggingly, hurling stones that they had placed in their campfires the night before, then removed and wrapped in cotton. The wind of their passage fanned the glowing missiles and ignited the cotton as the red-hot stones flew through the air. When the projectiles hurtled into the roofs of Cuzco, the very dry *ichu* covering them took only a moment to catch fire.

Today, all the Ancestors of the Other World were with Manco. The wind picked up again before night lifted, quickly fanning the blaze. The flames grew and grew, stretching to the sky and writhing like giant snakes slipping from roof to roof. Then all the *canchas* of upper Cuzco caught alight at once, as though the fire itself had become liquid.

The warriors unleashed another volley of stones. Thousands of projectiles whistled over the flames to the roofs of lower Cuzco, which promptly ignited like a cornfield at the end of a very dry summer. The fire jumped across the alleys, the gardens and courtyards, sparing nothing.

With his hands resting on a stone wall as broad as a road, Manco laughed gleefully.

'Look, Anamaya! Look at them run like rats, our almighty Strangers! Don't they remind you of insects when they feel death singeing their antennae?'

Anamaya nodded in agreement. Manco's analogy was correct. The Spaniards and the few Indians who remained loyal to them, including Canaries, Huancas, and members of other nations, were running in every direction in total disorder, their only purpose being to avoid the beams collapsing beneath the flaming roofs. But as soon as they appeared out in the open, safe from the flames, a blizzard of sling stones and arrows would fall upon them. Anamaya could already make out a great many corpses, as well as the crawling bodies of dozens of wounded whom no one dared to rescue.

The Spanish horsemen were gathering in the great square, which was the only place that was safe from both the fire and the barrage of stones and arrows, for it was too far from the towers of the Sacsayhuaman fortress. Anamaya tried to pick out Gabriel's blond hair amid all the movement of those distant, jerky silhouettes. But the Strangers were too closely packed one against the other, and in any case their hair was hidden by their morions. Others now arrived on the square, screaming and protecting themselves as best they could by placing their shields above their heads.

'What do you think, *Coya Camaquen*?' asked Manco, looking at her closely with an amused look on his face. He knew exactly what she was feeling.

'I think that it is a momentous battle and, like all battles, it is a terrible thing.'

'We are going to win,' said Villa Oma indignantly. 'Yet you don't seem pleased.'

'We haven't won yet,' replied Anamaya quietly. 'At the moment, all we've destroyed is Cuzco – *our* Cuzco – and not the Strangers.'

Her remark cut Villa Oma to the quick. He swept his hand out angrily in front of him, indicating the mass of Inca troops surrounding Cuzco.

'Look out there in the plain, *Coya Camaquen*. Look at our warriors covering the hills and the plain. An ant couldn't get past them. Do you really think that they can be defeated?'

'For the moment, all our warriors are outside the city, whilst the Strangers remain inside it.'

'It will not last. I shall give the order shortly. Our troops will soon sweep into the streets of Cuzco. Take a good look at the Strangers over there on the square! By this evening, not one of them will remain alive.'

Villa Oma was almost shouting. Anamaya said nothing. She knew what the old Sage, drunk with violence, was inferring. She tightened her lips to prevent herself from asking the question that had been burning on them ever since Gabriel and she had separated at Calca. If Gabriel were indeed the puma, then what would happen if he died?

'Anamaya's right,' said Manco dryly, snapping her out of her reverie. 'I am pleased by what you show me, Villa Oma. But it is still too early to celebrate.'

'Then wait for this evening!' growled Villa Oma with a hint of disdain. 'Look! Look over there . . .'

He pointed at the first wave of warriors entering the streets and erecting barriers to prevent the Strangers from fleeing on their horses.

'No!' ordered Manco firmly. 'No, we shall not enter the city tonight. It's still too early. More warriors will soon arrive from Quito. When they do, then we shall attack – and win.'

'But My Lord! There are already two hundred thousand of us, whereas there are only two hundred of them!'

'I said no, Villa Oma. We must continue weakening them. We must cut the water canals to the great square. We must starve them and make their every moment unbearable, until they try to break out into the plain, which you've flooded so that their horses will be useless. They will fall into our hands, and we will sacrifice their riders to Inti. Fear, Villa Oma! They must die of fear!'

Villa Oma's face twisted with rage. But he said nothing. In silence, he watched the city burn, watched the men scurrying and screaming through its streets. Anamaya could see his lips trembling, and his fists clenching as though involuntarily. The priest used all his strength to hold himself back from striking Manco.

'Villa Oma . . .' she began in a conciliatory tone.

'You shouldn't be here, *Coya Comaquen!*' squawked the Sage with vicious irony. 'If the Strangers are indeed as dangerous as Manco claims, you are putting yourself in grave danger by remaining here on this tower. You must return to Calca immediately.'

Anamaya turned her back to him, and allowed her blue-eyed gaze to lose itself in the sky, above the rising smoke and flames. She could at last allow her heart to feel the terrible anxiety that she had been suppressing.

Yes, she was trembling for Gabriel!

Yes, she hoped with all her strength and from the depths of her soul that he, and he alone, would survive. Not only because he was the Puma foreseen by the great Huayna Capac, but because he was the man whom she loved. And because to live without him was not to live at all.

CHAPTER 4

Cuzco, May 1536

A S HELPLESS AS A DOG AT THE END OF ITS CHAIN, Gabriel listened to the death cries of the victims outside and watched the city burn. When the smoke reached his window, he retreated back into his cell. He tore up what remained of the rags of his tunic and wrapped them around his face. He suffered terrible coughing fits, bent double. He had long since given up hope of seeing either the jailer or Brother Bartholomew again.

Indeed, hope had left him some time ago, and all he thought about now was being able to breathe, and surviving.

Half of Cuzco was already ablaze when he heard the much-feared thuds: the sling stones were now reaching the roof of his prison. The warriors were now within range. The dull sound repeated itself perhaps ten times. Ten volleys. And then a stone pierced through the thatch *ichu* of the roof, and landed close by him.

Almost immediately, thin plumes of brown smoke began to rise from the log beams supporting the roof. A little flame sputtered into life and danced around, growing. Like a golden snake, it reached the peak of the roof, zigzagged hesitantly for a moment, then slithered down the opposite side and ran along the walls. Within a minute, countless other flames were born, joining the first.

Then, all of a sudden, the thatch itself burst into flames.

Before Gabriel had a chance to react, the fire came roaring down from above him, as though it was trying to caress the ground. It forced him onto his knees. In only a few seconds, the heat became unbearable.

Gabriel cursed his chain, cursed Hernando and all the Pizarro brothers. He lay down flat on his stomach, trying to protect his face. But the heat burning his back was excruciating.

Then entire sections of burning thatch collapsed, sending sparks in all directions on impact. The flames doubled in size, but were now being drawn to the air outside, taking the smoke with them. Gabriel thought of the water skins that Bartholomew had brought him.

He crawled along the ground, braving the heat that burned off all the hairs on the backs of his hands. With his teeth, he tore the leather strap holding the wood cork out of the first gourd and splashed the water all over his face and shoulders. He drenched his entire body in water until every gourd but one was empty. The cold shock was so extreme that it left him trembling, his teeth chattering. He was still just conscious enough to catch a glimpse of the thatch finally giving way completely, directly above him. His movements limited by his chain, he dodged the burning thatch as it fell as best he could and curled up at the foot of a wall.

And then suddenly, as quickly as it had ignited, the fire went out.

Only a few flames continued to lick around the beams overhead, disturbed by a wind that carried the smoke away in tortured spirals. Cool air managed to find its way through the burning walls.

His arms and hands in agony, Gabriel grabbed the remaining water skin and gave in to the urge to drink and to splash more water on himself. It was the last of his water. *But too bad*, he thought.

Exhausted from fear, he stretched out on the ground and gave thanks for the little bit of coolness that the wind bestowed upon him.

Now the smoke rose up above Cuzco's walls, veiling the sky like a storm at twilight. The smoke gave the impression of being a physical manifestation of all the cries for help, all the death moans, all the sounds of dying and destruction that rose from the city.

Gabriel closed his aching eyes and ran his tongue, as dry as old leather, along his blistered lips.

He wondered how many of the Spaniards were still alive.

He felt as though he already had one foot in the kingdom of the dead.

That night, as during those that had preceded it, the air was thick with the wails of trumpets, war chants, and the furious insults shouted down at the city by a hundred thousand Inca warriors. The terrible cacophony echoed beneath the incandescent sky and pierced through smoke as thick as storm clouds, as though the Devil himself had extended the canopy of hell over Cuzco.

Exhausted and aching from head to toe, Gabriel dozed for a long while, hoping to find respite in the stupor of sleep.

A cry that stood out from the rest made him open his eyes.

He was unsure of what he was seeing before him. Three silhouettes stood stiffly on the wall above. He could see their torsos and limbs but not their faces. He could also see their weapons: spears and clubs.

Nothing moved for a moment, and he thought that perhaps he was still asleep, lost in a nightmare. Then another cry rang out from the shadows. One of the silhouettes raised its arm and threw something at him: a stone – a large stone with a rope attached! It bounced right next to Gabriel's leg. He immediately stood up and shouted without thinking:

'I am not your enemy!'

The three men hesitated, surprised at hearing their own language.

'I am not your enemy! I am with the *Coya Camaquen*!' cried Gabriel.

He instantly sensed the Inca warriors' hesitation. One of them said something incomprehensible, then waved his arms at him. Gabriel repeated:

'I am not your enemy!'

He yanked on his chain to show how he was bound. One of the men gesticulated and spoke some words that Gabriel still couldn't understand. Another Indian nervously shook the rope so that the stone attached to its end rolled between the Spaniard's legs.

Gabriel instinctively grabbed the stone and the rope and pulled them towards him. One of the warriors, meanwhile, let out a cry. The other two dodged quickly aside. The rope went limp between Gabriel's hands. One of the men on the wall collapsed as his companions cried out, already twirling their slingshots. The warrior fell like a sack onto the floor of the prison cell.

When Gabriel looked up again, the two warriors had bolted into the ochre night. The man who had fallen next to him was already dead, a quarrel from a crossbow so deeply embedded in his chest that only its end was still visible.

But Gabriel didn't have time to be surprised. His cell door creaked open and a shadowy form, like some black ghost, slipped into his roofless cell, holding a small cranequin, a type of crossbow, in its hand.

Gabriel stepped back, the chain clinking between his legs. His visitor let out an irreverent laugh.

'Well now, my friend, you don't recognize me?' said an instantly recognizable voice.

Gabriel was tongue-tied with surprise. The silhouette took two cautious steps forward.

'Holà, Gabriel! Have they torn out your tongue already?'

'Sebastian . . . Sebastian!'

'Here at your service, Your Grace!'

His tall, proud, black companion, a former slave, drew nearer and carefully set his crossbow on the ground. Then he embraced Gabriel warmly, no more concerned about sullying himself than Gabriel was. His only clothing was a sort of leather skirt to which was attached his quiver of arrows and a long dagger. He was otherwise completely naked, his black skin spattered with gray beads of sweat mixed with soot.

'Sebastian, disguised as the devil!' cried Gabriel with relief.

A broad white-toothed grin gleamed through the haze.

'This is the best dress possible, given the present situation. For once, my black skin is an asset and I'm making the most of it!'

Gabriel laughed heartily, feeling so relieved that it was as though he had just gulped down cool, fresh water. Sebastian prodded the Inca warrior's corpse with his foot and said:

'Well and truly dead. I arrived just in time, didn't I?'

'How did you know I was here?'

'Brother Bartholomew, of course. He told me that I'd find you stuck here like a rat. It took me some time to get here, because I had to get my hands on this . . .'

Sebastian pulled a steel awl and a little hammer from his leather skirt.

'Your fat jailer friend proved reluctant to be found. Still, he's a cheerful fellow, the kind of man I like: he confided in me that he had to father six children with six different Indian girls before one of them gave him a son. In any case, he had this damned awl, which is the only way to break your irons. Without it, all I could do would be to rip out the chain from the floor, and you'd have to carry it around with you.'

Sebastian set about breaking the irons as he spoke, setting the awl against the shackle that held the irons to the chain and striking it with small, precise blows with the hammer.

'Don't move, I'll be finished in a moment. Watch the walls, and make sure that our Inca friends don't return to surprise us with their company!'

The tinkling sound of his irons opening was, for Gabriel, more precious than the chinking sound of gold coins. As soon as they were off, he immediately breathed easier.

'There, you're free,' said Sebastian, affectionately taking Gabriel by the wrist.

'Sweet Jesus, I was sure that I was going to roast like a chicken between these walls,' said Gabriel, massaging his ankles, which suddenly felt as though they were being pricked by a thousand needles. 'I am deeply grateful to you, Sebastian.'

'By God, you *do* smell like roasted flesh!' said Sebastian, with an amused grimace. 'Come, we must go. But first . . .'

He drew his dagger and kneeled down beside the dead warrior. Without flinching, he plunged the blade into the corpse's chest.

'. . . I must take back my arrow,' he explained. 'It's too valuable, we don't have enough ammunition to waste.'

'Where are Hernando and the others?' asked Gabriel, averting his gaze from what Sebastian was doing.

'In the *cancha* on the great square. It didn't burn. Don Hernando placed slaves on the roof to put out fires as they started. A dozen of them were killed, but now we're all sheltered there, and the horses too. There, I'm finished.'

Without showing the slightest emotion, Sebastian wiped the blood off the short arrow with the dead man's tunic.

'Come, I'll lead you there,' chuckled Sebastian. 'I look forward to seeing the surprise on their faces when they see you alive and walking about!'

'Like this, in these rags?'

Sebastian's hearty laugh rung out over the cacophony of the city under siege.

'No, no, milord! I've something far more appropriate than that!'

To Gabriel's astonishment, Sebastian didn't take the shortest, most direct route back to the great square. Quite the opposite: in total silence, and with feline agility, he followed the route through the small alleys around the square, smoke still rising from the burned-out roofs of their houses. They came out onto a road that Gabriel recognized as the one leading to the palace of Hatun Cancha. Sebastian stopped in front of a door made of guanaco skin and pushed it open. The skin was still fresh – and hence damp – enough to have survived the blaze.

'Wait in here a moment,' whispered Sebastian, closing the door behind him. 'Don't go anywhere – I'll be right back.'

Sebastian disappeared into the smoke. Gabriel didn't recognize the *cancha*. Like most of the other buildings in the city, its roof had gone. Its walls, however, seemed to have survived well, and were decorated in the Spanish manner. Recently built walls covered in dun-coloured roughcast joined the long Inca structures so that the space within was surrounded by an unbroken barricade. Doors and windows had been fitted – real European doors and windows – giving the enclosure a familiar feel.

'All's well,' whispered Sebastian when he returned. 'I just wanted to check that we have no unwelcome visitors.'

'Where are we?' asked Gabriel.

Sebastian's laugh was as clear as a child's.

'Ho! Where are we! Why, we're in my palace, of course!'

'This is yours?'

'Have you forgotten that I'm rich? A true Croesus!'

Gabriel shook his head, smiling wryly. He looked at Sebastian, almost naked and holding a crossbow, and it was hard to imagine him as the owner of this palace.

'If the truth be told, I'd forgotten. And I'd forgotten precisely *how* rich you've become . . . what a house!'

'Oh, it's much better when you see it with its roof and furniture,' grumbled Sebastian, leading him in. 'Come, let's not stay here.'

There was a smell of stale smoke in the room they entered, a smell of soot and ash. Only the leather seats of the wooden chairs remained, all cracked, along with a few corner irons from a table and a candelabra's dented base.

'What a waste!' lamented Sebastian.

He pushed aside the charred debris of a bed and pulled to one side a carpet of *mantas* stitched together. The broad flagstones underneath looked perfectly ordinary. Before Gabriel had a chance to express his surprise, Sebastian wedged an iron bar between a couple of flagstones and levered up first one and then two more. By the faint light of the stars and a crescent moon that was at last finding its way through the clouds of smoke, Gabriel made out a heavy wooden trapdoor.

'Lend a hand,' said Sebastian. 'It's as heavy as three saw-horses.'

The trapdoor seemed to open into a well of darkness. Still, Sebastian made his way through the gloom until he felt the rungs of a wooden stepladder. He groped around with his hand until he found a piece of candle and a tinderbox.

'We'd better move quickly. There's no reason to let anyone see us!'

A few moments later Gabriel stood absolutely flabbergasted. His evident surprise gave Sebastian a feeling of deep satisfaction. They were in a cellar, an underground space that was both a comfortably appointed room and a warehouse full of clothes and weapons.

'Rich is what I am,' chuckled Sebastian, 'and in a city like Cuzco, you could say that the political situation is far from stable. I could well find myself poor again tomorrow, either because of the Indians or through a change of de Almagro's or the Pizarros' mood. And if there's one thing that I've learned from life, it's that black is what I am and black is what I shall always be. In other words, I'll always be a little bit the slave! So Prudence, God bless her, dictates that I don't reveal my treasures for all to see. You're the first person apart from me to enter here, and you see before you my insurance for hard times. In other words, what you see here in this cellar is an illusion. It doesn't exist.'

While Sebastian climbed back up the ladder to close the trapdoor properly, Gabriel, amazed, took stock of the treasures that his friend had accumulated. There were a few trunks filled with new clothes: fine shirts, doublets, split-sided stockings, and even bolts of velvet, cambric, and linen waiting for the tailor's knife. Coats of mail padded with leather and cotton hung from various wall-mounted hooks. Morions were piled up in baskets. Four saddles, richly decorated with silver, sat on trestles, and a large box contained swords, daggers, and two cranequins. Gabriel couldn't see any gold but he was sure that a few ingots were hidden away somewhere even more secret.

'I can't believe my eyes,' he confessed, amazed.

'Come, I've something else to show you,' replied Sebastian.

They went to the far end of the cellar, lighting their way with the candle. A narrow passage led into a cold room. Gabriel heard running water without being able to see it.

'Look,' said Sebastian, raising the candle so that its feeble light revealed a natural pool in the stone floor. 'It's absolutely freezing, but at least we can wash ourselves, then rest until dawn. What's more, we can barely hear the Incas' tumult down here. And tomorrow, you can choose yourself a fine tunic and a sword worthy of you. You'll cut a splendid figure!'

'Sebastian . . .'

'Now, now, Gabriel, don't argue with me. It gives me boundless pleasure to be able to offer you these trifles, and I will be even happier tomorrow when I see the surprise on some of our friends' faces when they see you walking about, well and truly alive. Ha ha ha!'

At dawn, dressed in clean clothes, with new boots on his feet, a thick leather tunic and chain mail covering his shirt, and a Toledo sword embellished with a silver-encrusted guard hanging against his purple velvet breeches, Gabriel left Sebastian's house. Smoke was still rising from the city. At least half of Cuzco was in Manco's warriors' hands.

The two men had to go back twice the way they had come, running as fast as they could, dodging sling stones, before they managed to reach the Spaniards, who were holding out in the only *cancha* still standing on the great square. Thick sheets, like enormous sails, had been hung over the courtyards with vast quantities of rope, to protect the conquistadors from the Incas' stones and arrows. Soldiers stood guard at the entrances, using unhinged doors as shields, and they immediately let Gabriel and Sebastian enter. Gabriel didn't recognize any of the faces and, in the jam-packed interior, no one paid him any attention.

Gabriel walked among the soldiers for a while, observing their worried faces, before he heard Hernando's voice suddenly ring out. Hernando stood between his brothers Juan and Gonzalo, facing a small troop of cavalrymen. Gabriel watched as he struck a hastily drawn map of the city spread out on a large table in front of him with his finger and said:

'According to the Canaries, all the alleys in the north of the city are now blocked by barricades between eight, ten, or even twelve codos high. In any case, far too high for the horses to clear. And it's the same here, in the east, and here, in the south. They didn't waste any time . . .'

'They're tightening the noose, I tell you! They're going to cut our throats like pigs!' cried a man, the back of whose doublet was burned through so that his shirt could be seen.

'Let's not turn into poltroons because a few flames singed our arses, Diego!' cried Hernando.

'The barricades in the northern part of the city are the most troublesome,' intervened Juan Pizarro. 'They prevent us from charging against the Sacsayhuaman fortress. And it's from up there, unfortunately, that the Incas are bombarding us day and night with sling stones and arrows. It is intolerable! It's as though we were ants at the mercy of giants!'

Hernando, irritated by Juan's disillusioned tone, interrupted him with a gesture.

'Brother, this is no time to wax lyrical. From now on, we must be especially careful about how we move around. We can no longer leave this *cancha* in small groups, or else we'll go down under a hail of stones – and we might lose our valuable horses. We'd best wait patiently and contain our rage, and then mount a massive charge towards the plain in two or three days. Let's be clever, and play on their nerves. Let us lead them to believe that we're weak and terrified, then break through their siege, shattering their lines as though they were made of glass.'

'Weak and terrified! If they've heard the cries that have risen from this city over the last few days, we'll have no trouble convincing them of that! We *are* weak, and they know it. How can you be so sure of your tactic. Don Hernando? There are two hundred *thousand* of them and just two hundred of us. And we have no more than fifty or sixty horses!'

'That's fifty more than were with my brother the Governor at Cajamarca, my lord del Barco! There, we defeated Atahualpa's hundred thousand warriors in a few short hours. It was God's will, and he gave us our strength. Never forget that a Spaniard with a good sword can cut down ten Indians like a peasant scything wheat, whereas they need fifty arrows to pierce through one of our leather and cotton breastplates. Contrary to what my beloved brother Juan suggested a few moments ago, we are *not* ants, gentlemen. And so what if we're frightened? That's good: it makes our balls bigger!'

Gabriel came further into the room, a room that stank of soot, sweat, and fear, and met Bartholomew's surprised and direct gaze. Gabriel gave him an amused smile and put his fingers to his lips, indicating that he should say nothing, while a young man, his eyes sunken from lack of sleep, protested vehemently:

'But Don Hernando, I don't understand! Why wait for tomorrow or the day after to charge? Why not charge right away, and get ourselves out of this death-hole?'

'Because we must not fail, Rojas. Given the unequal numbers, we will have but one chance. These last few hours have made us weary. Look around: whether horseman or foot soldier, we all need some rest. And so do you, perhaps more than anyone: you can hardly stand!'

'Staying holed up in here, Don Hernando, means giving them the city! Giving them the city means condemning ourselves to die like rats! And now you suggest that we should waste our time sleeping!'

'No, Rojas, we won't be wasting our time. We shall annoy the Indians by *not* moving. They'll wear themselves out with their shouting and by throwing their stones!'

'And what will stop them from simply coming here and burning us alive tonight? There are tens of thousands of them, Don Hernando. If they want to, they can jump over the walls into this *cancha* like fleas hopping into a priest's habit!'

'But they *don't* want to, my lord del Barco!' growled Don Hernando, growing livid with irritation. 'Don't you see that they're content to remain at the other end of the square, hurling stones at us? If they weren't frightened of us, of our swords and horses, then we'd all be dead already! They're frightened of us, del Barco! There may be thousands of Indians, but they are thousands of *frightened* Indians! One charge, I tell you, one charge, with all our strength concentrated, and we shall throw their rank and file into panic.'

'You delude yourself, Don Hernando,' interrupted Gabriel quietly. 'We aren't at Cajamarca. You were there, true, but so was I. I have just come from outside, and I can assure you that the fear that you say grips the Inca warriors is wishful thinking. On the contrary, they are very determined. Looking at your faces, my lords, and without wishing to offend you, I would say that fear reigns in here rather than out there!'

Standing his ground, Gabriel met their astonished gazes as each man turned to face him.

'Fucking hell!' spat Gonzalo. 'Who freed him?'

He took a couple of steps towards Gabriel. He was still limping from their last encounter. Juan grabbed him by the elbow, both to help him stand and hold him back.

'I am as overjoyed as you are to find myself still alive,' said Gabriel, glaring at him before bowing especially low, the mockery of his gesture clear to all. 'Having regained my liberty by my own efforts, Don Hernando, I forgive you for taking it from me and I put myself at your service for the fine battle that awaits us!'

Gonzalo shoved Juan aside and reached for his sword. But Gabriel's was already out of its scabbard.

'I could fight my lord your brother, Don Hernando, and we could well disembowel one another. But might I suggest that the moment is ill chosen? After all, you need as many men as possible and, in any case, no doubt there will be a great many opportunities to die during the coming days. Don Gonzalo might even choose to do just that himself!'

'Brother!' cried Gonzalo in a hoarse voice. 'You cannot allow this fucking mongrel of a spy to join us! You cannot take on this liar and murderer! He will betray us at the first chance he gets!'

'Why don't you shut your stupid mouth, Gonzalo?' replied Gabriel. 'There's nothing to betray here, except honor. Or have you so little of that left to realize it?'

'Enough!' cried Hernando. 'We will settle our scores later. Do not think that you have escaped justice, Montelucar!'

'It is not in my nature to flee justice, Don Hernando. It's just that one encounters it so rarely around here. I believe that I've proven that to you on more than one occasion.'

'My lords! Don Hernando! Don Gonzalo!' interrupted Bartholomew, raising his deformed hand. 'This is not the time for your squabbles.

Whatever grievances you hold against Don Gabriel, you must admit that he has fought the Indians as often, if not more often, than any man here. His advice must therefore be of some worth. Why not listen to him?'

'Very true,' agreed Juan Pizarro, looking at Gonzalo, 'Brother Bartholomew gives wise counsel. Let us leave our differences aside and join forces. Once the battle is over – and if we win it – then we shall have plenty of time to study Don Gabriel's defects of character!'

When Gonzalo made to reply, Hernando sighed and stopped him with a wave of his hand. Then he asked:

'Since you are so erudite, Montelucar, why don't you enlighten us with your wisdom? How should we deal with your Indian friends?'

'They have been observing us for years now,' declared Gabriel, addressing the whole company and ignoring Hernando's gibe. 'They have learned what our weak points are and how to put our horses out of action. The days when they panicked whenever we charged, and when they let us cut them down like hay, are over. They know how to sling their stones so that they break our arms or our horses' legs. As for hand-to-hand combat, they are far superior to us: they are far more agile, and far more efficient—'

'What grand news!' spat Gonzalo. 'You're not telling us anything we don't already know.'

'What they are waiting for, what they are *hoping* for,' continued Gabriel, totally ignoring Gonzalo, 'is that our arrogance gets the better of us, and that we give in to our impatience. They're hoping that hunger and thirst will drive us onto the plain, leaving us at the mercy of their troops. They hope that once again we will simply throw our cavalry at them, just as you have suggested, Don Hernando, in an attempt to break their stranglehold on us and escape beyond the plain. The difference this time is that they are expecting it, my lords! I promise you that, whatever path we take out onto the plain, we will find their resistance unusually light – until we start falling into their traps, into the pike-lined ditches that they have dug, and grow confused among all the hidden obstacles that they have created. Go ahead with your charge as you intend, Don Hernando – and our horses will all have their legs broken before we have even brushed an Inca neck with our swords!'

Gabriel's speech had its effect. He had effectively said out loud what others had been thinking. A long, discouraged silence followed.

'What do you propose we do, then, Don Gabriel?' asked Juan Pizarro eventually.

'Take the fortress!'

'You've lost your mind,' laughed Gonzalo contemptuously. 'That's impossible!'

'It's the only thing we can do to give ourselves a chance of survival. It's essential. You know as well as I do,' said Gabriel, turning towards Hernando, as though Gonzalo didn't exist, 'that without the fortress, we would not now be under siege.'

'Oh yes? And how do you plan to take it?' sneered Gonzalo. 'By jumping over its walls? Its tower and walls are nowhere less than forty-five to sixty codos high. Not to mention the barricades that block all its approaches.'

'We can destroy it this very night.'

A murmur rose from the men. Gabriel caught sight of them glancing at one another, their heads bowed in disappointment. Even Bartholomew looked unconvinced. Gabriel raised a hand and placed it emphatically over his heart.

'My lords, I have not lost my mind, nor do I want to lead you to certain destruction. I understand your fears. But the truth stands in front of us, more naked than ever. Either you die because of your prudence or else you die in battle. And it's not just that prudence is shame and fighting is glory—'

'Now he sounds like my brother Francisco,' said Gonzalo sarcastically to no one in particular.

'—It's that prudence,' continued Gabriel, still ignoring Gonzalo, 'will spell certain death for us, whereas attacking might well bring us victory. And a fair few of us may even survive.'

In the silence that followed, all eyes once again upon him, Gabriel stared Gonzalo up and down.

'Thanks to Don Gonzalo, I am indifferent to death. So this is what I suggest: tonight, I will set off and set fire to the barricades. I will go alone if I have to. We shall see what happens.'

'Brother, it's a low trick!' roared Gonzalo. 'He simply wants to escape and join the savages!'

'Don Gonzalo,' said Bartholomew with some feeling, 'reveals how little sense he possesses. If Don Gabriel had intended to flee once he'd broken out of your prison, surely he wouldn't have come to tell you about it!'

An unpleasant smile broke out on Hernando's face even before Bartholomew had finished. Hernando put his hand on Gonzalo's arm.

'What you propose suits me perfectly, Don Gabriel! I am curious to see how you fare. Perhaps someone here will lend you a horse. And if any of the gentlemen present care to accompany you, then I will let five of them go – no more. That way it won't be too great a disaster.'

'I am delighted, Don Hernando, that you are at last allowing some sense to moderate your ardent desire to see me take leave of this world,' said Gabriel affably.

'My dear Don Gabriel – if, at last, you wish to make yourself useful to your king and to bring some glory to Our Lord, who am I to stop you?'

'I'm coming with you,' Sebastian assured Gabriel a moment later.

'No,' said Gabriel, smiling. 'Although it amused me to play off the Pizarros' bad characters, I'm far less sure of succeeding than I pretended.'

'They, on the other hand, are sure of your failure, Hernando most of all. The way he looks at you, you would think that you were already a corpse.'

'Bah. Let them dream.'

'I'm coming with you,' repeated Sebastian, his gaze severe. 'Otherwise you'll have no horse: who else is going to dare offer you one?'

Seeing that Gabriel was about to protest further, Sebastian added:

'And you're not the only one who wants to show those gentle-men what loyalty and courage are.'

The two friends looked at one another for a few moments before Gabriel, moved, took Sebastian's hands in his.

'I am most indebted to you.'

'You've paid your debt in advance – well in advance, dear Gabriel. And there's nothing I enjoy more than baiting the Devil himself in your company. Come now, I want to show you my horses.'

The *cancha*'s inner courtyard, which had been carefully covered with canvas, had been transformed into stables. The thick smell of horse urine and dung assaulted their noses, and flies buzzed about in dense clouds. As soon as Sebastian and Gabriel entered, a few of the horses drew fearfully away, and a moment later all the animals began neighing, stamping the ground, and rolling their big, frightened eyes back in their heads, lurching violently into one another. They were all huddled together with no real space to speak of, and clearly they were still terrified by the fire and the fearful cries from the hills. Their fear was visible as their quivering, unkempt withers shuddered.

Sebastian whistled softly, and a superb mare, its coat as white as snow, approached somewhat hesitantly, its neck bent and its head forward as though looking for a comforting hand.

'This is Itza,' said Sebastian, stroking the animal's muzzle. 'You see, I'm not like you: I give my horses names.'

'What does Itza mean?'

'I don't know. But back when I was a slave, when I didn't even dare look a white man in the eyes, I met an old conquistador in Panama who spoke to me as a man rather than an animal. And he always said that word: Itza, Itza, as though it was some magic spell. I thought it suited this lady perfectly: she's lively, as quick as a flash, yet she's gentle. And here, we have Pongo.'

'I'm not going to ask you about the name.'

A gray, gelding came out to stand in front of the other horses, but drew no closer to the two men. It stood back a little, watching suspiciously as Sebastian stroked the mare.

'Pongo lost his balls, but he retained his bad character. And yet, we get along well. You shall ride Itza – I'm sure that she'll take to you.'

Without warning and as though on cue, the mare left Sebastian's caressing hand, turned to Gabriel, and rubbed her head on his chest. He patted and stroked her neck, returning her affections.

'What did I tell you?' chuckled Sebastian.

'Do you think any other cavalrymen will come with us?' asked Gabriel, his tone serious.

'What's important is not how many cavalrymen join us but how many of our Indian allies. They will prove far more useful.'

'No, that's not what's most important,' said Gabriel, grinning.

'Oh no? Then would your lordship care to enlighten me what is?'

'It's having an African like you as a friend.'

That night, after endless arguments, fifty Canary Indians and three Spanish cavalrymen volunteered to accompany Sebastian and Gabriel. The rest of the Spaniards formed a silent line and watched as the *cancha*'s door was opened. The only sounds were those of horses' hooves on the flagstones and Bartholomew's voice raised in prayer, while out on the hills the Incas kept up their caterwauling.

Don Hernando was closest to the door. He smirked as he bowed slightly and said:

'Good night, Don Gabriel.'

'Have no doubt,' said Gabriel in an equally even tone, 'that it *will* be a good night. And if you cannot find sleep, I suggest you glance over the walls. You may enjoy the spectacle.'

The men made the most of the darkness and the fact that the Incas weren't expecting anyone to leave the *cancha*, and they reached the first barricade with no difficulties. It blocked the largest of the alleys leading to the Sacsayhuaman fortress. The Incas had tied spiky bundles of wood to the log barricades, the thorns sharp enough to tear out the belly of any man or horse.

The Inca warriors' cacophony out on the hills covered the click-clack of the horses' hooves and the clinking of their harnesses. The animals' necks and heads had been carefully wrapped in cloth to protect them from stones, and the most vulnerable parts of their legs, as well as their chests, were armoured with thick leather. But all the gear weighed the horses down, and slowed their pace.

When the attacking party was nearly at the barricade, they suddenly heard the dirgelike tone of a *pututu* shell. A lookout had spotted them; he had sounded the alert. Within a second, Inca warriors swarmed out onto the tops of the walls of the surrounding burned-out *canchas*. Gabriel had just enough time to raise his shield to protect himself from the first volley of stones. He gave a berserk cry and, with his head down, urged on his mare at an irregular trot, staying as close as possible to the walls and holding his sword high to cut away at the Incas' feet and legs.

Behind him, the Canaries had bounded up onto the walls with bewildering agility and were already swinging their clubs and bronze axes. As the blizzard of stones ended, a terrible mêlée began on the walls as the Canaries and Incas engaged in hand-to-hand combat, both sides crying out horrendously.

'The oil, the oil!' screamed Gabriel to Sebastian.

As he turned Itza around and around on herself close to the barricade, whipping his sword through the air like a scythe, Sebastian and two of the Spaniards smashed a large jug of oil against the barricade. It took only one spark from a tinderbox to set it alight. A huge yellow flash erupted, blinding them, and someone cried out with joy:

'Santiago! Santiago!'

In the intense glow of the burning barricade, the merciless hand-to-hand fighting on the walls resembled some fiendish dance performed by men possessed by the Devil. The Canary warriors cried out with demented joy, hacking through their opponents as though the Incas were mere scarecrows. The blackened walls grew sticky with blood and guts, and the dead piled up on top of one another.

Gabriel, horrified, looked away and howled out at the top of his lungs the order to fall back.

'The next barricade!' he cried. 'We must burn another immediately, before they see what we're up to!'

Gently, he urged Itza into a gallop, the other Spaniards and Canaries following swiftly behind him.

And so it continued throughout the night. The barricades in one alley, and then in another, went up in flames. The same slaughter repeated itself four or five times. The raiders' task became more difficult with each new barricade they came to. But they had managed to draw close enough to the fortress to make out clearly its dark walls looming above them. Despite the men's exhaustion, and although half the Canaries had fallen, Gabriel was determined to destroy one last barricade. By destroying this one, he hoped, the road leading directly to the fortress would be clear by morning.

But things went differently this time. The Incas were expecting them now. Their volleys of stones and arrows were thicker than ever and were now far more difficult to weather. The Canaries, reduced in number and slow with exhaustion, struggled to climb atop the walls. Salvos of stones smashed into their faces and legs, breaking their bones and slowing their forward motion.

Gabriel pushed his agile mare to the limit and, miraculously, she bounded over a ditch, hidden under branches and earth, that the Incas had dug in front of the barricade. But the two cavalrymen following him weren't so lucky. Their horses fell into the lethal trench, breaking their legs. Gabriel heard the wounded animals' terrified neighs, and he pivoted Itza around just in time to see a hail of stones shower down upon his companions.

'Sebastian!' he cried.

'Over here!' the African giant shouted back. He was single-handedly holding off a pack of Inca warriors.

'There's too many of them, Gabriel! We have to retreat!'

But it was too late. The Incas were now rushing forth by the dozen, howling like demons. Gabriel abandoned his attempt to get to the barricade and set it alight, and instead charged in to help the two wounded Spaniards, whom the Canaries could no longer protect. Blood streamed from his sword. Suddenly, Sebastian cried out again, surprising him:

'Watch out! Gabriel, watch out for the fire above you!'

The Incas were firing burning arrows from the top of the

fortress, and the arrows fell like shooting stars slamming into the ground. The Canaries, suddenly petrified, stopped in their tracks, and terrible howls of pain rose up into the sky as arrows found their marks. Men ran around madly, the clothing on their shoulders and chests on fire. Out of the corner of his eye, Gabriel noticed the Incas on the ground retreating: another salvo was coming from the fortress.

'Damn the Devil, they've trapped us!' cried Sebastian. 'We're stuck between the barricade and the—'

He never finished his sentence: a burning arrow slammed into his leather breastplate, and the cotton padding immediately caught alight. Sebastian tried to beat out the flames with the back of his hand, but his armour impeded his movement. His horse panicked and began to buck around and around, the motion of the air only fanning the flames as other burning arrows slammed off its protected flanks. Gabriel came galloping up and drew his dagger. He cut away the burning sections of Sebastian's leather armour, flinging them to the ground.

Then something remarkable happened. Everyone, Spaniard, Canary, or Inca, saw it.

Another volley of burning arrows hurtled down. Yet not one of them touched Gabriel or Sebastian. They didn't even need to raise their shields to protect themselves. Arrows fell all around them, breaking on the flagstones or against the walls. But not one of them struck the two conquistadors. It was as though the missiles were deflected by some invisible force.

Gabriel launched into a gallop, his white mare as tireless as he. He charged the Inca line. Many retreated, but the braver among them still twirled their slings. Yet, like the arrows, their stones disappeared into the night without touching Gabriel or Itza. From the defensive circle into which they had retreated, the Spaniards and Canaries watched as Gabriel charged the Inca lines at full gallop, his blade pointed out in front of him, without touching a single warrior. Looking like some guardian angel atop his perfectly white steed, Gabriel forced through a passage for himself without shedding a single drop of blood. The Incas, petrified with either fear or amazement, offered him no resistance, and soon there was a clear passage through the alley.

'Follow me!' Gabriel shouted to his companions. 'Follow me – there's no danger!'

His men shook off their amazement and ran after him, crying, 'Santiago! Santiago!' Not a single Inca tried to stop them, and not one arrow, not one stone fell upon them.

For the rest of the night, it wasn't fear, hatred, or the urge to violence that churned in Gabriel's guts: it was a strange, intense, and irresistible impulse to laugh.

The exhilaration of the heroism of that desperate night was quickly dispelled by the events of the following day.

Around midday, not long after Gabriel, exhausted, had dozed off despite the relentless noise from the Inca drums and the discomfort of his own great hunger, he was woken by shouts and a great commotion. He grumbled sleepily, and was about to leave the shady corner near the horses where he had found refuge when Sebastian, his arm and shoulder now in bandages, appeared in front of him, along with Bartholomew. Both men looked grave.

'How are you feeling?' asked Gabriel the moment he saw Sebastian.

'Like a bride does the morning after her wedding night!' growled the big African.

'Are his burns serious?' Gabriel asked Bartholomew.

'Serious enough to cause him pain for some time to come,' sighed Bartholomew resignedly. 'But what I fear most is that his wounds may become infected. I need to treat him with an olive-oil salve, but finding that here . . .'

'I'm not some delicate maiden. My wounds will wait patiently with the rest of me for better times,' protested Sebastian, somewhat irritably. He pushed Gabriel back into his shady corner and continued:

'As for you, my friend, it's best that you remain inconspicuous for a time . . .'

'Why? What's going on?'

'We're out of water,' announced Bartholomew, 'except for a very few casks. This morning, the Incas destroyed the stone conduits that supply the fountains on the great square.'

'And why should that stop me showing myself?' asked Gabriel, astonished.

Sebastian looked at Bartholomew. Hunger and fear had hollowed their faces just as much as it had the rest of the Spanish contingent. Fever had dulled Sebastian's usually lively disposition. He was suffering a nervous tic in his wounded arm. As for Bartholomew, the skin on his face was as gray as his faded cowl. His skin was stretched so tight on his temples and hands that one could see the details of the bones beneath. Both men looked embarrassed when Gabriel repeated:

'Well, why should it?'

'Certain people feel that our barricade-burning expedition last night vexed the Incas,' murmured Sebastian, 'and that, without it, they wouldn't have thought to cut the conduits.'

'Who can believe such a thing?' said Gabriel, furious.

'Anyone Gonzalo can persuade to listen. What's worse is that the Canaries carried out a reconnaissance mission just now. The Incas have already rebuilt the barricades. All of last night's efforts were in vain. We can no more reach the fortress today than we could yesterday—'

'What of it? Of course they're going to rebuild the barricades,' Gabriel cut in. 'And we'll just burn them again and again! Are they not laying siege to us? What can we do but fight? Or else negotiate peace with the Incas. I certainly wouldn't mind that.'

'It's not just the barricades.'

'Oh?'

'No. It's also what else happened.'

'Oh yes? And what else happened?'

His question met with silence. Gabriel at last became aware of his friends' deep embarrassment.

'Fucking hell, are you going to tell me what this is all about?'

'You know very well,' murmured Sebastian, turning toward the horses.

'I know nothing!'

'People are saying all kinds of odd things about last night,' said Bartholomew softly.

'Such as what?'

'That you rode Itza through the hail of stones and arrows with impunity, whilst others fell.'

'What of it? We were lucky, very lucky – that's all.'

'No, that's not all,' said Sebastian.

'Sebastian, you're wounded. You were frightened, and you allowed free rein to your imagination. It's only natural.'

'Protest all you want, Gabriel, I know what I saw, and there was nothing natural about it. Itza returned without a scratch, whereas I have just spent the last hour seeing to Pongo's wounds.'

'Would you like to hear the rumor that was spread this morning?' interrupted Bartholomew. 'Gonzalo is telling anyone who'll listen that both the Devil and the Incas are with you. Those who were with you last night swear that they saw Saint James himself rise from you. Some even claim that the Sacred Virgin cleared you a passage.'

'Well, I didn't notice any saints,' said Gabriel with ill humor. 'And now I hear this rot . . . all that happened last night was a fight in which too many people died – and that's it.'

'No. Even the Inca warriors saw it,' Sebastian maintained. 'That's why they let us go. In any case, you know it very well: you drove them back with your sword without even touching them.'

'Sebastian's not the only one to have seen what happened, Gabriel,' continued Bartholomew. 'I've spoken with the cavalrymen whom you saved as well as with the Canaries. They all agree: the flaming arrows and the stones spared you as though by a miracle. Are you protected by God? Or is it . . . is it thanks to your friends among the Incas?'

'Brother Bartholomew, with all due respect, you have lost your mind! I know how susceptible the Inca warriors are during combat to anything that smells of magic. All I did was play on that susceptibility! I pretended that I feared neither their stones nor their fire. And it worked. Furthermore . . .'

But Gabriel's voice lacked conviction: his tone was unnatural. He could see both the doubt and the incomprehension in his friends' eyes.

'. . . Furthermore, I was lucky. It was luck, that's all . . .'

In truth, he wasn't so convinced himself. Sebastian was right: Gabriel *had* felt something strange happen to him during the battle. He had felt as though he had been empowered with a strength beyond any limits. But how could he admit such a thing without appearing mad?

'You must believe me,' he repeated in a muted voice. 'It's true that I don't care whether I die or live. But there was no miracle, and no magic, last night.'

'In your eyes, maybe so. But for those suffering here who don't want to die, it's not so simple,' replied Bartholomew. 'They are not so proud that they consider meeting Death a fine moment, Gabriel Montelucar.'

'What do you want me to do to convince you, Brother Bartholomew? Shall I go out into the alleys of Cuzco unarmed and prove that the Incas can slay me as easily as they can any other man?'

Bartholomew answered by raising his fused fingers to his face and deliberately making the sign of the cross before admonishing Gabriel:

'We don't ask so much of you. God will decide what path you take! But until He does, have the humility to behave like anyone else, and lie low. Don Hernando has forbidden any further action by his forces. That goes for you, too.'

They left him, and Gabriel remained lying on the ground. He gazed over at the massive stones of the unbreachable fortress and then beyond, up at the mountains. He laughed privately at his so-called luck, or his divine protection. 'Where is she?' he murmured to himself. 'Where is she?'

But the gods who had spared his life the previous night now refused him the answer that would have restored to him his taste for it.

*　　*　　*

Over the following five days and five nights, Cuzco became a maelstrom of pandemonium, death, and suffering.

The Inca warriors had learned from the Spanish attack during the first night: they not only rebuilt the barricades so that they prevented any more cavalry charges, but they dug more hidden ditches in front of them and posted guards over them day and night. Furthermore, in order to terrorize the Spaniards and deny them any rest, they maintained an incessant cacophony made up of the doleful wails of their horns and the sinister sound of drumming, alternating with the shrill, raucous chants and jeers of their warriors. Day and night, the archers and sling wielders on the high walls of the Sacsayhuaman fortress took turns bombarding the great square and the last *cancha* in which the besieged Spaniards remained holed up like rats.

Hunger, thirst, and the complete impossibility of rest – the endless din made unthinkable even the notion of sleep – sent many of the men temporarily mad. Some shrieked deliriously with their eyes closed, others sobbed like children. Some took to praying so incessantly and with such vehemence that Bartholomew didn't dare accompany them in their expressions of piety. Others remembered desperate methods of assuaging the craving for food and drink adopted during Governor Don Francisco Pizarro's earliest campaigns, and took to roasting earthworms and swallowing their own urine, even begging others for theirs.

On the fourth day, realizing that he wouldn't be able to restrain the demented, bloodthirsty men much longer, Don Hernando agreed to his brothers Juan and Gonzalo's request to lead twenty foot soldiers in a charge to retake Gonzalo's house on the other side of the great square, where they hoped to find a few of the pigs that they had brought from Cajamarca, along with some beans and perhaps even some cornflour. Gonzalo forbade Gabriel to join the attack, so Gabriel, along with a few others, formed a squad to protect Gonzalo's men from any flanking manoeuvre by the Incas.

It was only after four hours of fighting that Juan and Gonzalo's horses, trampling over Inca corpses, managed at last to enter the building. But the only pigs they found were dead ones – the animals' carcasses had become infested with maggots and had been left to rot. In the cellar the Spaniards found only one cask of flour that had been overlooked by the Incas. However, the discovery of a stone basin full of fresh water and fed by some invisible source, a fountain like the one in Sebastian's house, caused them to cry out with joy.

That night, this victory, slight though it was, restored some hope to the Spaniards. The Incas could no longer pound all of the Aucaypata, the great square, with stones. Men were ordered to fetch from Gonzalo's house every sheet, tablecloth and carpet that they could find. And the house was as full of fabric as a Cadiz warehouse.

They worked feverishly throughout the night, and their exertions made them forget about the clamour from the hills, their hunger, and their fear. While cavalrymen took turns keeping the great square out of Manco's troops' hands, foot soldiers, their thick-fingered hands more used to the sword or lance, sewed together the various fabrics, while others wove rope, raised stockades, or pulled free from the charred roofs those few beams that were still usable.

Hernando's modest success had made him bold, and now he was trying to break the noose that was strangling them. He sent his cavalry into skirmishes further and further away from the great square. But these actions soon proved more costly than useful, and threatened to weaken what little strength the Spaniards had left.

The same thing happened at each skirmish. Horses fell into the traps that the Incas had dug even in the terraces to the west of the square. Their riders were thrown to the ground and were immediately assaulted by dozens of Inca warriors, or else literally buried beneath a hail of stones.

On the evening of the fifth day, Juan Pizarro was brought in and placed on one of the cots in Bartholomew's makeshift infirmary. A sling stone had shattered his jaw and, despite his courage, he moaned with pain as the monk dressed his wound as best he could.

Bartholomew got Gabriel to help hold Juan still while he pulled at the wounded man's jaw so that the broken bones wouldn't overlap. Bandages and splints had been hastily prepared. By the time Don Hernando and Gonzalo had rushed to his bedside, Juan had fainted. Gabriel was astonished to see Gonzalo kneel by his brother's cot and stroke Juan's forehead as one would a child's. Tears welled up in his eyes, and his muttered words of comfort were indistinct as they left his trembling lips.

'Don't worry too much, Don Gonzalo,' said Bartholomew in a low voice. 'It's a painful wound, but not a fatal one. Your brother is as hardy as he is brave. He will be on his feet tomorrow, although he'll still be a little feverish.'

'On his feet to do what, by the blood of Christ!' cried Hernando, clenching his wrist.

His eyes met Gabriel's. For once, they seemed to be imploring him for help.

They all looked at the gap between the canvas stretched above them and the *cancha*'s wall. Those in the Sacsayhuaman fortress had already prepared for night, and a hundred torches glowed from atop its walls. In the dusk's failing light, the fortress's towers looked like a flame-colored dragon's head.

'It's up there that we have to go,' murmured Gabriel.

'Up there? You know that's impossible.'

'We must attack and take the fortress,' repeated Gabriel. 'It's all we *can* do.'

'You go too far! Nothing is better guarded than those towers. The roads leading to it are so steep that the horses slip and move too slowly to charge. We wouldn't cover a hundred paces before being massacred. The towers' walls are so high that we couldn't scale them even with ladders. We would have to take the fortress from behind. But before we could do that, we'd have to make it out of the city in one piece!'

'Don Hernando, you know as well as I do: there's no other solution. We must take Sacsayhuaman, at whatever cost.'

'Another one of your follies, like your attempt to destroy the barricades.'

'If we make it,' continued Gabriel, not listening, 'we will gain control of the noose with which they are choking us: we will turn it against them. Look at your brother, Don Hernando. How has his ordeal served us? There are only fifty cavalrymen left. It's our last chance.'

Don Hernando had a grave look in his eye. His doubts and his hostility to Gabriel were at odds with his hope.

'Let us first look after my brother,' he muttered. 'Then we'll think about it.'

'Yes, look after your brother,' said Gabriel. 'We need every brave man we have.'

For the first time, Gabriel detected in Hernando's glance something other than hatred and distrust. He thought he saw something like respect.

Gabriel looked into Gonzalo's red, tear-laden eyes, surprised by how affected he was. But then the angel-faced younger brother turned to him and spat:

'You're the one who should die, not him!'

But Gabriel sensed how terribly the youngest Pizarro brother was suffering, and he said nothing.

CHAPTER 5

Ollantaytambo, May 1536

THE SUN'S DISK WAS HUGE.

It rested on the air still separating it from the peaks of the western mountains like a huge, magnificent golden bubble, one that could at any moment burst open and engulf This World as a father embraces a son returned from a long journey.

Anamaya stood facing it, wide-eyed on the steep steps in the royal city of Ollantaytambo. She felt its heat on her face, on her chest and belly. She felt the sun's breath enter her.

'Inti, O Inti, shine Your light into our night.'

The closer the sun came to the mountains on the other side of the valley, the larger it grew. Anamaya could hear the priests behind her, standing on narrow terraces so steep that they seemed to have been built directly above one another. They stood facing the sun amid tall stalks of ceremonial corn, the corn still green except for those replicas scattered among it that were made of gold, and chanted:

> O Inti,
> O Powerful Father,
> You have travelled the Universe and made the day burn.
> O Inti,
> O Compassionate Father,
> You turn red, You become blood.
> O Inti,

May Quilla renew your blood,
May She embrace You and relieve You of Your weariness
In the Shadows of the Other World.
And we shall close our eyes,
We shall tremble like the stars until daybreak.
O Inti,
We shall tremble in the darkness and weep
Until You have rested,
Until dawn returns in the fire of Your gold.
O Inti.

Anamaya chanted the prayer with them as the sun seemed to grow heavier, floating gently down onto the mountains and then beyond, into the realm of the unseeable, leaving behind it a crimson glow as red as a heart cut open with a *tumi*.

The warmth within Anamaya's chest abruptly disappeared. A gentle but cold breeze came up from the mountains. The heavy stones of the buildings glowed red in the gloaming, and for a moment their surfaces seemed as supple and light as a child's skin.

And then an enormous shadow spread through the depths of the great Sacred Valley. The river's surface lost its shimmer amid the soft green terraces and became a giant black snake as cold as the eastern sky, which had already turned dark between the high peaks of the mountains. The narrow valley running down from them, ragged with sharp contrasts of light and shade, yawned open like a mouth, slowly swallowing the silent darkness creeping up it, a darkness that was also engulfing the city's streets, streets as neatly laid out as the pattern on a *manta*.

The *canchas'* roofs were already gray. The smoke from the braziers in their courtyards rose up straight, also gray. The silence in the city's narrow streets was gray, as were the terraces that fell away to the rivers, and the mountainsides disappeared into the same gray. And so the light faded until only one cliff face in the Sacred Valley remained illuminated with golden rays, as though Inti was applying one final polish to its stone with his red light.

For a few fleeting seconds Anamaya felt exalted, as though she was floating above everyone, borne up by a pair of wings. She saw the darkened valley with bird's eyes – the slopes of the now pale and foreshortened mountains, the houses of Ollantaytambo, which looked like wooden toys carved for children.

And then, at a single stroke, the sun disappeared, and even the sky turned gray and flat.

'O Inti,' she murmured, 'do not abandon us.'

Silence lingered on for a moment, as though every thing in the world was falling under the same evening veil of sadness. Then she heard voices from the bottom of the steps. She looked down and recognized the man arguing with the guards to let him through. Her heart began to beat wildly.

Anamaya almost set off down the steps to meet them before recollecting herself. She tightened all her muscles in an effort to hide her trembling. She yanked her *manta* tightly, too tightly, around her shoulders, and waited for the man to come to her. He was the young officer who had once escorted her to meet Manco at Rimac Tambo and who had helped her save Gabriel before the battle of Vilcaconga.

He had gained confidence in himself since then, and the features of his face and the set of his body had grown heavier, battle-weary. But even before he had reached her, she knew, merely watching him climb the steps as steep as a cliff-face path, with his mouth slightly open and his shoulders drooping, that he was bringing her bad news.

When he arrived at a point still five steps beneath her, he kneeled and bowed his head.

'I am at your service, *Coya Camaquen*,' he said, still catching his breath.

'Please stand, Titu Cuyuchi,' she replied a little nervously.

What she saw in his expression confirmed her fears.

'So?' she asked.

'May you forgive me my failure, *Coya Camaquen*, but we were unable to do it.'

Anamaya forced herself to take a few deep breaths to still her beating heart, then asked:

'Do you at least know if he's still alive?'

'He was when we last saw him. But that was five days ago.'

'Why didn't you succeed. Titu Cuyuchi?'

The officer waved his hand despondently.

'I had two men with me. As soon as the roofs of Cuzco had stopped burning, I waited until the darkest moment of the night before running along the walls until we reached the *cancha* that you had pointed out to me. You were right, the Stranger was there. We recognized him by his clothing, a peasant's tunic from Titicaca. He was tied to the wall with a chain—'

'A chain?'

'Yes. That was what confused us. We stood there a moment, wondering how to free him. Then one of my soldiers was hit by an arrow and died. All we saw was a black shadow. It was a very confused moment . . .'

'Did he say anything to you?'

'He said that he was your friend, *Coya Camaquen*, and that we shouldn't kill him. He hadn't understood that we had come to free him.'

Anamaya said nothing. She turned her gaze away from the horizon, the last faint red tint still lingering in the west.

'We had to flee,' continued Titu Cuyuchi. 'We didn't even see the faces of those who attacked us.'

'You didn't try again?'

'No, *Coya Camaquen* . . .'

There was a reticence in Titu Cuyuchi's tone. Anamaya looked at him closely.

'Have no fear. Speak freely,' she ordered him in a flat voice.

'The following night, the Strangers, with help from the Canaries, set fire to our barricades. They killed many of our warriors. I fought on the last barricade, where we managed to repel their attack. I saw him there. He was on a horse, and wearing Stranger's clothes, and . . .'

'And?'

But Titu Cuyuchi hesitated again before replying. His gaze strayed to Anamaya's shoulder, and then up, past it. As she turned around, she heard the Master of the Stone's soft step as he approached them. She was almost relieved that he was there. She repeated her order in a harsh voice, and loud enough for Katari to hear:

'Speak, Titu Cuyuchi.'

'He rode his white beast and fought like an immortal from the Under World! He sliced through our warriors as though nothing counted for him, not the deaths on our side, nor those on his. And then, something odd happened. We had surrounded the Strangers in front of the barricade, and our warriors on the great tower of Sacsayhuman were bombarding them with stones and flaming arrows. But the arrows and sling stones swerved away from him. I saw it with my own eyes, *Coya Camaquen*! Our warriors were so unnerved that they stopped fighting and let him pass.'

Anamaya shuddered and shut her eyes.

'Are you sure that it was him?'

'Yes, *Coya Camaquen*. I saw him as clearly as I see you now. He tried to plunge his blade into my belly! He was alive, and free.'

The officer hesitated, but then a smile lit up his severe face. He looked Anamaya directly in the eyes and said:

'But he burned our barricades in vain, *Coya Camaquen*. We rebuilt them the very next day. The Strangers no longer dare to come out of their hole. They will soon be defeated, and the Emperor will be able to return to Cuzco.'

'Thank you, Titu Cuyuchi. I know that you did everything you could. Now go – eat and rest . . .'

Night had fallen on the alleyways of Ollantaytambo by the time the officer went back down the steps. Anamaya stood as if frozen. She didn't dare look at Katari lest he should see the tears in her eyes. He drew near her, put his hand on her shoulder, and said gently:

'Your puma is free, *Coya Camaquen*.'

'Free? Or dead? Who knows? Was what I did wrong, Katari? When I saw that the Strangers had imprisoned him, I ordered Titu Cuyuchi to free him.'

'But the puma always frees itself,' replied Katari with a grin.

'Do you believe, as I do, that he's the Puma that Emperor Huayna Capac predicted would come?'

'When I treated him on the shore of Titicaca, I saw the mark on his shoulder. I put my hand on it, *Coya Camaquen*, and, like you, I sensed it.'

Anamaya shuddered again. Night now veiled the mountains almost completely.

'I made a mistake, Katari. I can no longer make good decisions, because my heart confuses my spirit. I suffer because I'm apart from him, and yet I'm frightened of getting too close. I accepted that I had to leave Gabriel because Villa Oma asked me to. He hates him. But my fear of losing Gabriel grows with each passing day. Oh Katari, am I frightened because he's the Puma, or only because the man I love is a Stranger?'

'I cannot tell you, *Coya Camaquen*.'

'You agree with Villa Oma, don't you?'

'No. Villa Oma is no longer the sage who educated you. He is a war-hungry hawk now. He sees only violence ahead of him.'

'Help me, Katari. How can I tell what is true and what is false?'

'You must heed the Ancestors of the Other World.'

'But I hear only silence.'

The last hint of light vanished from the top of the sacred town's highest building and from the rocky peaks overlooking it. The first stars twinkled in the night sky, and torches lit the streets of Ollantaytambo. Anamaya felt the warmth of Katari's hand on her shoulder.

'If you will trust me, I think I know a way whereby your husband the Sacred Double will allow you to travel to meet the Emperor Huayna Capac,' he whispered.

Anamaya could not tell, through the darkness, what it was that lay behind the twinkle in the Master of the Stone's eyes. But his words echoed in her soul for some time after he had uttered them (and they continued to do so in her dreams later that night after she had succumbed to sleep), and for the first time in many moons she felt a glimmer of hope that wasn't immediately destroyed by anxiety.

'I will wait for you,' she murmured to the night.

And she felt as though her puma had heard her.

CHAPTER 6

Cuzco, May 1536

G ABRIEL DIDN'T IMMEDIATELY RECOGNIZE THE MAN he saw approaching him on the evening of the tenth day of the siege.

In the half-light that accentuated the shadows cast by the shielding canvases stretched over the courtyard, the man appeared only as a silhouette, albeit one with an unusually large head. It approached cautiously, keeping away from the Panama slaves dozing on the rubbish-strewn ground. The ubiquitous filth made the place stink, and even the breath of the starving men reeked as though they were already exhaling the foul stench of death. Gabriel, like everyone else, cursed the insistent pain in his empty gut. It was almost a burning sensation, one that never let a moment pass without reminding him that all he had eaten in five days was a shred of meat torn from a dead horse.

When the man came closer, Gabriel made out the scarlet feather rising from the morion that he held under his arm, as well as the large bloodstains spattered across his doublet. As for the abnormal size of his head, Gabriel saw that this was because it was swathed in bandages, with only small openings left for the man's feverish eyes, his hooked nose, and his mouth from which he now spoke haltingly:

'Don Gabriel!'

His voice was so low and his words so ill-formed that they were only just comprehensible. Gabriel did not move from the empty barrel he was using as a chair as he returned the man's greeting with a barely civil nod and said:

'Don Juan. Well then, I see that you're on your feet again. And that Brother Bartholomew has padded your head admirably: you shouldn't feel a thing the next time a sling stone slams into it!'

Juan Pizarro stiffened at Gabriel's taunt and the fever in his eyes blazed. Both men sized one another up for a moment. Gabriel didn't bat an eyelid. Then Juan raised his right hand in an appeasing gesture.

'Don Gabriel, I have come to make peace with you,' he murmured in his unnatural, throaty voice.

Since Gabriel merely looked at him, saying nothing, Juan continued, pausing for breath between each sentence:

'I know what drove you to attack Gonzalo . . . I cannot say that I blame you . . . I am not a stranger to the love of a woman, Don Gabriel . . . as you know, my wife fell to my lot in an unorthodox manner . . . yet I love her as though God Himself had led me to her . . . my dear Inguill has often spoken to me about her friend . . . about your . . . about the woman whom my brother ill-treated . . . Gonzalo sometimes acts without thinking . . .'

Gabriel waved away Juan's embarrassment and said:

'Do not be mistaken, my lord,' he said sadly. 'I have found no mercy in my soul for your brother. Indeed, I am afraid that, should the occasion present itself, my heart and my honour dictate that I must take the same action . . .'

'In that case, you will find me confronting you, and for the same reasons. For honour and love are virtues I too value, Don Gabriel. Whatever his failings may be, Gonzalo is my brother, and I love him as such . . . and although it might surprise you, he loves me with the same absolute and burning sentiment, which I confess worries me at times: it's as though I am all that stands between him and his demons.'

'Then lucky for him that he is today guided by angels!'

Juan was about to answer Gabriel's gibe, but a sudden spasm of pain gripped him and it was only after a moment that he managed to respond bitterly:

'So be it, then, Don Gabriel: you would kill him and I would defend him. Isn't there anything better to do until then?'

Gabriel gestured dismissively in reply. This time, the grimace that appeared fleetingly on Juan's tense mouth was closer to a smile.

'Let us look to the moment,' he continued, approaching Gabriel so that his mumbled speech might be better heard. 'I have come to make peace with you so that we may make war together . . . Don Hernando called us together . . . the decision has been made to attack the fortress. It was your idea . . . even though I'm wounded, Hernando has nominated me as commander of all the lieutenants . . . this battle is mine.'

'Very well,' said Gabriel, now serious. 'But don't commit the same error as our Lieutenant-Governor: do not underestimate the Incas. I know their chief. His name is Villa Oma. He is both intelligent and tenacious. But above all, he dreams only of annihilating every last one of us. He derives his strength from this dream. Do not expect any sign of weakness from him, Don Juan. He would fight you with the stumps, were you to chop off his arms.'

Juan nodded, or at least moved his head as much as his bandages allowed him to. Gabriel noticed sweat beading on his exposed nose, despite the coolness of the evening.

'I am aware of this, Don Gabriel . . . which is why I want you at my side. You have the energy that I lack. If I falter, you will take my place.'

As though to give physical substance to his words, he roughly thrust his morion into Gabriel's hands.

'I want it to be on your head . . . I cannot wear it, because of my injuries. With you visible under this feather, each man will know what to do.'

'It is a great honour that you do me, Don Juan. I am most unaccustomed to it. Are your brothers of the same opinion as you?'

Juan lifted his aching head, and met Gabriel's sardonic stare. His voice was barely audible when he said:

'I told you, I came to make peace . . . and I am to pick the lieutenants . . .'

He let a moment pass, then continued:

'Our companions want you with us, Don Gabriel. Certain of them believe that you are protected by the hand of God, and that the Virgin Mary is with you . . . others believe that it's nothing to do with God, that you have acquired magic powers from the Indians, from your relations with them . . . your exploits the other night have made a deep impression on the men . . .'

'God's blood, how can you lend credence to these fancies?'

'Because I saw the same thing with my own eyes . . . and I didn't arrive yesterday, like many of the men here . . . no, it started on the beach at Tumbez, when we arrived . . . you should have died on that day.'

Gabriel sniggered:

'I am far too indifferent toward God for Him to even blink in my direction. As for the woman that you're thinking of, she taught me no magic. Indeed, I learned nothing of particular note from her, except that the Incas are human beings like you and me, that they are big or small, thin or fat, and that they suffer in both their bodies and souls because of us.'

'Oh, what does it matter to us whether God or pagan demons grant you your power?' interrupted Juan, irritated and breathing shallowly. 'What matters is that our comrades-in-arms now both fear you and see you as some sort of talisman, or lucky charm . . . they believe that, without you, we have no chance of succeeding.'

'Oh yes? Only yesterday, they believed that all was lost because of me.'

'Do you accept my proposal, Don Gabriel?'

'If I refuse, it's back to jail for me, right?'

'I have come to make peace with you, not to threaten you.'

Gabriel carefully set down the morion on the barrel. He absent-mindedly stroked its scarlet feather as he asked:

'How do you plan to enter the fortress?'

Juan gave an odd-sounding grunt and narrowed his eyes. Gabriel realized a moment later that this was the closest to a laugh that he could manage.

'By any way you think is best!'

Gabriel smiled, almost with Juan now, and traced an indistinct shape in the dust with the point of his boot.

'We must trick them. We must make Villa Oma and his lieutenants believe that we're trying to flee . . .'

He described a circle around the shape in the dirt representing the fortress.

'Here, the Carmenga pass. It leads out of the city to the north-west, and avoids the fortress. It will be a formidable task to reach it, and a greater one to climb it: it's a real steep-sided ravine. The Incas will rain death down on our heads. But if we succeed, then we will be out of their range of vision – they will no longer be able to watch our every move. We can then make a long detour and approach the fortress from behind. There are a number of entrances there, which may well prove vulnerable.'

'Then we shall do it . . .'

'Don Juan, no illusions! I can perform no miracle. Our chances of success are as slender as our stomachs.'

'Well, since there's no banquet planned for tonight, I think each man will have plenty of time to pray.'

Gabriel felt deeply troubled as he watched Juan Pizarro walk away, his step heavy and irregular. He had just agreed to serve his mortal enemies without a word of real argument (and, in the depths of his soul, he was as frightened of his mysterious invulnerability in battle as were his comrades-in-arms).

But he didn't regret his decision.

He even felt strangely joyful.

Dawn came and found fifty horsemen on their knees, with a hundred or so Canary and Chachapoya warriors looking on, impressed. The Incas, of course, hadn't ceased their terrifying cacophony once throughout the night. Now Bartholomew made his way through the close ranks of the Spaniards, giving the benediction to each forehead with his fused fingers.

Juan, his head wrapped in fresh bandages, and wearing real armour on his chest and thighs, received the benediction fervently. Don Gonzalo was kneeling beside him, his long, fine hair cascading down onto his steel armour that was decorated with fine gold chasing across the shoulders. He wore a scowl on his face. His lips hardly moved when he uttered the prayer of the benediction.

Hernando stood watching the ceremony from a little further back, standing in front of the foot soldiers who would soon be left to face the siege on their own. He was murmuring inaudibly to himself. He was the first to notice Gabriel arrive at the entrance to the courtyard, leading his white mare. Gabriel already had a round shield attached to his left arm, and he held the scarlet-feathered helmet against his leather-padded coat of mail with the other.

If Hernando's face betrayed nothing, then that of Gonzalo, who stopped short in mid-prayer, turned distinctly pale when he saw Gabriel. His eyes grew wide, and his mouth closed as he choked on the words of the *Pater Noster*. Gabriel thought that he was going to rise to his feet and challenge him. But Hernando's imperious gaze bore down upon his younger brother. The prayers ended, and the horses were brought forth. The cavalrymen glanced at Gabriel. Some bowed their heads, saluting him, others crossed themselves one more time. But none dared approach him, and instead they mounted their animals.

Gonzalo was lost in the general movement, while Hernando helped Juan clamber up onto his gelding.

Gabriel in turn donned his morion, pulling the strap tight beneath his chin. Brother Bartholomew came up to him.

'You were in my prayers, my friend. What's more, I saw you praying yourself earlier, when you thought no one was watching.'

'I hope you're not going to denounce me. It would damage my reputation. Yet still, Brother Bartholomew, you should be happy for me. Didn't you once explain to me that one doesn't have to believe in order to pray?'

'You believe more than you admit to yourself.'

Bartholomew placed his wooden cross against Gabriel's chest. His eyes had sunk deep in their sockets and exhaustion made his face look ten years older.

'Be careful. Watch out both ahead of you and behind your back,'

he said in a lower voice. 'Gonzalo is furious that Juan insisted that
you go with them. Try not to provoke him.'

'Don't worry. Everyone knows that I am protected by all the
powers, including God Himself.'

'Don't blaspheme! It's pointless.'

'Brother Bartholomew, if God does in fact exist,' said Gabriel,
looking directly and with the utmost seriousness at the monk,
'then today is that day for Him to convince me of it. Not by
preserving me from death, from which I do not shirk, and you
know why, but—'

'—But by purging the earth of evil at one stroke, preferably
beginning with Gonzalo Pizarro?'

'By the faith, brother, sometimes I wonder whether you are not
inspired by God Himself.'

'My God,' answered Bartholomew in a serious tone, 'is not a god
of vengeance, who punishes by the sword, but a god of love and
charity. And if you heed my words, you would do well to heed His.
As well as handling your sword properly when it's called for!'

Gabriel opened his mouth to make a sarcastic reply but then
he saw that Juan Pizarro was approaching. Gabriel could make
out more from reading his dry lips than from listening to his
halting words:

'It's time, Don Gabriel . . . I have divided our cavalry into two
groups. My brother Gonzalo is leading the second.'

His eyes sought approval, which Gabriel gave him with a nod.

'Let us go, then, with the Grace of God!'

They approached the *cancha*'s door, barricaded with beams, in
silence, as though they wanted to better hear the bedlam from
the hills and the trumpets wailing from the fortress. Even the
Canaries, normally so loquacious, said nothing.

Gabriel noticed Sebastian among the men removing the beams
from the door, his arm and shoulder still wrapped in bandages.
He grinned at him. For once, the African didn't return his smile.
His serious expression bore all the sadness of a real farewell. He
approached Gabriel and stroked his mare's mane. She responded
by nuzzling her head against his chest.

'Take care of her – and of yourself, my friend.'

'I shall bring you back some salve, so that you can come with us the next time,' joked Gabriel.

Now Sebastian smiled a thin smile.

'Good idea.'

At that moment Gabriel stood tall in his stirrups and shouted at the top of his voice:

'By Saint James, tonight we dine at the fortress!'

Behind him, fifty voices answered with a thundering:

'Santiago! Santiago!'

They were still shouting when the horses broke out into the great square, raising a cloud of dust through which the Canaries swarmed, also screaming like a pack of wild animals.

Only moments after the Spaniards and their Indian allies had passed the last walls of the *canchas* and reached the lowest of the terraces at the foot of the pass, a salvo of arrows whistled over their heads. They had been fired from too far away to be truly effective, and they thudded off the Spaniards' shields and the horses' armoured flanks without piercing them.

But now the Spaniards could see in front of them the line of Inca warriors, three or even four deep, blocking the road through the terraces to the west of the city. Juan turned to Gabriel. His eyes said what his mouth couldn't.

With his sword unsheathed, Gabriel shouted the order to increase their speed to a gallop. Itza immediately bounded forward and increased her pace, as though the command was all she had been waiting for. Her mane streaming in the wind, she seemed to be floating towards the enemy, her hooves hardly touching the ground. The other cavalrymen, a compact mass of flesh and steel behind her, moved as one in her wake, followed by the Canaries who, waving their axes and with their shields raised, ran on with astonishing speed, all the while howling at the tops of their voices.

For a brief moment, the Inca warriors squeezed closer together, holding their spears out in front of them and their clubs in their other hands. But everything happened too quickly, faster than the flight of the sling stones that ricocheted off the Spaniards' chain mail and breastplates. The Incas watched with wide eyes as the horses bore down on them. The ground itself shook, and the hammering sound of the animals' hooves rattled their own bodies like a vibration of fear. The scything blades of Spanish swords seemed to hack the sun itself into shreds of blinding light. Inca mouths gaped in agony as Spanish steel tore into their flesh while horses' hooves crushed their bones and staved in their chests. It wasn't long before the Spaniards had stabbed and slashed the Incas so fiercely that their faces were unrecognizable. They cried out in anguish as the horses, bucking around and around in tight circles, trampled not on stone or earth but on a yielding carpet of flesh and bone. Only then did the Canaries join the fray, adding to the general confusion. The ferocity of the battle doubled, and the dead fell quickly, clearing the way forward for the Spaniards as their swords cut through those Incas still left alive.

The Inca lines had to yield: some warriors flung their clubs at the Spaniards' heads before taking to their heels, while others effectively committed suicide by standing their ground and trying to thrust their spears into the horses' bellies or their riders' legs. But their heroism was futile.

Their chests and hocks now covered in blood, the horses extricated themselves from this tangle of death and galloped toward the first turn in the pass, beyond the reach of the slings.

His face covered in sweat and blood, his body aching from having swung his sword so much, his chest burning, Gabriel, out of breath, nevertheless continued shouting for the Spaniards and their allies to follow him.

He was exultant. His excitement rose above his indifference, his distaste for life. Now he felt a boundless sense of power.

'Santiago!' he cried once again, his voice hoarse from shouting.

And in the voices of the Spaniards and their allies as they answered him, in the whistle of falling arrows and the clashing of sword and ax blades, in the cries of agony and triumph, in the din of battle and the thunder of horses' hooves, Gabriel heard the mountains, the stones, the earth itself placing the mark of victory upon him.

But the Spaniards and their Indian allies had so far accomplished only the easiest part of their mission. The slopes of the Carmenga Pass proved as steep and as difficult to scale as Gabriel had feared, and it sapped the conquistadors of most of their strength.

For two hours, they climbed up and up the steep, winding road. Sections of the path had crumbled away, leaving spaces barely large enough for a horse to pass or even creating actually impassable crevasses or falls of scree. So until the Canaries, as busy as ants, had finished clearing away the scree or, squatting on their little square shields, bridging the crevasses, the expedition had to suffer the hail of stones flung down upon them from above.

Gabriel smelled the foul stench of fear rising up again from the Spaniards. Impatience and anxiety sharpened by hunger eroded the courage of even the hardiest among them. A stone struck a horse directly on its nose, injuring it, and it reared up in pain. It struck the horse in front of it with its forelegs, and threw its rider, who would have tumbled all the way to the bottom of the ravine had not two Canary warriors saved him. But the panic spread to all the animals in the vicinity, and the ensuing crush almost sent half a dozen horses and their riders plummeting down the cliff face.

'Dismount!' shouted Gabriel. 'Dismount and hold your horses by the bit. Force them to lower their heads!'

But, hearing the men murmuring in protest, Gabriel changed his tone and asserted as confidently as he could:

'We will pass! We will pass, because we have to!'

Yet Juan looked doubtful. In truth, all the men were haunted by the same thought: that the struggle for the Carmenga Pass would become a repetition of the battle in the Vilcaconga Pass. There, many years earlier and for the first time since they had arrived in Peru, the Spaniards had found themselves in such a dangerous situation that Gabriel, who had been at death's door, had survived thanks only to his tenacity and his love for Anamaya.

'It's the same situation,' murmured Juan, closing his eyes as though trying to shut out a nightmare. 'Them up there and us down here . . . and hampered by our horses.'

'No,' said Gabriel in a hushed voice so that Juan alone could hear him, 'there's no one up there. The bulk of Villa Oma's troops are behind us.'

'May God make it so!'

'I remember a rocky ledge, just below the summit of the pass. We can remount there, and then follow the terraces to the north-west. They'll think that we're leaving the fortress behind us. They'll think we're just trying to get away.'

Juan's only answer was to make the sign of the cross over his bandaged face.

'Watch out for the stones!' roared a voice. 'Watch out for the stones!'

Gabriel instinctively raised his shield over Juan, whose thickly swathed head prevented him from wearing a helmet.

'Protect yourself, Don Gabriel,' ordered Juan in a low voice.

This time, the stones fell so thick and fast that it seemed that the entire mountain was avalanching down upon them. The Spaniards held their shields over their heads, but many of these protective coverings cracked, and men shouted as their horses neighed in terror. Everyone, however, including Gonzalo, saw the deluge of stones miraculously miss Gabriel and his white mare, even though they were right in its path and even though everyone else, without exception, had their thighs, backs, and shoulders bruised by the missiles despite the protection of their shields and padded armour. And they saw that Juan was as safe from the stones under Gabriel's shield as if it were a solid roof.

But no one dared breathe a word. Instead, they tightened their lips and prayed fervently.

When the downpour of stones ceased at last and they had reached the ledge as Gabriel had promised they would, the Spaniards found that the Inca warriors who had been plaguing them from above numbered no more than fifty. They didn't dare approach closer than the range of a sling and the Spaniards only had to gallop at them briefly for the Incas to turn on their heels and bolt.

Gabriel listened to the Incas shouting to one another as they fled.

'They think we're going back to Castile!' he announced to his compatriots, laughing.

Their relief was as great as their terror had been a little while earlier. Their chests swelled with laughter, and for the moment they felt released from their exhaustion.

'Santiago! Santiago!' cried the cavalrymen before crossing themselves and lowering their eyes, as though they preferred not to know to what they owed their success.

Gabriel felt a chill settle on his soul.

He thought about what was to come, and the vision of it filled his mind's eye as though he had already lived through it.

It was only in the middle of that afternoon, after a number of detours, that the Spaniards reached at last an uneven platform, strewn with enormous black rocks, from which a gentle slope led down to the back of the Sacsayhuaman fortress. The fortress's high walls were built of massive stones so meticulously fitted together that it was difficult to imagine how human beings had been able to place one on top of another. What was stranger, however, was that there seemed to be no Inca warriors at all standing guard.

Juan ordered the men to stop and rest beside a gurgling spring. Some Canary warriors had been able to catch a few wild rats and even two llamas that had become separated from a herd – no doubt scattered by the war – during their march to their present position. Overjoyed, they carved up the animals and ate them raw, fires being forbidden.

For a long while, a curious silence reigned over the halted expedition. But after a few mouthfuls of meat, savoring the sickly taste of the blood that they drank, even the most exhausted men quickly recovered their energy and alertness. Gonzalo was the first to call for them to attack:

'It's time, my brother. We mustn't wait for night to fall. The Canaries have returned from their reconnaissance mission. The passages between the fortress's defensive walls are indeed barricaded but, as we thought, no Incas are guarding that part of the fortress. I suggest that our friend Don Gabriel exploit his . . . unusual gift to accompany the Canaries and open a passage for us. He can send us a signal when we are clear to charge. And as you are in no condition to lead one, dear brother, I suggest that you remain here with a dozen cavalrymen to reinforce us if we need it.'

Gabriel smiled thinly at Gonzalo's irony. His gaze met Juan's, and he put his crimson-feathered morion back on his head as he nodded and said:

'It's not such a bad idea.'

Then he caught Gonzalo's glancing stare and what he saw in it gave him the satisfaction that came only with the onset of revenge: he saw that handsome, cruel Gonzalo was afraid of him.

Gabriel approached the first totally undefended barricade on foot and surrounded by Canary warriors. It took them little time to breach it.

While the Canaries finished dismantling the stone barricade in total silence, Gabriel remounted his horse. He silently urged Itza into the maze of natural rock and thick walls that were the first line of defence around the fortress's great walls and towers.

He expected to hear an Inca lookout raise the alert at any moment.

But no such cry came.

No one saw or heard him. He passed alongside the little hill that hid him still from the great wall. Soon, he made out the walkway opening up ahead of him, and he slowed to a walking pace until he reached the edge of the vast, grass-covered space at the base of the fortress. He looked at the gargantuan stone blocks that made up its wall.

Gabriel's heart skipped a beat. No Inca warrior had spotted him. No stone or spear had been thrown at him. Not far in front of him, to his left, the main wall followed a zigzag turn. In it, he could make out a large, trapezoid gate that had been somewhat carelessly barricaded with stones and logs.

If they could breach it, they would reach the very heart of Sacsayhuaman.

He had seen enough: sure of the conquistadors' coming victory, he yanked on his mare's reins and galloped back to rouse up his companions.

'Everyone mount your horses!' Gabriel ordered when he was within shouting range of Gonzalo. 'The road is clear! Don Hernando is distracting them on the city side of the fortress, and they are completely unaware that we are here.'

As had been arranged, only Juan Pizarro and a handful of cavalrymen remained behind, ready to reinforce Gabriel's soldiers if necessary. The rest galloped as quietly as they could behind Gabriel on his white mare. They leaped over the dismantled barricade, hurtled past the Canary warriors, and charged the great trapezoidal gate.

It was then that everything went horribly wrong.

They heard a conch horn sound from the top of the round tower. A furious clamor immediately erupted from the top of the great wall. Gabriel was about to launch his forces across the terraces, terraces that had been empty a moment earlier, when he was appalled to discover a hundred, two hundred, possibly even a thousand Inca soldiers assembled in front of him.

Before he had even managed to halt Itza's flying gallop, he felt the air around him quiver as the warriors whirled their slings so powerfully that they might have been hurling cannonballs rather than mere stones. A moment later, and a hail of stones tore through the air and thrummed above him. The cavalrymen behind, still exposed on the walkway, screamed with pain as they were hit. The horses stumbled on the bouncing stones, throwing their riders forward over their heads, and already there were Inca warriors swarming forward to seize them.

Gabriel roared furiously, scythed his sword through the air and headed back to their rescue. His solo charge terrified Sacsayhuaman's defenders enough for them to move out of the way. The riders who had been thrown tried to yank their horses back up or else abandoned them, jumping instead onto the hindquarters of their companions' horses and bolting back the way they had come.

But still, utter confusion reigned among the Spaniards. The Canary warriors, surprised by the sudden appearance of the Incas, defended themselves poorly, and their hand-to-hand combat with the enemy obstructed the retreating cavalrymen. Furthermore, the ground was now so strewn with stones that the horses were able to move only gingerly. Only Gabriel's mare maintained its gallop, and he charged down on the Incas again and again in a futile attempt to force them back.

No one knew how long this madness lasted.

The Spaniards, their frustration heightened by the growing pangs in their empty stomachs, repeatedly beat early and pitiful retreats to the other side of the first barricade. Gabriel had to come to them five or six times and harangue them to get them to return to the fray.

But their advance was turned back time and again by the hail of stones, long before they ever reached the massive wall. They were utterly unable to follow Gabriel's white mare, and each time they had to hold their own horses back lest the animals should break their legs.

More than an hour passed, draining the Spaniards of their courage, and now the light was fading from the sky. Gabriel returned to urge them to make one final, heroic effort. But he had only just come up in front of them when a yell of rage exploded in his ear. He raised his shield by reflex and in doing so saved his own life: Gonzalo had brought his sword crashing down when he'd shouted, trying to cut Gabriel in half.

'Traitor! Filthy vermin!' screamed Gonzalo, a mad look in his eyes. 'At last, we see your true colors! May you be cursed to hell for having led us into this trap!'

'Don Gonzalo!'

'Shut up, you goat turd! I saw you! We *all* saw you: the Incas leave you alone! You've learned how to dodge their stones, and now you want to lead us right to them so that they can slaughter us at their leisure!'

Gabriel hadn't time to reply before Gonzalo was at him again, standing in his stirrups, waving his sword and screaming:

'Compañeros! Compañeros, listen to me: this man is not Saint James come to save us, but a filthy traitor and a devil! Do not follow him! Do not obey him, or he will lead you to your death!'

The Spanish cavalrymen, deeply weary after all their efforts and all their disappointments, stared at the two men, unable to distinguish the truth from the madness. Some crossed themselves, others bandaged their wounded legs, shattered by stones, still others pulled arrows out of one another's chain mail or from their horses' breastplates. But then the sound of galloping horses saved them from having to choose. Juan and his reinforcements were approaching them at full speed.

'Juan!' Gonzalo shouted furiously. 'My brother, you put out your hand to a viper, and he's bitten you! Montelucar has led us to our perdition. He's the Devil himself! The Incas were expecting us; they had probably even been warned! We will never make it into the fortress! We must go back down to Cuzco before night falls!'

'Don Juan,' exclaimed Gabriel, 'don't listen to your brother's nonsense! We still have one chance left: the Inca warriors are as tired of slinging stones at us as we are of receiving them. Soon they'll be too tired to even lift their arms! We must attack them one more time: I'll go alone if I have to!'

Juan didn't hesitate. He pointed at the fortress with the point of his sword and whipped his horse's flank. A moment later, the entire contingent had followed in his wake, despite Gonzalo's protests.

This time, once he was past the first barricade, Gabriel launched Itza down the side nearest to the hill, where he had spotted a few rocks stepped one above the other. His mare bounded up them deftly. He charged at the forward Inca line from behind, forcing them to rush back before they could turn and whirl their slings. His small, single-handed victory so inspired the Spaniards below that they cried out joyously with renewed hope.

A moment later, and Itza's white mane beneath the red feather of Gabriel's helmet seemed to be visible everywhere above the mêlée, and even seemed to be moving closer and closer to the great wall. It was a marvel to the Spaniards, who began shouting out victoriously.

But then a horrendous volley of stones and arrows fell upon them from the top of the great wall. Gabriel raised his shield like everyone else, and he heard the deadly patter of arrows slamming into his and Itza's padded armour.

A brief, unnatural silence followed. Then a terrible cry tore through the air:

'Juan! Juan! Oh, my brother . . .'

A hundred paces from Gabriel, Juan Pizarro fell from his saddle and crumpled onto the layer of stones now covering the grass. His bandage had come off, and the entire upper part of his skull was a bloody mangle of bone and brain. The excitement of battle had made him reckless and he had lowered his shield, leaving his unprotected and already wounded head exposed to the enemy's stones.

Gonzalo was already on his knees at his side, his mouth agape as he wailed and sobbed. He drew his brother to his chest and cradled him like a child, but it was pointless.

Gabriel felt an icy blade cut his heart and choke off his breath. He mechanically urged Itza towards the Pizarro brothers as all the other cavalrymen gathered around to protect them. They took up Juan's body and carried him away at a run. Gonzalo turned to face Gabriel, his handsome face twisted with grief and hatred.

'You killed him. You killed him, Gabriel Montelucar – you killed my beloved brother!'

Gabriel said nothing. All his hatred and biting sarcasm had left him. A moment later Gonzalo, overcome with grief, turned away from his foe and began sobbing like a child.

'I didn't fling the stone that smashed your brother's skull, Don Hernando, but it was I who insisted that we charge one more time. The final charge proved to be as futile as all those that had preceded it. Don Gonzalo is right to accuse me of bringing about your brother's death.'

Hernando didn't answer. His hard, emaciated face was barely visible by the guttering light of a candle-end. They could hear Gonzalo's wails of grief from the neighboring room, as well as Bartholomew murmuring a prayer.

It had taken them four hours to come down from the walkway in front of the fortress to the *cancha* on the great square of Aucaypata, and they had carried Juan's body the whole way, despite constant harassment by the Incas. Gabriel was so tired that he could no longer feel his arms or legs. He couldn't even feel his hunger anymore. His fingers were numb and his hand swollen from having gripped his sword for so long. His eyes had trouble seeing.

'But it's not true that I hoped for – and orchestrated – our defeat,' he continued.

Still Hernando said nothing. He seemed to be listening to the wails and the women's funeral laments that accompanied the Christian prayers next door. But then he said in a low voice:

'Juan was the only person in the world that Gonzalo ever loved. He always loved him, and passionately. Rather strange, don't you think?'

Now it was Gabriel's turn to say nothing. But he remembered the words that Juan had spoken to him that very morning.

'Gonzalo has never respected anyone but Juan,' continued Hernando. 'No woman, no man. He obeys me, but only just. And now, Juan's death is going to make him even madder than he was before.'

'The demons will be free . . .' murmured Gabriel.

Hernando looked at him for a moment, surprised. Then he repeated:

'The demons, yes . . .'

Next door, the Christian last rites had finished, but the laments continued still. Hernando made a weary gesture with his hand, as though he was trying to push away the thoughts that had occupied his mind. A thin – very thin – smile spread across his lips.

'People tend to die in battle, Don Gabriel,' he continued in his more usual ironic tone. 'It's happened before. Especially when you lose the battle. I'm a good Christian, and my brother's death grieves me. But what grieves me even more is that, despite all your promises and magic powers, we are still on the *outside* of that damned fortress! It seems that the stones and arrows spared you once again: but never has a miracle seemed more useless to me.'

'We shall see soon enough if it's magic or not,' muttered Gabriel, wiping his hand across his face.

'Oh yes?'

'There's at least one good thing to have come out of our attack, Don Hernando. While we diverted the Incas at the back of the fortress, you at last managed to reach the base of its wall on this side. I noticed earlier that our people are bivouacking there . . .'

'. . . For the moment. But tomorrow morning, the Incas will throw everything they've got at us to get us out of there. And they will succeed, because we haven't the strength to resist them for any length of time.'

'No. At dawn, I will climb to the summit of the tower – alone – and I will open a passage for you.'

'That would be madness, Gabriel.'

Hernando and Gabriel turned together to look at whoever had uttered these words. Bartholomew crossed the threshold of the room and said again:

'It would be madness. You'll never make it.'

'There's a window halfway up the great wall. It can be reached with a good ladder. Inside, I'm sure that there's a stairway leading to the base of the tower. The Incas have a way of getting up there: I'll find it!'

'You've lost your mind. By all the saints, today's action has sent you mad.'

'Don Hernando, order the ladder to be built. I need to get some sleep. But make sure that it's ready by the first light of day.'

'Don Gabriel, you'll be lying dead beneath an avalanche of stones before you get even halfway up the ladder,' remarked Hernando with cold circumspection.

'Well, I'm sure that my death will cause you little grief. On the other hand, I'm sure that you won't mind if I succeed, either. I've known worse deals, Don Hernando.'

At first, Hernando looked a little surprised. Then an odd little laugh came out of his dry lips.

'You are a strange fellow, Don Gabriel. Always this obsession with dying, then coming back from the dead! Always wanting to show yourself to be better than everyone else. Why, I may well end up sharing my brother the Governor's opinion of you, and admit that you have certain qualities!'

Gabriel ignored his comment and the sardonic look in his eyes. He took Bartholomew's deformed hand and squeezed it strongly.

'It is time to know, my friend Bartholomew. I must know! And this time, no one will have to follow me.'

Gabriel hardly shut his eyes that night. Whenever he did snatch a few moments of sleep, it was despite himself, and as for the rest of the time he spent it in a waking dream.

The visions that had thrust themselves before his mind's eye pursued him relentlessly, and never let his soul have a moment's rest. In them, he saw a rope tied to the crenellated ramparts of the round tower, the most forbidding of the towers, and the rope's end floating gently in the breeze. And when his injured hands closed around the rope, he sensed that nothing could prevent him from reaching the top.

It was a cold dawn. The ground was almost frozen over, and the sky was as white as a linen canopy. Gabriel was holding a dirty blanket around his naked torso.

He had been woken by a soft hand caressing his forehead and shoulders. He felt the hand's smooth skin and delicate fingers: a woman's hand, a forgotten gentleness.

When he opened his eyes and emerged from his deep sleep, his body still ached, and he looked into the young woman's face without recognizing her. He saw tears swelling in her eyes and dust daubed on her cheeks.

'You don't remember me,' she whispered, with the slightest of smiles. 'My name is Inguill. We met a long time ago, before Emperor Atahualpa's death. I was then a young girl serving the *Coya Camaquen*. She often spoke of you.'

Gabriel sat up and rested on his elbows, now completely awake.

'Did she send you?' he asked. 'Did Anamaya send you?'

She shook her head, her smile broadening slightly.

'No. I am Lord Don Juan's wife.'

Her voice cracked as she continued:

'Or was, until yesterday.'

'I know. I regret it tremendously. He told me about you.'

Gabriel saw a blend of grief and pride in Inguill's eyes.

'He chose me as a slave, and yet he loved me as a wife. And I loved him. He was gentle with me. His Ancestors of the Other World didn't want him to suffer too much. It is well thus.'

She nimbly reached into her *unku* and drew out a little jar, which she handed to Gabriel.

'We drew a little milk from your goats for our children. I've brought you some. You must drink it before climbing up the tower. It will give you strength.'

Gabriel grabbed her by the wrist.

'Why are you doing this?'

Inguill looked at him for a moment. She caressed Gabriel's shoulder with her free hand. Her fingers slipped over his shoulder blade and brushed over his birthmark.

'The *Coya Camaquen* is protecting you, and the Powerful Ancestors too,' she whispered. 'We all know that you are going to save us.'

Gabriel tightened his grip around Inguill's arm.

'How do you know? Why defend me from your own people? It makes no sense!'

Inguill broke away and stood up brusquely.

'Drink the milk. It will do you good,' she said simply before disappearing.

Only then did Gabriel notice Sebastian standing in the background and giving him a stony look.

'That woman talks rubbish,' he growled. 'Climbing that damned ladder up their damned tower is the worst idea you've ever had, Gabriel.'

Gabriel grinned as he rose to his feet.

'So, you no longer think that you saw Saint James reincarnate with your own eyes?'

'Oh yes, I do! At least, I saw enough to know that one of the two of you is an imposter. And I would happily put my money on it being Saint James!'

'Blasphemer!'

Laughing openly now, Gabriel embraced his friend.

'Look after Itza. She's a fine mare, and I'd like you to give her to me later, when this battle's over.'

'I'll give you your mare and much more, Your Grace. But first you must promise me one thing, by Saint James and the Sacred Virgin, by the Sun and the Moon, by my teeth and your beard and my own—'

'What?'

'Stay alive, you damned fool.'

The ladder was at least eight codos long, but still it only just reached the narrow window set high in the great wall. It took twenty men to raise it and hold it in the right position. It was made of roof beams and logs from the barricades, fitted together as best they could. They had run out of rope for the rungs, some of which were made from the shafts of broken spears and set so far apart that Gabriel had to pull himself up by his arms to reach them.

As soon as he was about four codos up, the ladder began to sway, and Gabriel made sure that he made no sudden movements. He climbed a couple more rungs, then heard people calling to him. He looked down and saw Sebastian, Bartholomew, Hernando, and the others on the ground dashing away from the base of the ladder. He immediately understood without having to look up. He bunched his head and shoulders tightly, hooked his feet solidly onto the rungs, and raised his shield.

As the stones slammed into his leather shield, he realized that he was almost enjoying the thudding sound that they made. Some of the heavier ones struck the ladder, causing it to shake violently. He had to hurry.

Grunting like a woodcutter, Gabriel ignored the missiles and began scaling the uppermost rungs. The ladder squeaked horribly, sagging like a belly whose owner was breathing too strongly. Gabriel kept his eyes fixed on the wall. He put the notions of up and down out of his mind, and ignored the stones whistling past him and sometimes smashing into his hip, or onto the ladder, almost crushing his fingers. He climbed with his feet and his knees. He didn't hear the shouts and cries ringing out all around him.

His companions had taken his fatigue into account: they had fixed the last rungs closer together, so that they were easier to climb. He felt as though he could practically run up them, and soon enough he found himself on the broad lintel outside the little window.

The pale morning light barely lit the inside of the room, but still he could make out a staircase and a number of dumbfounded Inca faces, normally so impassive.

The mere sound of Gabriel drawing his sword from its scabbard sent the dozen or so Inca warriors scurrying back, even though they were all armed with slings and bludgeons. They looked at one another stupidly, doing nothing, their curiosity making them immobile as much as their surprise. Gabriel cried out in Quechua:

'Stand back! Stand back! I wish you no harm!'

Waving his sword about as though it were made of balsa wood, he took three steps forward. But the warriors took the corresponding number of steps up the staircase. Each time he advanced, they moved back, maintaining the distance between themselves and Gabriel. Then one of the Incas said:

'It's the Stranger with the white beast!'

They stared at each other once again, utterly amazed, and Gabriel didn't know what to do next any more than they did. Then, wordlessly, the soldiers turned away from him and bolted up the steep staircase with astonishing agility.

Gabriel followed cautiously on their heels, breathing hard and holding his sword out in front of him. When he at last reached the light of day, he discovered that the rampart at the base of the tower was deserted. The warriors had run off to roust out their officers.

He could be seen from the neighboring towers. He heard shouting from them, and stones were slung. Yet none were thrown at him, only at the Spaniards still at the foot of the great wall.

Gabriel, encouraged by the ease of his adventure so far, walked around the base of the tower.

He looked up and felt a shiver run down his spine: he knew now that Inguill had been right – that everyone had been right.

There was no door or window that opened into the interior of the tower or led to its top. But there was a rope, made of agave and *ichu*, of the sort that the Incas used to build their suspension bridges, that was as thick as a man's arm. It hung down the entire height of the building, as though inviting him to climb it.

He could now *see* with extraordinary clarity what he had already seen in his dream.

His exhaustion and caution left him; his tense muscles relaxed. Unable to contain himself, Gabriel approached the top of the great wall, waved his sword and shield around, and cried:

'Santiago! Santiago!'

His companions down below, who were holding their shields close together, looked like tiny animals with dirty shells. Gabriel laughed like a madman and cried once again:

'Santiago!'

Then he flung away his shield, sheathed his sword, and took off his heavy chain-mail coat. He took a firm grip of the rope, a rope as miraculous as Jacob's ladder, and began his ascent. The thought that the Incas up above could cut it at any moment didn't even cross his mind.

But the exertion of hauling himself up four codos, with his legs and torso at right angles to the wall, the soles of his boots slipping on the stone, and all his weight on his arms, was enough to bring him out of his exhilaration.

His legs felt desperately heavy, and his feet slipped twice after he had set them poorly against the wall. Both times, Gabriel slammed into it with all his weight. He banged his knees and chest painfully hard and almost let go of the rope. He found himself short of breath once again, and his muscles tightened. Both times, he set himself right and continued his ascent. One codo, then another. He had six to go, perhaps more. He remembered Sebastian's words: 'Not long from now, you will fly down to earth like a true angel, except that you'll be ballasted with stones!' He chortled to himself and paused to rest, but his body weighed so heavily on his arms that he preferred to carry on climbing.

Gabriel was almost halfway up the tower when he felt a jolt through the stone. He looked up. A rock the size of a footstool was hurtling down at him, bouncing off the wall. He didn't have enough time to protect himself by hugging the wall. He closed his eyes.

Nothing, except a movement of air as the rock brushed past his shoulder.

He opened his eyes just as the rock smashed into the flagstones of the ramparts below, exploding into dust.

'I *am* protected,' he said to himself, his chest burning. 'Anamaya is protecting me! She loves me, and is protecting me!'

Gabriel was transported back into his elation. He no longer saw the stone wall of the tower in front of him – he saw Anamaya's blue eyes. He no longer felt the burning sensation in his lungs, or his exhausted arms, or his legs that would no longer bend. He climbed like a demon, like a monkey. The Spaniards down below watched him scale the last codo, and when he reached the edge of the little wall that ran around the top of the tower they cried:

'Santiago! He made it! Santiago!'

Gabriel collapsed and stretched his body along the top of the tower, struggling to regain his breath. He didn't have the strength to lift himself up. He listened for the sound of Inca soldiers coming to capture him.

But the only sound he heard came from far off.

Finally, he sat up. He was alone. The top of the tower was deserted. There was a turret in its centre that housed the top of a stairwell. He looked down, and saw that there were many flights, and that the steps were so narrow that one had to descend them edgewise. Gabriel saw no one. But he could hear voices rising up from the bottom.

Gabriel went back to the little wall at the edge of the tower. He cried out once again, he screamed at the top of his lungs, he shouted out his victory, yelling that he had taken the tower, and that they could all come and join him!

By midday, they were still fighting, and the Spaniards had taken a second tower. Gabriel had never left the first one, and no one had come to join him. He had grown horrified, but never weary, of watching the great spectacle of war. The ramparts of the Sacsayhuaman fortress were now strewn with corpses: at least a thousand, perhaps two.

Gabriel placed his aching hands on the little stone wall and saw that they were trembling. He couldn't feel anything anymore. He asked himself what madness had possessed him, how he had come to be like a drunkard emerging from his haze.

He didn't even dare think about Anamaya, nor did he believe the obscene notion that she had protected him to permit this horrendous carnage.

The pestilent stench of death assaulted his nostrils.

Sebastian's affectionate words now seemed to have been addressed to someone other than Gabriel.

Once more, he hoped that death would simply fall upon him, and that he wouldn't have to jump from the tower to forget the pleasure he had derived from being the catalyst of the present massacre.

'I thought I was master,' he sniggered to himself, 'when in fact I was nothing but a miserable slave.'

But still he never looked away, not even for a moment, from the unceasing spectacle of men dying.

That evening, Hernando Pizarro gave the order for the attack against the last of the fortress's towers to begin. It was the largest, but it had been built hastily, and its stonework was less than perfect.

When Pizano's men were halfway up the ladders, the Inca

general in charge of the defence of Sacsayhuaman stood alone
on the little wall at the top of the tower. Broad gold disks glinted
from his ears, marks of his high rank.

Gabriel watched, appalled, as the general rubbed dirt into
his cheeks so hard that he abraded his skin. The Inca warrior
picked up yet more dirt from between the tower's stones and
rubbed it into the wounds he had just opened, until his face
was unrecognizable.

Every Spaniard now stood stock-still, their eyes fixed on him.

The Inca soldiers stood just as still. It was as though an icy
wind had frozen everyone in their places.

Then the general stuffed dirt into his mouth, wrapped his long
cape around himself, and threw himself into the void.

There wasn't a sound until his body smashed into a pile of
sling stones.

Only then did Gabriel hear someone cry out from behind him.
He turned around and found ten Inca warriors staring at him. He
saw the hesitation in their eyes and the rope in their hands. One
of them raised his long, bronze club, ready to strike him.

Gabriel shook his head.

'No,' he said in Quechua. 'Don't bother.'

He slowly drew his sword from its scabbard and flung it over
the little wall.

'I won't fight anymore,' he said. 'It's over.'

The warriors bound him and led him into the night. As they
went, Gabriel listened to his Spanish comrades' drunken cries of
victory floating on the breeze.

He had wanted to die.

He had wanted to live.

Now, he wanted nothing at all.

PART 2

CHAPTER 7

Ollantaytambo, June 1536

I N THE *CANCHAS* OUT ON THE PLAIN, IN THE FORK BETWEEN
the two rivers, and on the slopes where the terraces and
temples stood stepped one above the other, hundreds of
fires burned. But there was no singing or sound of drums, no
cries of joy, no drunkenness. The only sound was the murmuring
of water, a haunting lament, filled with sadness, that permeated
Anamaya's soul.

The Inca warriors crossed the bridge, moving at the pace of
the defeated. They went one by one, wordlessly, their faces
impassive but their heads bowed. By the hoary light of the
full moon, their faces looked like tarnished silver. Deep lines
of exhaustion furrowed their foreheads and cheeks like so many
wounds. Their *unkus* were torn to shreds and covered in blood and
mud. Their limbs were weary, and their weapons dangled from the
ends of their arms like useless toys. Even those carrying swords or
those few leading horses taken from the Spaniards looked deeply
ashamed. They had lost.

When they caught sight of Manco and Villa Oma on the other
side of the bridge, their shoulders slumped further, as if the
weight of their defeat had become too great to bear. But still
Manco encouraged them with a small gesture or a few proud
words as they passed. Then they disappeared into the night. But,
despite their exhaustion, they found little rest in it.

Anamaya watched Villa Oma. The piercing gaze of the man she

called the Sage was lost in the distance, traveling along the length of the Sacred Valley to the hills above Cuzco, as though he was reliving the battle they should have won but hadn't. His face was taut with silent rage.

For once, Manco was not standing in defiance of him. His proud profile revealed only sympathy and encouragement for his defeated warriors. Anamaya was surprised by this expression of gentleness, a gentleness that had until now remained masked by the violence that had been corrupting Manco's heart ever since he had been humiliated by the Spaniards – or even, perhaps, since the day he'd been born.

Anamaya had hardly slept since Titu Cuyuchi had brought her the news of Gabriel's disappearance. Whenever she felt herself about to fall asleep, she saw a vision of the Puma pass before her mind's eye. And during the day, she was tormented by chimeras of its shadow. She continued playing the role of *Coya Camaquen*, maintaining appearances and saying the right things, and everyone – including the priests and soothsayers, who had come to respect her – continued to look to the *Coya Camaquen* for consolation or inspiration. But in the most corner private of her soul, she was a woman tormented by concern for her beloved.

And in this hour of defeat – a defeat made worse because it had been snatched from the jaws of victory – her concern for the man she loved was more powerful than any other feeling she had and she was almost ashamed of it.

'Come with me.'

Katari's voice was so low that it was practically a whisper, no louder than a bat flapping its wings in the night, and she wasn't sure that she had heard him right. She turned toward him. The young man tilted his head slightly, his long hair billowing down to his shoulders.

He didn't repeat himself, but motioned to her to follow him. She banished her preoccupations about Manco and Villa Oma.

The two young people walked beside the river, listening to its rumbling. They followed the low wall that ran alongside the flow, its carefully fitted stones indicating the water's sacred nature. Moonlight lit the path rising before them toward the city. There, they could see the fires burning in hearths of the houses and temples, looking like distant stars belonging to another world.

Anamaya's beating heart slowed a little.

Now she could hear the water gurgling in the canals that fed the fountains from the mountains above, and its music added lighter grace notes above the deep rumble of the Willkamayo River.

Katari suddenly stopped in his tracks. Anamaya stared at his broad shoulders for a moment before following his gaze toward the western mountains, above which Quilla's perfectly round disk hung suspended.

The black silhouette of a condor emerged from the night.

It was a gargantuan bird, a bird-mountain, and it was watching them. A rock jutting out was its beak, and above it another that was its head, its eye wide open, its ruff retracted between its two powerful wings. Motionless, it looked as though it was pointing down the Sacred Valley, protecting it, threatening anyone tempted to defile it.

After a long moment, Katari turned to Anamaya.

'It's time,' he said simply.

Once again, Anamaya found herself admiring the young man's calm disposition and the radiant wisdom emanating from him, from his broad, muscled body, and from his slender eyes, as elongated as a flaw in a *huaca*.

She didn't immediately notice that sections of the rock in front of them had been worked. Channels had been cut for water, and countless nicks marked its base, a sign that men had been coming here for innumerable seasons to commune with the gods.

They passed into the condor's shadow and were hidden from the moon. Anamaya followed Katari confidently, despite the darkness, stepping where he had stepped.

They walked around an enormous flat shale-stone set in the ground. Its shape seemed familiar to Anamaya. Embers glowed red in a small cavity carved out at its center, and Katari had little trouble using them to get a fresh fire burning. Anamaya looked up and scrutinized four small niches carved into the rock. She felt that she recognized the place.

As she stood there, getting her breath back from the walk, she was overcome by a strange feeling. Katari was communicating with her without speaking. She was almost frightened by the ease with which she instinctively surrendered to the power.

'There's nothing to fear,' he said gently.

'You were listening to my thoughts?'

Katari's laugh tinkled in the night.

'You should know that I listen to you even when I'm not at your side . . .'

She remembered Gabriel lost in the Salar desert. Her unease left her, and she smiled back at him.

'You said that you could help me . . .'

'I can. But first, all your fear must leave you. Also . . .'

Katari had already spread out his *manta* in front of him.

'Also?'

'We must be one to make the voyage.'

'One? But I need you to make it. What do you mean, Katari? I don't understand.'

'There is water, and there is stone,' said Katari. 'There is this world and there is the Under World, there is the Willkamayo and there is the Way in the stars, there is Inti and Quilla, there is silver and there is gold. Everything in the universe has its twin . . . but we can only see the one hidden in the heart of things if we know how to look.'

Anamaya's heart had leaped as soon as he had started talking. In her mind, she added: *There are Incas and there are Strangers.* But she didn't dare say it out loud.

'I still don't understand,' she murmured.

Katari glanced at her.

'You understand better than you say you do . . . but I can't explain it to you now. Simply remember that nothing you discover will be hidden from me. Do you trust me enough to do that?'

She watched him pull out a bundle of leaves from his *manta*. They had come from a forest plant, not a mountain one. He flung them onto the flames. A strong, acrid smoke rose up from the fire.

'You trust me enough to take me there,' said Anamaya. 'Let me give you what I—'

'I shall guide you, Anamaya, and yet you will be the one taking *me* there.'

She stared at the four niches and at the incredible outlines of the rock in which they were encased. She smiled. She knew what voyage he was talking about.

Katari looked away from her. He closed his eyes and swung his head from side to side, using his long hair to fan the smoke in Anamaya's direction. He began singing a monotonous chant in a language that Anamaya didn't recognize. The smoke entered her nostrils and soon it and the song filled her head, even her entire body. She felt both heavy with sleep and alert, almost incapable of moving yet utterly weightless. She saw him rise.

He sat next to her, holding in his hands a magnificent *kero*, a wooden vase incised with minute geometric patterns, the details of which she could make out with astonishing – even supernatural – clarity. A small amount of dark green liquid lay in its depths.

Katari pulled out two smaller, undercorated *keros*. They were made of raw, unhewn wood, still holding the shape of the branches of which they had once been part. Only the cavities within them had been worked by the hand of man.

He filled the two wooden goblets and handed one to Anamaya. They drank slowly, letting the liquid's soft flavour, something like that of unripe corn, infuse their palates and throats.

Katari's chanting had begun softly, like the distant murmur of a mountain stream; his voice had risen now, so that it almost drowned out the sound of the water coursing through the rock channels. Anamaya's entire body, from the buzzing in her ears to the dull thud of her heart, became entranced by the chant's rhythm. To her, the song seemed to emanate not from Katari's throat, but from the rocks and water around them, and from the mountain itself.

She heard a more high-pitched voice rise above Katari's monotonous chant. Suddenly, she succumbed to a violent spasm, as though a lightning charge had started on the nape of her neck, shuddered down her back and flooded each of her limbs. It happened again and again, and each time she surrendered to the sensation as though it was an amorous embrace. It was in fact pleasurable, and her pleasure took the form of a delicious sensuous explosion as wave after seething wave of feelings passed through her. Her belly felt hot, almost burning. Her happiness was so complete and so intense that she didn't register its duration.

The silence returned.

Blots of brilliantly intense glowing colors danced before her eyes.

The song had ended. All that remained was the sound of water: water streaming into the channels, flowing in the canal that ran along the Condor *huaca*, and rumbling in the river down below. But in the fraction of a second in which nature was suspended and all was calm, Anamaya's powers of perception became so sharp that she could see, hear, feel, and taste everything in the hollow night. Her ears heard every fluctuation of the wind, from the slightest breeze to strong gusts. She felt it caressing her skin, and she opened her mouth and nostrils wide to gorge herself on it. Suddenly, a bird's cry echoed through the air: the cry of a bird that she hadn't heard since she had been a little girl living in the middle of the forest. She inhaled the smells of the earth, the scents of its humus and dense vegetation loaded with nocturnal moisture.

Anamaya heard a shuffling on the stones nearby and opened her eyes. She saw Katari staring by the four niches in front of them. She looked at them, unable to see how deep they were. He reached for her hand, and she gave it to him without fear.

As they approached the rock face on their knees, a weak, milk-coloured glow lit up one of the niches. It was as though the light was coming from the rock itself. They lowered themselves still further until they were crawling, and again until their bodies were pressed against the rock. The white light from the niche now engulfed them completely. Anamaya felt a continuous tremor in the rock. She couldn't tell whether the niche had expanded to allow them to enter or whether they had shrunk to its size. It didn't matter.

At one point, without Anamaya being able to tell when, the feel of the rock on her skin turned from a scraping friction to a smooth caress, and she felt as though all the weight and anxieties of her body had given way to a very soft mantle, as though her flesh and the matter surrounding it had fused. She heard distant voices echoing within her, telling her that it was thus, once, that men had been born. But her rapture didn't allow her time to listen closely: limb by limb, her body was absorbed by the mountain, and the last human sensation she felt was Katari's hand wrapped around hers. She saw her fear off in the distance, a ball of flames traveling through the night, a ball of suffering in her mind, and the very great weight of the mountain brought her an unimaginable sense of lightness, as though one enormous mass had been canceled by another even greater, one that would absorb it piece by piece, fiber by fiber.

She was stone. She was the mountain itself.

The strangest part was that she had retained an unequivocal consciousness of herself. She was still Anamaya, but now an Anamaya suddenly enriched by an entire universe of sensations, one in which all things and all nature's aspects were combined. Before she had time to delight in it once again, all the fibers of her being began pulsing like a thousand drums, a thousand trumpets, a thousand rivers, or a thousand stars hurtling towards a colossal explosion. And at the center of this sensation of abundance, she felt her being shrink into a tiny ball, the only purpose of which was to make the immense effort of extricating itself from the rock – as though, finding herself ingrained in the utterly immovable stone, she wanted above all to avoid dissolving into it and disappearing.

She heard Katari speaking to her in a very low yet clear voice that came from within her: 'Come, Anamaya. It is time.'

She entered the other side.

Air.

The vibrations Anamaya felt were all that held her up – a gliding sensation, a lightness.

She was flying.

For the moment, she felt nothing other than the delight of it, a sense of power coupled with one of absolute and infinite freedom. It seemed to her that she no longer had eyes to see, nor ears to hear, and that her body had become a fragile thing, like a *balsa* drifting on a river of wind.

You are the Condor.

For a moment, after the thought had occurred to her, she was struck by the strangeness of it. Then she realized that Katari was no longer beside her, holding her hand, but that he was with her in her flight – that he had become the Condor with her and for her.

She let herself go completely, feeling no fear or reticence.

Anamaya realized then that she had passed through the night and that she was watching the sun rise; that currents of air were carrying her higher into the sky. The world lay unfurled beneath her wings in all its magnificence; the winding river lay at the bottom of the valley, silver-scaled like the snake Amaru, the god of wisdom, who had come to her so often. He was everywhere in the valley, coiled around himself, nestling in the emerald bower of the forest.

She gazed at the distant mountains. She was as high as they. Salcantay's snowbound summit and all the Apus of the Andes in their majesty offered themselves to her by the light of the rising sun. She heard Katari chanting joyful incantations within her: *'Hamp'u! Hamp'u!'* And it was as though the mountains scintillated in the light by way of reply.

She recognized them, of course: the young mountain and the old one watching over the city whose name must never be spoken aloud where the young girl she had once been had been admitted many years earlier. She glided over the stepped terraces of harvest-ready corn and over the buildings of the city itself, where the tiny forms of priests and astronomers, soothsayers and architects, were beginning to emerge to begin the daily ritual of saluting Inti's return.

Anamaya could sense the gazes of the men below looking up at the condor high in the sky, and she felt pleased by their fear and respect.

'It's here,' she said to Katari, 'that the Empire's secret of all secrets is hidden. The place that must exist beyond time is to be found here.'

Katari said nothing, but she felt his joy, and she flapped her massive wings to carry them higher into the sky.

'Villa Oma took me there when he was still the one known as the Sage and could communicate with the gods. But he has lost his way and forgotten how to go there, and will never find it again.'

'Look at the Sun triumph,' said Katari.

They were above a ceremonial stone in the heart of the secret city. The sun's rays were hooked in it, as they were every day before they spread to illuminate the world and divide time. The stone had been hewn in ancient times to acknowledge the eternal momentum of the Young Mountain, Huayna Picchu.

They glided above it, caught up in the harmony that emanated from it. They were moved by the synchronicity between Man's wisdom and Nature's order that was evident here. The stone looked as though it had been cut to receive light; the way it divided light from shadow was a prayer that echoed silently through the mountains. Its fragility was out of reach. Its beauty was memory itself.

Anamaya felt all these sensations pass through Katari at the same time, as though he was gorging himself on some intoxicating liquid – every temple, every terrace, every stone summoned in him the legend of the origins of the world, its water, its stone, and its peoples.

The sun warmed the muggy air slowly. All the perfect sounds of life, from pestles grinding in mortars to the crackling fires stoked by women, from the frantic chattering of squirrels to the unfolding of the blood-flowers of orchids, converged and were unified in this perfection.

Anamaya soared over the terraces and made out the invisible vein that crossed the Old Summit. It was the way she had taken many years earlier, when a condor had interrupted the priests as they were about to sacrifice a young girl. She remembered the look in the girl's eyes and the feel of her little hand clasping her own, and she remembered the childlike confidence and absolute trust that had been implicit in that grasp.

As they approached the summit, their flight slowed and grew

heavier. Her wings no longer carried her so well, and she felt suddenly very tired.

She landed just above the *huaca*.

She could hear nothing but breath – her own, Katari's, and the wind's.

'Look,' said Katari. 'Look into the depths of your own heart.'

Anamaya automatically looked at the Huayna Picchu, its slender profile rising up right in front of her. Her gaze fell into the abyss and was suspended facing the mountain, so that she could make out its every outcrop and bump. And then, a terrible and familiar form loomed up suddenly from it: the Puma.

The mountain had become the Puma or else the Puma the mountain in the same way as Katari and she had become the Condor. The magic spectacle fueled her passions and she felt a river of all too human emotions flow through her. 'Gabriel,' she thought to herself, at first timidly, and then, with gathering conviction: 'Gabriel!'

'It is he. He is in front of you, and he is waiting for you,' Katari said softly.

Before she had time to understand or even think about it, she was overcome with joy: he was here, right in front of her, and all her fears evaporated with the breaking day.

She hovered before the puma-mountain for a long time. She felt protected by its power. She understood now the meaning of Katari's profound intuition: nothing could harm Gabriel. The Apus were protecting him.

When the sun had reached its zenith, she unfurled her wings and set off again.

With a single wing-flap, Anamaya and Katari glided down towards the walkway in front of the temples. They hovered above it, invulnerable to the vertigo that seized ordinary men lost between the bed of the Willkamayo, rumbling far below, and the snow-capped peaks of the distant Vilcabamba Cordillera.

A small ceremonial stone stood by itself at one of the

walkway's corners. It had been expertly hewn, marking the Four Directions.

And it spoke.

The walkway was completely empty, but had anyone been on it, they would have seen the odd sight of a hovering condor facing the rock, absorbing the sun's heat. At least, that was how it would have appeared to those who could not truly see.

Only Katari knew that Anamaya had transformed once again into an innocent young girl, a pure and wounded child standing at the side of the great Huayna Capac who was in the twilight of his life. Katari saw her dressed in a white *añaco* held closed by a simple red sash, kneeling by the old rock-king, his gray-skinned body trembling, his ragged profile turned toward the snows, toward the Under World. He saw her leaning toward the king in perfect silence, listening to him speak.

Katari could hear every word.

You are with me, young girl with eyes the color of the lake.

And I will never leave you while you watch over my Sacred Double.

After which everything will disappear. He too will vanish.

You will see the Puma; he will bound here from across the ocean.

He will only come to you when he leaves you.

Although separated, you will be united as one.

And when everyone has left, you will remain, and the Puma will remain at your side.

Together, like your ancestors Manco Capac and Mama Occlo, you will beget new life on earth.

There will be wars just as there have always been wars.

Separations just as there have always been separations.

And the Strangers, in their triumph, will know misery.

And we, the Incas, we shall have to know humiliation, we shall become slaves to our own shame before we understand the long journey that we have made, a journey that our panacas, *driven by the lust for war alone and no longer inspired by Inti, have forgotten in their destructiveness and madness.*

But we shall not die.

Anamaya was, somehow, actually *in* the old king's breath as he spoke to her. Once again, she listened to him tell the story of the ancient times, of the creation of the world, of the confidence of the Incas born in the cradle of the mountains of Cuzco; she listened to him tell proudly of his military victories, and she listened to him despair over the war between his sons. He spoke about the ball of fire that had designated Atahualpa as Emperor and she remembered; he spoke of Manco, *the first knot of the future*, and she remembered.

I wanted to turn to stone, just as the Ancients of my race did, and remain still on the soft, green grass of one of Cuzco's mountain slopes.

War chased me away. I found refuge in the Secret City.

My stone opens to the Four Directions, just as I expanded the Empire of the Four Cardinal Directions; and yet it's a humble stone, for it will be all that remains of the Empire; a stone to which the Sun will hitch itself.

The Four Directions will remain in the heart of a pure man.

Today, there is already war between brothers, although they don't know it yet.

And there will be more war.

War visits the Sons of the Sun and war visits the Strangers. It is the sign.

The brother's blood and the friend's blood are shed far more than the enemy's. It is the sign.

The stone and the waters vanish in the forest. It is the sign.

The Stranger who worships a woman rather than his Ancestors is killed: it is the sign.

No seer sees it; the priests are baffled; the Sun hides itself from

*the astronomers; betrayal insinuates itself as a friend of the people;
the Ocean vomits Strangers on us, in ever-greater numbers. Soon it
will be time for you to flee in order to preserve what has always been
and what will always be.*

*But you will heed the signs, and you will remain with our people
until that moment when Inti has consumed the hatred dividing us,
and only women singing their grief over all the spilt blood will
remain.*

You will make no mistake.

*You will meet He-whose-stone-stops-time and he will stand in
front of me like you. But he will go to the place of origins whereas
you will take the road to the city whose name must never he
spoken aloud.*

*You will know what must not be spoken, and you will not
speak it.*

*You will say only what must be and will be, and when it has been
then two fingers of one hand will unite you.*

You will be free.

*You will take my Sacred Double to the end of his way, and he
too will be free.*

*Only one secret will remain hidden within you. You will have to
live with it.*

Never doubt me. Remain in my breath, and trust the Puma.

Silence returned, save for the eternal speech of the wind and the
river. Heavy black clouds filled the air and hid the sun.

Anamaya remained as still as Huayna Capac. Her hand was
resting on the dying old sovereign's body. Her old pain was
young once again, and the loneliness that she had done away
with returned now to grip her heart. She kept her eyes closed.
She shuddered. She sensed the presence leaving without actually
moving, heading to another shore, and she ached from being
unable to go with it and live with it.

Katari put his hand on her shoulder and restrained her suffering.

The entire valley filled with fog, and they could no longer see the summits. The golden corn on the terraces disappeared, the ripe *quinua* turned grey, and the temples looked as though they had been built from water stone. Shreds of clouds streamed around them, as if in a slow dance.

Anamaya took her hand away from Huayna Capac's corpse.

She could see only the stone, but she wasn't surprised.

She could feel Katari's broad palm still resting on her shoulder. She was still sad, but she felt that her friend had stopped her from embarking on a dangerous voyage.

They both looked to the west, where a halo of light was still filtering through the clouds on the black horizon.

Then the sky tore open as suddenly as it had closed. A rainbow had placed one base of its arch in the central opening of the temple of the three niches.

'Come,' said Katari.

Together, they rose into the sky.

Night had fallen on Ollantaytambo.

Katari and Anamaya were lying on the little wall that ran alongside the Willkamayo. Neither dared speak.

The sky was clear and the moon full. The condor rock stood clearly illuminated by its light.

'I had a dream. You were in it,' said Anamaya eventually, sitting up.

Katari didn't move, his eyes wide open and staring at the immensity of the star-speckled sky.

'I had the same dream,' he said without looking at her.

'How do you know?'

Katari didn't answer out loud, but Anamaya heard his voice echo from within her, and in a flash realized that the voyage that they had undertaken together had been real. Katari was right. She wanted to ask him if they had returned to their point of departure or if a day had passed. She looked at the moon but didn't find the answer.

'You will know what must not be spoken, and you will not speak it.'

Anamaya let the words resonate within her, and she suddenly felt the full power of Huayna Capac's speech. No, she was no longer the terrified little girl who forgot the past, the present, and the future; nor was she the *Coya Camaquen* who had to struggle continually to understand the mystery. The world was in place: that which had been revealed remained, and that which was secret remained so as well.

They heard a dull rumbling sound from the north.

Katari sat up.

At first, they wondered if it was a convulsion of the earth, one that would shake the rock and lift the river out of its bed. But the rumbling grow louder and they both realized its source at the same moment. It was coming from the mountain facing them, the one that rose above both the rivers, the one that stood guard over the Sacred Valley.

The mountain seemed to roar like a man racked by violent pain. They felt it tremble, they felt the breaking point of its tension, and they saw an enormous block break away from the rock face, leaving a gaping cavity.

A thick cloud of black dust slowly rose up and invaded the night, and still the mountain shook sporadically. Another almighty cracking sound signaled the breaking away of an entire side of the mountain, and Katari and Anamaya watched it fall away as best they could through the thick cloud of dust. After that, the mountain gave two more agonized cries, howling against the wounds that it was inflicting on itself.

They watched the spectacle with utter fascination, quickly forgetting their own fears. This upheaval of nature wasn't the mark of some divine rage against Man. It came from even further away. Merely to watch it was to be part of the secret.

The dust rose up, half blinding them. They were obliged to go to the channels cut into the rock and wash out their burning eyes. After, they remained by the water, waiting.

When the mountain had become completely quiet, they turned around. The dust cloud was slowly settling, revealing a dramatically changed view.

Anamaya cried out.

She saw Huayna Capac's face, clearly visible in the moonlight, disclosed in the newly exposed stone. It was his face as it had been in the hour of his death all those years ago, and as it had been during her dream – her flight – as a condor.

He was carved into the side of the mountain, as though some gargantuan sculptor had chiseled him there. He was the man of stone, a hundred times – a thousand times – bigger than any men of flesh.

His eyes lay deep in their sockets and his prominent nose accentuated the straight line of his forehead, a mark of his resolution. A long crack marked his mouth, and his chin was covered by a great beard of rocks. He was facing north, as though looking beyond the forest and toward the Secret City in its valley.

Anamaya knew then that the knowledge was within her.

CHAPTER 8

Ollantaytambo, Choquana lock, 16 June 1536

H IS HANDS TIED BEHIND HIS BACK, HIS FEET HOBBLED
with thick agave ropes that reduced the length of his
stride considerably, and guarded by a dozen warriors day
and night, Gabriel had been walking for three days.

After his capture at the fortress of Sacsayhuaman he had been
taken to a hamlet of wretched adobe houses beneath some arid
mountain. He had been kept there for many months. The old
woman who fed him didn't answer his questions any more than
did his guards. His questions became fewer as time passed, and
after the blind exultation of battle he had gradually slipped into
a state of apathetic despair. Gabriel had felt no more master of
his own fate then than he had been before, and he had allowed
himself to slide toward that fate without rancour, thinking that
it could only be death. The thought had crossed his mind that
it would have been better if his captors had killed him straight
away. But he banished the notion as irrelevant.

Three days earlier, they had come to fetch him at daybreak, and
had told him that it was time to go. Gabriel had said nothing and
since then he had barely exchanged three words with his guards,
who looked at him with that indifference with which he was
now so familiar. He knew that it actually hid a deep curiosity as
well as, most probably, fear. At sundown, he heard them talking
among themselves, but he was too exhausted to make the effort
to understand them.

He woke as though from a dream.

For all those weeks, Gabriel had lived like a man possessed: surviving Gonzalo's revenge, then the burning of his prison, then avoiding the Incas' arrows and sling stones before taking the tower. In his mind he watched himself accomplish all these things, actions that had won him his companions' admiration. But he couldn't shake the feeling that he was watching a play being performed in the theatre of his mind in which a masked actor was playing himself. It was as though he, Gabriel, had been asleep throughout, as though he had slipped out of himself. When he found himself tied up once more, powerless, and being marched through this valley locked away in the mountains, it brought him – disagreeably – back to life.

Gabriel could see in front of him only the backs of the porters' bare legs, their muscled calves like polished knotted wood. They bore enormous sheaves of *quinua*, which made the broad Inca road ahead seem as though it had been transformed into a field that was being ruffled by a fickle wind. Gabriel exhaled all the air in his lungs: the sheaves shivered. He breathed out again: still they shivered. Suddenly and absurdly, he felt an irrepressible urge to laugh. 'I am the master of *quinua*!' he cried in Spanish. 'I am the master of the corn!' He exhaled as though his lungs were the fountainhead of the winds. The Indian soldiers looked at him and clutched their spears and sling tighter: had the prisoner gone mad? Gabriel laughed so hard that he broke out into a paroxysm of coughing, and then stopped suddenly.

The river valley, which at first had been broad, became progressively narrower as they made their way up it. Cliffs, at the bases of which fortresses had been built, now rose up on both its sides. The river meandered from one cliff to the other, from one fort to the next. Hundreds, or perhaps even thousands of men wearing only their *hauras* were working to strengthen the forts. They had formed long lines to pass down enormous blocks of stone, while work teams built walls and put up wooden scaffolding.

But it was only when the soldiers urged him to ford the river that Gabriel saw the magnificent spread of terraces rising up through the valley, and, up above, an imposing building with a commanding view over its entirety. This structure was no less fascinating for being unfinished. Whether it was a temple or a fortress, he couldn't tell – and in any case, he knew that the Incas no longer made a distinction between the two.

His breath was cut short.

In that moment, the exhilarating and painful conviction came to him out of nowhere that he was going to see *her*.

Nightfall brought with it a cool breeze. Gabriel, passing through the straight streets, each one perfectly paved and lined by high, narrow doors leading into *canchas* under steep, thatched roofs, was struck by the bustling activity that filled the place.

It was a city under construction, teeming with endless activity and people speaking to one another not only in Quechua, which he had mastered, but also in Jaki aru and Pukina, Kollasuyu languages of which Gabriel had learned just enough to distinguish between them. Many of the town's peoples had never encountered a Stranger, and they struggled to hide their astonishment upon seeing him, with his long tangled blond hair and the beard that covered his face after weeks of imprisonment and, before that, combat. Upon entering the town, his guards had moved in closer around him, as though worried that he might try to escape, impossible though that would be, into the crowd.

They came to a halt in front of a *cancha* guarded by two *orejones*, as the Spaniards had taken to calling those Inca noblemen whose ears were distended by disks that, before the conquest, had been made of gold, but that since that time were more often made of wood.

Gabriel was shoved into the building with little ceremony. He was familiar with its layout. The courtyard was full of soldiers. Behind them were the women, some busy preparing a meal, others gathered timidly together in little groups at the back of the courtyard just in front of the staircase leading up to the first floor shared with the neighbouring *cancha*. Gabriel immediately recognized Manco sitting on his royal *tiana* in the center. He also recognized the emaciated and thin-lipped Villa Oma sitting on a bench, only slightly lower than the Emperor's, to Manco's side. Although his circumstances were greatly reduced, Gabriel felt that the young sovereign nevertheless exuded a far greater majesty and dignity than he had at the grand affair of his coronation on the Aucaypata in Cuzco. Gabriel couldn't help but be struck by the dark but inflexible will that Manco seemed to embody. The puppet king installed on the throne by Don Francisco had died. In his place had been born a warrior who had almost defeated the Spaniards at Sacsayhuaman, and whose troops were still laying siege to Cuzco. But the one person Gabriel couldn't see was Anamaya.

A heavy silence filled the room.

Gabriel looked from the Sage to the Inca and from the Inca to the Sage. Gabriel had learned from the Incas not to speak too soon, and to read the expression of his interlocutors' faces before opening his mouth. Villa Oma broke the silence first.

'The Stranger must die,' he spat, rising slowly from his *tiana*. There was fury in his calm. All those present were frozen in their places.

'He assaulted the tower at Sacsayhuaman. Many of our warriors died because of him. It is also because of him that the noble Cusi Huallpa sacrificed himself. The Strangers pretend that he has magic powers greater than those of any of our soothsayers, and that he is protected by their gods. These are ridiculous lies! Let us cut him into pieces and send them his skull; let us flay off his skin and make a drum with it and send them that too! That will show them that our warriors are far more powerful than their so-called gods! We should have killed him a long time ago. Only our weakness prevented us from doing so . . .'

Villa Oma turned towards Manco and, with an exasperation clearly too long suppressed, continued:

'. . . And it was to that same weakness that we relinquished complete victory over the mongrel Strangers!'

No one had ever dared attack Manco so directly and unambiguously in public. Gabriel was aware of the insult and, oddly, since it was his own life that was the subject of the argument, he felt a calm sense of detachment, as though he were an onlooker, albeit one watching others decide his fate. He looked directly at Manco, ignoring the Sage, and said in a calm voice:

'I am more indifferent to my own life than you are. My own people tried to take it from me, but God – or luck – let me keep it. You would take it for doing what soldiers do? Then kill me. It's not my place to say whether that is justice or merely a pointless cruelty that would offend your gods as well as the one that my own people worship.'

Manco still hadn't said a word. He seemed lost in his own thoughts, almost completely inert. Villa Oma grew exasperated:

'Let us do away with him, brother Manco! It will be the sign that the people and the gods are waiting for to give us a brilliant victory.'

'This man will not die.'

Manco had spoken without looking at anyone in particular. Villa Oma froze in his fury. He raised his arm, pointing at Manco. But before he had a chance to affront the Inca, he was interrupted by a commotion at the *cancha*'s entrance. Two *chaskis*, streaming sweat, entered the courtyard and prostrated themselves in front of Manco.

'Speak,' ordered the Inca.

Without raising his head, the older of the two began:

'Emperor, we bring you news of a brilliant victory. Our troops have destroyed an army of Strangers sent by their *kapitu* to reinforce those we have surrounded in Cuzco. We killed many of their men, and took many of their weapons and horses. These are being brought here, my Lord, as an offering to your glory.'

Manco remained as impassive as he had been when Gabriel had been led into the *cancha*.

'Sage Villa Oma,' he eventually said in a slow, measured voice, 'must realize now that it isn't necessary to carry out injustices to ensure great victories.'

Villa Oma's face was as green as the coca juice dribbling from his lips. But he said nothing. Without formally taking his leave, he cut through the crowd of astonished soldiers, shoved his way through the women, and swept up the stairs. When he reached the landing and was about to disappear onto the floor leading to the neighbouring building, he wrapped his *manta* about himself, spun around on his heels, and said:

'Manco, I have not forgotten that we are both sons of one father, the great Huayna Capac. Nor have I forgotten that you are the Son of the Sun. But Inti does what must be done to shine every day. Do you wish to bring eternal night upon us?'

The Emperor's soldiers moved towards the Sage after he had delivered this insult. But Manco stopped them with a wave of his hand.

'Let him be,' he said. 'The Sage is no longer the Sage. Anger and hatred have overcome him, and his words are meaningless now – mere noises that he makes when he moves his lips.' Looking at Gabriel, he continued, 'I too suffered humiliations at the hands of the Strangers. They wanted to take my wife from me – they treated me worse than a slave, worse even than a dog. But I kept silent, and in the secret places of our mountains, and with the help of our gods, I prepared for this war that we are going to win . . .'

Manco's voice rose in volume as he spoke, and the murmur of approbation from his audience rose into a corresponding clamor, until the entire *cancha* echoed with their cries.

'And now,' said Manco, once the clamor had died down, 'I wish to be left alone with the Stranger.'

He stood up suddenly, waving away the women who rushed forward to sweep the ground in front of him. He approached Gabriel and took him by the arm. The audience couldn't help but cry out in surprise, but the Inca himself remained indifferent. He led Gabriel into another room, the largest and most richly decorated in the *cancha*.

Apart from that which passed through the door, the room was devoid of daylight. Gold and silver vases and animal statuettes sat in niches carved into the walls.

'You know, of course, the reason for my clemency?' said Manco dryly.

Gabriel couldn't hide his surprise.

'No, Lord Manco.'

'No? And yet my reason is called by a name dear to your heart.'

Through the shadows, Gabriel saw the light in Manco's eyes flare up. Only a moment before, the Inca had seemed as serene as the thoughtful sage that Villa Oma had once been. Now, the Emperor seemed to share Villa Oma's present anger, and his eyes glowed with wrath.

'Anamaya is the reason you still live,' said Manco. 'If it was not for what I know you mean to her, you would have been killed on the day of your capture, and the dust of your body would now be fertilizing our fields . . .'

'I know it, noble Manco. But I also know that you meant what you said to Villa Oma! You may hate me, but you cannot prevent me from admiring you.'

'I am the Inca, Stranger! Remember that you look upon me now only because I wish it. Even your feelings are not your own!'

Gabriel did his best to keep control of himself. He said:

'In that case, you will allow me to keep the one thing that you cannot take from me: silence.'

Manco stared at him, saying nothing. Then he turned on his heels to leave the room. As he was about to pass through the door hanging, he turned, looked at Gabriel one last time, and spat spitefully:

'The Puma! The mighty Puma has come!'

CHAPTER 9

Ollantaytambo, evening of 18 June 1536

GABRIEL SANK INTO THE COLD NIGHT.

He was dozing on his hard mat, listening to the constant sound of water running through the town, when the Indian slipped into the room that Manco had given him. No one had told Gabriel whether he was free or still a prisoner. His wrists had been untied and his ankles unshackled. He had been given two women to serve him and two Indian attendants, taciturn Kollas, to protect him or perhaps guard him – he wasn't sure which. So when Katari slipped into his room, his heart leaped with joy: Katari was Bartholomew's friend, and above all it was Katari who had saved him on the shore of Lake Titicaca.

'Welcome, Master of the Stone! Are you here to bring me back to the world once again?'

To his great surprise, Katari said nothing, not even smiling at his joke or making some gesture of friendship. His face, with its prominent cheekbones, remained completely impassive beneath his long hair.

'Follow me,' was all he said.

Gabriel had had a chance to wash and to throw away the filthy clothes that he had been wearing since the attack on the tower. He was now wearing an ample Indian tunic made of alpaca wool. But his muscles still ached, and his body was stiff, as though he had just been in battle. He didn't question Katari, but simply rose and followed him through the heavy wool door hanging.

Katari spoke quietly with the two attendants there, and they stepped aside. Out in the street, Gabriel followed him past the silent *canchas*. Their sandaled feet moved silently over the flagstones. Katari crossed the great square without slowing and without saying a word, and soon they passed through a monumental gate. Gabriel followed behind as they climbed up six platforms linked by flights of steps. Then, despite the feeble light of the waning moon, Gabriel made out the base of a stairway before them, one that rose vertiginously in a straight line up the side of a hill. It was the hill on which he had seen the stepped terraces and massive structure when he had arrived earlier that afternoon.

With each step he climbed, Gabriel shed the weight of both his exhaustion and his concern at Katari's odd attitude. He saw in the shadows, beyond the terraces shored up with stones, a building with many niches, which he took to be a temple because of the quality of its walls. But his increasing shortness of breath, together with Katari's persistent silence, prevented him from asking the young man about it. Even when they reached the base of the massive walls enclosing the great temple that he had seen from the valley, Katari didn't stop or even slow down. The slope here, however, was a little less steep, affording Gabriel some small relief. Only when they reached a massive wall blocking the way further up the hill did Katari stop.

Gabriel bent forward, bracing his hands against his thighs, and inhaled deeply. When he had recovered his breath, he looked up at the Master of the Stone and asked:

'Now will you talk to me?'

Katari said nothing, but at least his face had lost that neutral expression which Gabriel had mistaken for hostility.

'She is the one who will talk to you.'

Gabriel felt the breath go out of him once again, but this time not from exertion. *Anamaya!* Ever since he had first seen Ollantaytambo, he had banished to a corner of his mind the thought that had jolted his heart like a bolt of lightning: seeing her, holding her . . . it was both so wonderful and so painful that he lowered his head and held it in his hands.

Katari pointed beyond the wall at the gentle winding path leading to the top of the hill.

'Go,' was all he said.

He turned and disappeared without further explanation or even a goodbye. Gabriel looked at the path, then set off. Each step he took felt as though his feet weighed a ton each. And he was trembling more than he ever had in battle.

Anamaya had been waiting alone in the little temple at the top of the hill since sundown. The small structure wasn't visible from the valley, which was why she and Katari had chosen it. When they had told Manco of their idea, the Inca had listened without giving anything away before agreeing and sighing: 'You know things that I don't.'

So Katari had overseen the construction of the building, carried out by a small number of his Kolla brothers, so that the secret would be kept. It had been built in only one day: a simple supporting wall and a small edifice with four niches, each one big enough to hold a man. Three nights previously, they had taken the Sacred Double there. They had wrapped it in *mantas* so that no soldier or priest or anyone else other than Manco would know about it. The Sacred Double was now installed in the first niche, facing south.

Anamaya hadn't looked at the Sacred Double in the same way ever since her Great Voyage. It was as though the knowledge that she had gained had quenched her thirst and done away with her anxiety. It was no longer he who held what she needed, but rather she who had to guard and protect him through the war.

And yet, when the last rays of the sun had disappeared beyond the mountains behind her, when she found herself in the company of only the night's cold and wind, she couldn't help but be overcome by the anxiety of waiting. Seeing Gabriel again, seeing him at last: she rose, stared out into the darkness, and listened carefully for his step. She remembered how she had glanced at Katari when the *chaski* had brought the news that the prisoner was on his way. She stopped her imagination from picturing herself running into his arms and holding him, or from imagining herself telling him all the things that she had kept to herself for so many moons. A jumble of Quechua and Spanish rested in her throat, and she felt the urge to both laugh and cry.

Anamaya looked at the immobile, eternal Sacred Double, and some semblance of calm returned to her.

She took a short stroll outside the building. The breeze's murmur had grown as distant as those of the two rivers. *'He will only come to you when he leaves you. Although separated, you will be united as one.'* Those were the words of the great Huayna Capac. Did they refer to what had been or to what was to be? Anamaya's blood raged as she asked herself more questions than the prophecy had given her answers. There was another door on the other side of the door of knowledge, and then yet another, and so it continued until the end of life in this world, until one reached the steps leading to the Under World.

A cloud hid the moon: the night turned pitch black. As the wind picked up again, Anamaya at last heard Gabriel's step. Then she saw his silhouette. She ran, not towards him but into the temple. He found her inside on the ground, her arms around the Sacred Double.

He slid down next to her.

They couldn't say a word or make a gesture.

They couldn't even look at one another.

The breeze picked up Gabriel's long blond locks and tangled them with Anamaya's black hair. They sat beside each other, only their shoulders touching. In their emotional turmoil, they couldn't tell their own trembling from the other's.

Anamaya pulled herself together first.

Slowly, she slid her honey-skinned hand onto Gabriel's shoulder, then let it slide between his *unku* and his skin. Slowly, she ran her hand over his chest, and Gabriel's entire body shuddered at her touch. She traced the mark of the puma, knowing from memory exactly where it was, and scratched him lightly. He moaned.

Then she held her body against his back in a grip of passionate intensity and fervently pressed her lips to the mark that foretold his destiny.

*   *   *

They rediscovered one another in the night.

Uncertain gestures preceded any words between them: a nervous giggle, a sudden tear. Gabriel's hand stroked sensuously through Anamaya's hair, again and again; Anamaya's nails trailed through his beard before she ran her palm over his cheeks, his chin, his entire face. They drew in deep breaths of one another, touched one another with their fingers, their skin, their tongues. They struck one another playfully, not painfully, but still hard enough so that the marks they left roused forgotten appetites.

Then the length of their prolonged separation and of the hunger that this abstinence had produced drove them into a furious embrace, and they clasped one another almost violently, so that there was a fierceness to their sweet pleasures. They rolled over and over like two young wildcats and bit one another playfully, each surprised by the fervour of the other's bite. Gabriel had the advantage of superior strength, but Anamaya had the reflexes of a forest animal, and she slipped away from him just as he thought he had her, only to jump on his back. He managed to turn around and take hold of her: with a single movement, he took hold of her *añaco* and an instant later it fell to the ground.

They stopped and stood absolutely still.

She was naked in front of him. The urgency of their desire to take one another quietened in the calm of the night. They stared at each other for a moment, and then it all began again, but more slowly this time, each gesture performed with a considered gentleness.

Anamaya held her breath as Gabriel's mouth approached her breast. He kissed it as though he intended to caress every pore of her body with his lips. His desire was so deep and so strong that he intensified it by being patient to the point of cruelty with her. Anamaya stretched towards him and encouraged him, calling him to her not with words but rather with soft moans, short, wordless cries that nevertheless conveyed her desire for him. But he continued kissing her as lightly as he could, despite the urgency rising in his loins that was gradually wearing away the restraint of his exploration. Finally, she took his head between her hands with such ardor that he raised his lips to hers from the smooth lower slopes of her body in one movement. He kissed her forever, kissed her as though he was drinking from a mountain spring after crossing the desert, kissed her as one loves, as one breathes, as one lives – he kissed her as though he had never kissed before.

Their clothes formed a bed on the ground, and they rolled around on it. If it had not been for the different colors of their skins, it would have been hard to tell that they were two separate people. Yes, they wanted to be *one*, the conquistador and the strange young girl from the forest, the Spaniard and the Inca. In that moment, all each of them had was the other's body, and Anamaya felt herself slipping into a place of happiness that reminded her of her journey with Katari. She came almost at the very instant he entered her, but as he continued the dimensions of her pleasure broadened to include the universe itself, the stars, and the streams hidden in rocky mountain chasms. As for Gabriel, he was happy as he thrust and thrust again, feeling as powerful as a waterfall whose roar filled valleys. He wasn't frightened of his body and all that was hidden in it, and he felt able to push back all his own limits. In one corner of his mind, he laughed at the irony of his past exploits. On his white horse, he had been but a boy. Only now was he a man.

They became covered in sweat in the endless frenzy of their passion, and their sweat's salty taste made them thirsty. The breeze picked up, the breeze died down, and the cold night reached them. But they didn't care: they stretched out the limits of the night, they smashed together like two stones, they flowed like rivers, they scratched each other's flesh like animals – they loved one another like a man and woman.

And even when, exhausted at last, they slipped into sleep, their love followed them.

They were lying at the Sacred Double's feet, their hands on one another's thighs, and with Gabriel's shoulder in the hollow of Anamaya's neck. Their mouths were open, smiling.

They were happy and, because of it, they were beautiful.

The first rays of dawn crept over the mountain ridges, waking Gabriel. He tightened his embrace around Anamaya. Together, they sat up and watched as the world was reborn for another day: the fury of the waters flowing down the Willkamayo at the point where they were funneled through a narrow gorge; the narrow summit of the Wakay Willca.

As it emerged from night's shadows, Gabriel noticed the enormous shape in the side of the mountain facing them. He turned to Anamaya, a quizzical look on his face. She looked back at him, without replying. But he felt the heat and even the light emanating from her, and without quite knowing why he sensed that there was some link between her and the monumental and mysterious figure in the rock.

He drew her closer still, and she surrendered to him. But all the while she kept her gaze fixed on Huayna Capac's face, for his words continued to reverberate through her mind like the rumble of the Patacancha river.

She spoke the first words that had passed between them since they had been reunited.

'Gabriel . . .'

The three syllables slipped from Anamaya's lips as softly as a breath. Her soul was a seething cauldron: there was so much that she wanted to tell him, and she didn't know where to begin, unsure of what he was allowed to hear. But then she succumbed to the urgency of her emotions: just as the light was now flooding through the valley and across the mountains, so she had to feel her soul filled by his voice as her innermost physical depths had been filled by his manhood.

'Tell me everything, Puma . . .'

Gabriel described to her those appalling days when he had come to believe that the war separating them would never end, when he had given in to despair and had wanted only two things: to rid the world of Gonzalo and his henchmen, and then to die. Anamaya smiled when he told her about the three Indians who had come to kill him in his cell, only to be thwarted by Sebastian's timely appearance. She displayed no emotion as she listened to his account of the battle for Sacsayhuaman, of Juan's death, of the strange feeling of invincibility that had risen up in him and that, along with his profound despair, had driven him to accomplish the most unimaginable and even absurd exploits.

'I didn't understand it then,' murmured Gabriel, 'and I still don't. I felt as though I was giving off light, and as though I was surrounded by it. I'd heard silly talk of magic, you know, but I dismissed it: stories of arrows bouncing off soldiers, of sling stones changing direction before they could hit them and then rolling harmlessly into the rocks. I don't believe those things any more than I believe in Don Francisco's beloved Sacred Virgin. And yet, I had to suffer it: for although I myself didn't believe it, my companions, those few brave men, did, as much as the rabble. They looked upon me not as a hero – which is something I know about and which is in the end only a very human sentiment, in which admiration and jealousy are mixed – but with a fear of the supernatural. But don't think that it made me proud. No, it only increased my indifference, if such a thing is possible. When I flung my armor off the top of the tower, I felt as though I was freeing myself. If I could have thrown my skin with it, I would have.'

Gabriel paused for a moment. Anamaya let his words echo through her without yet trying to fathom their meaning.

'And then, in a dream, I had the strangest impression of actually *seeing* you.'

Anamaya gave a start.

'It was as though I knew ahead of time what I was going to do, as though some messenger from nowhere showed me clear, lifelike images of what was to come. That rope hanging from the top of the first tower – I *saw* it well before I took it in my hands. And when I did grab it, I was already in some place beyond fear or courage, beyond doubt or duty: I was only doing what had to be done.'

'You are arriving, drawing nearer . . . you are almost here . . .'

'By leading the assault against your people?'

'You are here to save us.'

'The night before, or even the same morning as the assault, I saw Inguill. She said those very same words . . .'

'Accept them . . .'

Gabriel shook his head.

'Everything is still too new for me, for my mind. Sometimes I feel as though I'm separated from myself by a wall, a wall even thicker than those of the towers we took.'

'You will pass through the wall.'

Gabriel sighed.

'Well, for the moment, I've given up trying to understand more.'

'What happened after you took the tower?'

'When your people took me prisoner, they captured a dazed man, his spirit broken, who didn't resist at all. Why didn't they kill me? To this day, I don't know, just as I still have no idea why they kept me in that shack up in the mountains for an entire month, feeding me those damned shriveled-up old *papas*. You call them *chuños*, right? I'll never forget that taste of mouldy earth. And can you tell me why, one fine morning four days ago now, they finally decided to tear me away from that delicacy and bring me here?'

Gabriel sighed again, then said with a laugh:

'Well now, Princess-who-knows-all-the-secrets, can't you tell me?'

Anamaya hesitated and started gathering up their scattered clothes.

'It happened two moons ago, right?' she said eventually. 'During those two moons, I often dreamed that if I saw you again, I would spend the entire night with you. And now I've had that night . . .'

She stopped, leaving her sentence unfinished. But the time of his painful impatience was over. *Bartholomew*, Gabriel thought to himself. *If you could see me now, you might well call me wise . . .*

'I want to tell you everything I have learned,' Anamaya said at last, 'because you are part of what I've learned. You might even be the most beautiful part of what I've learned. But you must first pass through each stage, as I did.'

'I feel as though I've already passed through more than a few stages,' replied Gabriel with strained good humor.

'I know, my love, I know. But there is still so much you have to learn . . .'

'One terrible night many years ago we were standing by your Emperor Atahualpa's corpse. You allowed me a glimpse into that world then, didn't you?'

'I was very proud after I'd been nominated *Coya Camaquen*. I was proud that the Powerful Lords called upon me to transmit the secrets of which I was myself unaware. I was so confused! But yes, you're right. I wanted to show you then that there was another world behind our love, another world beyond the war . . .'

'Do you think I came near it?' asked Gabriel in a tone so beseeching that Anamaya couldn't help but laugh.

'My Puma is sometimes such a child,' she said, taking his hand and holding it between hers, as though to temper the jest of her words. 'But yes, of course you did: you drew near in great, furious bounds, without knowing where you were going, but always with your generous heart to buoy your spirit.'

'I'm with you now, right? We're together now?'

'*Although separated, you will be united as one . . .*' She had searched for those words fruitlessly for so long. And now that she had them, she almost regretted knowing them, for they left her tongue-tied. She was no longer the little girl under Villa Oma's tutelage who knew nothing, she was no longer the proud *Coya Camaquen*, nor even the woman in love. But as this thought passed through her mind, her heart rebelled: yes, she *was* still that woman in love, and no matter what secrets were revealed or what prophecies still lay hidden, she had to make her love live, she had to live it, gorge herself on it.

'Yes,' she said, 'you're with me.'

Gabriel calmed down. He looked out over the magnificent landscape that was being revealed by the rising sun. The face in the mountainside drew his gaze more than anything else, more than the eternal snows on the peaks, or the emerald rainforests below them. The face was only just visible in the weak light of dawn, but it was so extraordinary that it was impossible not to look at it. Anamaya watched it with him.

'Who is he?' whispered Gabriel timidly.

'He's the one who brought us together.'

CHAPTER 10

F ROM THE TOP OF THE GREAT STAIRWAY THAT ROSE through the sacred terraces, Gabriel looked down upon an amazing sight. The *canchas* at the bottom of the valley had been built long ago. But Manco had decided to make Ollantaytambo his principal bastion, and all the narrow terraces overlooking it had been transformed into an enormous building site. Gabriel had never before witnessed the Herculean efforts that went into erecting an Inca city, and, Manco having granted him a supervised freedom of movement, he returned to this spot day after day, enthralled by the progress of the construction.

In the Chachicata quarry in the distance, hundreds of tiny silhouettes worked busily on all sizes of blocks of stone that had broken away from the Black Mountain. The valley was filled with the rhythmic pounding of hammers and chisels, made of hard-stone or bronze, with which the tireless workers hewed the rock.

The valley was filled with people, from the foot of the mountain to the river bank. Thousands of men, each one with a specific task, began work at dawn. Some chipped away at the boulders that had rolled to the bottom of the valley. First they chiseled them into a rough, unfinished shape, thus ridding them of unnecessary weight, before transporting them by raft from one river bank to the other.

Others made rope or trimmed logs with which to haul and roll the rocks up the opposite slope, to the summit of Ollantaytambo. Hundreds of men pushed and pulled for hours on end. They levered the blocks up each section of terrain with enormous timbers, a slow, complicated system that took great effort but that allowed the boulders to be taken up safely and surely.

A great number of people were gathered at the end of the ramp along which the blocks were transported from the river to the construction site. Here, the work required more skill; using only stone or bronze tools, working in a cloud of white dust, men smoothed and polished the enormous stones so that they fitted perfectly together. Gabriel watched, enthralled, as a group of men flocked around a boulder three times taller than any of them that rested on a platform of logs and was secured by a web of rope.

Katari was in charge of this vast construction site. Gabriel occasionally caught sight of him supervising the alignment of a temple, or the building of a wall, or the shaping of a rock, in his own quietly efficient manner.

Gabriel never once doubted that Katari's efforts complied with a set of precise rules. But they were unlike any of those in his own, admittedly very limited, knowledge of the architect's art. Katari never had a plan in his hand, for instance, and he seemed to select the most unlikely and difficult locations on which to place his buildings. He could have expanded the town in the area between the two rivers in the valley, where there were only springs. But 'expanding the town' was clearly not his objective. Nothing being built was designed to be lived in.

And none of the new buildings mystified Gabriel more than the temple halfway up the slope, set on a vast esplanade that had been cleared to make room for a number of blocks already prepared. Only one of its walls had been erected so far, from four enormous blocks of rose-colored rock fitted together. This type of stone displayed an astonishing range of iridescence as the angle of the sunlight falling on it shifted throughout the day. Between each rock was what looked to the unknowing eye like a long stone reed.

As with all of the Incas' most magnificent buildings, no mortar held the huge trimmed stones together. Each block was simply hewn to fit perfectly with its neighbour, and the walls rose up majestically, mysterious and indestructible. Drawing closer, Gabriel saw that three of the rocks were decorated with stylized knurls. He tried to guess their purpose.

'Do you find them beautiful?'

Katari was sweating, but his almond eyes above his prominent cheekbones were smiling. His torso was bare, like those of all his workers. Gabriel admired his strong physique; his broad hands were covered in fine rock dust and looked strong enough to snap a man's back with little effort. A bronze key hung from a small gold chain around his neck.

Gabriel didn't try to hide his admiration.

'It's magnificent, Katari. I've never seen anything like it. I doubt even our best architects are capable of working such wonders.'

'We are not trying to build wonders.'

'What *are* you trying to do?'

'You already know that, better than you think.'

Gabriel was taken aback.

'What do you mean?'

Katari's smile widened.

'Don't the shapes of these stones remind you of something?'

Gabriel narrowed his eyes and stared at the enormous blocks. Slowly, a shape formed in his mind. It was a blurred shape and an ancient one, one associated with forgotten miseries . . .

'Taypikala!' he cried. 'There were stones like these there!'

Katari nodded.

'There's more. Come closer.'

Gabriel came up close to the rocks. It was midday, and their shadows were short. He saw that strange designs had been carved on their surfaces. He thought that he recognized the geometry of a double staircase. The upper flight rose up in the normal way, but the bottom one led down, inverted like the reflection of a mountain on a lake's surface. On another block set on its plinth, Gabriel brushed his hands over a relief cut in the form of a T-shaped key.

'I've seen this before,' he exclaimed, turning to Katari.

'In the same place,' said the Master of the Stone. 'Are you surprised?'

'I don't know,' said Gabriel frankly. 'I don't know what it means.'

'I could tell you that these hollows, cut with bronze keys like this one around my neck, are designed to help us set the stones in position, and that these knurls are used to secure the stones to transport them here, but . . .'

Katari fell silent, his gaze wandering to the northern horizon. 'But?'

'. . . It would be true. But that wouldn't be all there was to it. There's something else.'

Gabriel's curiosity was piqued: not only his curiosity, but also a desire to enter another world, one that he had skirted around for so long without suspecting it.

'Do you see the town down there,' said Katari, 'with its *canchas* and their courtyards and the rooms coming off them? The alleys are laid out according to a plan. Their lines are designed to cross. I've never seen one of your towns, Stranger, but ours no doubt didn't surprise you. But this one, on the other hand . . .'

Katari waved his arm all around him and looked at Gabriel.

'. . . Here, we want to pay homage to the gods with every building, every stone, every rock. We want to pay homage to the gods around us: our Father the Sun, of course, but also the Moon, Illapa the Lightning Bolt, and all those mountain peaks. Look at those terraces . . .'

All around were small terraces full of tall corn, as though the temple was embedded in them.

'As you can see, they aren't arranged in a haphazard way. They surround this temple like the sides of a jewel box. As for the temple itself, our astronomers have been watching the sky for a long time, observing the movements of the stars and the planets to determine its position, as well as the orientation of each of its walls. For us, both shadow and light are a form of homage to the gods . . .'

Gabriel thought fleetingly of the ancient abbeys and churches of his own country. His mind made a tenuous connection between the Christian cathedral masons and the Incas. But he was too absorbed by Katari's tale to dwell upon it.

'. . . What I'm telling you is no great secret,' continued Katari almost flippantly. 'All Incas know it. But what they don't know is that by approaching the stone, by looking at it and touching it, they can learn the most occult secrets of our history. They can travel back to the most ancient times, when even the Incas didn't exist.'

'You mean that the Incas haven't always been masters of this land?' Gabriel asked, surprised.

Katari burst out laughing.

'The Incas are only a very few generations of men, excellent but not invincible warriors, as both you and I now know . . .'

Katari glanced at Gabriel before continuing:

'They came after other civilizations of great spiritual strength. These remain mysterious even for us, and a whole lifetime is needed to understand even one glimmer of their history.'

'He who is on Lake Titicaca is already on the road leading home,' murmured Gabriel.

'You see, you know far more than you imagine! Yes, one must take the Taypikala road and the one to the Lake of Origin. The secret is in the stone and the water, in the mountain peaks forever reflected off Lake Titicaca. I was born near that lake. My father took up soldiering as a career. But my uncle, Apu Poma Chuca, the man who convinced the Inca Tupac Yupanqui to return the Sanctuaries of the Sun of Lake Titicaca to their original splendor, initiated me into the art of stones. But enough of all that: I want to show you something. Come here.'

Katari took Gabriel by the hand and positioned him directly in front of the two blocks on the right-hand side.

'Look carefully at those carvings.'

Gabriel had noticed them long before. There were three on each stone, equidistant from one another. They appeared to the naked eye to represent figures lying down, each one similar to the others.

'You must look at them properly, not just with your eyes but with your entire body. You must enter into them.'

Katari's voice grew lower as he spoke these words, and Gabriel heard it quiver slightly. He tried to follow the Master of the Stone's instructions without really understanding them. Slowly, the forms on the rock seemed to come alive.

'A – animals,' he murmured hesitantly.

'One animal in particular that you know well, my friend.'

'The puma!'

Katari looked at him, smiling.

'You have already learned our language. And you love one of our women,' he said emotionally. 'But I believe that this is the first time that you have realized that your own destiny is written in the stone.'

Gabriel blinked. He knew that what were in front of him were only the enormous blocks of a temple that was still being built. And yet, it was as if the whole world had suddenly changed. A lone cloud passed in front of the sun. The rose tint in the stones turned grey.

'Will you go further?'

Gabriel looked at Katari, amazed. How could he 'go further'? Katari seemed amused by his bafflement.

'Don't worry, my Brother from Beyond. Tonight, everything that you've seen will return to you in a dream, and that will banish your fear of knowing. Come: it is time to return to the village.'

Gabriel followed him down the steps that led back to the path beside the Willkamayo. Halfway down the mountainside, they heard the deep notes of a song fill the valley. Gabriel hadn't heard any signal, but all the workers at once stopped whatever they were doing. Those in the quarry, those toiling on the fortresses, on the fountains or on the temples, the stone workers, the carpenters, the bearers and those whose job it was to chisel the rocks – everyone in the valley turned as one towards the sun and sang a salute to it as it slipped behind the peaks of the western mountains.

Despite himself, Gabriel raised his own palms up to the sky and, without opening his mouth, silently joined the others in their Song to the Universe.

CHAPTER 11

'Sometimes,' said Gabriel, 'I feel as though Katari has thrown again his stone that stops time.'

'How do you know that he hasn't?'

They both smiled, and Anamaya's hand brushed against Gabriel's. Whenever they could be seen by others – that is, whenever it wasn't night – they were careful not to touch each other. But she nevertheless enjoyed startling him on occasion. Whether by scratching him lightly or surprising him with some gesture of affection and watching the thrill apparent in his reaction. They spent their days going from stone to stone, from the cool springs down the *collca*-lined road to the Sacred Double's temple.

In truth, they went wherever their whim took them, and wherever they paused their love took root and bloomed.

Gabriel was enchanted.

Some days were cathedrals of silence, dedicated to the contemplation of pure beauty, to the blue of the sky, to the passage of the winds. Then there were the days when they talked endlessly, telling one another everything and anything. They switched effortlessly between languages, at times without even realizing it, carried away by each other's words.

But whether the time passed in silence or in talk, Gabriel had the impression that his heart was growing fuller with each passing day.

Of course, there was always the mystery in Anamaya's blue

eyes, across which a cloud of doubt or the shadow of a secret sometimes passed for no apparent reason. Gabriel asked her no questions, and was content to reflect upon her answers: he was no longer the jealous lover or the naive, easily offended soldier. He felt like a man – not wise, as such, but certainly much calmer and even content. He surprised himself when, searching for a word to describe his state, the one that came from his lips was: *happy*.

Memories of his life came back to him in waves: his agonies as a spurned child, his youthful enthusiasms, Doña Francesca, prison, his dreams of freedom, of glory, his yearning to make a name for himself – he realized now that he had not once had the idea of letting happiness touch his heart. It was still such a fragile notion to him that he held back from surrendering to it completely. But when he closed his eyes and let the sun's warmth caress him, when he let himself bask in the glow of Anamaya's presence, it seemed to him that his life now was vastly superior to any of those alternatives in his youthful, callow dreams.

'Are you dreaming, Puma?'

'It doesn't matter which one of us is dreaming, as long as both of us are in the dream.'

They were halfway up the slope, well above the long, trapezoidal shape of the town below and a little below the end of the ramp from the quarry to the site where the great temple was being constructed – the temple that Gabriel could not contemplate without remembering what Katari had revealed to him. They were facing the mountain-sculpture that he had first seen with her that dawn. He never tired of looking at it, of pondering its mystery. Although Anamaya had told him all about her life, including her closeness to the Inca at the moment of his death, she stayed tight-lipped about the secrets that he had confided in her then. And with the perhaps mistaken forbearance that love engenders, Gabriel refrained from questioning her about it.

'Close your eyes,' she said.

He obeyed as docilely as a child. Anamaya gently caressed her lover's hand and silently asked him with her spirit to empty his own, to drain his soul of the war and everything associated with it, and to go with her to a place beyond desire, beyond emotion,

to the stone and the water. His body relaxed, and she sensed that
he had surrendered himself completely to her.

Yet she could tell him so little. Gabriel had to travel the road
himself. There was no other way. Only when he reached his
destination would he know what she did, would the words come
to his mouth. But until then, all she could do was show him the
path of the sun and the position of the stars – and hope that he
would learn to ride the wind and follow the course of the water.

'Now open your eyes.'

Gabriel rubbed his face as though he was coming to life for the
first time.

'What do you see?'

Gabriel's eyes shone impishly.

'Why, I see that I love you, my dearest. I love you completely,
with all that I have!'

'Don't make a move, Puma! Be serious – tell me what you
saw.'

'I saw what one sees when one closes one's eyes: I saw dancing
patches of color, and a stronger light where the sun was, where
I felt its heat. And although you told me to empty my mind, I
saw myself on my white horse and I heard the arrows and stones
whistling past me.'

Anamaya's heart beat hard in her chest as Gabriel asked:

'Someone has chosen for me, haven't they? That's what I'm
meant to believe?'

'I don't know the answer to those questions, Puma. You will
know everything that you're meant to know when they are all
within you.'

'Please, don't speak to me in riddles.'

'I know what I know through riddles. It's up to me to carry my
body toward those things that will allow me to decipher them.'

'Carry it, then,' said Gabriel, suppressing another laugh. 'Carry
it over here to me, and then you'll decipher a few things . . .'

Anamaya let herself lean into him slowly. He closed his eyes
again, but this time he couldn't help but feel the pure, simple joy of
having her against him, of feeling her passion and graceful reserve.
And Gabriel found it impossible to think of anything except love.

He suddenly reached out for her, but she slipped away from him like a cat, and when his hand closed, all it clasped was shadow and air.

She was standing up, watching the bearers unload their heavy burdens of *mantas* containing green and golden corn at the *collcas*.

'Villa Oma confronted Manco again this morning.'

Gabriel's face darkened. The war . . . they hardly mentioned it when they talked but they couldn't ignore what had almost torn them apart forever. He didn't dare ask her for news of it: he clung to the absurd hope that one day he would be told that it had ended in a great dance around the Aucaypata.

'Does he still want to turn me into a drum?'

'He blames Manco for not having attacked Cuzco earlier, and for having sent troops to attack the reinforcements that your Pizarro managed to send rather than concentrating all our forces on the city. He says that without some last-ditch effort, the battle is lost.'

'What does Manco think?'

'Manco is a warrior. The humiliations he suffered at Gonzalo's hands only strengthened his determination.'

'Perhaps, but that doesn't necessarily mean that he'll win.'

'He will fight until the end, even if this war cannot be won.'

'And you? What do you think?'

Anamaya looked away from Gabriel to the distance.

'I think that one day the war will be over.'

Gabriel laughed a sad laugh.

'Even I think that, despite not being initiated into any secrets.'

'Well, I *am* initiated into those secrets, and yet my ignorance is greater than anyone else's. I know that the end of the war will set us free, Puma. But until then . . .'

Anamaya came over, squatted beside him and put her head on his shoulder.

'Don't say it,' he whispered.

A line of quarrymen passed in front of them. Despite the men's diffidence, Gabriel sensed that they were watching them. He made to stand up, but Anamaya squeezed his hand, preventing him.

Yes, Katari had indeed thrown the stone that stopped time. But now she saw that it was falling back to earth – and falling much too fast.

The rumor traveled across the valley as quickly as did the churning waters of the Willkamayo. It was shouted from summit to summit before the *chaskis* themselves reached Emperor Manco.

A regiment from General Quizo Yupanqui's army, commanded by the proud Apu Quispe, was on its way, bearing a great many magnificent war prizes: Spanish weapons, clothes, and even horses. The prisoners of war were a few days' march behind.

The valley was filled with song, drumbeats, and the wail of horns. The workers paused from their jobs to admire the victors as they arrived. No one touched the weapons piled up on stretchers that were carried by bearers with the kind of dignity due an Inca's palanquin.

There were a dozen horses, each one surrounded by at least twenty terrified warriors linking hands to form a sort of mobile fence.

When the news reached Manco, he wanted to meet the victors, accompanied by a few of the Lords from his court; he asked Gabriel to do him the favor of accompanying him, of walking alongside his litter. Gabriel agreed before realizing how great was the honor that had been bestowed upon him.

They waited at the bottom of the Choquana fortifications. Even Villa Oma had come along, although he lurked at the back of the column and maintained a hostile and disdainful silence.

'I would like you to show me how all these things are used,' Manco said to Gabriel, smiling and stepping down from his palanquin. 'I wish to learn your people's ways.'

Gabriel saw that Manco was looking at the approaching weapons. He said nothing. All eyes were on him.

'I'm not sure that they will prove of any use to you, my Lord Manco,' he said eventually.

'Why, on the contrary, I'm sure that they'll be very useful. I don't understand what you mean. Please explain yourself . . .'

Happily for Gabriel, who was growing increasingly uncomfortable, the troops bearing the prizes now arrived.

As Apu Quispe prostrated himself at Manco's feet, the Lords silently approached the stretchers loaded with prizes. There were swords, shields, spears, morions, coats of mail, leather breastplates, and even small artillery pieces. Each of these things caused Gabriel's heart to leap, reminding him as they did of the battles in which he had participated. They banished any lingering doubts he might have had about the continuation of the war.

After the weapons on their stretchers came a number of bearers who unfurled their *mantas*. There followed two more stretchers, overflowing with useless luxuries that had been shipped from Spain during the previous two years: brocades and silks, bolts of other fine fabrics, jugs of wine, casks of preserves and other Spanish foodstuffs. There were even a number of pigs, still alive and squealing horribly. These beasts were looked upon by the Indians with visible distaste, despite their efforts to remain impassive.

But what the Indians most admired were the horses. It had not been so long since the Incas had wondered whether a horse and its rider wasn't in fact a single being with fabulous powers. Gabriel remembered how frightened Atahualpa's men had been at Cajamarca, much to the wrath of their Inca. Most of the Indians here had never had the opportunity to see a horse up close: the Spaniards had strictly forbidden them from going anywhere near not only the animals but also the conquistadors' steel weapons, on pain of death. Actually owning a few of these prized items filled the victors with pride.

'What do you say to all this?' asked Manco.

'It isn't worth half as much as your brother Atahualpa's ransom,' said Gabriel in a neutral voice. 'But you can be happy at having taken them.'

The Stranger's caution amused Manco, who smiled, turned away, and motioned to the victorious general to stand.

'Tell us of your victory, Apu Quispe. And be sure to speak up, so that no one among us remains ignorant of the Inca warriors' worthy deeds.'

'Your army, commanded by your loyal general Quizo Yupanqui, fell upon a column of Strangers made up of seventy cavalrymen and as many foot soldiers. They were heading toward Cuzco, to reinforce their countrymen there. We tracked them for days without them ever realizing it. Then we waited for them in the narrow pass of the Pampas River. They had just crossed the Huaitara Puna. We destroyed them with a hail of sling stones. We killed most of them. We took those who survived prisoners. They are following behind us, under guard. Here are their horses.'

The soldier was unused to expressing himself. He spoke in short, clipped sentences, and his harsh voice hardly carried any distance, while all the while he spoke he looked directly down at his sandals.

'Do you hear, Villa Oma?' said Manco, visibly delighted.

The Sage said nothing.

'There is more news,' added the general.

'Speak.'

The man hesitated, intimidated.

'Your general Quizo Yupanqui has learned that another Spanish regiment is on its way. He is preparing to destroy it also, with Inti's blessing. But messengers have reached us from the south . . .'

Manco's face lit up. His brother Paullu was in the south with his army, under the pretext of supporting the one-eyed Diego de Almagro's expedition there. He had orders to annihilate his 'new friends' as soon as he received word of the attack on Cuzco, and then to return to the Inca capital and join in the general uprising.

'Is my brother on his way?'

'Yes, my Lord. But—'

'But what?'

'—But de Almagro and his army are with him, and he is helping the Spaniards, as he has been ever since his departure. Furthermore, he has had several chances to turn on the Spaniards during battle. But not only did he not give the order, but actually allied himself with them.'

'My brother, allied with the Strangers? Why, if it weren't for the fact that you have brought me the news of Quizo's victory,

I would cut out your tongue and slice off your lips for uttering such an impiety!'

'In that case, you would have to cut off the lips and tongues of a great many of your Lords, Manco!'

Villa Oma's dry, sibilant voice surprised everyone.

'We all know that your alliance with Paullu exists only in your own mind!'

'My brother would never betray me!'

'You're right, Manco, after a fashion: he has no need to betray you *now* because he already did so a long time ago. Only your naivety and weakness prevent you from seeing it.'

Manco trembled with rage.

'You will be silent, false sage. It is only because of our father Huayna Capac and because of the help that you once gave me that I don't tear you apart right now with my own hands for speaking so irreverently.'

Villa Oma fell silent. But he did not avert his gaze. Gabriel's heart beat furiously. It was the first time that he had witnessed such explosive tension between the Incas themselves. It boded poorly for the future. The war had taken him in its grasp again far more quickly than he had thought it would, and he sensed that, this time, it wouldn't let go.

Manco, boiling with rage, walked up to the first of the stretchers piled high with weapons. He picked up a sword, and waved it about, quite comfortable handling it.

'I have learned, Villa Oma. I have learned from the story of the Great Massacre. I have learned that we were like innocents in the face of the Strangers, and that we let ourselves be massacred. I promised myself that it would never happen again. I learned of the terrible war between our brothers Huascar and Atahualpa, and again I swore that it would never happen again. Before he left with the one-eyed man, my brother Paullu and I took the blood oath – we reconfirmed how it has always been between us. Now, for the first time, we are taking the Strangers' weapons from them, we are defeating them in battle, we are laying siege to them, we can see their fear, their very real fear, in their eyes. And you call me weak; you tell lies about my brother!'

Manco windmilled the sword through the air, then pointed it at the sun.

'I will defeat them,' he howled, 'with our own weapons and with theirs. I will defeat them in the mountains as on the plains, on the rocks as on the sea, yes, I *will* defeat them, I will annihilate them and offer them as sacrifices to the gods in the hope that our nation will return to the peace and glory of the times before!'

Manco fell silent. The crowd, too, uttered hardly a murmur. Manco let the weapon fall to the ground and walked toward the horses. His men parted in front of him and prostrated themselves.

'I'm going to ride their horses,' said Manco with eerie calm.

'Who's going to teach you?' asked Gabriel.

'You are.'

CHAPTER 12

Ollantaytambo, summer 1536

A S HE SADDLED TWO HORSES, GABRIEL MAINTAINED a steady flow of soothing talk, punctuating his precise movements with a few affectionate pats. All gazes were fixed on him, and he moved carefully, wary of making any sudden movements. After girthing the big gray, he sized up Manco before adjusting the stirrups to his height. He had chosen a handsome chestnut for himself, seduced by its tawny coat and intelligent look. *You'll be the third*, he thought to himself, and smiled. Then he slipped on their bits ands bridles before going up to the Inca.

'We're ready to go.'

Manco was surprised. It was beneath the dignity of an Inca to leave himself open to a display of clumsiness in front of his Lords, and especially in front of thousands of his vassals. But Gabriel spared him that risk.

'We shall first walk along, leading them by the bridle, to the bridge, which we shall have to cross on foot in any case. We shall then mount them in the bend of the road, where no one can see us, before entering the town. Does this suit you?'

Manco, who had grabbed the bridle without hesitation, nodded.

'Don't listen to him, Manco!' cried Villa Oma. 'Remember who he is: it's a trap!'

'I prefer you when you're silent,' answered Manco as he moved away. Then: 'Not one of you is to move from here until you see me entering the town with the Stranger!'

The road from Choquana ran in a straight line, and was lined on each side by well-built low walls. Gabriel had first traveled along it as a prisoner, bound with ropes, and had admired then, through a thin layer of fog, the town, its terraces and its temples. He reflected on the irony of the thing: here he was now, leading a horse and alone with the Inca, a privilege that was no doubt reserved only for Anamaya and a very small group of the Emperor's court.

'Allow me to thank you once again, Lord Manco.'

Manco was trying not to turn around too often to check on his animal's unexpected movements, although it was actually following him perfectly docilely. Gabriel noticed that Manco was holding the bridle neither too tightly nor too loosely, and that the posture of his body displayed no tension or worry.

'I have told you already – it is not me that you should thank, but Anamaya. She spoke of you a long time ago now, and I know how sad she would be were you to die . . .'

'Then you also know that we have a common enemy.'

Manco's face darkened.

'That Stranger they call Gonzalo Pizarro is a monster who has emerged from the Under World, a monster who must be destroyed.'

'As you probably know, I've already tried to kill him. I risked my life doing so. Now I'm afraid that, since Juan was killed, his power will grow unchecked.'

'I don't understand all that,' said Manco, 'and I don't wish to. For me, all those brothers are Strangers who want to take everything from us. I know that Atahualpa trusted the *kapitu* Pizarro – and I know what happened to Atahualpa.'

'And yet you trust *me*.'

Manco said nothing. The two men made their way in silence. Gabriel admired the terraces rising up ahead of them. The rope suspension bridge was a hundred paces ahead, supported by its unusual stone column set the middle of the river.

Gabriel went on: 'I don't like those men, Lord Manco. I am not their friend. I fought when I had to fight. But Princess Anamaya must have told you that I have never failed to keep my word, and that what I most desire for your country is peace . . .'

'Are you their king? Do you command their armies?'

'Men like me will be needed, Lord Manco, when this war is over . . .'

'There's only one way to end this war, and that's for us to win it.'

Now it was Gabriel's turn to say nothing for a while.

'I have endeavored to learn something of your history,' he said eventually, 'and I have come to believe that your wisdom is more than equal to ours. But we need time, we need to negotiate, we need to exchange gifts . . .'

'I was forced to respect you, and I truly believe you to be a brave man. I consented that you keep the name "puma", bestowed on you by others. But now you speak to me of time and gifts, of wisdom and negotiation, even though your people have brought me nothing but death and destruction, pillaging, humiliation. Why should I listen to you and ignore our ruined temples, our raped women, the betrayals, the pillaging, my enslaved people? Why should I forget what I myself was subjected to?'

'Are you sure that you wish to cross this bridge alone with me?'

'You don't understand. I want you to guide me across the bridge. I want you to teach me how to ride these animals. I want you to show us how to use your weapons, as well as how to make them. I want you to help us.'

'I'm going to go ahead of you,' said Gabriel, blindfolding the horses.

'I've crossed other bridges!'

'In an Inca's palanquin!'

'No! Before I travelled in palanquins, I was a fugitive, a vagabond. Believe me, I've crossed bridges that you would never dare to set foot on.'

'Wait until I reach the central support column before crossing.

I'll wait there, and come to your aid if necessary.'

'It won't be necessary.'

They passed between the two pillars that marked one end of the bridge. Although impressed by Manco's determination, Gabriel nevertheless felt profoundly disturbed. Earlier that morning, at sunrise, he had still felt full of serene certainty. At that time, the light in Anamaya's eyes had answered all his questions. But Manco's words had perturbed him, and now he felt unsure. Those words bothered Gabriel more than the unnerving undulations of the bridge. They were impossible to ignore. And it was equally impossible to counter them with the awkward, prevaricating answers that he had given the Emperor.

The chestnut horse followed, remarkably composed.

'Be sure to step evenly, so as not to frighten your horse.'

'I know what to do,' Manco said brusquely.

He was visibly annoyed. Gabriel didn't embarrass him with any more advice. The young Spaniard felt the chestnut's breath behind him, and noticed that the bridge's movement didn't bother him as it once had. The water of the river seething below was now familiar.

Yet when he reached the solid platform atop the central pylon, Gabriel slipped and was forced to grab the thick agave guard-rope to stop himself from falling. At the other end of the bridge stood Anamaya — alone, waiting.

Sometimes, when Anamaya saw Gabriel in his Indian garb, she would forget that he wasn't one of them. Even though he spoke Quechua with an odd accent, and even though blond hairs covered his face when he had been unable to shave for a few days or longer, she felt that there was nothing of the Stranger in him.

But now, seeing him leading his horse across the bridge, she remembered in a flash their first meeting, near Cajamarca. She recalled the impression that the horses had made then on Atahualpa and his people. She shuddered at the thought before recollecting herself.

As Gabriel drew nearer, she saw the look of surprise on his face. Manco was fifty paces behind, leading the big white horse.

'Why are you here?'

'I too want to learn how to ride a horse.'

The road followed a bend that hid them from the prying eyes of Manco's Lords. And they were still too far from the town's gates to be seen from there.

Manco seemed unsurprised when he saw Anamaya, and said nothing when Gabriel adjusted the stirrups on his chestnut to her height. Gabriel instructed them in turn, showing them how to mount into the saddle without frightening the horse, how to hold the reins, neither too loosely nor too tightly, and how to make the horse walk.

A harvested *quinua* field served them as an equitation ring. He led them around one after the other, holding their horses by tethers. 'Go on!' he said. 'Easy!'

Anamaya liked the tone of Gabriel's voice when he gave orders. She liked, too, the confidence growing within her, as well as the feel of her naked legs around the large, living animal – a creature utterly strange to her, and with a power that she knew to be formidable. She watched as Manco, a dedicated yet impatient student, dug his bare heels into the white horse's sides, as though to show it that he was already its master.

When they had mastered walking, Gabriel led them into short trots. Anamaya was surprised as she watched Manco's handling: he seemed to have synchronized naturally with his white horse's rhythm. Then came her turn, and she found that she too adapted easily to the jerky rhythm, bobbing along like a twig floating down a river.

Gabriel was sweating.

'I want to go faster,' said Manco. 'I want to go as fast as you do when you charge!'

'A gallop?'

'A gallop.'

'You'll fall,' said Gabriel. 'You need more lessons. You need to get used to your horse first, and for it to get used to you . . .'

'I want to gallop today!'

Anamaya recognized the stubbornness that she had encountered in Manco on the day of the *huarachiku* so many years before.

Gabriel didn't say another word but simply unclipped the tether and glanced at Manco. The Emperor slapped the horse and urged it on with a shout, but the animal hesitated and threw its head around, as though trying to see who was riding it. So Gabriel, clenching his teeth, whipped its flank with his end of the tether. The horse, clearly irritated, immediately took off at a nervous trot down the middle of the field. Manco was jerked around like a puppet and lost his foothold in the stirrups. His hands reached for something to hold onto. He grabbed onto the animal's mane, but his thighs had lost their grip on its barrel. The white horse hadn't gone thirty strides before Manco slipped undignifiedly off its flanks and back over its croup, letting out a raucous cry as he fell heavily to the ground.

'Why did you let him do it?' asked Anamaya at Gabriel's side.

'Didn't he ask to?'

Manco picked himself up and glared furiously at the horse, which had stopped a few paces on and was now eyeing him suspiciously. The Inca walked back to Gabriel and Anamaya, making a deliberate effort not to massage his bruised limbs.

'Well?' said Gabriel. 'Do you believe me now?'

'I want to try again!'

Gabriel sighed.

Gabriel kept Manco practicing until dusk. The Emperor never once wearied of being thrown, always picking himself up without any further murmur or sign of vexation.

A servant came to fetch the chestnut. He stood a little out of the way, his back to the Sapa Inca. Anamaya watched Gabriel and admired the quiet way he spoke and his patience. She sensed the violence and tension in Manco gradually fading and soon the Emperor was feeling quite comfortable on the horse.

When the sun had finally slipped behind the mountains, Manco eventually agreed to stop.

'You will teach us,' he said to Gabriel. 'You will teach my Lords as well as myself. Then you will teach us how to handle a sword, then the gunpowder . . .'

'I will do nothing of the sort,' said Gabriel.

'Isn't Gonzalo your enemy?'

'I laid down my arms when the last tower at Sacsayhuaman was taken, Lord Manco. I swore then that I would never take them up again. Not against your men, nor against my own.'

Anamaya looked at the two men facing one another. Gabriel made an effort to move slowly as he unsaddled the white horse, revealing its sweat-sodden barrel. Manco stood perfectly still, rage in his gaze.

'What does "being the puma" mean?' asked Manco, turning to Anamaya. 'Does it mean eating our corn and our *quinua*? Does it mean distracting you from your duties to the Sacred Double? What kind of puma refuses to fight? I know that none such as this live in our mountains.'

'He's speaking the truth,' Anamaya said calmly.

'The truth?'

Manco looked at her, then at Gabriel, then back at her. He felt a violent impulse rise up inside him, swiftly followed by a sense of the ridiculous. He said nothing. The evening songs were now echoing through the valley, from terrace to terrace, as the gloaming gilded the *canchas*.

'The war is happening whether you want it to or not, Stranger. The war is happening because it has to, ever since you and your people came here and violated our country . . .'

'I don't disagree, Lord Manco.'

'Then how can you be on neither one side nor the other?'

Gabriel felt oddly calm, as though a truth was at last revealing itself to him after having stayed hidden for so long.

'Perhaps "being the puma" means exactly that,' said Anamaya. Once again, Manco said nothing. He raised his hand against

Gabriel, but without any real threat in the gesture. He didn't understand his own motive. Gabriel remained stock-still. Manco managed a slight smile.

'Put that saddle back on the horse, Stranger-who-doesn't-fight,' said Manco. 'Put it back on, Puma-who-doesn't-hunt, and watch!'

Gabriel obeyed, then helped Manco climb back into the saddle.

The Inca went off toward the town, first at a walk, then at a trot, and finally at a gallop, kicking up a cloud of dust behind him.

When Manco was no more than a black spot against the walls of the town, Gabriel and Anamaya heard a clamor rise up from there, louder than the chants and deeper than the trumpets and drums.

Gabriel walked over slowly to the servant holding the chestnut by the bridle. The man had remained with his back turned throughout. 'Go,' Gabriel said to him. He never looked up, gazing only at the ground as though Gabriel was himself the Inca. The servant ran off into the dusk.

Gabriel rose effortlessly into his own saddle, enjoying the familiar feel of its leather and the warmth of the animal beneath him. He leaned down towards Anamaya and held out his arm. She took it, and he lifted her up to him.

They headed back at a walk, as slowly as they possibly could. As the darkness gathered and gave them the protection of its black veil, they found no need for words to feel a mutual, powerful yearning.

It was the yearning of a cavalryman holding the woman he loved in his arms.

It was the yearning of that day at Cajamarca, when Gabriel had rescued Anamaya from being trampled during the massacre, and when their destiny had appeared to him for the first time, like a cool breeze blowing from out of the dust and the blood and the sweat of conflict.

CHAPTER 13

IN THE COURTYARD OF THE ROYAL *CANCHA*, SHADOWY
figures slipped busily through the night, their straw sandals
rustling along the ground. Whether it was to Huayna Capac,
to Atahualpa, or to Manco, the gods required that duty should be
done to the Inca – the Son of the Sun – in accordance with the
established rites and customs. What had been would be again.
The past would become the future. The Inca's clothes, made
from the finest vicuña wool, were made to be worn only once.
He never touched his food with his own hand. And each hair
that fell from his head was carefully stored away. Thus, he was
always surrounded by an endless, well-ordered and silent ballet
of activity.

There was a fountain in the middle of the courtyard. It was
a simple square stone from the middle of which water spurted.
Four grooved channels carried the water in four streams at right
angles to each other across the courtyard. The water's energy thus
passed through the center before being carried away to irrigate the
Empire of the Four Cardinal Directions.

As time passed, Anamaya began to notice critically those
things that she had formerly taken for granted. She questioned
everything, even the air she breathed. Ever since she had had the
vision, she had been aware of the secret crack at the heart of the
Empire: that which was eternal had to be – but not everything
was eternal. And perhaps a symbol such as this one, the fountain,

which at one time she had thought would last forever, was to exist, in the perception of the gods, only for as long as a hummingbird took to flap its wings.

Anamaya heard two voices from the other side of the door-hanging: one, both tender and admonishing, belonged to Manco, and the other to his favorite son, little Titu Cusi, whose mother had died giving birth. Manco's wife, the gentle and beautiful Curi Ocllo, now lovingly cared for the child.

Manco hadn't occupied himself with his son at all while he'd been in Calca. But once they had reached Ollantaytambo, he had had the boy brought to him, and now not an evening passed when the Emperor didn't spend some time playing with the child.

'Faster! Come now, use your heels!' said Manco in his deep voice.

'Faster, faster!' cried the little boy in a high-pitched, overexcited voice.

Anamaya passed through the door-hanging without the two impassive warriors standing guard at the entrance to the Emperor's private quarters making any attempt to obstruct her.

In the torchlit room, she saw Titu Cusi riding on his father's back, urging him on with great swipes at his backside:

'Faster, horse! Faster!'

Manco bounded around on the carpets and pillows that covered almost the entire floor area. The room's luxurious furnishings seemed even stranger, in Anamaya's eyes, than the sight of the Inca-cum-horse ridden by a little boy and bounding around amid the feathers and the finest *cumbis*.

'Look, Anamaya!' cried Titu Cusi. 'I can ride a horse, just like my father!'

Manco now slipped his son gently off his back and took him up in his powerful arms, hugging him tightly.

'Go, now,' he said, putting the child back on the ground.

The little boy, whose long black hair framed an impish and intelligent face, dashed across the room, crying:

'I will be back for another lesson tomorrow, Horse! Be ready!'

Anamaya smiled at Manco.

'Of all his brothers, he's the one, isn't he?'

Manco's face darkened.

'He's the oldest. And he's the one who has the most flair, the most confidence. He was raised by Curi Ocllo. He was nursed on the milk and the strength of the woman I love. Whenever I hold him in my arms, I think of how much I love the *Coya*, and for a moment I forget about the war and about your absence.'

His last two words resonated like the beat of a drum.

'My absence?'

'I know that you're here, and I know that you're looking after the Sacred Double, but . . .'

'But?'

'I feel as though you've already left with him, and that you're indifferent to the outcome of our war.'

'You're wrong, Manco. I rejoice when I hear of our victories, and the news of our defeats makes my heart heavy. But your father Huayna Capac's words are always in my mind, and they concern a time after the war.'

Manco laughed dryly.

'So, there's to be a time after the war? You've always been at my side, Anamaya. It was you who urged me to lead the uprising. And now you speak to me of a time after the war! Now, at this decisive moment! My beloved brother Quizo Yupanqui has failed in his attack on Lima. He died in battle. Luckily Illac Topa and Tisoc and many others have taken over. But what about you? There was a time when it seemed to me that you would hurl sling stones yourself, to further our cause in the war! What happened to you that you now only want to speak about a time "after"?'

'I will tell you, brother Manco.'

Anamaya spoke to Manco for a long time. She affectionately recalled their long acquaintance, which had begun when she had been a young princess who had narrowly avoided death. He reminded her of the snake that she had removed from his path; they spoke of Guaypar, Manco's sworn enemy, and about how there was now a rumor spreading that Guaypar had resurfaced, leading an army alongside the Spaniards. But throughout their conversation, Anamaya felt a hesitation within her as she recalled Huayna Capac's words: *'You will know what must not be spoken, and you will not speak it.'* What was she to tell Manco, and what was she to keep to herself?

'I promised that I would stay at your side, and I have. I promised it when you found me with the Strangers. You know how I've kept that promise ever since.'

'I spoke to Katari, but he told me nothing. I speak to you, and you too tell me nothing. I know that you've kept your promise. And you know that you've never heard me reproach you. Have you seen how the Sage Villa Oma looks at you? Have you ever heard me say a word to encourage him in his attempted intimidation of you? But your silence . . . your silence makes my heart heavy, your silence echoes through my soul at night, and sometimes I ask myself . . .'

As he told her of his doubts, Anamaya heard Huayna Capac's thundering voice: *'. . . We, the Incas, we will have to know humiliation, we will become slaves to our own shame . . . But we will not die . . . The brother's blood and the friend's blood are shed far more than the enemy's: It is the sign.'*

'. . . I ask myself, why am I fighting if Paullu and you – who have both been with me from the beginning – turn away from me? Even Villa Oma is thinking of making his own war. Illac Topa is in the north and Tisoc is in the south, but they only rarely send me reports. Each of us on his own! It's madness!'

Anamaya wanted to give Manco an answer, but she realized that she didn't have one. She couldn't tell him that, according to Huayna Capac's words, he was hopelessly doomed. And so her silence imprisoned him in an unavoidable war in which he was alone, like a child fighting against shadows and trees.

'You were the one who urged me on,' continued Manco, 'who called me 'the first knot of the future time'. But it meant nothing, it was mere noise, as empty as the wind, nothing more . . .'

'You are brave, Manco. The flame of honor blazes within you.'

'But it's useless! If I learn to ride a horse, then the horse will die. If I learn to wield a sword, then it will smash into pieces. If I send off a thousand arrows, they'll all fall back to the ground . . .'

'What your father told me,' said Anamaya regretfully, 'is unclear even to me. I turn the words over and over, and they are in my mind when I'm awake and in my dreams when I sleep. They are enigmas that I decipher differently each time I think about them. The more I consider them, the more ignorant I feel. All I know is that the destruction has a purpose. But I don't know what comes after that.'

'Is that purpose our own?'

'Ask Katari: he's the one who knows time.'

Manco turned a black stone with sharp corners around in his fingers. He dropped it at her feet.

'The man who can do anything can do nothing,' he sighed. 'Isn't that so?'

Again, Anamaya stayed silent.

'But there *is* something,' said the Emperor.

'What?'

'The Puma.'

Anamaya's breath quickened, and the anxiety that had left her now returned and almost overwhelmed her.

'If he's the Puma, then he should help us. But his words prove that he is nothing.'

'He can help us without picking up a weapon.'

Manco brushed aside her objection with a disdainful wave of his hand.

'What kind of friend refuses to fight when his enemy attacks? A coward, nothing more.'

'You know that he's a brave man.'

'Yes, I know. But I also know that if Villa Oma ever hears what your mad Puma said, he'll be executed on the spot, and I'll be powerless to stop it. You don't want to know what's being whispered about him on the terraces and in the quarry. All the men here would like to see him ritually sacrificed—'

'You can't let that happen!'

Manco breathed quietly, letting a moment pass. Then:

'That's what's so strange. No, I won't let that happen.'

CHAPTER 14

Ollantaytambo, October 1536

THE FACE IN FRONT OF GABRIEL HAD SCREAMED BEFORE
its owner had died. Now the mouth was twisted into a
rictus of suffering and atrocious fear. But the eyes would
never tell what had happened, because they had been torn out
from their cavities, and in their place was a mass of putrefied
flesh and blackened, hardening crusts of blood.

Nauseous, Gabriel turned away from the sight to stop himself
vomiting.

The broad avenue leading from the *canchas* to the Willkamayo
River was filled with the kind of hustle that one would expect in
a market place in Spain. But instead of merchants haggling over
fabrics or spices, there were only corpses.

The avenue was lined by two walls in which dozens of niches,
each one about the size of a man, had been carved. And there
were indeed men displayed in each one, for the admiration of all.
The Indians, usually so impassive, now pointed them out to one
another, talking loudly and laughing.

The most prized trophies had been placed in the niches closest
to the *canchas* – the bodies of a dozen Spaniards. Their bones had
been removed, and they had been turned not into drums but into
windbags, literally. Their flayed skins had been sewn up again and
then inflated, so that they formed grotesque balloon parodies of
human bodies.

Gabriel, though sickened, couldn't help but ponder on the cruel irony: these men, created by God in His own image, had been recreated by foreign gods in the image of their crimes – deformed, loathsome, unnatural. And yet their essential humanity could still be seen clearly in these lifeless puppets, as though the Indian warriors' cruelty had peeled back their skin and revealed the true nature of the man-monster within each of them.

Each corpse was attached to a stake and had its own niche.

Gabriel choked back his revulsion and fear and forced himself to look carefully at their faces to see if he could recognize a comrade. It was true that he had hated most of his fellow soldiers and that by confronting the Pizarros, as well as through his relationship with Anamaya – which they had never understood – he had isolated himself from them. But now he surprised himself by suddenly feeling close to his countrymen – a belated kinship, as though he himself had been tortured and killed by bands of howling, joyful Incas intoxicated by their first taste of victory after the many bitter humiliations of defeat.

He was profoundly happy not to recognize any of the Spanish corpses. No doubt they were reinforcements recently arrived from Panama. They all had something of the aghast and terrified look of young men who had come to find gold and instead had found death.

After the Spaniards came the corpses of black slaves from the Panama isthmus, and then those of the conquistadors' Indian allies, although these last hadn't been given the same treatment as their masters.

They had simply been decapitated and their heads stuck on spikes wrapped in horse skin, to some of which a mane or tail or even hooves were still attached. Gabriel thought of pagan idols: these were grotesque versions of the demigods that some Indians had at first imagined the conquistadors to be.

Poor gods . . . the slaves' white teeth had all been wrenched out, and the multicolored feathers of the headdress of one Indian, who had evidently been a chief when he was alive, were now black with dust and mud and hung down over his forehead, pathetically broken. Some of the Canary caciques still had their coloured headbands, although these had slipped down past their vacant eyes to the blood-encrusted space where their necks had been.

In the middle of the loud, busy crowd, Gabriel suddenly felt brutally and inescapably alone.

He jumped into the air when a hand landed on his shoulder.

'Katari!'

The Master of the Stone wore a grave look on his face.

'Let's not stay here.'

Gabriel followed him. The two men made their way through the narrow alleyways between the *canchas* toward the steep flight of steps leading to the Great Temple. Gabriel began to breathe easier once there was some distance between him and the macabre spectacle in the avenue.

When they reached the Temple's esplanade, they sat down on a stone block not yet hewn and fitted to the wall. Gabriel saw that two more giant monoliths had been placed in position since he had first seen the Temple, both of them separated from each other and the rest by a thin stone spike shaped like a reed.

'You are in danger,' said Katari.

'I've been in danger ever since arriving here,' said Gabriel quietly. 'And in any case, I'm in less danger than those poor souls down in the avenue. What barbarity . . .'

Katari said nothing for a moment, then:

'A dead man is a dead man.'

'You're right. He's not any more dead because he's been chopped up into pieces, or because his balls have been sewn into his mouth, or because he's been turned into a skin flag or a balloon . . .'

As he spoke, Gabriel became aware that his words were bitter with a cutting irony. He realized that although he had thought that he had become a stranger to his fellow Spaniards he still considered himself, deep within, to be one of them.

'The men who did those things would like me to teach them how to use our weapons so that they can kill more people and fashion more abominable trophies for themselves. But they don't know me: I shall never again take up arms. That is how it is.'

'Even if it costs you your life?'

Gabriel was surprised to hear a slight quiver in Katari's voice.

'My life . . .' murmured Gabriel. 'Do I really know what it is, my life? It's been taken from me and given back without my consent so many times . . .'

'You are the Puma,' replied Katari in a serious tone. 'You must survive.'

Whenever he was with Anamaya, his love for her made Gabriel so breathless that his mind grew fuddled. When he was with Katari, on the other hand, he felt unusually lucid.

'Not if I have to take up arms to—'

'I know, I know,' Katari interrupted impatiently, 'and I'm not saying that you have to. But Anamaya and I cannot protect you for much longer, and soon Manco will no longer be able to resist Villa Oma. The Sage sees this blood-sodden victory as an unhoped-for opportunity.'

'Well? What should I do?'

'You must leave.'

'When?'

An explosion boomed out before Katari could answer.

As they raced down the steps toward the *canchas*, Gabriel's heart beat furiously. But he wasn't sure whether it was because he was alarmed by the possibility of yet another horror, or because he now knew for certain that he would have to leave Anamaya once again.

Villa Oma's long, thin, corpselike arms emerged from his blood-red *unku*.

'Do you want to end up like them?' he screamed, pointing at the dead bodies in the niches.

He was talking to two Spanish prisoners who were trying to maintain some modicum of dignity but who were both trembling from head to toe. Gabriel could imagine the horror that they must have been feeling at the sight of their slaughtered and mutilated companions.

'What's going on?' he asked in a determined voice.

'Why, here's the Puma of the Shadows!' yelped Villa Oma.

Gabriel stood facing the Sage. A crowd had gathered around them, but he could see neither Manco nor Anamaya. Katari was still at his side and, more importantly, *on* his side, the only one supporting him in this blindly hostile crowd that had the taste of blood in its collective mouth, spurred on by the fear emanating from the two bound prisoners.

'Our warriors tried to use your weapons that spit fire,' said Villa Oma. 'But all they managed to do was frighten themselves without hitting their target.'

He pointed again at the niches. Not only had those Spaniards died in terror, but now their cadavers were being used for target practice.

'And these two,' continued Villa Oma, waving wickedly at the prisoners, 'were pretending to help us. But they tricked us, and the fire exploded in one warrior's face.'

'What happened?' asked Gabriel, turning to the Spaniards this time.

'They packed too much powder into the arquebus. It exploded,' said the younger of the two in a blank voice.

'It was an accident,' Gabriel said to Villa Oma.

'An accident? No, it was a trick by those mongrel Strangers. Now they shall die!'

Some Indians grabbed the two prisoners, who offered little resistance, and shoved them towards the niches. The Indians pulled out the stakes on the ends of which two heads were fixed. They laughed as the heads came off and fell into the dust.

Gabriel stood in front of the two Spaniards.

'I want your men here to know who you really are, Villa Oma.'

The crowd fell silent. Villa Oma was so taken aback that he too said nothing.

'When I was in the south, I saw how the most ignoble of my companions inflicted terrible suffering on your people. I tried to tell this man about it,' Gabriel said loudly, pointing at the Sage. 'He had the power, then, to stop it, for his opinion, along with Paullu Inca's, was important to the Spaniards. Yet he did nothing . . .'

'Don't listen to him!' screamed Villa Oma. 'He's lying!'

But the crowd remained silent and listened to the Stranger.

'Oh, he'll tell you that he was preparing for the war, that you would at last wreak vengeance on the Strangers. But I tell you that this man you call Sage is in fact a madman whose cruelty knows no limits and who will ultimately lead all those who follow him to their deaths! War is what it is, I grant you. But if you kill these two men here, then Inti will unleash his wrath against you!'

This was the last straw for Villa Oma. He cried:

'Listen to him, invoking our gods! How dare he! Tie him up with the others, so that he may share their fate.'

Some soldiers came forward and grabbed Gabriel. Others scooped up gunpowder from a powder keg and stuffed it into the two Spanish prisoners' mouths. Still others advanced, holding firebrands.

Gabriel fought furiously, but to no avail. He looked around for Katari.

'Enough!' thundered Manco.

The Inca had come through the crowd unseen by Gabriel. Soldiers and noblemen made way for him. Only Villa Oma stood his ground, facing the Emperor. A steady trickle of green coca spittle dribbled from his lips down his chin.

'Prostrate yourself before your Emperor!' Manco ordered Villa Oma.

The Sage had, for a long time now, exempted himself from the natural gestures of respect due to an Inca. His bloodshot eyes stared defiantly at Manco for a moment before he bowed, very slightly.

Gabriel at last saw Anamaya, half hidden behind Manco.

'Look around you, Manco!' said Villa Oma. 'See that the *pachacuti* has already begun, and surrender to a force greater than yourself. Some of us used to call the Strangers gods. Look what we've done to them now.'

Villa Oma pointed to the niches, at the horrors that had once been men, horrors held up by bronze-pointed spikes.

'It is the beginning of the upheaval, it is peace returning, for us and our people . . .'

'The *pachacuti* began a long time ago, Villa Oma. My father

Huayna Capac was its first victim. Yet he guides us still from beyond.'

Villa Oma wasn't listening. If one listened closely, one could hear him murmuring to himself:

'There is something ancient and impure in you . . .'

Anamaya's blood had run cold when she had seen that Gabriel was in danger. She took no comfort now from Huayna Capac's imprecise words, and she was frightened of visions in which she saw nothing, and prophecies that prophesied anything.

Most of the Indians in the valley had gathered in the straight and narrow alleyways running between the *canchas*. They had put down their tools and abandoned their fields and had converged on the town. Anamaya sensed them baying silently for blood and death, an urge whirling within them like the turbulent waters of the Willkamayo, and she felt as though she alone was resisting it. She looked up over the heads of the crowd at the Ancestor, and begged him for his help.

'You do not see clearly, Villa Oma. Your eyes have grown red as Atahualpa's did, and your heart is drowning in a lake of blood. You secretly cast curses, and you secretly make sacrifices, and you kill and kill, but you have forgotten that you are nothing without the Ancestors, nothing without the gods surrounding us . . .'

'Something impure . . .' repeated Villa Oma, louder now, as though he hadn't heard a word that Manco had said. 'I remember the woeful day when, disregarding my advice, his spirit shadowed by illness, the great Huayna Capac refused to give the Puma the body of an impure little girl, and then even placed her at his side and confided secrets to her that no one had ever before or has ever since known. I should have taken her from him and have done away with her, because now, instead of being eaten by the Puma, she has drawn it forth from the earth so that it can consume us all . . .'

'For the last time, Villa Oma, silence! Anamaya has never betrayed the Incas. You forget that she has never stopped performing her duties as *Coya Camaquen*, the *Coya Camaquen* chosen by Huayna Capac himself, and that you yourself guided her along the way. Anamaya is the tradition, she is what was before and what will be . . .'

Villa Oma fell silent. His thin body shook inside his *unku*, and the red tunic billowed like a wave of blood. Instead of words, from his lips issued a froth that mixed with the green juice of the coca leaves he was always chewing. His copper skin turned gray.

Then, making a supreme effort to stiffen all his limbs and control himself, he said, with a tone of regret:

'I must go. Farewell, my Lord.'

Walking jerkily, he made his way toward the river, alone.

Despite Villa Oma's obvious fury and hatred, despite all that had widened the rift between them until it seemed too great to cross, Anamaya heard in the Sage's last words the echo of that respect which he had refused to give Manco and yet now bestowed upon him by distancing himself. She heard the echo of an old, fraternal alliance that had soured into enmity.

CHAPTER 15

IMMEDIATELY AFTER VILLA OMA DISAPPEARED, SOLDIERS surrounded Gabriel and took him through the growling, hostile crowd to Manco's *cancha*. Gabriel could no longer see the reassuring faces of Anamaya, Katari or even Manco, and he felt like a flimsy basket being carried down rapids by a raging torrent.

When he entered the *cancha*'s courtyard, the women moved away from him. He soon found himself alone beside the fountain of the Four Directions, his heart still beating furiously after his scrape with death, his mind revisiting the belligerent exchange of words between Manco and the Sage. A part of him was wondering whether, once again, he had been protected by some mysterious force, whether some unseen power was watching over him after all.

'Are all the Strangers like you?'

A little boy, his eyes agleam with curiosity, was staring at Gabriel without any trace of fear, even though the child was only four or five years old.

'Oh, there are many much nastier than me!' replied Gabriel, grinning.

'What's your name?'

'Gabriel.'

The little boy pondered upon this, a serious expression on his face.

'That's a strange name. It doesn't mean anything.'

'Some of your people have told me that it means "puma". And you? What's your name?'

'I'm Titu Cusi. I am the son of Lord Manco, and one day I will be Inca.'

'Well, I'm sure that you'll be a powerful emperor, and that you will also rule your people benevolently . . .'

But the little boy was no longer listening; he rushed over to his father, who had just entered the courtyard, surrounded by a guard of Lords and soldiers. Manco leaned down to his son and smiled, and Gabriel saw how tenderly the Emperor hugged his boy. But when he stood up Gabriel saw that his black-eyed stare was once more hostile, impenetrable.

'Come,' said Manco. 'Follow me.'

Gabriel, Anamaya and Katari followed him through the door-hanging into the royal chamber.

'Lord Manco,' began Gabriel, 'I know that you are indifferent to my gratitude. Nevertheless, I wish to thank you from the bottom of my heart.'

Manco looked at him without saying a thing. Gabriel didn't dare look away to Anamaya or Katari.

'Had Villa Oma known what I now know, you'd have been dead before I arrived,' said Manco eventually.

'What do you know?'

'Your people are coming. A powerful army, including many cavalry – commanded by one of *kapitu* Pizarro's brothers – and supported by thousands of traitors.'

'Gonzalo?'

Despite himself, Gabriel's heart pounded with rage as he pronounced the hated name.

'Hernando.'

He shrugged.

'You know that I'm not one of them.'

'I don't know *what* I know about you. But I have with me here the only two people for whom your life is worth anything. Count yourself lucky that they are also the two people I value most.'

'What are you going to do?'

'Let's sit down.'

Manco took his seat on his *tiana*. Gabriel, Anamaya, and Katari sat at his feet, on a pile of soft vicuña and guanaco wool blankets spread over the ground. The light of the torches played on their faces, and Anamaya in particular looked as though she was covered in a fine layer of gold dust.

'Our spies have been telling us for days that the Strangers are preparing to attack us. We are going to fight them, and defeat them so completely that what few survivors remain will go to the Governor and convince him to leave us in peace . . .'

'You're mistaken, noble Manco.'

An expression of anger flashed across the Emperor's face.

'You doubt our victory?'

'Victory in battle is never a sure thing. But that's not what I mean: they won't leave. Even if you defeat those who are coming now, others will follow, and then others after them. Believe me, I know Pizarro better than anyone: he never gives up.'

'He doesn't know me!'

'Lord Manco. No one here doubts your courage. But I beseech you, please think about it – unless you want to become like Villa Oma. You must face the reality of how strong the Spaniards really are.'

'Silence!'

'Let me give you one final piece of advice, although no doubt you'll ignore it: seek an honorable peace, endure without complaint whatever humiliations the Spaniards impose, save what can be saved, and secretly send a group of young men to learn for themselves how to use the Strangers' weapons. I'm not talking about their steel blades, their gunpowder, or their horses. I'm talking about their language, their god, and their customs.'

'I cannot do that.'

'I know how you feel, Manco. I accept that you're going to do what you consider necessary.'

'I cannot do that . . .'

Manco repeated himself as though he was alone in a dream. Gabriel had spoken passionately and sincerely. For a moment, the room was filled with silence, the torches flickering.

Then Manco turned to Anamaya and asked:

'What do you say, *Coya Camaquen*?'

'Win this battle, Manco. You have no other option, and nor do we. But afterward, heed those words spoken in wisdom.'

Manco reflected for a moment. Then he looked at Katari.

'And you, my friend, Master of the Stone?'

Katari said nothing. He stood up, approached Manco, and took him by the shoulders. Manco stood to meet him, and the two men embraced briefly. Then Manco sat back down on his *tiana*.

'Leave me now. I want to be alone.'

CHAPTER 16

Ollantaytambo, November 1536

AT DAWN, KATARI WRAPPED ANAMAYA AND GABRIEL IN *mantas*, so that they were cloaked up to their necks. Without wasting any words, and walking quickly, they climbed the steps to the Great Temple, hoping to avoid prying eyes. Anamaya sighed with relief as they passed through its outer wall.

They were hidden by the hill now, and no one would dare come to the little temple with the four niches where the Sacred Double was waiting for them.

Gabriel and Anamaya kissed for what seemed a time without end, their hands on one another's faces. They embraced with the eagerness of their first cleaving together and with the sadness of the last. Caressing each other's skin was a voyage of discovery as momentous as crossing oceans or climbing mountains. They joined themselves together like the links of a single, indestructible chain.

When they separated finally, their eyes were brimming with tears.

'I'm leaving,' said Gabriel.

'There's no other way,' replied Anamaya.

The first rays of the sun struck the Sacred Double's gold surface at the same moment that they illuminated the mountain crests.

'I don't want to be sad,' said Gabriel.

'Nor do I. Everything is happening as Huayna Capac told me it would. The mysteries are being unraveled, and you are still here. You will be here at the end . . .'

'I know that you're telling me what little you can. I know that I must make my own way, and learn on my own. That is the lesson that I forget sometimes. But sometimes I remember it. When I spoke to Manco, I was no longer frightened. I knew that everything within me was as it was meant to be. Do you think I'm becoming a good puma?'

He spoke these last words with a gentle irony, and Anamaya leaned against him. He continued:

'Your love has revealed everything to me. Your love has made all this possible and bearable, even the anguish of having to leave you once more without knowing when I'll see you again.'

'He said to me: *"He will only come to you when he leaves you. Although separated, you will be united as one."*'

'Your venerable old Inca was a cruel man!'

They both laughed softly, like children. They looked at the Ancestor from the same dizzying perspective as the Sacred Double in the southern niche.

A shuffling sound startled them. Katari appeared in front of them.

'It is time,' he said.

They climbed up the Ancestor Mountain by a narrow, poorly paved path. Both Katari and Gabriel bore a heavy stone, wrapped in a *manta*, on their backs.

They had passed through the hustling *canchas*, where every man was preparing for battle, without seeing a sign of Villa Oma; then they had walked past the well-stocked *collcas* before leaving the town behind. At the base of the slope, Katari had selected a stone for Gabriel, and it was this burden that was now digging into the young Spaniard's back and shoulders, making every step he took agony.

And yet, Gabriel made no complaint, nor did he feel any need to ask why he had to carry the stone. He followed in Katari's steps, noting how the Master of the Stone moved with the ease and grace of an alpaca. Katari's load didn't seem to weigh him down any more than his long hair that floated freely behind him in the breeze.

From time to time, they turned around to watch the Inca troops deploy. Hundreds of fearsome Antisuyu archers had emerged from the forest and joined the Inca ranks. A barrage had been built downstream on the Willkamayo and the water level had risen, making the river harder to ford. And Gabriel, the man who had sworn that he would no longer bear arms, now felt a painful ache in his body. It was as though he was sharing the Spaniards' efforts as they approached – and as though he was only now facing the stark and strange reality of not being among them, riding on his white horse, holding his sword, sweating beneath his morion and chain mail. And another, unexpected thought rent his soul in two: he knew that Sebastian would be among them, and that he wouldn't be there to help defend his friend and even perhaps save his life.

Gabriel gritted his teeth to prevent himself from crying out in fury at his impotence. He hooked his hands into the folds of the *manta*, distracting himself by bending forward and concentrating on the back-breaking weight of the stone.

Gradually, pain and exhaustion produced the desired numbness, and he felt paradoxically aided by his burden.

They reached a flat, rocky platform the size of an esplanade. Gabriel set down his stone and almost collapsed, so great was the pain that shot through his back. Anamaya's warm gaze offered him some support, and he slowly straightened his body, feeling crushed by the physical effort as much as by the sudden doubt that had overcome him.

'We're here,' said Katari.

Gabriel was completely lost. He looked to Anamaya for some explanation.

'We are above the Ancestor's face,' she said.

Katari squatted and took a bronze chisel from his *chuspa*. He began working the stone he had borne up the slope, his movements precise and meticulous. Then he did the same with Gabriel's.

'Look,' he said.

On one stone, the Kolla had carved the shape of a puma, and on the other that of a snake.

'Strength,' said Gabriel, 'and Amaru's wisdom.'

'Well done,' said Katari, smiling. 'You know our gods. Soon, a temple will be erected here to crown Huayna Capac's head. Those searching for the Inca's power will come to it to pray and make oblations.'

Then the fog scattered, and bright morning light illuminated the mountain slopes; a young sun brought out the colors in the terraces and put a sparkle in the water.

It was a beautiful day to die.

When the crowd down below surged forward suddenly, Gabriel became aware of the imminent danger. His body stiffened so abruptly that it was painful. Anamaya turned to him and said, tenderly:

'You're pale.'

And indeed, the blood had drained from his face, even though his heart was beating furiously.

'I can't,' he said.

'I can't let them die without me . . .'

Anamaya put her hand on his.

'Do you want to fight?'

'No!'

The cry had burst forth from his mouth, uncontrolled.

'Do you want to die with them?'

'I thought that I was . . . protected . . .'

'You are – from everything except yourself.'

Anamaya gazed down at the slopes and terraces that were covered in warriors.

'Let him go,' said Katari calmly.

At that moment, the first battle cry erupted.

It was as though Anamaya's blood had suddenly turned to ice, freezing her entire body. She was unable to move a limb.

Gabriel's first few steps had been slow, painfully so. At the first bend in the road, he stopped, as though to turn back. But he didn't.

Quite the opposite: he was almost hurtling down the slope when Anamaya saw him last, a man moving like a sling stone.

She saw the Antisuyu archers on the terraces below, and, on the left bank of the Willkamayo and the slopes rising from it, innumerable warriors armed with slings.

Anamaya focused her mind on the stone where Huayna Capac had spoken to her, but he didn't say anything more. She had no way of knowing whether the Puma was dashing toward his death like some untamed beast, or whether he was going to cross the Ocean again – in the other direction, back to his own people.

Katari remained at her side. He finished chiseling the two stones with which the temple would be founded.

'You had forgotten that the Puma is also a man,' was all he said.

Anamaya nodded, but without believing him.

Gabriel raced down the slope, the blood throbbing in his temples. It was as though the decision had been made for him, without any conscious thought of his own. As he ran, breathless, he began to have doubts. As he came closer, it seemed to him that the mountain and the whole valley were growling, as though thousands of drums were being beaten within the depths of the earth, causing it to pulsate.

The ominous sound was the voices of frightened men, shouting to give themselves courage, combined with the stamping of thousands of feet, the clashing of thousands of weapons.

Halfway down the slope, Gabriel suddenly found himself above the terraces where the archers who had come from the forest had taken up their positions.

He stopped in his tracks, daunted by the sheer number of warriors; even after so many weeks in Ollantaytambo, he was amazed by how many fighters had been hidden in the mountains. Behind the archers was another mass of Indians armed with spears, clubs and spikes. He immediately noticed that some of them had donned Spanish armor that had been lost in battle. He saw Indians wearing morions, leather breastplates, even coats of mail. Some Inca officers, amazingly, were carrying swords.

Far away, on the other side of the river, Gabriel saw the Spanish forces approaching. They were still too far off for him to make out their individual faces, but he recognized Hernando Pizarro by the plume in his helmet. He was riding at the head of the column. There were about a hundred cavalrymen, followed by at least thirty thousand Indian warriors, made up mainly of the Spaniards' usual allies, the Canaries and the Huancas. But their ranks had been swollen still further with Incas hostile to Manco.

Gabriel felt his blood surge upon seeing them, and he elbowed his way through the mass of tightly packed Inca warriors, swearing the whole while, until he had managed to push through a few ranks.

But when he reached the archers, he had to stop. Dejected, he realized that there was no way he could get through them.

Gabriel saw Manco's proud silhouette standing at the end of the terraces. He was riding his white horse, handling it well, and he bore a spear in his hand, its tip glinting in the sun.

Anamaya could not see the plain or the Spaniards moving across it, but she knew they were approaching by the heightened tension that she could sense in the Inca ranks. She heard a tumultuous crashing of drums and a cacophony of horns rising from the slopes of the mountain atop which sat the Temple, whose doors had been walled up. She realized that Manco and his battle advisers, instead of using the element of surprise that had served them well before, preferred now to show their adversaries that they were expected. And to show them in such a way as to fill them with dread.

She closed her eyes and conjured up a vision of Gabriel. Where was he now? Had he managed to cross through the lines? Against all reason, she imagined him worming his way through the Inca ranks, diving into the river, and joining his people, jumping on a horse and grabbing a sword. He had often told her of how he had taken Sacsayhuaman, and she had no trouble now imagining him leading the Spanish attack.

'She opened her eyes only to be blinded by the sun. 'It's no longer possible,' she murmured. 'He swore never to take up arms again. He's come so far . . .'

But Anamaya found no comfort in her own words: wherever Gabriel was, whatever he meant to do, he was in the middle of a battle, and she could not help but think of the possibility of him dying.

'Santiago!'

The all too familiar Spanish war cry echoed across the valley and reverberated within her.

'Santiago!'

She recoiled in fright. Katari came up to her.

'Stay,' he said. 'Wait. Banish your fear.'

But when Anamaya looked at him, she saw the worry in his eyes. She felt her heart tighten.

As soon as Manco saw Gabriel, he made his way over to him. The ranks of his soldiers parted, making way for their Emperor.

'Why are you here?' Manco demanded brusquely. 'Have you come to fight alongside us?'

Gabriel said nothing. He simply stared intently at the Inca.

'Or do you want to join your people? And die with them?'

Manco said this quietly, and Gabriel understood his confidence.

'If that's what you want to do, then I won't stop you crossing over to them,' said Manco, pointing at the plain.

Gabriel remained frozen on the spot.

'Are you sure? You don't want to? In that case, come and join my Lords,' said Manco. 'You've nothing to fear. Come and see what's waiting for your people . . .'

The cry of 'Santiago!' had caused some ancient instinct to boil in Gabriel's veins. It was a call to battle that, if he had let it, would have given him the will to act upon Manco's challenging offer, leave the horde of Incas and join his own people. But gritting his teeth, he said nothing.

With precise coordination, the Incas sent a hail of sling stones and arrows down upon the Spaniards, causing the vanguard first to halt, then to retreat. Then two cavalrymen detached themselves from their company and charged at the Incas' outer defences. Without being able to see their faces, Gabriel could still recognize them both by their immense size: de Candia and Sebastian – the black giant riding a white horse and de Candia mounted on a black one. Gabriel's pulse pounded as he recognized Itza – of course, the mare that Sebastian had given him.

It was as though his past was galloping back toward him.

Katari removed the bronze key that he wore around his neck and handed it to Anamaya. Her blue eyes were pale, her expression distant.

A deafening cacophony rose from the terraces, and the air was shrill with the whine of falling missiles. Each volley of arrows was like a cloud of stinging insects plunging from the sky to devastate the land below and the sling stones fell like diving hawks.

Anamaya turned to the north, toward the Secret City where she had met Huayna Capac. Katari turned with her.

'*Until that moment when Inti has consumed the hatred dividing us . . .*' she murmured.

Katari continued:

'*. . . And only women singing their grief over all the spilt blood will remain.*'

'Do you think that this is it?'

Katari opened his powerful hands, the natural lines in his palm criss-crossed by the scars of his work.

'No. Not all the signs are there.'

'And him? Can he die?'

'I told you, the Puma is a man, and a man must die. But that man is the Puma.'

Anamaya smiled.

An explosion shook the air itself.

* * *

Gabriel watched, fascinated, as the Indian bombardment forced Sebastian and de Candia to retreat, despite their bravery. They wheeled around and joined a troop of cavalry that headed off to attack the Temple. Seeing it from below, with its formidable walls, the Spaniards had no doubt mistaken it for a fortress. Its defenders seemed at first to fall back, but then two Chachapoya Indians broke the legs of the lead horse with a sling stone, causing the rest of the cavalrymen to panic, and they beat a hasty retreat. No cavalryman dared attempt another charge.

Gabriel could see that the Spaniards were hesitating. For the first time, they were facing the prospect of a pitched battle without having an obvious upper hand. The time when their horses had afforded them automatic advantages of speed and surprise was long gone, their artillery was next to useless, and Manco seemed to have taken their every move into account when he had organized his defensive lines.

Even the regiment of foot soldiers that Hernando had sent around the mountain to attack the Temple's walls was repulsed by a hall of sling stones.

Gabriel heard a culverin fire. The noise came from the Inca side, from somewhere midway along the terraces. Although the explosion undoubtedly did no harm to the Spaniards (it was a miracle, thought Gabriel, that the long cannon hadn't exploded and blown the heads off its amateur Indian gunners), it caused a proud murmur to run through the lines of Inca soldiers.

The blast was heard by all the warriors waiting along the terraces and slopes. It coincided with a triumphant roar from Manco as he ordered his forces to charge.

The Incas, moving as one, surged downward toward the Spaniards. Gabriel, powerless and unable to see anything, felt the earth shaking underfoot. He concentrated on not getting trampled by this tide of screaming men, a tide rolling down the mountainside and overwhelming everything in its path, a tide full of rage amassed over months of humiliation and fear.

When he recovered his footing, all Gabriel could see on the plain was a fog of confused movement: in fact, it was dust kicked up from the earth, it was a mist of sweat, it was the flash of swords scything through the air – and it was the strange sight of Manco in the middle of the fray, mounted on his white horse, spear in hand and wearing his *mascapaicha* on his forehead, charging at the enemy like a demon afraid of nothing.

Gabriel fleetingly remembered the first riding lesson that he had given the Inca emperor.

'I didn't want to make war,' he murmured. 'And yet I make it all the same.'

Despite their furious resistance and the considerable damage, that they inflicted on the Incas, the Spaniards and their allies were gradually forced back. Their cavalry charges became less and less effective, no longer cutting deep into the enemy ranks. Gabriel watched Hernando's crimson feather retreat further and further across the plain, like a tattered red sail on a rudderless, drifting raft.

Gabriel was surprised when he noticed that the light was failing: he felt as though the sun had only just risen.

He looked away from the battle toward the mountain peaks, the Apus that Anamaya and Katari had taught him to recognize. Then he looked back down at the two rivers. And froze in horror.

A hundred or so Indians were diverting the flow of the Patacancha toward the channels that they had dug weeks ago.

Gabriel immediately realized what they were doing.

They were going to flood the plain. They were going to drown the Spaniards.

CHAPTER 17

Ollantaytambo, November 1536

DARKNESS FELL ON THE MOUNTAIN LIKE THE SHADOW of a condor's wing that was as big as the sky itself. The din of battle down below grew dimmer, as though it was somehow slipping away into the distance. There were fewer war cries but more agonized moans, and the explosions had ceased completely. Anamaya felt suddenly cold. She pulled her *manta* tighter around her shivering body.

'I wonder where Villa Oma is,' she said.

Katari thought about it for a moment.

'He probably took refuge in an underground *huaca*, where he's casting curses in the hope that we are defeated, thus confirming his jaundiced and utterly wrong prophecies . . .'

'I would have thought that he would have joined Manco for the battle.'

'His anger imprisons him alone on an island lost in the middle of nowhere.'

'He's still the Sage to me . . .'

'And he's also just a man, like the Puma. He has never really understood why the powerful Huayna Capac confided the secrets of Tahuantinsuyu to a strange little girl with blue eyes rather than to him.'

Anamaya looked lost in a dream.

'Still, for me, he'll always be the Sage,' she repeated.

Katari's laugh carried gently into the night.

'Why are you laughing?'

'I've been trying, for a while now, to see, behind the *Coya Camaquen*'s façade, the little girl that you were when you arrived before the great Inca Huayna Capac. I think I just heard her for the first time.'

Anamaya laughed with him.

'Why did you give me the bronze key?'

'One day, when all the signs have been revealed, we too shall be separated. I shall go to the Lake of Origins, whereas you will head back to—'

She interrupted him, putting her finger to his lips.

'Please don't say the name out loud.'

'You'll need this key. With it, you will open the stone.'

'How will I know?'

'You'll know.'

The nocturnal breeze picked up, carrying the sound of the men on the battlefield away from them. Curiously, Anamaya was no longer cold.

'What about him?' she asked.

Gabriel watched the water rise with frightening speed and flood the plain. It reached the level of the horses' girths, and then the animals could hardly move, stuck in a lake that had suddenly risen from nowhere and that threatened to swallow them up. He watched as a cavalryman fell from his saddle. In the water, he whirled his arms about, desperately trying to stay on the surface while at the same time getting rid of his heavy gear.

As night gradually enveloped the valley, the Spanish retreat was detectable only as a dwindling noise. It occasionally flared up again when a battle cry rang out, or a trumpet, or the sudden clamor that occurred when the Incas caught a lagging Spaniard or managed to topple a horse.

Gabriel felt a heaviness that he could not shake off overcome his body and weigh down his limbs.

Although he hadn't fought that day, he suddenly felt very old, as though he'd been crippled by his non-existent wounds. He closed his eyes and saw an Inca and a Spaniard, each of them sometimes on horseback, sometimes on foot, wielding a sword or a sling. He had difficulty banishing the vision from his mind. Yet in his soul he wanted to be engulfed by it, like a warrior who, surviving a battle, collapses at its end, when everything is over and he can no longer be beaten by anything but his own all-consuming weariness.

He saw Manco returning on foot, leading his mud-covered horse by its bridle. The Emperor looked Gabriel up and down without saying a word, his black eyes gleaming with pride, his being still charged with the fever of battle. Victory was a drug stronger than any number of jars of *chicha*, stronger than ten thousand coca leaves.

Manco handed Gabriel his horse's reins and headed toward the *canchas*, an exhausted victor.

Gabriel followed in his steps.

The path was so steep and in places paved so badly that it was risky to travel down it, particularly at night.

Yet Anamaya and Katari descended sure-footedly, guided only by the occasional glimpse of moonlight and the instinct of those who had traveled across all the skies.

As they drew closer to the Willkamayo and the springs they heard the clamour of the *atiyjailli*, the victory songs already being sung, in which the noble feats of the battle's heroes were hailed. The earth had not yet finished drinking the blood that had been spilt upon it, and corpses still floated in the river. Anamaya saw a woman facing her from the river bank. She was holding against her belly the *manta* containing her husband's clothes, a husband whom she had followed to a senseless war. Her expression was blank, her gaze lost in a place beyond the Four Cardinal Directions.

Just outside the *canchas*, they came across men staggering along. Some were lying in the mud and in their own vomit, still singing drunkenly about their famous victory over the demigods who had come from across the ocean. The Strangers had once more become the fabulous creatures that they had been many moons ago, when they had been described as invincible, as half-man, half-horse, with hands that sliced through flesh and silver sticks that spat fire. But according to the legends now being invented by the drunken, victorious warriors, Viracocha himself had created the Incas from stone, and had made them so strong and brave that even with their arms sliced off they repelled the attackers. They had also become the masters of water and hail.

Anamaya and Katari heard this story again and again as they made their way through the narrow alleys between the *canchas*. Even the womenfolk, gathered around the fires grilling guinea pigs, told it. Everyone spoke of the warrior who had hurled the stone that had broken the leg of the first horse, and of the soldiers who had diverted the Patacancha. They recreated the scene by imitating the sound of arrows or stones whistling through the air, telling how so-and-so had grabbed onto a horse and toppled its dead rider from his saddle, leaving the corpse to float down the river. Everyone spoke at once, as though there weren't enough words to recreate the joy of the victory.

Anamaya was frightened.

She couldn't find Gabriel. She stared at every silhouette she came across in the dark, hoping it was him. But she didn't dare ask anyone if they had seen him. *Seen the Stranger? I hope he's buried in the Under World.*

Her heart was pounding when they at last reached the tall, trapezoidal door that opened into Manco's *cancha*.

The Inca was standing amid a gaggle of his Lords, wearing a coat of mail over his *unku*, his spear lying at his feet. He was waving his hands around, describing some particular action, and Anamaya saw that the men were still covered in blood and mud; grime covered Manco's face, and his eyes glinted with pride and hatred. The men surrounding him laughed and smiled almost familiarly, and the great deference normally accorded an Inca now gave way a little to the camaraderie of fighting men. The room fell silent as Anamaya and Katari entered.

'Well, *Coya Camaquen*, presumably my father had told you of our victory. No doubt that's why you've taken so long to join us.'

Manco signaled to two women to bring him more *chicha*. They poured it from a jug into his finely worked gold goblet. Manco drank slowly.

'And you, Katari? Have you been slinging stones from the top of Pinkylluna Mountain?'

The two young people said nothing. The Inca's cheeks were flushed from the drink and his eyes burned.

'They don't reply,' he said, turning to the Lords. 'Either they scorn us, or else they're ashamed . . .'

'We have laid the foundation stones for a new temple,' said Katari, 'that will one day crown the head of our Ancestor, Huayna Capac – your father.'

He spoke calmly, fearlessly. Manco lost his murderous look. He pointed at Anamaya.

'I captured an animal during the battle,' he said, his rage abating. 'I want to give it to you.'

'What animal?' she asked gently.

'A puma. I understand that you're attached to them.'

Manco motioned toward the far side of the room. Two soldiers brought Gabriel forward. His face was impassive.

'I'm giving him back to you, Anamaya. He's yours.'

Anamaya forced herself to remain still, despite every atom in her body urging her to run up to Gabriel and take him in her arms.

'Your puma can keep his life – on one condition.'

Anamaya returned Manco's unflinching gaze, her own blue-eyed stare steady.

'He must disappear before Inti throws his first rays into the sky of the day after our victory. Tomorrow – before dawn. Do you understand me?'

Anamaya remained silent. She waited as Gabriel walked unsteadily toward her. He was clearly exhausted. They stood side by side without touching, facing Manco. Then they passed together through the crowd, and she felt their hostility, their lust for vengeance. They wanted to tear him to pieces.

As they passed beneath the stone lintel that was decorated with a carved condor, Manco called out after them:

'Tomorrow before dawn, d'you hear?'

He sounded completely sober.

Night closed in around Anamaya and Gabriel as they left the *canchas* behind.

She led him past the springs, then along beside the Willkamayo toward the condor *huaca*.

They said nothing for a long time, and didn't even dare touch one another. They had only been apart for a few hours, but they both had to recover their breaths and slow their beating hearts before they could speak.

The night was cool and clear, and as they walked they left behind all the horrors of the battle. Soon, there was no thought of defeat or victory, no memory of fighting, no mental echoes of the cries of hatred and triumph.

When they reached the rock, Anamaya stopped. She took Gabriel by the hand and made him lie down on the low wall that ran alongside the river. They closed their eyes together and emptied themselves of violence, letting their souls and bodies join with the water's eternal flow.

Then she stood up and led him down to the water's edge. She undressed him tenderly. His *unku*, still drenched with sweat, slipped to the ground. The water was so cold that Gabriel almost cried out from the shock. Anamaya led him toward a flat, black rock whose top showed through the river's surface in the middle of the current. He stretched out on it, the cold water flowing around him, and Anamaya rinsed him carefully with her hands, washing away his exhaustion. Gabriel surrendered until he was no longer able to distinguish between her hands and the water. He felt his weariness slip away from him and sink into the river. The images haunting him slowly disappeared, and slowly he emerged from the hand-to-hand combat that he had never fought. A delicious sense of well-being overcame him, and even the first stirrings of desire. Then Anamaya made him sit up and led him back to the river bank.

She had brought him a soft wool *unku* in her *manta*.

They climbed back over the little wall and returned to the path. They passed beneath the silhouette of the condor *huaca*.

'I didn't want to leave,' said Gabriel.

'I know.'

They spoke in low voices, not for fear of being overheard but to create a sanctuary for themselves in the night. They spoke of everything except their coming separation – a separation that they knew would be upon them all too soon, despite the night's illusion of timelessness.

'I thought that I had to be close to them. I didn't want to fight your people, I wanted to be like the grass beneath their horses' hooves, within a hand's reach of the wounded, within their sight. I felt as though I was *meant* to see that crimson feather in that bastard Hernando's helmet. I even felt fondness for him, and though I was ashamed of it, I couldn't help it. I knew that they were going to lose the battle, but if I had come down from the mountain, I would have looked like a traitor.'

'A voice said that you weren't meant to die, but another said that you would be trampled and torn to pieces. One voice told me that we would find one another again, and another said that I'd lost you.'

'You were there with me. When I saw Sebastian and de Candia approaching at a gallop. I turned towards you. I wanted to tell you . . .'

Anamaya laughed. Then, in a serious voice, she asked:

'Are they still alive?'

'I don't know. I hope so. I saw them disappear beneath a hail of stones and arrows, and I remember willing myself toward them and wishing with all my heart that the force that had protected me during the battle of Sacsayhuaman should now protect them. I prayed to a variety of gods – my own, all of yours – and I said, "Whoever you are, ignore my disbelief and save my two friends. Don't let them die now."'

'Then they're still alive.'

'You mean, I have that power?'

'I mean that power exists. Come.'

They climbed through the rocks into the *huaca*. Newly sensitive to the Incas' beliefs, Gabriel felt an energy vibrating through the place. He said nothing, letting Anamaya lead him from stone to stone.

She stopped in front of a rock about as tall as she was, its slender form telling that it had been worked by man, although no chisel marks were visible. It was the same shape as a mountain that rose in the distance but was now hidden in the night.

'This is the place,' said Anamaya.

Gabriel's heart skipped a beat.

Anamaya stopped herself, surprised by her own words. She had spoken without thinking – the words had just come out. The lingering remnants of her fear disappeared: those secrets that she was meant to keep from Gabriel were now right in front of him. He had to know.

'It's a place,' she said, 'that is close and yet very far, and its name must remain secret. Of all those in Ollantaytambo, only Katari and I have traveled there. He carved this stone in the shape of a mountain that no one here has seen, and which rises up over there, above our secret sanctuary. On that mountain's side . . .'

Gabriel let Anamaya's words flow through him without trying to understand them. They penetrated through every pore in his skin, and marked him.

'. . . A face is being carved. It's the Puma's face.'

Anamaya paused. A moment passed before Gabriel realized that she was talking about him. Still unsure, he squinted through the darkness, trying to make out anything at all carved into the rock. But he saw nothing.

'You don't see it,' she continued, 'and yet it's there. Katari told you that your destiny is written in stone. Here it is, directly in front of you.'

Gabriel suddenly felt an intense heat invade his body, a feeling unlike either the blood-colored, ash-flavored fury of battle or the honeyed taste of carnal love. His entire body shuddered, and he felt at one with the world. He felt amazingly grateful.

'I see it,' he murmured. 'I see it!'

He saw the Puma's fangs emerge from the rock, ready to

bite, ready to tear to pieces. But Gabriel wasn't frightened. He was intoxicated with inexplicable and magnificent joy, beyond laughter, beyond tears.

At last, he thought, *I have arrived.*

CHAPTER 18

Ollantaytambo, November 1536

ANAMAYA AND GABRIEL LAY NAKED AGAINST ONE another, entwined around one another, wrapped up together as though they had been sculpted from a single block of stone. They had plunged into one another deeply, almost without moving. Their light, fleeting caresses brought them intense, exquisite pleasure. They shared their breath with the breeze.

Their happiness was complete. It made all the strange twists and turns that their fates had dealt them seem obvious, even necessary. They were united in the certainty that all was well without having to explain it. Their emotions floated as though on a gentle lake by the light of the half-moon.

Occasionally they lay so perfectly still together that they almost stopped breathing, and they could well have been carved from stone. At other times, they flowed together as though they were part of the river that they could hear rushing past outside, and within them as well.

They spoke without moving their lips; their words were their hands, their grammar their heartbeats. They were like light and shadow, their two bodies dancing in the middle of the universe.

Anamaya broke away first.

Gabriel felt no pain.

He watched her slip on her *añaco* gracefully before passing him his *unku*.

She sat down beside him. She gazed into the darkness at a spot on the mountain where Gabriel thought he could make out a few niches carved into the rock.

'I'm going to tell you about a journey,' she murmured.

Anamaya told Gabriel about her expedition through the stone and her flight as a condor over the Secret City.

He listened as she told him about the rock that spoke to her, and about seeing the old face of the great Inca Huayna Capac. He remembered that she had served the Inca a long time ago.

Anamaya told Gabriel what the Inca had told her, and although not all of it gave him any insight, he kept it in his heart. It didn't unravel all the mysteries surrounding him, but as he listened to Anamaya's soft voice, he felt a peace enfold him, a sense of release that he had never known before. He was overjoyed to realize that he had not only laid down his weapons but that he had been freed from the grip of the very spirit of war.

He realized that it was war that had forced him to remain on the move his whole life. He knew now that he had been displaced by war ever since that sad day when the man he hadn't been able to call 'father' in public had freed him from jail, only to scorn him.

Gabriel felt as though he was watching his life replay itself and that Anamaya was watching it with him. He wondered whether that was how she had felt when she had flown over the mysterious valley with Katari. He saw his battles, his conflicts both physical and spiritual, and his struggles with himself as well as with others. He saw them not as a Stranger, but with new-found acceptance, with a sense of peace that made him want to whisper, 'Oh yes, I remember that trifling thing – is that all it was . . . ?' Of course, this didn't diminish his affection for his few friends, or lessen the love for Anamaya burning in his soul.

He tested the extent of his love and was dazzled by its brilliance, by its almost infinite power. He explored his own fears.

And then that landscape disappeared, and he heard Manco's severe voice echoing like a bell from its tower: *Before dawn, before dawn.*

Gabriel thought he could make out a slight glow atop the Ancestor Mountain.

Anamaya clasped him to her.

'You know what I know,' she said. 'Nothing remains hidden from you. Now you must live the life you're meant to, before coming back to me. We have to wait for the signs to be revealed . . .'

'How will we know that they have?'

Anamaya remembered asking Katari the same question when he had given her his bronze key.

'We'll know. You'll know it as soon as I do.'

'Will we have to wait long?'

Gabriel said this anxiously, suddenly. She hadn't expected it. It was as though the child in him had re-emerged and was demanding his happiness right away, threatening to throw a tantrum if he didn't get it.

Dawn was upon them.

A pale yellow light grazed the mountain peaks. Night was withdrawing. Each moment was another grain of sand that slipped between Gabriel's fingers. Anamaya answered his question by kissing his lips lingeringly.

They stood up together, still holding one another, kissing each other almost violently, then tenderly, alternating between the extremes of their passion. And then, with an effort that wrenched the breath from his lungs, Gabriel tore himself away from her.

'I love you,' she said.

He looked at her. All the memories that he had of her face, all her smiles and all her tears, melted into one. He looked into the serene lake in her blue eyes. He thought he saw a mountain peak reflected in it.

She put her finger on his lips.

'I love you,' Anamaya said again, louder now.

She looked at the Ancestor Mountain before turning away. *'Remain in my breath, and trust the puma.'* The words gave her the courage that she needed.

Gabriel turned around and began making his way down toward the riverside path, all the while sensing Anamaya standing still behind him.

He didn't turn around for fear of losing his determination and not being able to do what had to be done. He knew what that was now. He understood it and accepted it in his innermost heart.

He began walking more quickly toward the *canchas*.

As Gabriel crossed the bridge, he blinked as the sun's first rays touched his face.

PART 3

CHAPTER 19

Lake Titicaca, March 1539

E ARLY DAWN, AND A THIN FOG SLIPPED SLOWLY OVER
the Island of the Moon. The lake was still hidden, and
only the very slight sound of waves lapping on the pebble
beach betrayed its existence.

Gabriel was sitting on a low wall that ran along the rim of the
highest terrace, his back to Quilla's temple. The air was cold, and
his skin was covered in goose bumps despite the large blue wool
cape he had wrapped around himself. He was, as always, deeply
moved by the prevailing serenity of the sacred place, a place that
he now knew well.

He liked that time of day when the sky and the lake were of
the same milky, fluid hue, the light gradually brightening from
its centre. And although he felt profoundly alone, he also felt as
though he was being borne up by a sense of the power of the new
life now unfolding with the dawning day.

Soon the morning breeze blew stronger, ruffling his blond hair
and rippling through his long beard. It came from the south,
scattering the fog into long, thin strips and pushing it north
so that it resembled a pack of white horses galloping through
the blue of the sky. The little island's grass- and shrub-covered
slopes appeared; and the ceremonial terraces, neatly divided by
brown and ocher stone walls, now lay unveiled. They descended
in orderly stepped rows right down to the somber waters of the
lake, its shore streaked with the foam of small waves.

Soon, Titicaca, in all its vast magnificence, was visible. Gabriel could make out the vertiginous Apus to the north and east – the Ancestor-Mountains, the haughty guardians of the Lake of Origin. Night's shadows gradually withdrew from the mountains' folds and ravines as the last streaks of fog dissolved in the blue sky. The sun tinted with gold the cotton clouds caught on the eternally frozen peaks of Ancohuma and Illampu, those same clouds that skimmed over the mountains' harsh screes, cliffs, and seracs.

The other mountains were, in their turn, very quickly crowned with solar gold too. The blue of the lake's water grew deeper and denser, and the banks seemed to rise straight up from it. Like a peacock showing its resplendent feathers, the thousands of geometrically arranged terraces on the western shore unfurled their whole range of greens. For a short moment, Gabriel felt as though he was witnessing the birth of the world.

The last strands of fog in the north, directly ahead of him, scattered abruptly to reveal the lunar orb, the Moon-Mother. She was enormous, perfectly round, and hung suspended directly over the mountains reflected in the lake. She stayed there for a long moment, long enough for Gabriel to become absorbed in her faraway contours and shadows, and to watch her nocturnal brilliance slowly fading in the growing light of day.

And then the sun rose swiftly over the big Apus and threw its blinding illumination across the world. The lake's surface, so somber a moment before, now shimmered so brightly that it was impossible to look at it directly.

The moon's disk began to fade slowly.

Voices began intoning behind Gabriel, startling him:

> *O Mama Quilla, how cold was the night!*
> *O Mama Quilla, hold us tight,*
> *O Moon-Mother, embrace us!*
> *The Sun has suckled the milk of day at Your breast,*
> *The Sun has spilt the milk of life in Your womb,*
> *O Mama Quilla!*
> *May You rest in Titicaca's depths,*
> *May You cross through night's shadow,*

> *May You return to us in the unborn tomorrow,*
> *May You swell our wombs and breasts.*
> *O Moon-Mother,*
> *In the World Above,*
> *In the Under World,*
> *Embrace us,*
> *For we are Your daughters,*
> *O Mama Quilla!*

He turned and saw a dozen old women chanting.

With their arms raised, they focused their pale eyes on the moon's increasingly diaphanous sphere. They sang farewell to it once again, their cracked lips moving together, vocalizing from toothless mouths. They marked the end of each line with a sway of their hips, their long capes lined with silver plaques undulating in time with their movement. Gabriel saw that although their faces were wizened and old they moved their bodies with youthful grace.

The women were standing in front of the Temple of the Moon, which consisted of a number of buildings set around three sides of a perfectly proportioned courtyard. Thirteen doors, with lintels and frames lined with ocher stone as delicately worked as *mantas*, opened onto thirteen small rooms, cubicles set next to the upper terraces. A young girl in a white tunic stood in front of each door, her bosom covered by a silver plate.

Gabriel shivered. He straightened himself and waited for the end of the prayer, feeling the stiffness in his muscles.

When the priestesses finished their chant, three adolescent girls emerged from the temple. Two of them had vicuña wool *cumbis* draped over their arms, the material so finely woven that it seemed to be weightless. The third came up to Gabriel and handed him a tunic decorated with a simple red-and-gold motif.

Wordlessly, he took off his coat. Beneath it he wore only boots, a shirt and velvet breeches. The young girl helped him slip his head through the tunic's narrow neck-hole. From the neck down it covered him almost entirely, so that of his boots only the toes were visible.

Gabriel could smell the animal odor of the wool and door hangings. He took one last glance at the mountains, now iridescent in the morning light, before bowing to the oldest priestess.

'I am ready, daughter of Quilla,' he murmured respectfully.

The old women surrounded Gabriel and led him into a dark room, lit only by a few burning candle-ends. Each woman threw a handful of coca leaves into a glowing brazier.

Fussing noisily, they urged him toward a long, dull-coloured door hanging. One priestess pulled it aside and disappeared into an unlit, narrow passage that bent at an odd angle. Five more old women disappeared behind her. Gabriel felt hands pushing him into the pitch-black passage.

As soon as the door hanging had fallen back down behind him, he could see nothing. He held his hands out in front of him, feeling his way along the cold wall. Its originally roughcast surface was surprisingly smooth, as polished as leather by the thousands of hands that had felt their way along it.

The passage forked off to the left and narrowed considerably. Gabriel stopped, but an old woman behind him, so close that he could feel her breath on the back of his neck, impatiently ordered him to continue. Gabriel had to shuffle sideways to pass through. His chest brushed along the wall. He advanced cautiously, still feeling his way with his out-thrust arm, before negotiating a gap only just large enough to let him through into another room, much larger than the first and filled with smoke.

On one of this room's walls were four arched niches that were pierced with small square holes through which thin beams of daylight passed. A huge, slightly bulging silver disk, twice as large as a man, gleamed on the opposite wall. Its convex surface distorted the mirrored images of the women moving around the room. Thick smoke billowed from two large baked-clay braziers, painted in rich colors, that stood below the disk. Dried llama-dung was being used as fuel, and its acrid stench was mixed with that of burned flesh and guts, the heady odor of smoldering coca leaves, and the sour reek of sacred beer. The smoke was so thick and the smell so ancient and ingrained that the walls themselves seemed to give off the fetor.

Gabriel covered his mouth and nose, stepping back despite himself as he did so. But now the old women crowded around him. Some grabbed his hands, his arms or even his neck, others took hold of the folds of his long tunic. They led him to the center of the room, moving as a large, single body. The harsh smoke eddied around them. It irritated Gabriel's eyes, but he nevertheless watched the women's grotesque reflections in the silver disk as they began chanting:

> O Mama Quilla, hold us tight,
> O Moon-Mother, embrace us!

The senior priestess stoked the embers in the braziers and only then did Gabriel realize that the devices were shaped like roaring pumas. She threw more coca leaves onto them, followed by some small plant roots. Their smell as they burned was very strong, something like incense, and it overwhelmed all the others. But the smoke the roots gave off irritated Gabriel's eyes even more, so that tears formed beneath his eyelids. The women tightened their grip on him and began swaying from side to side, leading him so firmly along in their dance that he felt like a doll in their hands. They sang plaintively:

> O Moon-Mother,
> In the World Above,
> In the Under World,
> Embrace us,

The senior priestess broke away and stood to face them. She raised her right hand and touched the silver disk. Their distorted images in it moved with increasing frenzy. She picked up a jug of *chicha*. Still swaying, she tilted it forward and spilt the bitter liquid all around, even on the embers in the braziers, and chanted:

> O Quilla, drink for us!
> O sweet Mother, drink for him!

The air in the room had become quite unbreathable. Gabriel gasped for air, his mouth wide open, tears rolling from his smarting eyes. He felt as though there was sand grinding under his eyelids. He wanted to rub them to stop the burning, but the old women holding on to him never gave him the chance. He could barely see the senior priestess placing the resplendent *cumbis* woven by the temple virgins on the braziers, the fabric's bright colors reflecting for an instant in the silver disk.

The smoke died down for a brief moment before coming back twice as thick, heavy and black. The old women's swaying grew increasingly frenzied.

The *cumbis* on the braziers twisted as they burned, their delicate wool fibers dematerializing into tiny green and blue flames that consumed their ornate geometric designs. Their beautiful colors crackled and flared. One after the other, the bolts of fabric in the braziers turned to ash. Gabriel felt the smoke fill his mouth like some abrasive paste and burn his throat and lungs. Each breath he took required enormous effort. He clenched his fingers on the women's shoulders, and they bore him up with amazing strength, considering their great age, never once ceasing their chant.

Gabriel opened his eyes with great difficulty, but he could barely see the silver disk or the senior priestess through the smoke. He felt choked and nauseated but the old women held him ever tighter.

And then, suddenly, they fell silent and stopped swaying.

He watched the smoke dance in front of Quilla's silver disk. The smoke rose up in coils of various colors. One whorl was pure white, another yellow, another brown, almost black. Some were gray at the bottom, green in the middle and red at the top. They danced haphazardly to and fro. The heavy smoke near the top of the room twisted back down toward a thick, smooth, rising bank of vapor, then drifted up again before dispersing into diaphanous strands, their mottled tints mingling together. Opaque wisps spiraled up against the silver disk as though trying to bore a hole through it.

The room was dark and menacing: its walls seemed to be closing in on them like a giant fist squeezing shut. Gabriel felt his throat constrict, as though he was being strangled. All the muscles in his legs, his back and his shoulders suddenly felt so heavy and simultaneously so weak that he could barely stand. His heart beat as though it was trying to burst out of his chest. He kept his eyes open despite the pain, and he thought he glimpsed a face in the silver disk. But a moment later there was nothing, and he was convinced that he was about to die. He saw blood flooding his eyes and mouth. He saw himself falling into the abyss.

Unable to cry out, Gabriel tore himself away from the hands holding him. He pushed the old women aside, flinging them to the ground, and rushed at the gap in the wall and so out of the room. He scraped his palms and forehead as he moved too quickly through the narrow passage, bolting toward the temple's exit. Gasping for air, he emerged into the cold, bright morning.

Gabriel lay recovering on the temple's grass-covered walkway.

When he eventually looked up, he saw the oldest of the priestesses standing a few paces away. A gaggle of young girls stood behind her, in front of the Temple's doors. They were all, oddly enough, smiling and laughing, and the old priestess, her grin broad and toothless, uttered a high-pitched laugh.

'I warned you, golden-haired Stranger!' she guffawed. 'I told you that you wouldn't be able to take the Smoke of the Encounter! Only very old men and women can stand it and travel into the silver disk.'

Gabriel ran his hands over his throbbing head. He sat up and glared at the woman.

'Well, maybe I failed the test,' he grumbled, 'or maybe it's *you* who can't produce the Smoke of the Encounter?'

The very old woman laughed again. But this time her laugh was as short as it was dry.

'Your words are nothing more than a ripple on the lake,' she flung back at him, her tone serious now. 'You asked me to take you through the smoke to the *Coya Camaquen*; I told you that you wouldn't make it. Thrice you've tried, and thrice you've failed.'

'Maybe the *Coya Camaquen* can't hear me. Maybe she's gone to the Other World.'

The old priestess grimaced contemptuously as Gabriel voiced his fear.

'You are arrogant, golden-haired Stranger. You cannot stand the smoke, so you pretend to know what Quilla's silence signifies better than I do! Know that had She wanted to, She would have drawn your last breath from you in there. Quilla's domain has always been denied to men still in their prime. It has been thus since the dawn of time! And yet the *pachacuti* has begun building, and our Mother the Moon needs you.'

Gabriel shrugged. He turned aside from the old woman and her criticisms and walked away, taking off his long tunic as quickly as he could. But the priestess ran after him, grabbed his wrist, and commanded:

'No! You cannot leave like this. You must serve Quilla until She has forgiven you your impiety.'

'What do you mean?'

The woman said nothing, but simply pointed at the young girls.

'Follow the daughters of the Moon and do everything that they ask you.'

'No,' protested Gabriel. 'I've had enough of this stupidity for today!'

'Follow them,' repeated the priestess, not releasing his hand. 'It is Quilla's will. She will answer all your questions.'

'Apinguela! Apinguela!' cried the young girl in the prow.

'Apinguela! Apinguela!' chorused the twenty young women in the boat, pointing at a gentle-sloped little island, very low in the water.

Gabriel stood up awkwardly to see what they were pointing at. He took hold of the long reed-vessel's mast. But the craft's motion on the small choppy waves forced him to sit down again. His useless effort was met with a teasing laugh. The women began chanting fervently:

> *The Sun,*
> *The Moon,*
> *Day and night,*
> *Spring and winter,*
> *Stone and mountains,*
> *Corn and cantuta.*
> *O Quilla,*
> *You are the milk and the seed,*
> *You open your legs*
> *To receive the passion of the night,*
> *O Quilla, it is Your will that*
> *He who leaves Titicaca*
> *Is already on the path home.*

The wind blew from the south and filled the strange-looking sail made of tightly braided *totora*, a fine and supple reed. It was almost as efficient as a Spanish canvas sail. The hull was made of the same material, bundled together in large bunches on which the young women lay. The vessel had no keel, no rudder, and no oar, and it moved forward by fits and starts, steered only by the set of the sail and with long poles where the lake was shallow enough. It took them almost an entire day to reach the little island that the Daughters of the Moon called Apinguela. And not once throughout the day did they stop their laughing and singing.

Gabriel was the only man aboard. For hours, he had been the focus of their attention and the butt of their jokes. But not one of his shipmates would give him a straight answer when he pestered them with: 'Where are we going? To do what? What does Quilla want with me?'

'You'll see, you'll see,' they replied, chuckling. 'Mama Quilla is thinking only of your happiness!'

Nor had they allowed him to help steer the craft. They stuffed him with *chicha* and fruits of the jungle. His belly full and his senses dulled by the sun beating down like a white flame on the lake, he had fallen asleep for the better part of the day, only to wake with his heart in his mouth.

The wind now carried evening's coolness to them, and the

shadows of the rocks on the little island's approaching shore were long in the light of the setting sun. All the women were silent now. The only sounds were those of the creaking rigging on the mast and the reed hull cutting through the waves. The Daughters' expressions were taut, serious, watchful.

Gabriel, surprised, stood up again. He ran his gaze over the island shore, looking for some sign of life or some boat coming to meet them. But there was nothing on the island's slopes except jumbled slabs of rock from the cracks of which grew tufts of *ichu* or bushes stunted by the wind.

'Apinguela!' cried the girl in the bow again.

The girl closest to Gabriel pointed to the island's eastern point.

'There,' she said quietly, pointing at a shadow bigger than the others on the face of one of the rocks where it rose from the lake. 'Apinguela! Our Mother the Moon's womb is open.'

Gabriel made out a yawning cave at the water's edge. In the rock was a giant fissure that led into the island's heart.

The Daughters of the Moon began busying themselves even before they entered the cave. While some dropped the sail, others began steering the vessel with long poles. Still others took out some glowing embers that they had brought along in a clay bowl and with them lit a dozen torches. In the middle of the craft, meanwhile, four women removed the *cumbis* that were wrapped around a stone urn and fifteen gold figurines of llamas and small-breasted women, their arms held across their breasts.

As the barque slipped through the huge crevice, Gabriel felt a warm breeze coming out of the cave. The flames on the torches flickered for a moment, and then they were in. The air in the cavern's interior was still and warm. The cave's walls, from the waterline to the top of the natural vault, were smooth and covered with a thin layer of moss. The water was perfectly still, without a single ripple on its surface, and was so clear that they could make out the shallow lake bottom by torchlight alone.

All the women were standing in silence and facing forward.

Gabriel tried to stand too but a number of firm hands forced him back down.

The large craft moved deeper into the cave, the women pushing it along with their poles. They reached a point where the cave split into two shadowy passageways. The Daughters of the Moon took the one on the left, which was larger and which grew suddenly deeper so that the bottom of the inlet could no longer be seen through the emerald water.

The unexplained heat grew more intense here. Sweat beaded on Gabriel's forehead and streamed down his spine. The passageway grew narrower, and the rounded edges of the *totora* vessel squeaked quietly against the moss.

They went a further eighty *codos* or so, then stopped. Gabriel was stunned to see an enormous silver disk, at least as large as the one in the Room of Sacrifices in the Temple of the Moon, blocking their way.

The women silently placed their torches in holders carved into the mossy walls. They began chanting quietly again.

Then everything happened so quickly that Gabriel had no time to protest or even to understand what was going on.

In no time at all, the youngest of the Daughters of the Moon whipped off their clothes and dived into the water. Then those still on the vessel undressed too. Gabriel, embarrassed, sat up and leaned against the wall of the cave. He wanted to look away, but the women, instead of being abashed, came over to him and removed his tunic, then went on to tear off his shirt and yank down his breeches.

'Hola!' he cried, trying to push them away. 'What are you doing?'

His voice echoed loudly through the cave. The silver disk seemed to tremble. But he was answered only with laughter. The women were more forceful now, and tore away his underclothes. Then, because he was still resisting, they bound his wrists together with a thin but strong-fibred rope.

'God's blood – you're all mad!' cried Gabriel, his voice again reverberating in the confines of the cave.

Yet his shock, his embarrassment at his nakedness, and the

chicha-induced intoxication still throbbing through his head made his resistance as futile as that of a newborn babe.

As he clumsily tried to free himself from the rope binding his hands, the women deftly tied its other end around the stone urn's long, chiseled neck.

Gabriel saw two Daughters of the Moon lift it up and realized, too late, that they intended to throw it overboard.

The urn went over the side of the boat with a splash. Gabriel made one last-ditch effort to hold it back but the rope cut deeply into his wrists. He gave a furious, desperate cry as he was yanked over the side behind it. He had just enough time to take one last gulp of air before his face slapped against the water and he was dragged under.

Gabriel was surprised to find the water as warm as the air in the cave. The further down he went, the hotter it became. His descent was short, a few fathoms at most. He touched the rocky bottom with his fingers and looked up through the clear water to see the light of the torches reflected on the surface. But they seemed completely out of reach.

He tried again to untie his hands, but in vain. And then all the Daughters of the Moon appeared around him, swimming like mermaids. Some were holding the little gold figurines, which glinted in the water like fish scales.

Gabriel's lungs were running out of air. His chest felt as though it was burning, and he began to panic.

The women continued darting around him, brushing past him, stroking him, touching him. He wanted to cry out for them to release him. But the women just carried on dancing around him, their underwater ballet becoming slower and slower. He saw them lift the cover off the urn and put their statues into it.

His temples were pounding furiously, and the fire in his lungs now spread throughout his body, surging through his muscles as though his blood was boiling. The sensation of drowning dulled his senses. He thought he could still feel the Daughters stroking his face, his buttocks, and his belly. He struggled and kicked, banging against them. But they simply pressed in closer to him. He felt their thighs and arms around him.

Then something gave way.

Gabriel stopped thinking about life or death. He felt a woman's body against his, and he recognized Anamaya's warmth. He surrendered.

Immediately he felt relieved, transported, protected.

He looked for his lost but never forgotten beloved's face.

But before he could find it, the tongue of fire licked the inside of his lungs once again. A raucous cry tore its way from his throat.

His eyes closed as he realized that he was breathing once again.

His naked skin slipped wetly against the girls' arms and breasts as they passed him along to the vessel.

Gabriel found that breathing gave him as much pain as being almost drowned had.

I didn't see her face, he thought, desolate with grief.

He shuddered and convulsed. His teeth chattered. He felt himself being wiped down, the women's hands stroking him and making the blood flow again through his veins. When he opened his eyes, his vision was blurred by tears of emotion. But he could see the Daughters of the Moon smiling down at him.

'I didn't see her face,' he murmured.

'Mama Quilla only reveals herself when she deems it fit,' replied one of the women gently.

'Not Quilla's face,' Gabriel protested. 'Anamaya's!'

'Quilla is every face,' said another woman.

At last, warmth returned to his body, thanks to the women's caresses.

He made a final effort to conjure up a mental image of Anamaya, to gather together all her features in his mind's eye. He wanted desperately to make her real enough to touch with his fingers.

But his attempts were in vain.

All he could feel were the insistent caresses of the Daughters of the Moon on his body, and the light touch of their lips as they moved across his flesh, seeking to pleasure him. He felt their fingers tightening around his erection, and without looking he knew that thighs were parting over his loins before being lowered onto his yearning manhood.

Gabriel surrendered to their warmth, seeking solace for Anamaya's absence.

CHAPTER 20

Vilcabamba, March 1539

'LISTEN! LISTEN!'

Anamaya stood up in the river, the water eddying around her waist.

It was a moment of great beauty. The distant sky glowed softly in the gap between the canyon's walls, gold merging into red like a perfectly woven *cumbi*, and yet a very pale blue lingered at its zenith.

For the first time in many days it hadn't rained and the jungle's humidity was less stifling. Dusk brought life back to the river banks set between the steep sides of the canyon that were cloaked in dense vegetation.

'Listen,' whispered Anamaya again, looking intently upstream.

Curi Ocllo, Manco's young and very beautiful wife, had been cavorting in the fast-flowing water not far from Anamaya. She regained her footing on the river's pebbly bed and stood stock-still. Her body was more thickset than Anamaya's, but perfectly proportioned. She squinted, put her hands over the brown areolae of her breasts, turned towards the valley, and then shook her head with incomprehension.

'What do you want me to listen to?'

Anamaya waved to her to be quiet. She stared intently at the highest foliage hanging over the river in which they were bathing. She saw branches bend and long, hanging strands of leaves shiver as though from a gust of wind. But she realized that it was only a group of impish monkeys made playful by the coolness of dusk.

And in fact, the jungle was echoing with noises, but only the ordinary, reassuring kind that always preceded dusk in the forests of the tropics. Weaver orioles gave their typical gurgling cry in short bursts, and their song rose above the ceaseless patter of the blue-white waterfall whose mist-cloud penetrated the green depths of the jungle. A flight of small green parrots flew over the river, emitting ruffled squawks, much to the annoyance of a dozen local red and blue macaws. For a moment they gave a furious cackle, calling from their nests hidden in a crevice in the cliff. But then things settled down again, the murmur of the water underlying the other ordinary sounds.

'I'm listening. But I hear nothing unusual,' said Curi Ocllo.

She slid back down up to her neck in the cool water as Anamaya, still tense, ran her gaze over the river banks where a group of turtles lay basking on fallen logs.

'It was only a bunch of parrots, that's all,' said Curi Ocllo, smoothing down her thick hair.

'No,' said Anamaya. 'I'm sure I heard something.'

Anamaya let herself slip back into the water and watched Curi Ocllo's round, finely featured face as she approached. Anamaya felt the young woman's hands rest tenderly on her shoulders.

'Well, then, what you heard was audible only to a *Coya Camaquen*. Something that doesn't reach the ears of an ordinary woman like myself.'

'Maybe.'

'Not "maybe"' – absolutely!' declared Curi Ocllo, vexed. 'Everyone knows that you and the Master of Stone can accomplish marvels!'

She waved away a cloud of tiny white butterflies. Then she floated gracefully on her back over to the low muddy bank. With her eyes closed, she surrendered her splendid naked body to the current's caress.

Anamaya smiled. She was about to answer when suddenly her expression changed once again and she looked up, her eyes searching, her ears listening intently.

She felt a kind of breath or murmur come down the river and envelop her. It was nothing tangible, just an inexplicable sensation. It could simply have been a cool gust, the barely audible whisper of the wind sighing through the dense jungle. But she couldn't stop herself from thinking, from hoping, that it was something else. She sensed a presence. Was it the puma's breath?

Gabriel!

For a few seconds, Anamaya's whole being was filled with a sense of him. A shudder passed through her belly, and she held her arms across her breasts, her nipples hard. She strained to hear as clearly as possible. The invisible murmur enveloped her again. She thought she felt Gabriel's hands and breath on her quivering skin. She was so overcome with emotion that she closed her eyes involuntarily.

She whispered his name without realizing it.

And then the spell lifted as abruptly as it had fallen upon her. Its coolness evaporated into the jungle's warm air in an instant, like a reflection flashing across a mirror.

Anamaya relaxed and opened her eyes. Everything was as it had been before. The sky had grown more red and the shadow between the foliage-covered cliffs had grown deeper. The monkeys were welcoming the coming night with excited hooting cries, the parrots were shrieking at the macaws to keep them away, and little clouds of butterflies were gracefully rising up in the mist of the waterfall.

'What did you feel?' asked Curi Ocllo nervously, now curled up on herself in the water.

Anamaya laughed softly, bringing herself back to reality. Manco's young wife, her eyes dark and warm, looked at the *Coya Camaquen* with a mixture of curiosity of fear.

'You *did* see something!' she exclaimed. 'You were so strange just now, so absent . . .'

With an embarrassed laugh, Anamaya slid deeper into the water. She felt an unreasonable fear that Curi Ocllo could see on her skin the mark of Gabriel's mysterious caress that had been sent to her by the Ancestors of the Other World, and she hid her nakedness.

She scooped up water from the river eddying around her and splashed it over her shoulders and the back of her neck.

'It's difficult to explain.'

'You mean that it's forbidden to talk about it.'

'No, it's not forbidden. Just difficult to explain and difficult to understand.'

Curi Ocllo pursed her beautiful, still childlike lips in a sulky pout. She tilted her head back so that her thick hair streamed in the current like some dark seaweed, and her round breasts rose from the river's surface like two golden water stones.

'We should go back now,' said Anamaya.

Curi Ocllo uttered a little laugh, both teasing and jealous, and her belly shuddered.

'I know what you don't want to tell me, *Coya Camaquen*. You thought of the Stranger you love, didn't you, the one that you call the Puma?'

Anamaya hesitated for a moment, then smiled and admitted:

'I didn't *think* of him. I felt him.'

'You *felt* him? Felt him as though you were in his arms?' exclaimed Curi Ocllo, standing upright now, wide-eyed.

Anamaya only laughed and nodded. She took the young woman's hand in hers and led her to the river bank where their clothes hung from the low branches of a ficus tree.

'Does he often come to you like that?' asked Curi Ocllo.

Anamaya waited until she was out of the water before replying. Her voice was slightly muted, as though the confidence that she was about to impart was more of a confession.

'He doesn't really come to me. But his presence surrounds me. He's searching for me, thinking of me.'

'I don't understand.'

'I told you that it was difficult to explain. Wherever he is, he remembers me; he wants to be close to me. So he tries to pass through the Other World to reach me.'

'How is that possible?'

'It's possible because he's the Puma . . . and no doubt he has priests and priestesses helping him!'

Anamaya laughed at her own words. Curi Ocllo finished dressing and glanced at her, both suspicious and confused.

'I'm not making fun of you, Curi Ocllo,' continued Anamaya quietly. 'There's much more to the world than what's visible. The Powerful Ancestors are watching over us. We must trust them.'

'Yes, yes, I know. You all say that – you, the priests, the Master of Stone. But it seems to me that the Powerful Ancestors don't watch over everyone equally. Maybe they've even turned away from Manco and me . . . and almost all Incas!'

The young woman's voice quivered with anger, and she began crying. Suddenly she dashed toward the path that had been cut through the jungle, as though she was about to flee.

'Curi Ocllo!'

She halted. 'How long have you been apart from the Stranger, Anamaya?' asked Curi Ocllo in a hard voice, her back still turned to Anamaya.

'Twenty-eight moons.'

'And during those twenty-eight moons, you've never known where the one you call the Puma has been?'

'No, I haven't.'

'And yet, despite all the time that's passed, he's never forgotten you nor you him. In spite of all that time, you still feel close to him and he to you.'

'Maybe.'

'Not maybe. Certainly! I'm sure that you see him in your dreams, and that you even lie with him in your sleep! Twenty-eight moons! I'm sure you're right: the Powerful Ancestors are protecting you both and don't want you to be apart. You and a . . . a Stranger!'

Curi Ocllo turned on her heels and stood defiantly, facing Anamaya.

'And why? Will you tell me why, *Coya Camaquen*?' she shouted, and for a few moments the jungle's din ceased.

'I don't understand your question, Curi Ocllo,' replied Anamaya gently.

Pain and despair racked the young queen's beautiful face.

'I've only been apart from Manco for four moons,' she sobbed, 'and yet I sleep without dreams, and when I swim, I swim alone.

Wherever I go, my beloved husband is absent. The Powerful
Ancestors wrap me only in cold solitude. They ignore me, *Coya
Camaquen*, and I think that they don't even support Manco
anymore.'

'Manco is doing what he must do,' said Anamaya quietly. Her
heart sank – she understood only too well the truths that were
overwhelming Curi Ocllo. 'He loves you,' she continued. 'He loves
you more than he loves any of his other wives.'

'He loves me, but I cannot reach him. My bed is empty. He
loves me but I don't feel his hands or his lips on my skin. He loves
me, but my tomorrow will be as cold and frozen as a winter's day
atop the highest mountain.'

'He's fighting a war, Curi Ocllo. Manco's fighting the Strangers.
He's fighting a terrible war.'

Tears streaming down her cheeks, Curi Ocllo shook her head.

'No, Anamaya, and you know it better than me: Manco's not
fighting a war – he's *losing* one.'

'Curi Ocllo!'

'Who can deny it? Emperor Manco, my husband, is alone, and
his strength is diminishing. His brother Paullu has joined the
Strangers. Sage Villa Oma is waging his own war on the side.
You and the Master of Stone, you're both here in Vilcabamba,
hidden in this newly built jungle city, and you're both always
dealing with the Powerful Ancestors, and are far from Manco, far
from my beloved. And I'm here too – even I am not at his side!'

'Curi Ocllo,' murmured Anamaya, taking the young woman in
her arms. But she couldn't deny what the queen was saying.

'He's so alone! The Strangers have captured his son Titu Cusi,
the one he loves most! He's surrounded by traitors! They even
took the mummies of the Powerful Ancestors from Cuzco . . .'

Anamaya was deeply saddened. She couldn't think of anything
to say to soften the impact of these terrible realities. She simply
stroked the young woman's tear-wet cheeks and murmured:

'Don't think that I'm abandoning Emperor Manco, Curi Ocllo.
I've always been close to him; he's always been like a brother to
me. Nothing that we're doing here in Vilcabamba is against him.
Quite the opposite: the Master of Stone has built a city where

your beloved Manco will one day be able to live, and to live as a Son of the Sun should.'

Curi Ocllo shivered and broke away from Anamaya's embrace. Recovering her pride, she wiped away her tears. But then she grimaced with pain once again. Like a lost child, she cried:

'Oh, Anamaya, I'm so frightened of what tomorrow might bring!'

The sun had almost set by the time Anamaya and Curi Ocllo reached Vilcabamba's outer walls. The newest Inca city had been built to the precise plans of Katari, the Master of Stone, and it induced a mysterious sense of serenity.

Its terraces and *canchas* were meticulously arranged around the great ceremonial square in front of the Temple of the Sun, a long building with ten doors. The walls of the rooms were coated with ocher roughcast that glowed gold in the failing light. Like a jewel, the Temple captured the setting sun's rays even as the nearby river and agricultural terraces disappeared into night's shadows.

And night had already descended upon the lower slopes of the mountains to the north and upon the sinuous valleys of the Pampakona to the east, valleys covered in forests of cedars and giant *caboas* from which rose ribbons of fog.

The two young women heard the faint cries of birds, and slowed their pace through the wet grass. They kept their gazes fixed on the peaks still aglow on the southern cordillera. And then the light abruptly disappeared, leaving the firs and glaciers and the two women in darkness.

They heard frogs croak loudly from nearby, and then fall silent just as suddenly. Curi Ocllo jumped and grabbed Anamaya's arm. Wordlessly, she pointed toward a thick clump of bushes beside a wall. The broad leaves moved unnaturally, and a young puma emerged. Its coat, still light in color, gleamed in the darkness.

It moved toward them sinuously, moving lightly on its powerful paws.

Anamaya involuntarily held her breath. She heard Curi Ocllo give a little cry of fear.

The puma was so close now that they could make out the white rims of its eyes and the pale edging around its ears.

It stopped two paces from Anamaya and looked into her eyes. It opened its jaws slightly and let out a long, soft growl.

And then it turned and bounded away into the bushes.

Anamaya and Curi Ocllo stood absolutely still for a moment, petrified, listening to the soft padding step of the feline creature as it headed away into the jungle.

When Curi Ocllo, her bosom heaving as she gasped out the breath she had been holding in fear, turned toward Anamaya, she saw the happiness on her friend's face.

'You were right,' the young Inca queen whispered. 'He *was* there. He stayed close to you.'

CHAPTER 21

Lake Titicaca, Copacabana, April 1539

'LORD GABRIEL!'

The child standing in the doorway was no more than twelve years old. Yet the severe expression on his face aged him by a few years.

'Leave me be, child!' growled Gabriel. 'Let me sleep or else I'll slice you into pieces and feed you to the pumas.'

'Lord Gabriel, you mustn't sleep anymore,' replied the child, utterly unimpressed.

Gabriel sighed and opened his eyes.

'By all the saints! It seems that my slumber does indeed displease you, Chillioc. Why do you wake me, boy, when it is not yet day?'

'Someone's coming, Lord Gabriel, someone's coming to see you.'

'Indeed?'

Gabriel now focused his attention on the child, who was still standing at the threshold. He could hear the noise of the women out in the courtyard preparing the morning meal.

He sat up in his hammock, careful not to set it swinging, and asked the boy:

'Who is it? And how do you know?'

'The *chaski* said, "A Stranger is coming on a horse. He is old and tired. He is already past Copacabana and is coming from Cusijata!"'

The child shrugged, then added:

'If a Stranger's coming all the way here, then it must be to see you.'

Gabriel couldn't help but smile. He got up, the hammock swinging gently behind him.

'Fetch me my tunic, Chillioc,' he ordered. 'An old and tired Stranger, you say? Does he have white hairs on his face?'

'I don't think so. The *chaski* only said that you couldn't see his face because it was entirely covered by cloth. And also that he wasn't far away and that he would reach your *cancha* before his shadow had shortened even by a hand.'

Gabriel finished dressing and looked at the boy, intrigued. When he came out into the long courtyard, the servants, busy around the hearth set under the sloping roof, greeted him with smiles and invited him to eat. He declined and grabbed the child by his neck, drawing him near.

'Well now, Chillioc, I'm going to have to thank you for waking me. Come and meet the Stranger with me.'

What Gabriel and Chillioc saw first looked so strange that it took even Gabriel a few moments to realize that it was a horse and rider. The approaching figure looked more like a pile of blankets, both Spanish and Indian, moving of its own accord along the terraces overlooking the lake.

'Whoever he is, he doesn't seem to be in the best of health,' said Gabriel to the child hurrying behind him.

When the strange rider was no more than thirty or forty cobos from them, he stopped. The man hidden beneath the pile of *mantas* looked as though he was about to fall from his saddle.

'Hola!' cried Gabriel, approaching him quickly now, 'Hola, *compañero*! Who are you?'

But no reply came from the pile of blankets. Gabriel, suddenly cautious, slowed down and urged Chillioc back.

'Stay here, child. Don't come any closer. The rogue might have a crossbow hidden under his rags.'

The boy obeyed reluctantly and gave Gabriel a reproachful look.

Gabriel looked at the man and horse for a moment. Both were so utterly still now that they might have been dead. But he could make out no sign of a weapon. In fact, not even a glimpse of the rider himself was visible beneath the blankets. Gabriel, worried, wondered whether the exhausted hack had been carrying a corpse all these leagues.

'Hola! Hola, *compañero!*' he shouted again, louder now.

His cries startled the horse so that it shied back a few paces and turned slightly. Only then did Gabriel notice the long monk's robe hanging over the rider's boots, their heels worn through, and a hand clenching the reins – an instantly recognizable hand, the ring and middle fingers joined together.

'By God! Brother Bartholomew! Chillioc! Quick, Chillioc, come and help me!'

Gabriel approached the horse, reassuring it with soothing words. As he stroked its cheek with one hand, he took its bit firmly in the other.

'Come closer, Chillioc. Don't be frightened.'

'I'm not frightened, Lord Gabriel.'

'Good. Come and take a hold of this strap. Stand still, don't yank on it.'

As the boy held the animal still, Gabriel pulled off the blankets. What he found horrified him. Bartholomew sat slumped over the saddle; he had either fallen asleep or was unconscious. His cowl was torn to shreds, and his face was barely visible through swathes of old bandages, brown with coagulated blood.

'In the name of God,' growled Gabriel, grabbing Bartholomew's hand. 'Brother Bartholomew! Brother Bartholomew, wake up!'

But the monk's eyes didn't flicker. The hand that Gabriel held between his own was so thin that it seemed devoid of flesh. Gabriel considered for a moment. Then he let go of Bartholomew and turned to the boy.

'Come here, Chillioc.'

He took hold of the boy around the waist and lifted him up onto the horse's rump, just behind the saddle.

'Hold on to my friend and make sure he doesn't fall,' he explained, guiding Chillioc's hands to the pommel. 'There, hold

onto that. And hold on tight. I'm going to lead you to the
cancha.'

Gabriel looked at the child: Chillioc was grimacing with dis-
gust, his face pressed against the foul-smelling blankets. Gabriel
smiled wanly.

'Don't worry, boy. He stinks – but then, all Strangers stink when
they first arrive at Titicaca!'

It was only long after the women had carefully cleaned his main
wound that Bartholomew came to. His eyes, set deep in their
sockets, swiveled as they searched his surroundings. Eventually
he emitted a hoarse sound from between his chapped lips.

'Gabriel?'

'I'm right here, my friend.'

Gabriel waved the women away and held Bartholomew's emaciated hand. They smiled thinly at one another, and Gabriel sensed
his friend's relief as the monk's breathing grew more regular.

He had never seen Bartholomew naked before, but what he
had seen while helping the women cut away his rags had, quite
simply, shocked him. The priest was so thin that the skin on his
ribs and hips was stretched to splitting point. His legs and arms
were covered with bruises and unhealed wounds.

They had carefully unwrapped his old, begrimed bandages to
reveal his face. They had found a long gash from his temple
to his left cheek, cutting through his flesh and grey-speckled
beard. The suppurating, infected wound had smelled awful,
was poorly cicatrized, and had a few translucent worms wriggling beneath its crust. The servant girls had screamed at the
sight of it.

Now it had been thoroughly cleaned, treated with ash and the
acidic sap of a jungle root, and covered with a green plaster, which
gave the monk the appearance of having two faces.

'I don't know what happened, old friend,' murmured Gabriel
affectionately, 'but they did their worst to you.'

'I made it! Thanks be to God, I'm here with you; that's all that
matters.'

Bartholomew smiled briefly and shut his exhausted eyes before adding:

'I thought that I'd never make it. But God knows when to intervene . . .'

'Perhaps next time he could intervene less violently,' quipped Gabriel, picking up a bowl. 'Here, a little *quinua* broth. You must eat. Your stomach is as thin as a feather in the wind.'

But Bartholomew swallowed only four spoonfuls before pushing Gabriel's hand away.

'I've been traveling for eleven days to reach you. We were coming back from the south, where the Pizarros crushed the insurrection of Manco's general, Tisoc. He was taken prisoner, and . . . oh, it's unspeakable! Such horror, Gabriel, such horror day after day!'

He spoke in a dry, halting voice. Gabriel knew that Bartholomew needed to talk. And he knew only too well what kind of images were haunting the monk. Had he not been haunted by the same ones for months and months?

'Children, women, the old!' said Bartholomew hoarsely. 'Massacres and tortures, day after day. And when Tisoc was taken, his troops defeated, Gonzalo ordered an even more horrendous atrocity. He had deep ditches dug and lined with sharpened spikes, and he threw men into them, and women too, after raping them. He set houses full of people alight, burning them alive! Oh, Gabriel . . .'

'I know, Bartholomew, I know. I saw all that when I went south with de Almagro a few years ago. I've never forgotten it. It cannot be forgotten.'

Bartholomew clenched his bony fingers around Gabriel's tunic and clung to him as though frightened of surrendering to the horrors plaguing his memory.

'I remembered your words, Gabriel: "I didn't add to the suffering, but I didn't prevent it either, which is the same thing." I understood what you meant, and like you my inaction filled me with shame. Oh, Lord, I think I even insulted you when you tried to open my eyes to the horror . . .'

'Bartholomew—'

'No, let me finish. My throat is infected from the air that I breathed there, my nose is still full of the stench of children burned alive. If I sleep, I see them . . . Oh Christ! Christ! The flames that consumed them burn within me, they're scorching me . . .'

Gently, Gabriel and the servant girls wiped Bartholomew's forehead and torso down with clean and fresh sponges. But nothing could stop the monk raving:

'I found them chained together. All women, not one older than twenty. But I was caught. The beasts, the beasts! Being a servant of God saved me from nothing. No doubt the Lord wanted to infuse the suffering of all His children into my flesh. Jesus did it! Yes, He wanted to mark me, Gabriel! Because they are His children too. Everyone must realize that the Indians are also God's children . . .'

'Easy, Bartholomew, easy . . .'

'. . . But at least the women got away before the sinners beat me and called for my head. I succeeded, Gabriel! A few, at least, managed to escape. Too few. Only twenty children. There are so many more, Gabriel, so many more!'

Bartholomew was almost delirious, his voice by now a high-pitched screech. Gabriel placed his hand on his friend's forehead to quieten him.

'Be still, my friend. I'm here. You're being taken care of.'

'I fled. I traveled only by night, so that they wouldn't follow me. Beasts. They are beasts from hell . . .'

'We're going to give you a potion, Bartholomew, you're going to sleep.'

'No, no, I have to tell you everything!'

'We'll have time for that tomorrow. You must rest now.'

'I've come to ask something of you, Gabriel, something important. Only you can—'

But Gabriel signaled to the women, who had in any case already understood what they had to do from the feverish pitch of Bartholomew's voice. They lifted the priest by the shoulders and gently lifted him up. They passed a little brazier of burning herbs under his nose. Almost immediately, he slumped back, docile, and they poured a liquid down his throat. He was asleep within moments.

It was only two days later, in the evening, that Bartholomew at last recovered his spirits and was able to eat a proper meal.

Gabriel had had his friend's bed set up in one of the rooms giving onto the lake shore. Women had watched over him day and night through his coma, administering potions to him until his fever began to subside. And as soon as the monk opened his eyes, Gabriel had fruit and coca-leaf tea brought to him, making sure that his first meals were easy ones. Bartholomew was so hungry that his fingers trembled as he devoured everything that was given to him.

'I owe you my life, Gabriel,' he declared in a raspy voice, breaking a long, slightly awkward silence and wiping his mouth.

'In that case, we're even. I would have been roasted alive in that Cuzco prison long ago if it hadn't been for you.'

'I suppose I said a lot of cretinous things during my delirium?'

'Unfortunately not. You spoke only the truth. But forget about all that: I am delighted that you're here with me, and relieved to see you eating with such appetite.'

'These fruits are one of God's wonders,' murmured Bartholomew, nodding, 'as though they were plucked from the Garden itself.'

The women had carefully wrapped a bandage around the monk's head, and now he yanked it aside unthinkingly so that he could get at the juicy mangoes and guavas better. The fruit seemed to bring life back to his emaciated face. As he ate, Bartholomew let his gaze wander over the deep blue of the lake.

At that late hour of the day, the mountain peaks were linked together by an unbroken layer of thick clouds. The reflections of the vertiginous slopes had become indistinct in Titicaca's surface, the colour of which had grown darker and more opaque.

'I'm beginning to understand why you came here,' said Bartholomew, smiling thinly. 'You were right when you told me that it was hard to imagine a more beautiful or peaceful place.'

He fell silent for a moment, a pained and serious expression on his face, before continuing:

'After having seen what I saw these past few months, it's now as though God has at last granted me some rest. Perhaps He wants to show me that there is still peace and harmony somewhere at least in our troubled world.'

Gabriel glanced at him, astonished. The thick bandage distorting the left side of the monk's face and wrapped around his skull only accentuated his weariness. Gabriel smiled wanly and nodded.

'I was in no better condition than you are now when I discovered this earthly paradise, Bartholomew. And I thought much the same thing myself, although without any consideration of God. And indeed, it seems to me that Titicaca is in fact meant to be our refuge from a world turned too inhuman—'

'Inhuman!' spat Bartholomew bitterly. 'Inhuman is the right word! I'm saddened to admit, Gabriel, that you were far wiser than I. How right you were to leave us and stay away from the Pizarros after that horrific battle that destroyed Cuzco. May the Lord forgive me: you tried to warn me, but I didn't want to hear. It's only now that I understand what you said to me when I came to you in your cell and the Incas were about to destroy us: "For the peoples of this country, there are no longer any good Strangers or bad Strangers. In their eyes, we all deserve to be annihilated. This is what Hernando's diplomacy has brought upon us; this is what giving free rein to de Almagro and hell-hounds like Gonzalo has caused." You were so right, so right. And now three years have passed, and all that has happened is that things have become – and are still becoming – far worse.'

Bartholomew's chest shuddered with emotion. He fell silent for a moment and closed his eyes. Then he asked in a barely audible murmur:

'Gabriel, how can God allow such a thing? When will He end His chastisement? Dear friend . . . sometimes I wish that I was the one through whom He will administer His punishment to those monsters!'

Gabriel saw the tears welling up in his friend's eyes, and his sense of propriety urged him to look away. They were united in a brief silence, contemplating the lake. Outside on the shore, children's cries and adult voices accompanied the departure of a vessel leaving for the islands.

Gabriel took up a sliced mango and stared at its flesh as though its sweet flavor concealed some obscure, unidentifiable poison.

'This country is like this fruit. It only wants to present us with its richest flavors. Here, on Titicaca's shore, I sometimes feel that I am at the threshold of a wondrous, open world, one that is expecting us, even offering itself to us, but one that we obstinately refuse to see. I feel that peace would enrich each Spaniard more than cartloads of stolen gold.'

'Oh, peace!' exclaimed Bartholomew sarcastically. 'For my part, I don't ask so much. I would be satisfied if Don Francisco and his brothers conducted themselves with a little restraint instead of endlessly exacerbating the suffering. As though the war with the Incas wasn't enough, there's now a civil war raging among the Spaniards!'

'I knew that one-eyed de Almagro had been condemned by Hernando.'

'The truth is that Don Diego de Almagro was murdered. He made a fatal mistake. After the siege was lifted, when the Governor's brothers were greatly weakened, he took the city under his control and imprisoned Hernando and Gonzalo. I can assure you that I tried to dissuade him, not because I wanted to help Hernando but because I knew that de Almagro's coup would be a disaster. But alas, what is the word of a man of the cloth worth to an obstinate old man convinced that he has been the Pizarros' dupe for years? Not a night passed when de Almagro didn't have nightmares about Atahualpa's ransom, about all that gold portioned out at Cajamarca, gold that the Governor had not allowed him to share in. His hatred and lust for vengeance blinded him to reason. To take Cuzco for himself was one thing, but to throw the Pizarro brothers into jail – well, that's just like picking up a scorpion by the tail. They got rid of him as soon as they could, and when they did so they showed about as much emotion as if they were slaughtering a chicken.'

Gabriel shook his head.

'I've too many bad memories of de Almagro to grieve for him. And I see that Hernando and Gonzalo haven't changed their ways at all.'

'They're mad! All of them are utterly mad! Their side immediately took the lust for vengeance that had been de Almagro's as their own, as though it had been a ball stolen from the other team! And, indeed, two sides *were* formed: those supporting the Pizarros and those thinking only of making their own fortunes. And all anyone thinks about is annihilating the other side.'

Gabriel couldn't help but laugh sardonically. Bartholomew looked at him reproachfully and prodded at his bandage as though beneath it was all the suffering of Peru.

'The truth, Gabriel,' he sighed, 'is that soon we, the Spaniards, are going to destroy ourselves. And we're going to do it far more effectively than the Incas ever could. May God Almighty forgive us. Unless He has decided that it's time to punish every man who has contributed to the horror here in the New World.'

Bartholomew spat out these last words vehemently. Gabriel said nothing for the moment, simply staring at the blue of the lake. Then he asked:

'Does that mean that the war against Manco is winding down?'

'Manco is losing the war. During his brief dominance, de Almagro confused the Incas by naming Paullu, Manco's brother, as Sapa Inca. Many Indians rallied to Paullu. Now Manco is alone, and his position is weak. He lost a series of battles, and he retreated further and further into the forest, as though its trees were his only defence. Furthermore, he suffered two terrible blows . . .'

Bartholomew hesitated for a moment, even though Gabriel was giving him his full attention.

'. . . His son was captured: A young boy named Titu Cusi . . .'

'Titu Cusi!' murmured Gabriel. He remembered the look on the face of the child playing in Ollantaytambo. He remembered the boy asking him, 'Are all Strangers like you?'

'Also, Inca Paullu took all the mummies of Manco's clan with him to Cuzco. No doubt you know better than I do what effect that had on Manco.'

'For the Incas, whether lords or peasants, if the mummies are with one Noble Lord rather than another, it means that the one who has them has the Ancestors' support,' grumbled Gabriel, frowning. It was a very important factor.

Bartholomew closed his eyes and squeezed the juice of a blackish-brown prune between his cracked lips. Immediately, his expression became almost one of relaxed well-being.

'Paullu is an odd character. I'm not sure whether we should admire the wisdom of his pragmatism or be heartbroken at his cowardice. But in any case, he always seems to be on the side of the strong: first de Almagro, now the Pizarros. And no matter who he's allied himself to, he never hesitates to make war against his brother Manco. He never reveals what he's thinking. He was with us during that horrific expedition to the south. He didn't once try to stop the massacre of his own people, nor did he take issue with the capture of Tisoc, Manco's general leading the rebellion.'

'So,' murmured Gabriel, 'Manco's alone.'

Bartholomew stared at him intently, an unvoiced question apparent in his look. But he decided not to ask it and said merely:

'I heard it said that he's founded a new Inca city, very far to the north of Cuzco. Apparently it's in the jungle rather than in the mountains, and is utterly inaccessible to us. But, to tell you the truth, after what I've seen these last few months I think that his reign and his rebellion will soon be nothing more than a memory.'

A heavy silence fell between them. Bartholomew broke it first, asking hesitantly:

'Is my impression that you've had no news of Anamaya correct?'

Gabriel shook his head and attempted a thin smile.

'It's been almost thirty months since I last saw her. I don't even know if she's still alive, if she's still in this world.'

Another silence; then Gabriel continued, with feigned lack of concern:

'But it's not surprising: we had agreed upon it. I accepted it for a long time. I told myself that our separation wouldn't last for ever, that the war would soon be over, or that Anamaya would come to me because she wanted to. And then the truth became clear to me. Much time has passed, and I'm beginning to forget what her face looks like. It's unbearable, and yet I have to accept it. If I try to find her, I'd be endangering her. She still can't leave her people, not the way things are. Even less can she come to me.'

'The way things are?' asked Bartholomew in a low voice. 'Are you referring to that gold statue that she calls her husband?'

'Certainly – the Sacred Double,' said Gabriel, smiling. 'You know, Bartholomew, despite all your efforts to respect the Incas, I doubt that you understand what it means to them.'

'What does it matter whether I understand?' answered Bartholomew, somewhat ill-temperedly. 'What matters is that Gonzalo and Hernando still covet that . . . that object. The mere idea of all that gold drives them mad.'

'Their madness to the Devil! They'll never have it.'

Gabriel spoke with such serene confidence that Bartholomew looked at him closely once again, as though he was hearing a new, unfamiliar voice speaking from his old friend's mouth.

'You seem very sure of that. You know as well as I do that to find it they're capable of leaving no stone unturned in the whole of Peru.'

'They'll find nothing under every stone they turn,' said Gabriel, still smiling. 'We Spaniards can heap suffering on the peoples of this land. We can kill them and rob them. But look at that lake, Brother Bartholomew. Look at those mountains . . .'

Gabriel waved toward the slopes that, in the play of the light, seemed to dissolve into the pale blue sky at their peaks just as their bases melted into Titicaca's cerulean depths.

'It is indeed very fine,' said Bartholomew. 'And yet—'

'No,' interrupted Gabriel. 'It's not about beauty. All of what you see lives. Mountains, stones, water . . . everything here exists in a world parallel to our own, just *like* our own, and yet you and I don't know how to see it.'

'What do you mean?'

'I mean that the Incas can see the invisible. More than that, they know how to sense its breath and receive its support. They can sense life wherever it is, and however it manifests itself. It's true that they're no stronger than chickens under the sword's iron blade; and, indeed, one day they may well be exterminated like chickens. But the essence of the land will remain: it will live on. Nothing will prevent the Incas from taking away their knowledge of the world that exists in the mountains, the stones, and this very lake – a world that we can neither see nor hear. There are forces at work here far more powerful than anything that any Pizarro can hope to command.'

This time Gabriel spoke with passion. Bartholomew had a sad and gloomy look in his eyes.

'Well, that's not a very Christian way of seeing the world. Gabriel, I've heard that since you've been here, you've been participating in the Indians' pagan ceremonies.'

For a brief second, it looked as though Gabriel was going to lose his temper. But instead he laughed ironically and shook his head.

'It doesn't matter what people say about my life here. It suits me perfectly.'

'Are you sure about that?'

'Are you starting an inquisition?'

'I'm a man of God, Gabriel, and I'm your friend. But don't imagine for a minute that I am willing to accept that you abandon and even, maybe, scorn the work of Christ, and the hope that it brings to each one of us!'

'I will abandon my respect neither for mankind nor for life itself. That should be comfort enough for you.'

Bartholomew scrutinized Gabriel. Tension racked his emaciated face. Then, as though overcome by exhaustion, he nodded.

'No doubt you're right. But it's a strange thing to admit.'

Gabriel put his hand on his friend's arm.

'I am at peace with myself, Brother Bartholomew. My soul is at peace.'

The monk shuddered feverishly. His lips began trembling violently. He shut his eyes and murmured:

'I don't doubt that your soul is at peace, dear Gabriel. But, alas, mine is not. Far from it. I am exhausted, and I think I'll sleep a little now. But will you do me a favor? While I sleep, open those leather saddlebags. In them, you'll find some pages I wrote. For the love of God, please read them.'

'I won't do it for the love of God, Brother Bartholomew. But for your friendship, certainly I will.'

Bartholomew didn't emerge from his deep, deep sleep until nightfall. He opened his eyes and saw Gabriel sitting beside a brazier a few paces away. He was contemplating the lake and the mountains that were already veiled in darkness. On his knees he had a large leather case containing a bundle of sheets of paper covered in neat, compact handwriting.

'Gabriel . . .'

Gabriel turned around and smiled. And yet, it seemed as though some of the shadows that he had been contemplating had remained in his eyes. Bartholomew pointed at the leather case and said:

'Did you read it?'

'I read it. There are so many horrors and injustices chronicled in these pages that the world it depicts could be Hell itself.'

'And yet – and I can swear it to God – I have written only about those events at which I was personally present. I have written down everything that I have seen since setting foot here in Peru, omitting nothing. I have listed every injustice and humiliation inflicted on the Indians, every violation of the laws of God, of Rome, and of our own country. Everything!'

Gabriel looked down at the leather case, perplexed. Then he placed it at Bartholomew's side.

'Yes, everything. But you are reckless, dear Bartholomew. Should the Pizarro brothers or their friends find these papers, you're a dead man.'

'That's precisely why I traveled only by night to get here,' sighed Bartholomew.

Gabriel smiled, but his tone was serious when he said:

'I'm afraid that it won't be enough. Burn these pages, Bartholomew. Burn them now – in this brazier, right here. Or at least hide them somewhere very secure. They're no use to you now in any case: who wants to read such depressing prose!'

Bartholomew sat up and uttered an enraged yelp. He crawled from his bed and grabbed the leather case, waving it over his head as he cried:

'Burn them? Hide these truths from our King Charles who must be made aware of them? Spain must know what is happening here! Rome too will be horrified when the pope reads these pages!'

Gabriel shook his head, smiling sardonically.

'Your fever has made you delirious, friend. Have you forgotten the gold? Do you really think that anyone across the ocean cares how it's obtained? Do you imagine that any king or pope will cease covering their palaces in gold merely because the savages here are being ill-treated? Come now, Bartholomew! You know very well that Don Francisco and his brothers can continue playing the tyrant so long as they continue sending treasure back to Europe!'

'You are mistaken! You are utterly mistaken, Gabriel!'

Bartholomew stood up unsteadily. His indignant cries were so impassioned that two servant girls and Chillioc, who was carrying a torch, came rushing in. Gabriel nodded to them to calm them down while Bartholomew, beside himself, grabbed hold of Gabriel's hands and continued to shout:

'No! No! I will not have you say such things! Not you, Gabriel! There *are* good men in Spain, there *are* men of good will in Rome! There are good men at Court and in the Church! There are men who believe that the Indians are children of God just as we are!'

'Perhaps. But, alas, they are over there – not here.'

'That's why they must be told!'

'And even if they knew . . .'

Beneath his bandages, Bartholomew looked demented. He blinked constantly, apparently involuntarily, and a thick vein pulsed visibly in his neck. He held himself as taut as a bow, and Gabriel was concerned that he was going to faint at any moment.

But instead, the monk put his hands on Gabriel's shoulders and spoke intently:

'Listen to me, Gabriel. There is someone in Spain, a man of the Church, who is trying to ensure that all the people living here in these mountains are treated with respect, that they're allowed to live with dignity. This man is a Dominican called Las Casas. He is the kind of educated man that you and I like and admire. He has read Erasmus—'

'One man, Brother Bartholomew! He's but one man alone, like you, like me. And he is so far from these mountains . . .'

'No, he's not as alone as you think. His influence is far-reaching. He has the ears of some important people. He has already managed to have Pope Paul III issue a papal bull declaring that all the Indians on earth be treated as humans . . .'

When he saw Gabriel's sardonic smile, Bartholomew, grimacing with the effort it cost him, drew himself up to his full height, standing erect and shaking with rage. With his skeletal hand, he pointed at Gabriel's servants standing at the back of the room, wide-eyed with incomprehension, and declaimed:

'*We consider that the Indians are truly men and that they are capable of understanding the Catholic Faith. We declare that, notwithstanding whatever may already have been said or may be said in future to the contrary, the said Indians are by no means to be deprived of their liberty or the possession of their property, even though they be outside the faith of Jesus Christ; and that they may and should, freely and legitimately, enjoy their liberty and the possession of their property; nor should they be in any way enslaved; and we declare that the said Indians and other peoples should be converted to the faith of Jesus Christ by the preaching of the word of God and by the example of good and holy living.*'

Short of breath, his bandaged head nodding slightly, Bartholomew finished his declamation and grabbed young Chillioc, pushing him in front of Gabriel.

'Such are the words and the will of the Holy Father! I swear, on this child's head, that it is true. I swear it solemnly to Almighty God that the Sacred Office wants what we want!'

Gabriel reached out and stroked Chillioc's terrified face.

'Don't be scared, Chillioc,' he said in Quechua. 'My friend is taken by fever. Help me put him back to bed.'

Bartholomew protested, but his exhaustion was stronger than his fury, and by now he could hardly stand. As the child and Gabriel urged him back to bed and pulled a blanket up over him, he asked in a broken voice:

'Do you believe me, Gabriel?'

'I believe you.'

'Then take these pages to Spain. Take them to Las Casas. He needs them.'

Gabriel froze, taken aback.

The torchlight played on their faces, distorting them. Bartholomew's bandages looked like a bizarre mask.

'Me?' Gabriel asked.

'Who else but you has the will and the courage to do it? See how this child looks at you, Gabriel,' insisted Bartholomew, taking Chillioc by the hands. 'If you take these pages to Spain, then he will have a future as an adult.'

Seeing Gabriel frown and turn away, the monk continued:

'What are you waiting for here? For Anamaya to come back to you? You know that it won't happen like that. You are alone. You're wasting your time here, contemplating the landscape of Titicaca while those you pretend to defend are being destroyed. Take these papers to Toledo, take the truth to where it will have the most effect. Who better than you to tell the King about this country? Help me, Gabriel. Not for the sake of God's cause – I know that you've rejected Him. But for the cause that you cannot forget, and that fills your heart with sadness.'

Gabriel stared unblinkingly at the monk for some time and said nothing. But Bartholomew saw the look in his friend's eyes, and he knew that his words had had their effect.

A milky dawn spread over Lake Titicaca. The morning fog dissolved into strands. In the gaps, the gray water of the lake could be seen, as well as the gray walls lining the terraces. At the bottom of the large bay facing the sacred islands of the Sun and Moon, a few plumes of smoke rose from the houses of Cusijata.

Gabriel stood halfway down a steep rocky hillock that jutted out into the lake and admired the enchanted place one last time. It was the only place where he had managed to find peace since that March day in 1532 when, after having almost perished in the South Sea, and accompanied by Sebastian, he had first stepped onto the beach at Tumbez, one of the first conquistadors to set foot on Inca land.

That had been seven years ago, almost to the day. Seven years of hope, of battles – sometimes of glory. Almost seven years of love. And yet, in those seven years, so little happiness, just a few fleeting moments stolen from the war and the tragedy.

Anamaya! Even just whispering the word to the gentle morning breeze made Gabriel's body tremble as though the entire surface of his skin was being tattooed with his beloved's magical name: *Anamaya!*

And now he was going to return to Spain an entirely different man from the one who had left it seven years before. He was going to go back to Spain without looking back, without even kissing Anamaya's lips one last time. He was going to leave and slowly forget the smell of her skin, the warmth of her thighs. His memories of her guiding him on voyages into the strangeness of the world were going to slip irretrievably away.

Gabriel couldn't believe that he could do it.

But the monk's words had harrowed his soul throughout the night. They had been reasonable and utterly persuasive words, despite Bartholomew's overexcited state. Gabriel had tried to turn a deaf ear to them as best he could, but to no avail. And then, suddenly, other words had come into his mind, words spoken by Anamaya. They were words that she had addressed to the 'Puma' and that had carried the incredible and bizarre message of a long-dead Inca emperor:

*You will see the Puma; he will bound here from across
    the ocean.
He will only come to you when he leaves you.
Although separated, you will be united as one,
And when everyone has left, you will remain, and the Puma
    will remain at your side.
Together, like your ancestors Manco Capac and Mama Occlo,
You will beget new life on earth.*

They were words that he had heard but had not understood, words
locked in his mind the way a mystery is held in a strongbox. But
now the meaning of the words became crystal clear to him: yes, he
had to leave. At last, he understood how he was going to get back
to Anamaya: not by diving into Lake Titicaca, but by crossing the
ocean, by going back to Spain, by surrendering to what appeared
to be a coincidence but that was in fact his destiny – a destiny
bestowed upon him unwittingly by Bartholomew. Bartholomew,
he realized, was the servant of the Inca Ancestors as much as he
was a servitor of Christ!

A sound of something moving in the bushes startled Gabriel
out of his thoughts. He turned around but saw nothing. Then
Chillioc emerged hesitantly from a clump of foliage. He seemed
reluctant even to look Gabriel in the eyes.

Gabriel smiled tenderly and held out his hand.

'Come here, Chillioc.'

The child placed his little hand in the Stranger's, and Gabriel
had him sit down at his side.

'You should be sleeping,' he reprimanded the boy affectionately.

'I couldn't. I saw that you were awake, and I followed you.'

Gabriel squeezed the boy's hand. They sat together in silence,
watching the fog's slow dance over the lake.

'Are you going away, Lord Gabriel?'

'What makes you ask?' said Gabriel, surprised.

'I saw it in your face when you were talking with the sick
Stranger.'

'Yes, I'm going away, Chillioc. You saw right. I'm going to
miss you.'

'Why do you want to leave? Aren't you happy here with us?'

'I am happy,' said Gabriel, smiling 'Very happy.'

'Well then?'

'Well, it's time that I leave and return to someone. And there's something I must do.'

The child looked at him, his eyes full of sadness and incomprehension.

'If you leave,' whispered Chillioc, 'the Strangers who hate us will come here. Everyone will be so frightened.'

'That's one of the reasons why I'm leaving,' said Gabriel, his voice tight with emotion. 'So that you'll never again be frightened of Strangers.'

'Do you think that's possible?' asked the child, wide-eyed.

'Perhaps. I don't know. But I do know that it's impossible to live without trying to make it so.'

CHAPTER 22

Vilcabamba, June 1539

'I LOVE BEING IN YOUR PRESENCE, SACRED DOUBLE,' WHISpered Anamaya. 'I've been your wife for ten years now, enough time for the four seasons to alternate the heat and the cold of our world ten times. Ten times has another year been added to the distance between now and the day of my birth. I was a child when Emperor Atahualpa ordered me to accompany you for ever, to become the *Coya Camaquen*. Now I'm a woman older than Emperor Manco's wives and concubines. And yet when I'm with you I feel as though time passes without touching us.'

Anamaya smiled tenderly. She was squatting on her heels at the gold statue's side. The Sacred Double had been set in front of the Great Temple of the Sun at Vilcabamba on a stela built by Katari. She spread the offerings at his feet, as she had done a thousand times before: honey, fruit, river fish and young corn. Then, adhering to strict ritual, she scattered coca leaves on the embers glowing in a painted bowl shaped like the serpent Amaru.

Oh beloved husband, she thought, bowing to the statue, *accept these offerings brought to you by your devoted* Coya Camaquen.

The bitter, dry smoke rising from the coca leaves plumed upwards, slowly twisting around the gold statue in a long and lazy caress before vanishing into the morning haze of a new and warm day.

The little city in the middle of the jungle gleamed resplendently in the dawn, as it had done every morning since the rainy season had ended. Beyond the tip of the Sacred Stone to which the sun hitched itself each daybreak, the great ceremonial square and the walls lining the terraces abutting the royal *canchas* emerged from the opulent jungle. Soon the maze of alleys, flights of steps and bridges would in turn emerge from the shadows. Not a day passed when Anamaya didn't admire the perfect harmony of the city's design, a design that Katari seemed to have created out of nothing, as if by magic. The temples, the houses of aristocrats and common people alike, and the warehouses were so well proportioned and laid out in the jungle that if one walked only a quarter of an hour from Vilcabamba, it disappeared from sight like a mirage.

'I love your company, Sacred Double,' continued Anamaya quietly, 'it calms me and fills me with hope: I feel that Emperor Huayna Capac protects us through you, protects us while war rages all around us, destroying everything. For a long time, Sacred Double, I didn't know how to love you, or even how to hear you. I was too young. I feared you. I feared your silence and your body made of gold. I feared my duties as your wife. I feared the wisdom that your presence gave me: it infuriated the Powerful Lords and filled them with jealousy.'

Anamaya paused and reflected. A group of Chosen Virgins, carrying *cumbis* destined to be offered to the Sun Father, passed by the temple's high, trapezoidal door. When they saw that the *Coya Camaquen* was at prayer, the young girls bowed their heads, and out of respect kept their gazes fixed on the flagstones.

'Your presence, O husband,' continued Anamaya, smiling tenderly and a little wryly at the young *acllas*, 'has turned a simple mixed-blood girl into a widely feared woman!'

Now a serious expression returned to Anamaya's face, and she stroked the statue's shoulder.

'The thing *I* fear most, Sacred Double, is that you will prevent me from loving the one who was assigned to me by Emperor Huayna Capac. I fear your jealousy. I fear that you'll try to keep me from the one who, despite his long, long absence, makes my heart beat and my body melt like snow under Inti's caress. Yes, O Sacred Double, I dread your jealousy!'

Anamaya anxiously scrutinized the gold face in front of her. Its dark gaze grew lighter in the growing light of day. The shadow that it cast stretched away beneath its powerful nose and over the fine contours of its lips, which seemed suddenly to smile faintly. Anamaya closed her eyes and, in one breath, made her confession to the statue:

'O Sacred Double, how many times I feared your wrath whenever my mouth or soul spoke his name – Gabriel – or whenever his hands or lips touched my skin! Forgive me my stupidity, beloved husband. I now know that such fear was needless. Three moons have passed since the Puma's breath touched me that evening by the river. Since that moment, and ever in your presence, Sacred Double, not one night has passed when the Puma hasn't come to me in my sleep. We are together in every dream, Sacred Double. We caress one another and love one another as a woman and a man blessed by Inti's light. I run my fingers through the hairs covering his cheeks; I feel his face quiver beneath my touch; I see the fire in his eyes when he desires me and when he enters me with as much strength as he did during the nights we shared in Cajamarca, Cuzco and Ollantaytambo. Night after night, Sacred Double, his heart caresses mine. In every dream I have, I see him turn into the Puma, and I know that he hasn't forgotten me. Every morning, I wake up feeling serene and confident. At last I understand Emperor Huayna Capac's words. Yes, the will of the Ancestors is being fulfilled. And I, the *Coya Camaquen*, will soon accompany you to them, where you will be at peace.'

Anamaya remained absolutely still, deep in her devotion. Her eyes were still closed, and she had bowed deeply to better receive the gold statue's silent reply.

It was only after some time had passed that she suddenly became aware of someone sobbing quietly nearby. She straightened herself quickly and found Manco's young wife prostrated a few paces away, her face wet with tears.

'Curi Ocllo!'

'Help me, *Coya Camaquen*! Please, help me . . .'

'Curi Ocllo!' Anamaya exclaimed again, getting to her feet and reaching out to Manco's wife. 'What's wrong?'

'A *chaski* announced last night that Stranger soldiers have left Cuzco. They're advancing through the Sacred Valley. They're coming here . . .'

Curi Ocllo's large, dark eyes looked into Anamaya's searchingly, desperately, as though trying to impart all her fear to the *Coya Camaquen*. Anamaya simply frowned. Curi Ocllo sobbed louder now, bent double, and cried:

'The thing I feared most is becoming reality, Anamaya! Oh, it's too terrible! May Inti save us!'

Anamaya urged the young woman to her feet and wiped the tears from her face.

'I don't understand your panic, Curi Ocllo! Manco is in Vitcos with three thousand warriors. He'll repel the Strangers, just as he's done before. They don't know how to fight in the jungle.'

But Curi Ocllo, far from being reassured, simply sobbed louder. Anamaya sensed the young *acllas* behind her looking at them surreptitiously. She wrapped her arms around the young queen's trembling shoulders and led her out of the temple.

'Calm down, Curi Ocllo,' she whispered tenderly. 'It won't do for the Daughters of the Sun to see you in this state.'

Curi Ocllo mumbled an apology. The two women walked out onto the great ceremonial square. Anamaya headed for the broad stairway that led out of Vilcabamba and toward the cornfields beside the river.

'Tell me what's bothering you so much,' she asked as she invited Curi Ocllo to sit down on a low wall.

Curi Ocllo took a few moments to gather herself.

'Five moons past, Manco wanted again to take Cuzco from the Strangers. But he didn't even get close to the City of the Puma because his brother Paullu was returning there with thousands of soldiers from the south, where he had just defeated old and faithful Tisoc—'

'Yes, yes, I know all that,' interrupted Anamaya impatiently. 'I even warned Manco that his offensive would prove useless. He mustn't try to fight Paullu.'

'But it's not Paullu who wishes Manco the most harm,' murmured Curi Ocllo, looking away. 'It's my brother, Guaypar.'

Anamaya stiffened as Curi Ocllo continued in a muted voice:

'Guaypar gathered a large force of northern warriors some time ago, and now he's offering them to Paullu. He doesn't care that Paullu submits to the Strangers like a woman submits to a man who doesn't love her. For years, he's hated Manco as much as I've loved him. All his thoughts focus on one thing only: destroying Manco. And I don't even know why.'

Anamaya shuddered and shut her eyes. She reached for Curi Ocllo's shoulder and clasped it affectionately.

'I know why,' she whispered.

Curi Ocllo's words had transported Anamaya back into the past, and now she relived those cold, bright days during the *huarachiku* in Tumebamba. All of them – Manco, Paullu, Guaypar – had been little more than children then. And at the time she had been too, and Villa Oma had barely started educating her, although it was true that she was already under Atahualpa's protection. She remembered the terrible race. She remembered Manco's fear when he came across the snake, and she remembered Paullu's deep, fraternal love for his brother. And she remembered also Guaypar's violent and hateful nature, already manifest then. She remembered Manco and Guaypar fighting around the fire, two mere boys consumed by rage, baying for blood, drunk on *chicha*, brawling through the night, each prepared actually to kill his opponent, until one of Manco's uncles separated them.

'The lesson has been given, and none shall forget it,' Manco had said. To which Guaypar, consumed by hatred and shame, had answered: 'You are damned, Manco! You will burn before reaching the Other World. Your soul will never be free!'

And Anamaya remembered more: she remembered Huamachuco, where Guaypar had asked her to become his wife as the Strangers were advancing on Cajamarca. She remembered Guaypar telling her. 'My soul lives only for you, Anamaya! Just thinking of you makes me burn up inside.'

'Yes,' she repeated. 'I know what divides them.'

'I want to stop them from killing one another, Anamaya. Manco is my beloved husband! I have never wanted any other man. But Guaypar is my brother. I love him, too.'

Anamaya said nothing. She couldn't bear to look into Curi Ocllo's eyes, so horrified was her expression.

'Please help me, *Coya Camaquen*,' implored the young woman.

'But how? How can I help you? How can I stop what must be?'

'Let me go to Manco. He needs me. And I want to be at his side when Guaypar confronts him. I'll stand between them if I have to.'

'No, Curi Ocllo,' said Anamaya gently, 'I won't allow you to do such a foolish thing. What Manco and your brother face is too ancient and too strong for you to ward off. You cannot prevent them from opposing one another if that's what must be.'

'No! Never! I will never abandon them!' screamed Curi Ocllo. 'I'll go to Vitcos without an escort if I have to! Shame on you, *Coya Camaquen*! Shame on you for abandoning your lord—'

'Curi Ocllo!'

But Anamaya wasn't quick enough to hold the young woman back and Curi Ocllo bolted away toward the center of Vilcabamba, screaming the whole way. Anamaya took off after her, but gave up after only a few paces.

O Inti, she prayed silently, tears streaming down her face, *this day began with such hope and happiness, yet already it is more mournful than the dark clouds atop the mountains.*

CHAPTER 23

Cuzco, June 1539

GABRIEL WAS SHOCKED AT WHAT HE SAW AS HE approached Sacsayhuaman. Most of the fortress for which so many men had fallen and where he had forged much of his own legend had been destroyed in the flames of battle. The towers now lay in ruins, and the hordes of warriors who had once sent a storm of arrows and rocks down upon him had, of course, long since disappeared. But the gargantuan stone blocks still stood proudly, although now they guarded nothing but wind and a mystery.

Bartholomew halted his horse and pointed.

'Do you see that?'

There were children playing in the quarry overlooking the fortress, little figures chasing one another, catching each other and rolling around on the ground. Their strident cries could be heard across the hills.

Gabriel smiled.

'There are no victims in a children's war.'

'Yes, but they grow up quickly. And there's nothing easier than learning how to kill one's fellows.'

Gabriel nodded.

They passed through fields in which wheat, barley and oats were now being cultivated as well as the native corn and *quinua*, and they were surprised to discover small and enclosed cabbage patches lining the road into town.

The City of the Puma extended from the foot of the great walls, which now had grass growing on them. Gabriel remembered how deeply enchanted he had been the first time he had seen it. He called to mind Anamaya's face, now so distant, as it had been then when she had stood at Manco's side. And he remembered Pizarro's subsequent triumph.

Bartholomew drew some clothes out of a saddlebag and offered them to Gabriel.

'We're about the same size,' he said shyly, 'and I thought that—'

'I don't need them.'

Gabriel spoke quietly, but firmly. He felt Bartholomew's stare upon him. But he knew that this time he wasn't dressed as an Indian for the same reason as he had been when he had returned in disguise to Cuzco, determined to kill Gonzalo. This time, he wore his simple tunic as a mark of his solidarity with this new world. He wore a greyish-brown *unku* on which the women of Titicaca had, at his request, woven a black puma.

'It took time for me to become what I am now, Brother Bartholomew. I'm not going to start disguising myself as what I no longer am.'

Bartholomew's silence showed both respect and curiosity. A few moments passed before he made one last attempt:

'You know what they're going to say, don't you?'

Gabriel didn't bother to reply to the question. Instead, 'Let's press on,' he said, digging his heels gently into his horse's sides.

He was untroubled in the way only a man determined to do what must be done can be.

As Gabriel entered the town, he noticed immediately everything that had changed since he had last been there.

The most noticeable, even spectacular change was the filth. The canals running down the middle of the roads, in which limpid water had once flowed, were now clogged with every conceivable kind of dirt: he saw, among even less attractive items, potato peelings and half-eaten cobs of corn. The stagnant water gave off a nauseating stench, as did the horse and pig dung covering the streets.

'The gifts of civilization,' said Bartholomew sardonically when he saw the look on Gabriel's face.

Gabriel looked up.

Cuzco had been put to the torch and all the thatch that had burned had been replaced with tiles. It made for an odd architectural combination, these noble Inca palaces roofed with Spanish tiles. Gabriel also noticed that some of the trapezoidal Inca doorways had had sills added to allow wooden doors to be set in them in the Spanish style, each door equipped with a large lock.

'The Indians never knew theft,' said Bartholomew, 'and they used to bar their doors with a simple pole only as a sign that they were absent. The lock and key, another one of our gifts . . .'

Two pigs chased a rabbit at full pelt down the street and passed between Gabriel's horse's legs. The animal sidestepped nervously. Gabriel noticed the stares he was attracting and he reflected that he, a Stranger in Indian garb, was causing more of a stir than were the Indians who had taken to wearing Spanish accessories over their traditional clothes: here a pair of gloves, there a leather belt, another wearing breeches. He noticed that only those Indians of the Inca tribe still proudly wore their traditional dress unaltered.

When they arrived at Aucaypata square, a great many memories came flooding back to him: the time the mummies had been solemnly brought here, and Manco's coronation. But Gabriel's mental voyage into the past was interrupted by the sound of a bell ringing, and he froze upon hearing that deeply familiar ancient sound. He looked at Bartholomew, stupefied. The priest pointed to the spot where the Sunturhuasi, that mysterious building, had once dominated the square.

Where there had been a tower crowned with a conical roof there was now a construction site. Not a single stone had yet been placed, but the scaffolding had already been erected. The workmen had hung a single bell from one of its beams, and its peal echoed across the square, causing all the Indians to turn and face it.

'*El Triunfo!*' said Bartholomew. 'They've started work on it already, and have named it after their victory during the siege. Apparently a painter is coming from Spain to commit to canvas the miracles that took place here . . .'

'What miracles?'

'The miracle of the Sacred Virgin putting out the fires, accompanied by an invincible knight on a white steed.'

'Oh yes, I vaguely remember that miracle,' said Gabriel.

'Few are the men who have no need to believe in miracles that give them the will to live.'

'So I'm beginning to realize.'

Gabriel took Bartholomew to the road leading to Hatun Cancha. They stopped in front of a modest palace with a guanaco hide hanging over its door. Gabriel dismounted and handed his reins to an old man, who had clearly made horse-minding a profession.

'What are you doing?' asked Bartholomew.

'Someone's expecting me,' said Gabriel calmly.

'When did you set up this meeting?'

'In another life. You're the one, after all, who wants me to believe in miracles. Do you want to come with me?'

Bartholomew waved his joined fingers in the air, declining Gabriel's offer, and smiled before wandering slowly away.

Passing through the palace was like parading through some extravagant theatrical production. What with its antechamber, its long corridors, its Indian valets in livery, and its young servant girls, Gabriel had the comical impression of having been suddenly transported onto a stage and charged with playing a role for which he hadn't been given the lines. He was waiting impatiently in a room crammed with wall hangings when a thunderous laugh made him turn around.

'Sebastian!'

'Don't you recognize this place? Ha! I must admit, it was in far worse condition then . . .'

Gabriel remembered the palace's fire-blackened walls and burned-out roofs, the state it had been in when Sebastian had brought him here to equip himself after freeing him from jail.

'I was the one who was in a far worse condition,' he sighed.

The two friends embraced affectionately. No matter how perceptive and understanding Brother Bartholomew might be, Gabriel knew that he would never share this kind of intimacy with him, the intimacy of brothers-in-arms who have lived through many an adventure together. Eventually, the two men released one another, laughing and slapping each other's backs. Gabriel looked at his friend.

Sebastian was dressed in the most extraordinary manner: he wore brightly colored breeches and a fine lace ruff of the sort favoured by Pizarro. But Sebastian looked at Gabriel with equal astonishment.

'What strange things you wear,' they said almost simultaneously before breaking out into laughter again.

'I have to make an effort to stand out from the black slaves arriving here from Panama,' said Sebastian. 'And what about you? Have you been crowned Inca?'

'I'll be Inca the day you're named Governor.'

'And why not? Ours would be a fine alliance: first we would celebrate our victory by roasting Gonzalo on a spit, then we would devise a prosperous reign of peace – after having first filled our pockets, of course, as an insurance against hard times!'

'You look like you're pretty well insured now.'

Sebastian made a face.

'You can't imagine how difficult it is,' he said. 'A daily struggle. I'm utterly exhausted.'

He snapped his fingers and, without his having to say a word, two young servant girls hastened forward with a carafe of liquid that glowed deep red in the torchlight and two silver goblets on a silver platter.

Gabriel's palate had lost its taste for wine, but his face flushed when he swallowed a mouthful.

'Not so bad,' he said, clicking his tongue. 'But it has nothing on what we drank at . . . what was that inn called?'

'The Bottomless Jug!' roared Sebastian. 'Ah, I remember that dear charlatan of an innkeeper and his unforgettable wine well . . . but you're right, nothing could match it.'

There was a note of nostalgia in Sebastian's voice. Gabriel let a moment of silence pass between them.

'Tell me about yourself,' said Sebastian eventually. 'There's a rumour going round that you've become some kind of great Lord over there on Lake Titicaca's shores . . .'

'I'll tell you all about it later, Sebastian. First, I need you to bring me up to date with events . . . I know only what Bartholomew has told me. You might begin by telling me about your fortune.'

'Well, I'm a rich man, as you can see, yet I feel as threatened as I did when we first met, when I was still but a poor slave, protected only by the good de Candia . . .'

'Why do you feel threatened?'

'De Almagro was my protector, even though I was a somewhat reluctant protégé – he had his failings, but he could never forget that I had saved his life! In any case, ever since his death, I've felt the noose of hatred and jealousy tightening around my neck. Like I told you, there are more and more penniless blackamoors arriving every day, and when a good Spaniard sees me in my splendid garb, when he sees my three concubines, he tells himself that I am an insult to the natural and divine order of things. No doubt there'll be one who, soon enough, will take it upon himself to set upon me down some dark alley, chop me into pieces, and feed me to his foul swine.'

'Can't you be more . . . discreet? Can't you keep all your wealth hidden under that flagstone, in that cave where it used to be?'

Sebastian burst out laughing.

'To hear this from you, of all people!'

'What? It's not the same thing.'

The African grinned at him.

'You're right. It's not the same thing. I don't know what your motives are, but I cannot forget what I told you once: there's an ocean between us that no pilot, no matter how able, can cross. That's how it is.'

Sebastian drank slowly, enjoying his wine. He extended his goblet to one of the young girls, smiling at her tenderly. She filled his cup.

'I refuse to change my ways, even if I have to die. It cost me too much effort to get what I have – I had to suffer too many humiliations and play too many tricks. I'll never forsake it for a poor and uncertain life. If I have to die tomorrow, then it will be with my Toledo steel sword in my hand, and my blood will run onto my lace ruff.'

'I understand.'

Sebastian waved his hand through the air, as though sweeping away all his pessimism.

'Bah, you haven't come here to hear about my blighted destiny. You've come for her, haven't you?'

Gabriel stiffened.

'The blue-eyed princess, I mean,' said Sebastian redundantly. 'You've heard the news, then . . .'

Gabriel's heart beat like the bell on the *Triunfo*.

'I've heard nothing. Brother Bartholomew told me nothing about her. What's happened?'

'The expedition, by the blood of Christ! You haven't heard about the expedition?'

Gabriel sat up on his chair and knocked over his goblet. The wine splashed over the thick wool carpet.

'Tell me, by God!' he said, almost shouting. 'Tell me what's happened.'

'They left at least two months ago, on the Governor's orders,' said Sebastian somberly. 'Three hundred men under Gonzalo's command, plus a large number of Indians led by Paullu and other Inca captains hostile to Manco. They went into the jungle with one aim: to capture Anamaya and the great gold statue that they know is always with her because she's married to it, in some way or other.'

Silence.

'Why her?'

'They believe that Manco is weak, now that he's separated from his generals, and they think that taking her will be the final blow to his morale. They think that all they'll have to do then is track him down and finish him. But the truth is that they're all obsessed with that gold statue. Surely you've heard tell of de Candia's misadventure . . . ?'

'No, but save it for another time. I'm sure it's very amusing. Do you know if the expedition achieved its goal?'

'I doubt they have, or we would have had news of their triumph. And Paullu wouldn't have returned to rally reinforcements from Don Francisco. He's here at this very moment.'

Gabriel seized Sebastian by the hands and said:

'I must see them. Where are they?'

'No doubt at the Governor's place, at La Cassana. Unless they're at Paullu's palace at Colcampata, which he acquired at the time of his coronation.'

Gabriel headed for the door, preceded by the two young servant girls. He pushed them aside gently.

'Sebastian, might I ask a favour of you?'

'What?'

'I don't want to talk about it now. But if I did, would you do it?'

Gabriel heard his friend sigh, and quickly stopped himself:

'Forgive me. Pretend I said nothing.'

'I cannot pretend that you said nothing. I don't know what mad scheme you have in mind but, unfortunately for me, yes, I will help you.'

The two friends embraced briefly. Then Gabriel darted away, leaving behind the servants in their livery and the servant girls who looked suspiciously like concubines.

Bartholomew was waiting for him outside. Gabriel jumped onto his horse, saying nothing.

'Where are we going in such a hurry?' asked Bartholomew.

'To Colcampata. Why didn't you tell me?'

'I don't—'

'Don't lie to me, Brother Bartholomew, and don't lie to yourself! Don't tell me that you didn't know about Gonzalo's expedition!'

'You know very well that you can't do anything on your own, Gabriel.'

'I'll be the judge of what I can and cannot do.'

They headed off, their horses' hooves clacking on the stones. Gabriel did his best to quieten his anger, and to curb the fathomless dread that had taken hold of him.

CHAPTER 24

Cuzco, Colcampata, June 1539

A CROWD HAD GATHERED ON THE SQUARE AT COLCAMPATA. Although Gabriel mostly kept his gaze focused on Don Francisco Pizarro, he glanced around from time to time at the thick vegetation in which the City of the Puma was set, here in the heart of the mountains. He now understood the eternal force of the place better than ever, and how it stayed and would continue to stay far from the stench of swine and the other abominations brought by its conquerors. He could feel its powerful life-force, dormant for now but ready to leap forward and roar at any moment.

Mummies had been installed in the niches carved in the palace's perfectly built walls. Gabriel was moved when he recognized the mummy of Inca Huayna Capac.

'Paullu asked for them,' whispered Bartholomew in his ear. 'He felt that the "legitimate" Inca should not be separated from his Ancestors.'

Gabriel nodded, but kept his gaze fixed on Don Francisco Pizarro, his old protector.

The Governor looked older and bonier than ever; but although he seemed to have shriveled with age, he still radiated the energy that had always been his. His clothes were entirely black except for his white hat and leggings. The only sign of his immense wealth was the very fine lace ruff that he wore around his neck. Through his black eyes, he was focusing all his attention on the person facing him, who was sitting on a *tiana*, as befitted an Inca. Gabriel recognized Paullu.

Cuzco's latest Inca was of the same size and age as his half-brother Manco. But the similarities ended there. Whereas the rebel in the jungle had features that seemed to have been chiseled in stone by a sculptor, Paullu was round. And although it wasn't actually fat, his face still gave the impression of a flabbiness of the kind that comes from surrendering to life's easier pleasures. Only his eyes revealed his strong will and his quick mind.

The two men conversed without the aid of interpreters: Paullu spoke perfect Spanish.

As Gabriel and Bartholomew joined the circle of Indian Lords and Spanish hidalgos, Pizarro turned his head toward them.

Gabriel met the old captain's gaze and felt a wave of old, old emotions come over him. He looked into those black eyes deeply embedded in their sockets, stiffened, forced a smile, and bowed very slightly.

'What I need to know before I help you, Lord Paullu,' continued Pizarro, 'is the likelihood of the expedition being a success.'

'It is very likely, Governor, it is almost a sure thing . . .'

Paullu's voice retained the raucous intonations of Quechua. Gabriel heard a hidalgo behind him spit and mutter: 'This mongrel would have us all killed in that damned jungle . . .'

'I hastened back here, at your brother Gonzalo's insistence, to rally reinforcements. Manco's troops are powerful and well organized.'

Pizarro's eyes flashed at the mention of Manco's name.

'Are you sure that you can destroy that dog?'

'I cannot call my own brother a "dog",' said Paullu politely, 'even though I think that he's made a terrible mistake by leading his rebellion beyond what is reasonable. But to answer your question: yes, we can defeat his army. But on one condition . . .'

Paullu, sure of himself, paused for effect.

'What condition?' asked Don Francisco impatiently.

'Your Honor knows how dependent your men are on mine to guide them through the forest.' Paullu looked defiantly at all the Spaniards present. 'You know that your brothers Hernando and

Gonzalo, were they here, could testify that my loyalty to you has been the decisive factor in a great many battles . . .'

'I have no doubt of it, Lord Paullu. We know what we owe you. And you know what you owe us . . .'

Pizarro let his gaze linger on the Royal Fringe hanging over Paullu's forehead.

'A good alliance – a good *friendship* – is based on a good equilibrium,' said Paullu, more softly now. 'What I want to say to you, Governor, is that it is absolutely imperative that I return to the forest with my troops and with reinforcements. I must return to your brother Gonzalo and make sure that the expedition achieves its aims.'

'When do you want to leave?'

'Tomorrow or the following night. Time is running short. But think for a moment, Governor: as soon as victory has been won, you can go back to building Lima, your beautiful City of Kings . . .'

'And you can return to ruling over your beloved Cuzco.'

'Certainly, I'm not indifferent to the city of my Ancestors,' replied Paullu, gesturing discreetly at the mummies watching them from their niches.

'So be it, Lord Paullu. You may proclaim that, by order of the Governor, you are free to recruit as many men as you deem necessary.'

'I need Yungas, Governor, more than mountain men. Yungas from the coast, used to a humid climate . . .'

Pizarro made another impatient gesture.

'Do as you see fit, my dear Sapa Inca. You know your Indians better than I do. Just make sure you win.'

Pizarro was the first to rise from his seat. He gave the merest flicker of a bow to the Inca, who remained utterly impassive. Gabriel reflected that the slightness of the Governor's gesture captured all the ambiguities of the relationship between the two men.

The Inca dignitaries moved away.

Murmurs immediately rose from the Spanish ranks: '. . . can't trust that traitor . . . he was a friend of de Almagro . . .' But Pizarro restored silence by simply raising his hand. His authority was more absolute than ever. No one openly contested it.

'Enough,' he said. 'We need him, but he also needs us. He's too cunning to betray us at this stage. He wants us to get rid of his beloved brother first . . .'

He spoke these last words with an amused irony.

'Now leave, the lot of you. I want to be alone with—'

He turned to Gabriel. Fresh murmurs rose from the assembly. Not everyone present had previously met the Spaniard dressed as an Indian, but everyone had heard the legend of the proud knight protected by Santiago who had taken the fortress single-handed.

The old conquistador and the man who had been like a son to him were left alone on the square.

'Well then,' began Pizarro. 'What kind of thing is that to be wearing?'

Gabriel couldn't say how many hours Pizarro and he spent together.

Noon came and went, the sun slipped down the warm blue vault of sky, the mountains turned gold, evening's shadows grew longer – and still they talked.

The Governor showed real pleasure in renewing his friendship with Gabriel. He asked him all about life on Lake Titicaca's shores, and teased him about the native women; Gabriel had Pizarro tell about his beloved Lima, the founding of which had so absorbed him. They talked of the past, of Seville and Toledo, of the audience with the King and the terrible crossing to the New World. The initial reserve between them dropped away as they talked, and the Governor relaxed and waved his white hat about like a rag or flag or sail, emphasizing whatever point he was making.

'I've been asking myself a question, Don Francisco.'

'What is it, my boy?'

'I've heard tell that, during your first expedition, your men were on the point of abandoning you, and that you drew a line in the sand to show where poverty ended and fortune began, where the past was buried and where the glorious future could be found . . .'

'Yes, on Gallo Island,' murmured Pizarro dreamily.

'They say that twelve men crossed that line and came over to you.'

'Yes. What is it that you want to know?'

'I want to know if it's true. If that's the way it really happened.'

Pizarro said nothing for a moment. Then a smile replaced the severity of his expression.

'Aren't you friends with some of them?' he asked. 'Haven't you asked de Candia?'

'Yes, but he only laughs. I want to hear it from your mouth.'

But Pizarro gave nothing away, or else he was enjoying the conversation too much to end it by giving an answer.

'Well, I've heard something too,' he retorted. 'I've heard that a cavalryman with features exactly like yours, although not dressed in the odd manner that you are now, galloped on a white horse through a storm of Indian arrows, passed through blazing fires and with the protection of the Sacred Virgin – who appeared at his side – took the three towers of the fortress on his own. Is it true?'

Now it was Gabriel's turn to smile.

'Why, you have so many friends, Don Francisco. Haven't you asked them?'

'Yes, and they all swear to me that it happened just like that, by Christ. With the notable exception of my brother Gonzalo, of course.'

Gabriel burst out laughing, and the old conquistador joined him.

'These legends,' murmured Pizarro, 'which of us can say if they're true or not? So many memories come to me as though from out of the fog. Sometimes I wake up in the morning convinced that I'm in my village in my beloved Extramadura, making a bell, absolutely sure that that's what I've done all my life. Then I remember where I am, and what I've seen, and I become old again.'

'And yet, here you are.'

Gabriel waved at the country surrounding them. Night was falling, and torches were being lit here and there. The two men shared a moment of silence together, each lost in his own thoughts, each privately dwelling on the shared past that had brought them together.

Then Gabriel heard the Governor almost whisper to him:

'I need you, son.'

Gabriel's body stiffened as though he had been slapped in the face. Despite the affection that bound him to Don Francisco, despite the respect that he had for him, he sensed a dark, unbearable menace in those words.

'I'm alone once again, as you know very well. Hernando murdered the one-eyed de Almagro and has gone to Spain to justify himself to the King. God knows what his fate will be. I don't pretend not to know that you hated him, but he's the only one who has more brains than *cojones* – forgive me the expression – but you know my opinion of the others.'

'Then why did you leave Cuzco in Gonzalo's hands?'

Gabriel tried to say this as calmly as possible, but he couldn't hide the reproach in his words.

'Because, despite all his failings, he's one of my own people, and the only one I can trust. All these captains arriving from Spain with their ten horses and fifty infantrymen, they think that they can do whatever they want, and they expect the treasures of Peru to be just handed to them.'

Pizarro set down his hat on a low wall overlooking the town. He took Gabriel by the arm and leaned toward his ear, as though about to share a secret.

'You know that I'm living in concubinage with an Indian princess . . . we've baptised her Doña Angelina . . . well, you can't imagine the lengths to which I have to go to hide my love for her! And as for my darling little Francesca, my daughter by Doña Inés Quispe Sisa, why, not a day passes when I don't want to run to her and take her up in my arms. I haven't seen her for weeks now, and I miss her, Gabriel, I miss her so much.'

Don Francisco's eyes glistened with tears.

'I only want one thing,' he continued. 'I want to live with them, eat simple meals with them, wash the food down with a goblet of wine diluted with water, keep my old body going by playing children's games in the country, teach my daughter the games I used to play as a child – skittles and royal tennis. Do you think that I enjoy riding from dawn to dusk down impossible roads, leading these armies, winning over *caciques*, racking my brain whether I should trust Paullu or not . . .'

'Then make peace!'

Silence. Pizarro picked up his hat and rolled it like a clod of earth between his hands.

'Peace! You use grand words these days, I find.'

'Don't you see, Don Francisco?'

'I see some kind of demon, my boy – a Spaniard disguised as an Indian who throws around words that are above his station . . .'

The old man's face grew taut with cold fury, and it was hard to believe that this was the same man who just a moment before had been the sincere, doting father. But Gabriel felt overcome by a force that he had never felt before. All his limbs relaxed and his body was filled with a soft euphoria. He said confidently:

'Have you ever listened to the words of those who don't tremble at the mere sight of you? Do you know that your soldiers respect none of your laws? That they persist in pillaging this country, killing its inhabitants, and reducing them to slavery? Do you think that this brutality will bring peace with the Indians?'

'First I have to win the war against this damned Manco. We'll establish peace and harmony afterwards . . .'

'No, Don Francisco, you don't see at all. The lust for war is everywhere. It infects all your men. You allowed de Almagro to be murdered . . .'

'I didn't know . . .'

'Come now – you didn't know? Just as you didn't know that Atahualpa was going to be executed? You knew, Don Francisco, but you turned your head away and averted your gaze until the deed was done. And now the desire for vengeance corrupts the air itself. Each man hates his neighbour and dreams only of grabbing as much as he can, everyone feels that an injustice has been done to them, and that violence is the only law! And now you are so blind that you cannot see in your lieutenants' docile eyes which of them is going to betray you, which ones are perhaps already plotting to take your life . . .'

Pizarro tried many times to interrupt but Gabriel's impassioned statement left him no opportunity. Now, though, he raised his voice mockingly and said:

'Come now, my boy, they would never dare!'

Gabriel paused for breath, then said:

'You had – you still have – the chance to be remembered in the history books as the man who conquered a land and made a nation of it! But you're squandering that opportunity.'

'I cannot do anything else, Gabriel!' cried Francisco in despair. 'I know your courage, and I know your generosity, and I'm prepared to listen to whatever you have to tell me. I don't deny that much of what you say is true, and sometimes, when I'm alone at night, I pray to the Sacred Virgin, I cry and beg for mercy for the crimes that are being committed. I have no harsher judge than myself, not even you. No one, apart from Almighty God, knows what I know! But what you're proposing is impossible, don't you see, it's simply impossible . . .'

'Is it true that the purpose of Gonzalo and Paullu's mission is to capture Anamaya and the gold statue?'

'Yes, and Manco as well. But Gonzalo convinced me that Manco would be easier to take if we have his priestess in our hands, as well as that gold statue with God knows what magical powers . . .'

'And then there'll be peace, you say,' said Gabriel, but sarcastically, almost hissing it through his teeth. He continued:

'Do you really think that by simply destroying what they hold most precious you'll make peace? No, it'll be the opposite, Don Francisco: you will simply cause more war. When – or *if* – you get rid of Manco, you'll have to deal with Villa Oma, the Sage turned warrior, and then with Illac Topa. And when they fall, others will rise behind them. And when, in turn, you're finished with them, you'll have to face your own men, you'll have to remain forever on your guard, unable to trust anybody at all. Don't you see that by behaving like this you're leaving everybody, Spaniards and Indians alike, with a legacy of war, one that they'll never give up?'

'You don't understand, Gabriel. You're still too young. I know all that. But I also know things that you don't. Over there,' he said, pointing to the west, 'they're growing nervous, and news has reached me that they plan to send a viceroy here. If I don't take Manco and crush his rebellion first, then it'll be finished.'

'What will be finished? Your power? The extortions and murders?'

'My dream. My dream will be finished . . .'

Don Francisco's pale, thin lips quivered as he spoke these last words, and Gabriel held back from continuing his castigation of the aged leader. He had nothing to say about the substance of the dream of an old man, a man who had risen high above his humble origins; he knew that each man has his own secret, his own pathetic and magnificent dream.

Both men paused to gather their breath. Their anger subsided, evaporated into the night, was absorbed in the stones – absorbed, perhaps, into the wisdom of the mummies that had been observing them.

'Let me go to them,' said Gabriel. 'Let me take them the order to negotiate a peace with Manco immediately. You know that I know him well. I'm probably the only Spaniard that he'll agree to talk to.'

'No.'

Gabriel tensed. He walked a few steps across the square. All his emotions had fused into a deep tiredness, a weariness that was the sum of all his years in Peru, of the immense sadness of being unable to convince the man whom he had both hated and most admired.

He stared at the mummy with the broken nose: Huayna Capac. A wave of long-forgotten emotions passed through his body, and he shivered as though he had suddenly been transported through the night to the terraces overlooking Ollantaytambo.

He turned around.

Francisco Pizarro hadn't moved.

'Adieu, Don Francisco.'

The Governor still didn't move. Gabriel turned away and made to head back into town. Suddenly he heard the old man's voice from behind him:

'What are you going to do?'

Gabriel turned to face him, but he could no longer make out Pizarro's features through the darkness.

'I've thought about the story of what happened on Gallo Island, Don Francisco. I believe that you really did trace that line in the sand with the tip of your sword. And I believe that, sooner or later, every man has to choose: which side is he on?'

He paused and filled his lungs with the cool night air.

'I believe that there comes a point in every man's life when, like you, he can draw his sword and trace a line in the sand. I think that every man has a choice.'

'What are you going to do?'

'What I must.'

Gabriel disappeared into the night.

CHAPTER 25

Cuzco, June 1539

'**Y**OU'VE LOST YOUR MIND!' HOWLED SEBASTIAN.
        Gabriel raised his hands to appease his friend. He had
never seen him so enraged.

'Calm down.'

'You're telling *me* to calm down?'

'Let me explain it to you again—'

'Do you take me for some dumb nigger?'

Gabriel lowered his arms, defeated.

'I take you for my friend.'

Bolts of fury flashed from Sebastian's eyes. A single torch and
a few candles on the small inlaid table at which the two men
were sitting were the only sources of light in Sebastian's palace.
His servants and women had gone to bed, and the two men spoke
in low voices.

'Does a friend,' continued Sebastian, calmer now, 'wish for the
death of his friend? Does he commit suicide alongside him?'

'All I'm asking—'

'All you're asking is for me to bankrupt myself by financing an
expedition into the depths of the jungle to save one Indian girl
– I can get you fifty much prettier ones simply by snapping my
fingers! Oh, and to devise a peace that no one wants. Oh yes –
I was forgetting – *and* to help a gold statue escape, a gold statue
that will in any case end up in the smelting forge at La Cassana
anyway, or else in one of those noble hidalgos' palaces. Let me

tell you again, my friend: you've lost your mind. And if I listen to another word from you, then I'm as mad as you are.'

'And so am I,' said a third voice from the shadows. 'I am struck with the same insanity, or one very like it. But I still want to believe in the truth of it.'

'You do, Bartholomew?'

The monk came forward into the light. He stared at a sketch of the Sacsayhuaman fortress.

'Can it be,' began Sebastian, 'that since Bishop Valverde's return you have lost your position in this fine city's religious hierarchy?'

'What do you mean?'

'Doesn't your office make you their ally?'

'My friend, my office – and its burden – has made of me the witness and, for far too long, the accomplice of horrors and those who carry them out. I didn't come here to help massacre the natives in God's name. And this man – your friend – represents my opportunity to end it. Two years ago, when his Holiness Paul III issued his papal bull, I believed that we had won a decisive victory. But that hasn't turned out to be the case. I wanted Gabriel to go to Spain and bear witness to what is happening here, to insist upon the King's intervention in the name of God's law. Yet I understand what you call his madness, and I would go with him if I could . . .'

Sebastian looked from one man to the other.

'And may I know how – purely out of curiosity – you're going to find men to go with you?'

'I've got a few friends,' said Gabriel, smiling.

'Who? Our old comrade de Candia has already lost half his fortune trying to get into that damned jungle! If I'm to part with my gold, may I at least know the names of these friends?'

'Wouldn't it be better for you not to know, so that you can enjoy your prosperity the more?'

'How gracious of you, Your Grace! He gives me permission to enjoy my prosperity! What touching generosity . . .'

'Sebastian—'

'Never mind "Sebastian". You would ruin me and have me killed – and you want me to *thank* you?'

Gabriel and Bartholomew fell silent. There was no more space left in the night to argue, to convince Sebastian, to cajole, to complain, to joke around. All that they could do was to look at the ex-slave's face, and to see the expressions of anger, of doubt, of temptation, and of resistance pass across it.

'What if I refuse?'

It was a moonless night. Gabriel and Bartholomew hurried through the darkness along Cuzco's alleys. They crossed the Aucaypata and headed down toward the Temple of the Sun. Hurrying along beside it, Gabriel gasped in shock: its walls had been demolished, and only the heavy stones of its foundations remained, no doubt either because its conquerors hadn't had the power to destroy them or because they planned to build on top of them.

'What have they done with the garden of gold?' hissed Gabriel. 'Turned it into a trough for their pigs?'

Hidden in the night, he remembered the Inca's prophetic words that Anamaya had revealed to him on their last night together, the meaning of which had remained a mystery to him. But he knew that it was his faith in that prophesy as much as the love in his heart that now made him prepared to defy anything.

When they reached the Pumachupan *canchas*, he put his hand on Bartholomew's shoulder. The monk said nothing, but simply turned to him and smiled. His scar was a dark shadow across his face. He didn't hesitate as he headed toward a door leading into a modestly built *cancha*.

'It's here,' said the monk.

The *cancha*'s courtyard was dark and deserted. They woke a few guinea pigs as they entered, and the animals darted between their legs, squealing.

Then a torch came toward them at chest hight. Its light blinded Gabriel, and he shielded his eyes. A familiar, throaty voice spoke to him in good Spanish.

'Welcome, my lord.'

Gabriel discerned the outline of the dwarf silhouetted behind the torch. He followed him, fearing nothing, feeling as though he had come across an old friend. They had only ever met by night and had never spoken more than a few words to one another, but the dwarf had always been there to help Gabriel get closer to Anamaya. And now, once again, he was going to help.

He led them through a door whose humble hanging belied the luxury that lay behind it. It was as though the dwarf had been crowned Inca of a miniature kingdom created for and ruled over by him, and destined to be known by him only. Everything in the room was exceptionally valuable: the goblets, jars, and trays were all of gold or silver and decorated with jewels. There were vicuña wool carpets and a table made of precious wood and inlaid with emeralds, like the two chairs and the bench around it. Gabriel noticed the familiar shapes of llama and condor figurines in the room's niches, but he also saw some items that were far more terrifying than anything he had yet seen in the Inca world. The most surprising was an icon of the Virgin. What was more, everything was particularly small, as though it had all been made on a scale befitting the dwarf by artisans working in his court.

The dwarf invited them to sit, which they did as best they could. The time when he had worn a long red robe, the only robe he'd possessed, its fringe always dragging in the dust, was long gone. He now wore yellow linen breeches, a yellow doublet, and a four-pointed hat of the sort that Gabriel had seen on Kollas by Lake Titicaca's shores.

'I'm afraid this place is far humbler than my house in Yucay,' said the dwarf. 'But I am happy to welcome you here, nevertheless.'

'Your destiny has brought you good fortune, it seems,' said Gabriel, smiling.

'A slave I was, and a slave I shall always be. But in the meantime, I allow myself to enjoy – discreetly – what Fate has given me, and I watch my sons grow. They are five and seven years old, yet they are both already taller than me. Which proves that Fate knows how to be seduced. But you haven't come to listen to my life story.'

'We have come to ask you for help.'

The dwarf laughed and slapped his thighs with his disproportionately large hands.

'Who would have thought it? Who would have thought it, indeed?' he said over and over.

When the dwarf had finished laughing, his last 'Who would have thought it?' lost in a hiccup of mirth, Gabriel explained that he needed a guide and a dozen men to take him to Ollantaytambo, and to guide him through the impenetrable jungle where Gonzalo was hunting down Anamaya and Manco.

The dwarf asked no questions. He looked seriously at Gabriel for a long time.

'I have always taken you to her,' he said.

Gabriel nodded.

'When do you want to leave?'

'This very night.'

The dwarf whistled through his teeth.

'We will go to my house in Yucay. I'll gather the men we need there. But do you have enough gold?'

'Yes, he does.'

The door hanging lifted and Sebastian's giant shape appeared.

'He has it,' said Sebastian, lowering his head as though the smallness of everything surrounding him obliged him to shrink himself. He continued:

'He doesn't want to waste any time, I assume?'

Sebastian laughed at the surprised look on Gabriel's face.

'It's worth risking torture just to see that look on your face, Your Grace. Come on, let's hurry, my neck hurts just standing here.'

The four men went outside. Gabriel, moved, took Bartholomew's arm and squeezed it. The two ex-slaves walked side by side in front of them, not speaking a word. The dwarf trotted along but the giant still had to restrain his pace so that the smaller man could keep up. They passed by a number of silent *canchas* before coming out onto the paved road to Collasuyu.

When they had passed the last of the houses and they could see nothing ahead of them but crop fields and the dark outline of the mountain behind which lay Yucay, Bartholomew and Sebastian stopped in their tracks. Sebastian whistled softly.

Two Indians appeared, leading a white shape through the night.

'Itza!' cried Gabriel.

'I told you that I'd keep her for you.'

'Itza!'

'The range of your vocabulary amazes me. Will you say it a third time, I wonder?'

Ignoring his friend's jibe, Gabriel stroked the mare's muzzle affectionately. When he turned to face his friends, his eyes were aglow.

The monk raised his joined fingers toward Gabriel.

'You'll allow me to bless you,' he said, smiling. 'May the One True God be with you!'

'And don't forget your big *cojones*,' muttered Sebastian. 'Keep them tucked well between your legs.'

Gabriel looked at his two friends before embracing both of them briefly. He opened his mouth, about to thank them.

'Don't say a word,' growled Sebastian. 'You bore me already. You're going to sob like a woman, I know it. You're going to cry, "Itza! Itza!" and I hate that kind of thing. Now hurry.'

Gabriel hesitated, then turned aside and climbed effortlessly into the saddle. He and his horse galloped away into the night.

CHAPTER 26

A NAMAYA WATCHED THE MEN AND WOMEN WORKING on the terraces below Vilcabamba for a moment before approaching them. Under Katari's watchful eye, women were kneading clay before carefully spreading it inside wooden molds. Then men would carry the gleaming, thick slabs to a spot a little further away, where they would sit and fold the slabs over themselves on their thighs, before carefully setting them to dry in the sun on a bed of leaves. Further away, other men put the dried, light gray wedges into a round furnace.

Anamaya joined Katari. He watched as he called to one of the workers to bring him a clay slab that he had just folded over itself. The Master of Stone quickly etched an outling of a little snake into the still-soft substance with a reed stylus.

'What are you doing?' asked Anamaya. 'What are these clay slabs for?'

'To cover your roof, *Coya Camaquen*, and to keep you dry from the coming rains.'

Anamaya screwed up her face and looked on without comprehension.

Katari etched another snake on another slab. He worked so quickly and easily that the snake appeared as suddenly as a real reptile would from the grass.

'These are what the Strangers call *tiles*,' he explained, his eyes gleaming. 'Once these clay slabs have been baked, all we have to do is set them over the frame of a roof for the building to become absolutely rainproof. I decided to do your roof first, *Coya Camaquen*, as a homage to you. Then we'll set them over all the *canchas* of Vilcabamba, and make our Emperor's new Royal City truly beautiful.'

Katari showed her the tile that he had just decorated and added:

'My only worry is that our men's thighs are smaller than those of the Strangers, so our tiles are not as large as those I watched being made in Cuzco. We're going to have to adjust the frameworks of our roofs to accommodate the difference in size.'

'You surprise me, Master of Stone,' said Anamaya, smiling softly. 'You, the guardian of our Ancestors' knowledge, the custodian of our traditions, are going to replace Inca roofs with something invented by the Strangers?'

'Why not? Are we not to learn from others? We learned how to work gold and silver from Chimu goldsmiths, after all, and pottery from their ancestors, the Mochicas, and weaving from the people of Paracas. These tiles are a wonderful invention. They do away with the tiresome work of cutting *ichu* and replacing rotted roofs every four seasons. Should we ignore this knowledge merely because the gods haven't yet taught it to us? Tiles won't diminish the beauty of our buildings and walls in any way, because everyone knows that we, the Incas, build better and more beautiful buildings than any other of Viracocha's peoples!'

Katari's face and voice betrayed uncharacteristic enthusiasm. Anamaya was moved. She watched the workers' efficient ballet.

'What you say makes me happy, Katari. It means that you believe that our people must continue to evolve and live in hope despite the war, despite Manco's weakness, and despite Emperor Huayna Capac's dire predictions.'

'Let me address as one the two questions that you are asking me, *Coya Camaquen*,' replied the Master of Stone in a serious tone. 'Firstly, I believe that it's ill-omened to ignore new knowledge and new skills. It can only displease the Powerful Ancestors who, through the strength of their will-power, cause everything in this world to exist as a mark of their presence.'

Katari raised his arm and pointed beyond the muddy terrace they were on to a gang of children squatting and admiring a dozen horses grazing in a field.

'Manco captured those animals during the battle of Ollantaytambo. He was very proud of himself when he brought them here. But what can we use them for? Only he knows how to climb on their backs. And now, unfortunately, this jungle is our only territory, and these animals cannot move through it. What's more, we don't know how to make the metal soles they need for their feet. So how can those horses serve us, other than by filling our children with wonder?'

'Well, they serve Manco's pride,' said Anamaya tenderly. 'They show that our Emperor isn't always the victim of the Strangers' power.'

A thick and odorous smoke was now rising from the round kiln nearby. Anamaya soberly contemplated the men and women working around it. They remained unaware of Katari's artwork on the tiles.

'I'm flattered that you should want to tile my roof first,' she said. 'But I won't see the result for some time. I have given Curi Ocllo permission to join Manco, and I've decided to go with her.'

Katari gave her a surprised, worried look, and Anamaya answered his question before he had even asked it:

'For almost a whole moon, I have been forbidding her to leave Vilcabamba. But she cries more than she eats and is wasting away. In any case, she may be right: Manco may well find comfort in her company.'

'But why are you going with her?'

Anamaya hesitated for a few seconds. She watched as some workers called to one another and fed green branches into the furnace in order to keep the temperature of the baking tiles stable.

'I promised Manco that I would stay at his side. We've been apart for some time now. Also, Curi Ocllo fears that her brother Guaypar will confront Manco; there's an old enmity between them for which I feel partly responsible. But will I be of any use to the Emperor?'

Katari, doubtful, shook his head.

'That is not your proper place, *Coya Camaquen*. Manco's enmities are like the *ichu* roofs in this town: they are old ways that don't keep the rain from dampening our beds nor the Strangers from winning battles. And in any case, traveling through the jungle now, while the Strangers approach, is unsafe—'

'We'll have a strong escort,' interrupted Anamaya, placing her hand affectionately on the Master of Stone's wrist. 'Katari, I'm entrusting you with the Sacred Double. Take good care of him. I shall return as soon as I can. I have the feeling that soon we shall have to take him to the secret place.'

The small expedition – Anamaya, Curi Ocllo and a detachment of warriors – advanced cautiously through the jungle for three days, following the river, before sighting the fortified palace set on a rocky spur at Vitcos. Despite Katari's anxiety, they had met with no trouble apart from finding a way through the tangle of dense vegetation, vegetation so profuse that it had very quickly swallowed up the path that had been cut by the previous expedition.

Curi Ocllo had shown real courage, and had never hesitated to step out of her palanquin whenever the narrowness of the path demanded it. And now that they could see the walls of Vitcos looming over the valley, her impatience was so great that her hands trembled. Her face had lost the ugly, anxious furrows that had marked it in Vilcabamba and she had recovered the beauty that Manco so adored. Her eyes sparkled and her lips were full and soft. She looked like a very young girl as yet untroubled by experience of the world but also had the air of a grown woman who knew that her beloved would soon look upon her and call her to him.

When they reached the bottom of the steps leading to the fortress up its steep northern slope, the column came to an abrupt halt. As the officer commanding the fifteen warriors escorting the women approached their palanquin, Curi Ocllo called out:

'Why have you ordered us to stop, officer? We're almost there . . .'

The officer bowed respectfully and, with the subtlety of one long accustomed to this type of ceremonial gesture, twisted slightly so that his bow was addressed to Anamaya as much as to Curi Ocllo.

'It's true, *Coya*, that we are almost at Vitcos,' he said, 'but that is exactly why I wish to ask for the *Coya Camaquen*'s permission to send an advance party of two soldiers to the fortress, to warn the Emperor of your arrival.'

'It's unnecessary,' protested Curi Ocllo, pouting. 'His own sentinels will warn him. Anyway, it would be marvelous if I could surprise him!'

She giggled, turned to Anamaya, and pleaded:

'There's no point wasting any more time, right?'

'Officer,' asked Anamaya, 'do you think that it's absolutely necessary to send scouts? The *Coya* is right: the Emperor's sentries will warn him of our coming.'

The escort's commander, troubled, hesitated before bowing again and answering:

'In truth, *Coya Camaquen*, I want to make sure that Emperor Manco is actually in the fortress.'

'Why wouldn't he be?' cried Curi Ocllo. 'We would know if he'd left it. He would have sent a messenger. Oh please, Anamaya, we're so close!'

'It would be stupid to take unnecessary risks,' Anamaya said.

Tears immediately welled up in Curi Ocllo's black eyes. Anamaya couldn't help but smile at the girl's caprice.

'Officer,' she sighed, 'send a scout with news of our arrival. But let us not linger here; we shall press on without waiting for his return.'

Curi Ocllo, as uninhibited as a spoiled child, threw her arms around Anamaya's neck and held her tight.

'Thank you Anamaya, thank you! You can't imagine how happy I shall be to be with Manco at last!'

*   *   *

The expedition was within two sling-stones' throw of the fortress when the scout returned at a run. The officer halted the column again.

'*Coya Camaquen*,' he announced, 'there's no one there. Vitcos is empty.'

'Empty?'

Curi Ocllo cried out in despair.

'The Emperor and his men seem to have left several days ago.'

'But why?'

'Perhaps there are Strangers in the area, *Coya*.'

'In that case, officer,' ordered Anamaya, 'we mustn't linger on the path. Let's get to the fortress as quickly as we can. Since it's empty, we can stay there and defend ourselves in it, if we have to.'

When they passed through the bailey, they found that the buildings and courtyards were indeed empty.

Anamaya and Curi Ocllo were worried. They stepped from their palanquin and walked across a perfectly square courtyard bordered by low buildings. The soldiers accompanied them as they made their way toward the buildings facing the palace's entrance. A narrow passage leading off at a right angle led them to the fortress's most outlying point.

The spot gave them a splendid view. The edifice here had been built on a rocky outcrop atop a steep slope that fell away to the river. It was a long, heavy structure, with a raised patio and fifteen magnificent doors with white granite lintels. The snow-covered peaks and slopes of the Apus towered around the place, which seemed to have an indestructible quality about it, as well as a curious serenity.

'I don't understand!' cried Curi Ocllo, her voice breaking. 'Why would Manco leave without sending even a *chaski* to meet us?'

'It's only a slight setback.' Anamaya, staring at the forest on the surrounding slopes, tried to calm her. 'Most likely he has retreated to the little fort at Machu Pucara.'

'But why? Why didn't he warn us?'

'Perhaps the officer is right: the Strangers may be closer than we thought. We must be extremely careful. I'm going to send a messenger to Machu Pucara so that Manco can—'

But just then terrifying howls erupted all around them, interrupting her. Anamaya's group stood frozen with shock.

They could see nothing at first, as though the cries had risen spontaneously from the landscape itself.

And then the source of the noise came into view.

A hundred, maybe two hundred warriors from the north. They wore the colours of Quito on their tunics and leather helmets on their heads. Holding their shields out in front of them, they surged forward from behind the long building where they had been hiding.

They brandished bronze-headed clubs and axes and twirled their slings. Their spears were pointed forward menacingly.

The officer commanding the escort for Anamaya and Curi Ocllo quickly yelled orders to his men. His handful of soldiers formed a futile barrier around the two women and held their spears out before them. But they had hardly taken up their position when a volley of sling stones whistled down upon them, killing two of them on the spot. Curi Ocllo's scream rose above all the other sounds and seemed to intensify the assault's ferocity.

The fight was so quick and violent that Anamaya had no time to realize what was happening, much less to flee. The escort's officer was the last to be killed, his skull split open with a studded club.

Silence fell.

The northern warriors surrounded the women. Curi Ocllo fell to her knees. The fighters looked at them blankly, and the young queen grabbed hold of Anamaya. The soldiers' ranks parted, their shields clanging together, to allow someone through. A high-ranking Inca officer appeared. He wore fine ear-lobe plugs, a cape threaded with silver, and had a small fan of blue and gold feathers fixed to his helmet. His face was hard and bony, and his eyes looked unusually small and set well back in their sockets. Both women recognized him. Curi Ocllo jumped up and dashed toward him, crying:

'Guaypar! Oh, Guaypar, my brother!'

She collapsed at his feet, overcome with emotion. Guaypar stepped aside without even glancing at her trembling body. His well-defined lips curved in a thin smile. He came right up close to Anamaya, who simply looked at him with utter contempt.

'We've been waiting for you, *Coya Camaquen*. To be honest, we came all the way here just for you.'

'If that's the case, your welcome was atrocious, Guaypar.'

Guaypar's smile broadened. Anamaya could see Curi Ocllo sobbing behind him. Soldiers were already binding her hands.

'I don't worry myself too much about blood relations, Anamaya. My sister disowned me a long time ago when she married Manco, that traitor and usurper—'

'Know that my fate is tied to hers, Guaypar!'

'That's for me to decide, *Coya Camaquen*! But I'm sure you'll understand my impatience. I've been dreaming of this moment for so long.'

His eyes gleamed with arrogance and hatred and, for the first time in a long while, the twin venoms of doubt and fear coursed through Anamaya's veins.

'Do you remember that night at Huamachuco? It was before the coming of the Strangers, when Emperor Atahualpa was waging war against Huascar the Mad.'

Guaypar smiled as he asked the question. But his expression was somehow as icy as his tone of voice. Anamaya returned his smile and replied:

'Yes, I remember.'

She was half sitting, half squatting on the ground in one of the fortress's smaller rooms in which Guaypar's men had put her. They had tied her arms and legs to a heavy log, doing so without undue brutality but without respect for her rank either. The log dug into her back and forced her to maintain a twisted, uncomfortable position. All along her spine she felt a sharp pain and it was spreading through her shoulders too. Yet she forced herself to smile as she said again:

'I remember. You had just been made a captain for having captured Huascar's generals at the battle of Angoyacu.'

A surprised look came into Guaypar's dark eyes. Anamaya could see his chest rising as he breathed in deeply. He looked away from her, toward the patio where his troops were noisily settling themselves. A thousand questions sprang to Anamaya's mind, but she held back from asking them, forcing Guaypar to spit out his long-harbored resentments.

'That night, I told you that you were the most beautiful woman in all of Tahuantinsuyu. I told you that no other woman could boast half your beauty, and that no mouth or eyes could be compared to yours . . .'

Although he stood firmly on his feet, looming over the bound Anamaya, Guaypar nevertheless seemed to be defending himself rather than dominating her. His ceremonial ax, made of silver and gold, trembled slightly in his hand. He was ashen-faced, as though the poison of his memories was polluting his flesh. He continued:

'I gave you more than words: that night, I asked you to become my wife. You refused.'

'If you remember that, then you also remember why,' Anamaya replied quietly.

Guaypar laughed bitterly and said:

'Oh yes, the Sacred Double! You told me, "I can't, because of the Sacred Double!" But now there isn't a single Noble Lord in all the country who doesn't know how the *Coya Camaquen* displays her fidelity to Emperor Huayna Capac's Sacred Double by spreading her legs for a Stranger! A Stranger who disguises himself as an Indian and who is scorned by his own people as much as he is hated by ours! And if it weren't for your protection, then—'

Guaypar didn't finish his sentence. But he made a slicing gesture through the air with his hand, showing what fate he had in mind for Gabriel.

The pain in Anamaya's back forced her to close her eyes for a moment and gather her thoughts. Outside, she could hear noises and shouts: more troops had arrived. When she opened her eyes again, she saw officers on the threshold of the room, waiting for Guaypar's orders. But none of them dared interrupt him.

'What do you want of me?' she asked, trying to mask her agony.

Guaypar paced the length of the room twice without answering, as if he hadn't heard her question. The he stopped in his tracks, stared blankly at the activity outside, and said in a muted voice:

'I said something else to you back then. Don't you remember?'

'You always said a lot, Guaypar. If you're asking me what are my memories of your words I can sum them up in just one statement: yours were always words of hatred and violence, right from the beginning.'

'No!'

Guaypar's rage twisted his features and startled the officers waiting just outside.

'No!' he cried again, squatting down to Anamaya's level, 'I loved you from the beginning. But you, Anamaya, you who were nothing, not even a princess with Inca blood, you who were just a girl from the forest – you rejected me time and again the better to seduce Atahualpa and Manco!'

'So jealous for so long,' sighed Anamaya, shaking her head. 'Poor Guaypar. How can anyone live so long consumed by so much envy?'

'I told you a long time ago, Anamaya! I couldn't have forgotten you even if I had wanted to. Not one season, not one battle passed when I didn't think of you! Every woman I've taken into my bed has only brought you to mind. I never once fought the Strangers without keeping an image of you in my head. And I always knew that this day would come, a day when I could at last make you suffer the same kind of torture that your contempt for me has caused me to endure!'

Every inch of Guaypar's face was tense with hostility, and his barely repressed violence made his words as heavy as stones. Moving with the deliberate slowness of a madman, a blank look in his eye and his lips quivering, he raised his hand to caress Anamaya's cheek. Yet he didn't touch her. He simply let his fingers hover just above her skin, and he moved them over her body from her hairline down to her breasts.

'What do you want of me?' whispered Anamaya with great difficulty.

'First, I want to use you to catch Manco and kill him. Then it'll be your turn. Then I'll take Paullu's place and become Emperor.'

'You're mad as well as stupid,' murmured Anamaya, shutting her eyes. 'You have no idea about the future. Your hatred is leading you to the Under World, and you will never return to your Powerful Ancestors.'

'Nonsense, *Coya Camaquen*! I've never been duped by your impressive words, Anamaya. I don't believe in your magic. Huayna Capac was too sick and senile to impart the slightest power to you. It was all a hoax invented by Atahualpa to dupe the Cuzco clans. And you made the most of it, didn't you?'

'What does it matter what you believe, Guaypar? You can kill me. You can weaken Manco, and maybe even defeat him. But don't delude yourself into thinking that you can alter your own destiny, even less that of the Empire. You will never be Emperor. Inti has already decided what paths his sons shall take.'

Anamaya stared into Guaypar's eyes. Her blue gaze indicated nothing of the pain searing through her arms, back, and shoulders. Guaypar, nonplussed by her calm, stood up and moved away. His face had grown even grayer, and his eyes seemed to have retreated still further into their sockets.

'What have you done with Curi Ocllo, your sister? Do you want to kill her too? She loves you almost as much as she loves Manco, but your contempt blinds you to it.'

Guaypar waved his hand through the air as though sweeping away Anamaya's reproach, but he didn't have time to reply. Guffaws rose up outside, and they could hear the sounds of steel clattering and of Spanish boots stamping on the flagstones.

'Why, I find you already at your task, Lord Guaypar!'

Anamaya immediately recognized Gonzalo's voice, long blond hair, and fine features. The years had inflicted on his handsome face only a few crow's feet around the eyes, while the turn of his mouth had perhaps grown more severe. When Gonzalo Pizarro sniggered, she noticed that he was also missing a tooth from one side of his jaw. He looked at her with the pride of a hunter regarding his prey, vanquished at last.

A dozen Spaniards milled about behind him, each wearing metal helmets and high-legged boots, and with their breeches dirty from their trek through the jungle. Each man rested his hand on the hilt of his sword. The little room filled up very quickly. Sensing that all gazes were fixed on her, Anamaya forced herself to keep her expression impassive, even though the Spaniards' boots were level with her face.

'Allow me to congratulate you, Lord Guaypar,' continued Gonzalo in the same cheerful tone. 'You've done an excellent job. I had imagined that it would prove far harder to flush this precious princess out of this godforsaken jungle.'

Guaypar's expression was set firm now, and he showed no reaction to the Spaniard's unctuous words. Gonzalo leaned forward, took Anamaya's chin between his gloved fingers, and tilted up her face brutally.

'I see that you cannot hide your joy at seeing me again, my lovely princess!'

Anamaya said nothing. But she didn't show a trace of fear when she stared directly into the Governor's brother's eyes – stared with such intensity that Gonzalo was taken aback. He looked away, uttering a nervous snigger as he did so.

'She's always been like this,' he explained to his companions as he puffed out his chest like a male peacock displaying its tail feathers. 'Provocative and sure of herself. It's going to be a real pleasure interrogating her. Lord Guaypar, have you asked her where she's hidden the gold statue yet?'

A chill ran down Anamaya's tortured spine. Everything became instantly clear to her: Guaypar and the Strangers were looking for the Sacred Double. They hadn't captured her by accident. She saw her fear confirmed in Guaypar's hate-filled gaze.

'When Manco is deprived of both you and his Father the Sacred Double,' he murmured to her in Quechua, 'he'll be as helpless as a child.'

'I thought that you had only contempt for my influence over Manco,' said Anamaya, mockingly.

'What does it matter what I think! Manco is the one who believes in your powers, although they haven't helped him much up till now. When he hears that we have you, he'll be terrified. He'll take it for a sign that the Powerful Ancestors have forsaken him. And then I will finish the fight that we began that night of the *huarachiku.*'

'Guaypar!' cried Anamaya. 'Guaypar, you can't! Atahualpa called you his brother. Inti's blood passes through your heart. You are an Inca: you cannot allow the Strangers to desecrate the Sacred Double! You know very well what they'll do with it: melt it down into ingots that they'll carry away across the ocean. It will spell the end for our people. Guaypar! If that happens, no Son of the Sun will ever again stand tall in the light of day! Not you, and not anyone else. Kill me, Guaypar, and kill Manco, if that's your aim. But do not lead the Strangers to the Sacred Double, lest you destroy that from which you yourself were born! I beg of you, Guaypar! I'm not the one asking this of you: the Powerful Ancestors themselves are begging it of you through my mouth—'

'Holà, enough!' growled Gonzalo, raising his hand as though to catch Anamaya's words. 'So much talk, so many words, Lord Guaypar! I'd prefer it if they were in Spanish. What's she telling you?'

'I told him that I look forward to dying,' replied Anamaya before Guaypar had a chance to open his mouth. 'And that I prefer death to helping you find what you're looking for.'

'Oh, my pretty little friend,' Gonzalo retorted, winking at his companions, 'those are words spoken in ignorance. You cannot imagine how much I'm going to enjoy convincing you to change your mind!'

'Lord Gonzalo,' interrupted Guaypar slowly in Spanish, 'let me take care of the *Coya Camaquen.* I believe I know where the gold statue is. Soon, I'll lead you there, just as I led you here . . .'

'Indeed?'

Gonzalo raised an eyebrow, his expression suddenly suspicious.

His face twitched nervously, and he tried to appear defiant as he stated, his voice cracking:

'That is not how I see things, my dear friend. I know that you've found your sister here, Manco's pretty wife. Let *her* take you to him. I'm sure that you'll find a way to convince her to do you this little favor! And when you meet with Manco, you can tell him that this one' – he pointed at Anamaya – 'is with us, and that I'm . . . I'm making conversation with her. I'm certain that he'll pay you close attention.'

Guaypar shook his head.

'What's the point of finding Manco if it isn't to do battle with him?'

'Why, nothing's preventing you from killing him, if you can, Lord Guaypar,' chaffed Gonzalo. 'But didn't you explain to me that, without this girl, Manco is like a worm lying on a rock heated by the sun?'

As the Strangers ushered him out of the room, Guaypar looked back at Anamaya. This time, there was less hatred than weariness in his gaze.

CHAPTER 27

Vitcos, Machu Pucara, July 1539

IT WAS LATE AT NIGHT.

A dark-lantern had been placed at Anamaya's side. She had
had nothing to eat or drink since her capture. The pain racking
her body hadn't let up once, and made it so difficult to breathe that
she had to put all her effort into doing only that. She had quickly
forgotten her hunger and thirst.

Anamaya forced herself to keep her eyes open despite everything that she was suffering. She wanted Gonzalo to see in them
her total indifference to him.

He had returned alone to the room in which she was being
held. He had taken off his doublet and was holding a dagger, and
she could barely make out his face by the lantern's scant light.

'I like you when you're silent,' he murmured, fondling his blade.
'If it takes a while to make you talk, my pleasure will be more
intense, and last longer.'

He sniggered as he straightened up, stepped back out of the
light and slid behind her.

'Did you know that Gabriel's disappeared? He's gone, he's flown
away . . . some say that he's already back in Spain, others that he
drowned himself in the lake.'

Anamaya didn't flinch. She concentrated all her effort into
staying still, denying Gonzalo the pleasure he was seeking. She
said nothing, and showed not the slightest emotion.

'I might have taken you as my wife, years ago. I didn't find you displeasing then. I even spoke about it with my brother Juan. Do you know that your beloved Gabriel led Juan to his death?

Gonzalo slipped his blade between Anamaya's skin and her tunic.

'I loved Juan. Wherever he is now, whether in heaven or hell, I want him to hear your screams when you feel the kiss of my blade.'

He jerked back his knife and cut through her tunic. It slipped away and left her shoulder and one breast bare. Still she remained absolutely still.

'You're strong,' whispered Gonzalo into her neck. 'But now you're going to learn that I'm stronger than you.'

He walked around in front of her again and looked her in the eyes.

'I'm going to do to you what your warriors did to my *compañeros*. But I'm going to do it my way . . .'

He pressed the point of his blade against her shoulder and slid it down to her breasts.

'First, I'm going to remove some of your skin, here,' he said in an even voice. 'First one nipple, and then the other . . . they say that a woman won't die from such a cut, but that it's incredibly painful. Especially if one fills the wound with salt.'

He smiled. He waited in vain for her to react.

'There's another technique that I've seen: you spread a little gunpowder over the wound, then set a match to it. The advantage of that is that it staunches the bleeding.'

Anamaya was no longer listening. She let his words buzz around her like the pointless noise that they were. Gonzalo talked on and on, exciting himself with his own litany of tortures. But Anamaya felt an inexplicable serenity fill her heart and soul. Her fear was lifted from her, and even the pain in her back seemed to diminish. Gonzalo vomited an endless stream of words, revealing all his vilest thoughts and desires, yet he remained as impotent as a child who wants to hunt and kill animals that exist only in his imagination.

'But before I indulge myself in any of these pleasures,' said Gonzalo, picking up the lantern and standing tall, 'I'm going to let my dear companions enjoy you. You will give them your pretty body before I whittle it away. I'm sure that at least twenty of them will find you to their taste before your vagina becomes worn beyond use.'

With a smug laugh, he raised the door hanging and added:

'Of course, princess, you can avoid all these troubles. All you have to do is lead us to the gold statue. You have my word that once we have the statue, you'll interest me no more than does my horse's shit. So, what do you say?'

Anamaya hadn't said a word since he had come in with his taunts and threats. With all the refinement of a princess, and with a drop of sweat pearling above her lip, she said:

'No.'

Anamaya woke and realized that she had dozed off.

She could hear a sound through the complete darkness of her prison: it sounded like something moving through the bushes.

Her arms and legs were so numb that she could no longer feel them. But she could still feel the sharp, needling pain in her back and shoulders.

The rustling grew louder. It stopped suddenly, then began again, slowly.

And then a few clumps of *ichu* fell on her, and she understood. What good fortune that the roof was made of *ichu* and not of those new tiles of which Katari was so proud.

'I'm over here!' she whispered. 'Over here! I'm the *Coya Camaquen* . . .'

Bigger clumps of straw now fell through the darkness. She felt the freshness of the nocturnal breeze caress her naked shoulder. Bound as she was, she couldn't look up properly, but she nevertheless caught a glimpse of a silhouette through a hole in the roof.

She grew fearful suddenly. What if it was one of Guaypar's men?

She stayed quiet and held her breath as the man jumped, supple as a cat, to the ground.

Nothing happened for a moment. Silence reigned.

Why was he staying so obstinately silent?

Anamaya felt his fingers touch her naked flesh. With one hand he found the ropes binding her while he caressed her neck and temples with the other. She trembled, terrified, about to scream, when he whispered in her ear:

'Anamaya.'

She almost fainted. Her heart melted, burning through the core of her being like a lava flow.

'O Noble Lords, thus have You willed it!'

The voice whispered again: 'Anamaya!' She felt strong arms wrap themselves around her. She felt an indescribable happiness rise up and explode in her chest.

'Gabriel? Gabriel!'

'Yes, it's me. Shhh, don't make a noise – there's a guard outside.'

'Oh puma, my puma! I knew that I should trust you!'

'Shhh, wait a moment . . . I'm going to cut these ropes . . . gently now . . . those bastards didn't skimp on the rope . . .'

'How did you know?'

'Quiet – don't be impatient.'

When Anamaya felt the ropes slacken, she tried to kneel and take Gabriel's face in her hands, but her knees gave way under her. As the blood rushed back into her veins, she felt a prickling sensation in her legs as though they were being pierced by a thousand agave needles and she collapsed into his arms.

'Gently now,' he repeated, and she could hear the smile in his voice. He kissed her temples and her eyelids as his lips searched for hers.

But when his hands found the tear in her tunic they clenched convulsively and he said:

'Are you hurt? What did they do to you?'

'Nothing,' she said, smiling too. 'All they did was talk. They want the Sacred Double, and they tried to frighten me.'

'Yes, I know. I set out on Gonzalo's trail as soon as I heard what they intended to do,' Gabriel explained as he tenderly massaged Anamaya's stiff muscles. 'I caught up with them in four days. As

I didn't know where you were, I thought it best to let them lead me to you.'

'It's been so long,' breathed Anamaya, taking his face in her hands at last. 'So long! But I never once believed that we had been separated for ever! And a few days ago, I began feeling your presence near me . . .'

Gabriel put a finger to her lips. They heard someone walking outside and remembered the guard. Gabriel held Anamaya tightly in his arms and murmured in her ear:

'I refuse to be apart from you ever again. Ever. Don't ask me to do it: I'll refuse.'

Anamaya, cuddled against his chest, gave a little laugh.

'I won't ask you,' she replied. 'From now on, we shall stay together for ever.'

And in the ensuing silence, they remained in each other's arms as though all eternity was concentrated into those few moments and their wish was being fulfilled.

Then Gabriel pointed at the hole he had cut in the roof and said in a low voice:

'Gonzalo is so sure of himself that he put you in a very inadequate cell. There's a thick branch hanging over the roof. It leads to a tree beyond the outer wall. We'll climb down it and be outside the fortress. The dwarf is waiting for us there. He'll guide us to Manco at the little fort at Machu Pucara.'

'I thought that was where he was.'

'If we walk all night, we can reach Manco's camp before Gonzalo and his henchmen find out that you've escaped.'

'Yes,' agreed Anamaya, rising slowly to her feet. 'We must hurry. Curi Ocllo was with me. But Guaypar took her prisoner and Gonzalo wants him to force her to take him to Manco. We must get there before they do.'

'You're right,' said Gabriel. 'There's not a moment to be lost.'

Yet he took the time to clasp her to him once again before leading her away.

*   *   *

Emperor Manco wore a gold breastplate over a black and white checkered *unku*. His elongated gold earpieces dangled over the shoulders of his long vicuña cape. He wore the *llautu*, the royal fringe, on his forehead, and from his gold-covered, woven-reed helmet rose the three feathers of the *curiguingue*, marking him as Inti's son.

He was standing upright on his battle palanquin, itself supported by ten men. He held his ceremonial spear in his left hand, and his right rested on the pommel of the sword hanging from his waist. It was the most finely worked of all those brought to him by his warriors. His stare was as stony as the peaks of the highest mountains. His lips and eyes were so still that it was impossible to tell if he was breathing or not.

The officers and troops around him hadn't seen their Emperor don all his finery like that for many moons. They knew that it meant that something important was going to happen that day.

At dawn, when the night's fog was still hanging over the river's cold waters, Manco had given his generals the unexpected order to muster the men into ranks outside the old fort's outer walls as if they were on the great ceremonial square, the Aucaypata, at Cuzco. Intrigued, they watched him closely as he stood in front of them, smiled, and said:

'Last night I learned that the Strangers are sending us an important envoy. I wish to give him the proper reception.'

And as soon as Inti's first rays pierced through the jungle canopy, trumpets sounded, announcing the visitor's arrival.

The thousands of warriors had formed five ranks, just as they would have done had they been on the Aucaypata. Their lines stretched right into the jungle and bristled with spears, pikes, standards, and long-handled clubs. Behind Manco stood a dozen officers, clustered around arquebuses taken from the Spaniards.

They all remained absolutely still as Guaypar approached with Curi Ocllo a few paces behind him.

When they were a hundred paces from Manco, the *Coya* collapsed to the ground, tears streaming down her face, and shouted loud enough for all to hear:

'Forgive me, my Emperor! Beloved husband, you are the only

one whom I love and obey. I beg you, forgive my brother Guaypar. He wishes you no harm!'

Some of the soldiers saw a smile flicker across Guaypar's face. But Manco's officers were already swarming around him. They grabbed him by the arms and, although he resisted with all his strength, forced him to prostrate himself before Manco. A grizzled old general fetched a heavy stone and dropped it on Guaypar's shoulders, growling:

'Pay homage to your emperor or die, filthy traitor!'

'You're nothing but a coward, Manco!' shouted Guaypar in reply. 'You need your thousands of men to meet me, whereas I come alone.'

Manco said nothing. He simply looked down upon Guaypar, snarling contemptuously. Two of his officers held the butts of their spears against Guaypar's neck, forcing him to keep looking down at the ground. Yet he continued to shout:

'You are not your father's son, Manco, you're not his match! If it hadn't been for the *Coya Camaquen*'s plotting and Villa Oma's madness, you would never have placed the *llautu* on your forehead. My brother Atahualpa would never have designated you as his successor . . .'

As he continued screaming, Curi Ocllo rushed to him. Her whole body was trembling, and she clenched her silver *tupu* so tightly that blood trickled from her hands. Terrified, she cried:

'Shut up, Guaypar! Shut up! You cannot speak to my husband the Emperor like that!'

Curi Ocllo tried to cover Guaypar's mouth with her bloodied hands. But Manco signaled with a glance to a soldier who grabbed Curi Ocllo by the arms and dragged her away.

'Anamaya is my prisoner,' growled Guaypar, still looking at the ground. 'She will lead me to the Sacred Double. It's over, Manco! The Powerful Ancestors are with me now!'

Manco stepped forward and drew his sword from its scabbard in one smooth movement. Curi Ocllo's wails grew louder.

'Anamaya no longer has your father Huayna Capac's support,' Guaypar continued. 'But the Strangers have made me a promise. If you end the war and return to Vilcabamba, they will let you live.'

Manco waved his men away with his sword. He smiled and said:

'Stand.'

Guaypar rose, letting the stone fall from his shoulders. Manco's menacing smile grew broader.

'Poor Guaypar. You still haven't learned the lesson I gave you all those years ago at the *huarachiku*. Look here.'

Manco stepped away from him. The ranks opened and allowed Anamaya and Gabriel to pass through.

'Poor Guaypar,' mocked Manco, still wearing that sinister smile. 'Your words echo through the jungle, as loud and as terrifying as a parrot's squawk!'

At that moment a trumpet sounded a long wail. An officer ran up and shouted:

'There are Strangers approaching, my Lord! They are only a hundred sling throws away.'

As Manco raised his sword above his head, Curi Ocllo rushed forward and collapsed at his feet, crying:

'Don't kill my brother! Oh Manco, spare him, spare him out of love for me!'

'You should never have brought him here, *Coya*,' growled Manco. 'It is better that I cut off his head than that he should relieve me of mine. Your brother is fond of the Strangers' steel: well then, let him swallow it!'

The blade of Manco's sword whistled as it described a wide arc through the air. Guaypar's head shook strangely. He had a surprised look in his eyes as his head fell from his shoulders and a gusher of blood fountained from the stump of his neck.

Curi Ocllo let out a horrified, animalistic cry. She clasped her brother's convulsing body to her, his jetting blood covering her face and chest.

Anamaya and Gabriel rushed to her. Manco was already telling his generals to order the men to scatter into the jungle. Utter confusion reigned for a few short minutes as the thousands of warriors broke their silence and their perfectly formed ranks and bolted toward the north.

'Come with us,' begged Anamaya, shaking Curi Ocllo by the

shoulders. But the young woman remained huddled over Guaypar's body. 'Don't stay here. The Strangers will take you prisoner. Come with us . . .'

But Curi Ocllo had buried her face in her brother's chest, and she remained there, shaking her head and uttering little cries like a badly wounded animal.

'She can't hear you,' said Gabriel, unable to prise Curi Ocllo's fingers from their grip on Guaypar's corpse.

They heard arquebuses being fired in the jungle.

'Come on, Anamaya!' cried Gabriel, taking her around the waist and wrenching her away from Curi Ocllo. 'We must go or else they'll take us too!'

And as they ran to the north with the tail-end of Manco's troops, Gabriel turned around one last time and saw Curi Ocllo, her hair drenched with blood, still with her arms wrapped tightly around Guaypar's headless body, as though she wanted to slip with him into the abyss.

PART 4

CHAPTER 28

Chuquichaca, March 1540

THE AFTERNOON LIGHT FILTERED DOWN THROUGH THE thick canopy of treetops whose leaves and branches hid the blue of the slowly darkening sky. Animal cries and birdsong echoed through the jungle's immensity, presaging the coming dusk and plunging Anamaya back into the world of her childhood.

She sat on the bank and watched the river run by. She thought about her mother.

The rumble of the rapids upstream carried her into her dream. She became almost unaware of Gabriel to her right. They were sitting on a narrow stretch of sand amid a tangle of long-dead branches polished smooth by the current. She saw herself running barefoot toward her mother's open arms. It was a recurring dream, and it usually ended as a nightmare: the memory of the sling stone striking her mother's forehead, and of her mother's body suddenly becoming a dead weight in her arms. Anamaya would wake in a cold sweat, overwhelmed by her loneliness.

'Where are you?'

Gabriel's voice was like a cool breeze off the water, drawing her gently out of the daydream of her childhood. Since leaving Curi Ocllo to her despair and her brother's corpse, Anamaya and Gabriel had traveled for six moons by themselves in the jungle, far from Manco and far from the war. Their understanding of one another had grown deeper with every dawn and every dusk. They had reached a point where they could even dispense with words to realize the fullness of their love, remaining simply and perfectly in one another's company, silent yet communicating on a level far deeper than that of mere speech. A mere glance or a slight brush of the hand was enough to fill either of them with happiness.

'I was taking a long trip . . .'

'Was I there?'

Anamaya smiled.

'No. I was with my mother.'

The sun disappeared behind a cloud and a shadow fell upon their faces.

'You've often mentioned your mother,' said Gabriel, 'and I know that you meet her sometimes in the Other World. But why don't you ever see your father?'

Gabriel had never before asked her that question so directly, and Anamaya's throat grew dry.

'I don't know. His face remains indistinct in the night.'

'Anamaya . . .'

Gabriel reached for her hand, and she surrendered it to him before continuing:

'It's as though my mother's death has erased everything that I lived through before. What's left is very hazy . . .'

'"*Only one secret will remain hidden within you. You will have to live with it.*" Isn't that what Emperor Huayna Capac told you?'

'Yes. You remember his words well.'

'To me, they're your words. And perhaps that's the secret. Or perhaps it's something else: while I was waiting for you at Titicaca, I tried to reach you on the spirit plane. I asked the Daughters of Quilla to help me. One of them spoke of you as "*the girl with the eyes the color of the lake.*" She said, "*There's no great mystery. Our Mother the Moon dropped water from the lake into her eyes because the one you seek unifies the beginning and the end of time. She carries the Origin in her eyes. And as for you, you're going to have to learn to see if you want to find her!*"'

Gabriel chuckled at the memory of the priestess's displeasure with him. A fragile smile lit Anamaya's face as a quail called from nearby.

*   *   *

They had taken off their *unku* and *anaco* and were bathing in the river. The silt-laden water felt pleasant against their skin in the warmth of the sun. Two turtles sat on a branch that stuck out of the water, their heads extended far out of their shells toward the sun, absorbing as much heat as they could. Six little turtles sat beside them, completely immobile.

The blue streak of a kingfisher passing overhead sometimes flashed across the river's surface, and the occasional catfish slapped the water with its tail. Butterflies pirouetted above a pool of water on the river bank and filled the air with color.

Anamaya and Gabriel took turns diving under the water, their laughter mingling with the splashes they made. They wrapped themselves around one another like two water snakes coupling as the trail of foam that they left behind them was carried away by the current.

They saw a dugout canoe approaching from downstream, making use of the counter-current that ran alongside the river bank. The two men standing one at each end of the canoe, each of them holding a long pole, often had to duck to avoid the overhanging branches hindering their progress. When they were level with Anamaya and Gabriel, they looked briefly at the couple in the water and nodded before carrying on. They steered in toward the bank, where they would disembark and carry their pirogue beyond the rapids.

Gabriel stretched out on the sand. Anamaya leaned over him and rubbed his back and shoulders with some leaves that gave off an odor both sweet and peppered, and which induced a mild light-headedness. Gabriel surrendered to her long, gentle massage that was as gentle as a caress. Anamaya had taught him that his body was more than just a mass of bones and nerves, a powerful instrument eager to conquer; she had shown him that it was also a source of gentleness and tenderness as well as of potent desire.

Evening brought with it a cool breeze, and Anamaya pulled her *manta* up over them both. She brought her knees up to her chest and cuddled up against Gabriel. He put his lean arms around her, his muscles as finely honed as blades of Toledo steel.

'I feel that the time is coming,' she whispered.

'How do you know?'

'Everywhere, everything is fading. It's the time of signs. I'm frightened and I'm happy. I'm so eager to take you there.'

'Where?'

'Over there.'

'You can't leave Manco yet. You have to stay with him.'

'He's the one who's leaving us, Gabriel. He's the one who's leaving and going into the jungle with all his rage. Guaypar is dead, of course, and Gonzalo has returned to Cuzco. But others will come, and then others after them. We don't know what's happened to Villa Oma, but we know that his war is leading him nowhere. Illac Topa is still resisting, but he's alone, and he spends most of his time on the run. Manco has ruled over nothing but shadows for many moons now. The Empire of the Four Cardinal Directions no longer exists. Vilcabamba is a capital without a country – the Incas have no more peoples to subjugate, no more lands to conquer. They are far from their mountains, far from the land first turned by Manco Capac and Mama Occlo's mattock.'

'But it can't just disappear without a trace!' protested Gabriel.

Anamaya nodded.

'Oh, there'll be a trace. We must wait for Katari,' she said. 'It was he who advised us to leave Vitcos for a while, and it will be Katari who will call us when the time has come. We must trust him.'

Suddenly they were interrupted by cries. They sat up to look and saw children holding sticks and running toward them along the river bank from a hundred paces upstream. They were chasing a wooden object that was floating gently along, following the caprices of the current. Every now and then one of the children would jump into the water and direct the object back toward the bank before another would strike it with his stick, sending it back out into the middle of the river. It occasionally disappeared into an eddy before reappearing and continuing its slow progress.

'It's a basket!' exclaimed Anamaya.

'Let them play . . .'

'Wait – there's something in it.'

When the basket was level with them, some of the children dived into the water. Encouraged by the laughter and urgings of those who had remained on the bank, they grabbed the sides of the basket and dragged it out onto the stretch of sand. Curious and smiling, Anamaya went up to it.

The basket was unusually large and its cover firmly secured with an agave rope. As Gabriel joined them, the overexcited children pulled at the lid with all their strength.

The cover snapped open with a loud crack. Anamaya screamed in horror before the children had even realized what they were looking at.

CHAPTER 29

Vitcos, March 1540

ANAMAYA SHUDDERED WHEN SHE SAW THE ELEGANT lines of the Vitcos palace atop its rocky outcrop. She remembered only too well the empty fortress and Guaypar's terrible surprise attack, her capture, and Gonzalo's threats. Her body remembered the cold touch of his steel dagger on her skin. Gabriel, as though he had sensed her unease, wrapped his arm around her shoulder and shared his warmth and strength with her.

'I refuse to be apart from you ever again,' Gabriel had said to Anamaya when he had set her free. Since then, the full meaning of those few words had become only clearer to her – along with a horrible visual memory that haunted her and that she couldn't get out of her mind: that of Curi Ocllo's crumpled skin in the basket, flayed from her corpse and bunched up in the foetal position, looking as though she had been trampled to death. Her face had been intact despite the river water that had found its way into the macabre vessel in which they had found her floating. What had been most sickening was the echo of the beauty that had once been hers that lingered in her profaned skin.

They had set the vile basket on a litter of branches and reeds and had set off for Vitcos, escorted by a few warriors.

What had happened for Manco's adored wife to be so atrociously mutilated? Who had had the sinister idea of sending her flayed hide floating down the river in the absurd if ultimately successful hope that the terrible thing would be discovered and taken to Manco?

Manco! Even just thinking about his suffering wrenched Anamaya's heart. Despite all her efforts, she hadn't been able to protect the Inca from this horror, and it was impossible to know what its consequences would be.

Despite the great physical and emotional toll that the jungle exacted from those traveling through it, they had made sure, every evening, to submit offerings to Curi Ocllo's soul as it wandered through the Other World. They had burned coca leaves and beseeched Mama Quilla to support her during her difficult journey to the Under World. Once, Anamaya discovered Gabriel with his hands clasped, his eyes closed, and his face tilted up towards the jungle's thick canopy.

'What are you doing?'

'I'm praying to a god in whom I don't believe.'

'If you're actually praying, doesn't that mean that you *do* believe?'

'I'm praying for her, for her soul to find peace.'

Anamaya didn't press him. But she could see a light in the darkness of his grief, and she knew that the Puma and she were closer than ever. Neither the war nor the gods would separate them again.

As they drew nearer the palace, with its fifteen doorways holding up their white granite lintels, Anamaya saw a group of soldiers, spears in hand, coming to welcome them. They had recognized the *Coya Camaquen.*

They passed through the narrow door that led to the top of the hill where the palace and the fourteen buildings attached to it were assembled in a single *cancha.* The soldiers led them in silence, their faces impassive, to where Manco was sitting on a large patio.

As they'd passed through the palace, Anamaya had instinctively tightened her grip on Gabriel's hand.

'Where have you been?'

Manco's voice thundered through the courtyard that was bedecked with orchids, their dizzying perfume permeating the air. A young puma, captured in the jungle, grew restless in its bamboo cage set in an enormous recess in the wall.

Manco ignored the porters as they set the basket at his feet. His eyes, sunken deep into their cavities, stared fixedly at Gabriel and Anamaya. All present – Manco's servants and soldiers, lords and concubines – lowered their heads and held their tongues. Fear seemed to rise from the very stones.

'We were where the Willkamayo and the Vilcabamba meet,' replied Anamaya.

There was an infinite calm in her voice that troubled Manco. He looked away and considered the basket at his feet.

'What have you brought me?' he asked.

Bowing with the submission that every Inca subject owed his or her Emperor, Anamaya approached him. She didn't say a word as she raised the wicker cover.

Manco froze, his mouth agape, as though all the air was rushing from his lungs. He fell to his knees and grabbed the edges of the basket.

A howl tore through the air.

It wasn't a human cry. It was wordless, the scream of a wounded animal spewing out the pain that was tormenting its guts. Everyone present in the courtyard bent almost double, as though trying to disappear into themselves. They often had cause, in these troubled times, to fear their Emperor's ire or distress. But what they were listening to now was unlike anything that they had yet witnessed.

When Manco at last recovered his breath, his whole body succumbed to a series of spasms. He grabbed Curi Ocllo's face and raised it above him, the flaccid hide of what had once been his wife's magnificent body – the joy of his nights – hanging below it. He screamed again.

Anamaya reached out to him. She brushed his neck and felt the tension in it. But just as her fingers stroked his skin, he jerked away from her as though her touch had burned him.

'Manco . . .' she whispered to herself.

He didn't weep. He was like a storm that rumbles through the night, shredding the darkness with bolts of lightning, causing the world to tremble to its very foundations.

'No! No!'

Those were the first words in a human language that came from his mouth. But they brought him no relief, no balm, and they were as inhuman as the involuntary cries that had first burst from his throat.

'No! No!'

All Manco's defiance was concentrated into those words: his refusal to submit, his refusal to lose, his refusal to be taken prisoner, his refusal to give up, his refusal to accept that life could be so cruel. But despite all this he remained like a hunted animal beset by a scraggy horde of predators. He was a mass of flesh and bone still attached to life only by the fiber of his unequalled and atrocious rage.

His people slipped out of the courtyard one by one, going as quietly as possible in the cowardly hope that he wouldn't notice them, sticking close to the walls as they headed for the doors, their faces covered in the sweat of fear.

Only Anamaya remained squatting in front of Manco, who kneeled on the ground still screaming, but less loudly now.

Gabriel brushed his hand over Anamaya's back and left as well. She glanced at him tenderly before looking back at Manco.

'Manco,' she murmured again.

She looked at him. The young Inca looked like an old man. His body and face seemed older and more exhausted than Huayna Capac's had been when she had kept him company in his time of dying. And whereas Huayna Capac had known the secrets, Manco knew nothing anymore, and wanted nothing. He had forced his eyes deep into his skull with blows from his fists and his skin, furrowed with profoundly careworn lines, had turned a lustreless gray.

'Manco . . .'

He raised his head slightly and stared at her.

'I . . . I can't . . .'

Then, with only Anamaya as a witness, he surrendered to the bitter and futile tears of despair.

*   *   *

That night, the courtyard filled with people again. Manco didn't move, despite the rain that began to fall. He had let Anamaya dress him in his finest clothes, and now the drizzle caused the feathers in his *curiguingue* to droop slightly. A silver platter lay in front of him, and a pretty concubine stood by, ready to fulfill a command that wouldn't come.

'Speak,' he said.

The dwarf overcame the fear in his gut, remembering that ever since the great Huayna Capac had found him under a pile of blankets, he couldn't die.

'Two women came to me in Yucay and told me what you must hear, my Lord.'

'Why did you wait so long?'

'I was frightened, my Lord. I was frightened of this secret that is too heavy for me.'

Driven by his sense of his own powerlessness and weakness, the dwarf knew that he had no choice but to speak the plain truth. All those present feared an outburst of rage from Manco, but he only sighed through his thin lips.

'Speak now,' he said, pointing at the basket. 'Your secret is not yours to keep.'

'Governor Pizarro had received your messages of peace. As a reply, he had sent you a mare, a black slave, and other precious gifts. Fate had it that one of your commanders came across the convoy and, thinking that it would please you, he sacrificed the mare, the black slave, and a few others. Those who escaped returned and complained to their *kapitu*, who became enraged.'

Anamaya felt raindrops trickle down her neck under her *añaco*. But she could no more move than could the others.

'He gave Curi Ocllo to be raped by his brother Gonzalo, then by his secretary, and then by some Spanish soldiers, and perhaps even by some Indians allied to the Strangers. When they saw that her thighs were covered in blood and sperm, they were satisfied. He then ordered that she should be executed.'

Gabriel was chilled to the bone, horrified by the dwarf's words. He remembered the Governor's voice and the affectionate way he had squeezed his foster-son on the shoulder. Now he felt sick at the thought of every moment that he had shared with his old tutor.

Manco wasn't looking at the dwarf. He wasn't looking at anyone. His eyes gazed blankly into the falling night, to the snow-covered peaks, to the Apus who had forsaken him.

'Curi Ocllo distributed her jewels and all her other possessions to the Inca women in her entourage. She didn't say one word in anger or resentment. She only asked that her body be placed in a basket and released on the river, so that it would find its way to you.'

The dwarf's sepulchral voice was the only sound in the courtyard.

'One of my women gave her a band of fabric, and Curi Ocllo thanked her and embraced her. Then Curi Ocllo blindfolded herself. As they tied her to a post, she said: "If I have spoken even one false word, let my still-beating heart be fed to the puma. You would harm a woman to assuage your rage? What could you do to a woman such as me? Hurry, so that your appetites may be satisfied." They say that many were crying, even Spaniards. Then some Canary Indians shot their arrows into her and pierced her with their spears, and she didn't let out even one cry of pain during her agony. Afterwards, they lit a giant pyre to burn her, but it was against Inti's will, and her body remained intact despite the flames. That night, my women collected her and put her in this basket, as she had requested.'

Katari slipped through the crowd until he reached Gabriel. He gripped his arm discreetly and whispered: 'We must go immediately!' Anamaya turned around and looked at them quizzically.

'And then?' asked Manco.

'Sage Villa Oma was there. He had been captured at Condesuyu, and they had brought him to Yucay also. He cursed them, although he was shackled in chains, and he called them worthless dogs for what they had done to your wife. So they burned him alive . . .'

Unlike the dwarf's description of Curi Ocllo's end, which had been met with stunned silence, the description of the Sage's death was greeted with groans and curses. Manco raised a hand, restoring silence.

'Even as the flames licked his feet, the Sage called for support from Huayna Capac and all the Sapa Incas, Chalkuchimac and Atahualpa . . .'

'Did he call for me?'

The dwarf hesitated for the first time, and his voice lowered still further.

'No one heard your name, my Lord, but no doubt he died too quickly to call on all those he needed. After the Sage, they burned your general, Tisoc . . .'

Katari led Gabriel away, and Anamaya saw them disappear through the crowd. No one noticed them leave in the confusion provoked by the dwarf's litany of executed Inca commanders.

'They burned Taipi and Tanqui Huallpa, Orco Huaranca and Atoc Suqui . . .'

Manco didn't flinch once, nor did he once look away from the darkening sky. While every other person in the courtyard shuddered with shock as the name of each executed warrior was enunciated, the Emperor seemed to retreat more and more into himself. But Anamaya noticed his clenched hands. Although she didn't know where Katari had taken Gabriel, she was glad that her beloved Stranger had left.

'. . . Ozcoc, Curi Atao,' continued the dwarf, compounding the horror shared by all. It was as if each star in the sky had gone out, leaving the world in a deep and final darkness.

'Villa Oma was right,' said Manco at last. 'We should have destroyed them before they destroyed us. Chalkuchimac was also right. They often showed weakness, yet we never exploited it. We deluded ourselves with false signs, we believed in comets and pumas . . .'

Manco wasn't looking at Anamaya, but his hatred and despair were almost palpable.

'Leave me,' said Manco, lowering his gaze onto his subjects. 'I am alone.'

In a bedlam of clashing spears and pikes, shields banging together, sandals shuffling along the ground, and rising and falling voices, they left.

Only Anamaya remained.

'You too,' said Manco.

'I've never left you. You know that I've never left you.'

'Once, I believed that you were going to help me make the Empire of the Four Cardinal Directions grow as no previous Inca had ever done. I believed, as did my father, and as the Sage had convinced himself was true, that you were an omen from the Lake of Origin, sent to make us aspire to greatness. But you had none of that in you, and the prophecies that you bore in silence brought me only humiliation and destruction. Leave – now!'

'You refused to heed wise words and follow the path, Manco. You listened only to your anger, just as you did that very first day, when you unleashed it pointlessly against Guaypar . . .'

'And now Guaypar is dead, Villa Oma is dead, Tisoc is dead, my beloved Curi Ocllo is dead – they're all dead, and I shall die soon too. Is that your prophecy? Are you a woman sent from the Under World to make me suffer?'

'Your son Titu Cusi lives yet, and you carry the hope of so many others . . .'

'So many others?'

Manco brought his hand up to his forehead and tore the royal band from it.

'My power is like this feather,' he spat, waving it contemptuously, 'brought to me on a gust of wind, and taken away on another.'

He laughed a short, bitter laugh.

'See what remains of my power!'

He jumped up and approached the cage. The young puma was asleep. He considered it in silence. Then he murmured:

'You must grow up first before you can help us, right? You weren't found by chance, were you? Who knows, perhaps you're an omen.'

Manco opened the wooden door and grabbed the sleeping animal. In one savage thrust, he plunged his *tumi* into the puma's heart, then snapped its spine and broke its neck with a fury that had risen uncontrollably from the bottom of his soul. He broke each of the animal's legs, tore out its eyes, wrenched its jaws apart, and turned around, his arms covered in entrails and blood.

'Do you still want to stay at my side, lover of pumas?'

Anamaya was struck dumb with horror. But she forced herself to say:

'I cannot abandon you. Yes, I want to stay with you.'

'No!'

Manco raised his bloodied hand at her. There was little menace in his gesture, but it nonetheless indicated their ultimate separation. Yet Anamaya overcame her repulsion, went up to him, and took that hand between her own.

'I will leave if you wish it. But remember that until now I never once left you. Remember that ever since that first day, when your father Huayna Capac confided in me, I have done nothing but obey.'

Manco said nothing. He withdrew his hand from Anamaya's grip. She didn't know if he had understood her words, lost as he was in his lonely, violent trance. His voice was like that of one speaking from the Under World when he repeated:

'No.'

As Anamaya walked away from the patio, leaving behind the gathering pool of puma blood mixing with the rain on the ground like a puddle of red mud, she thought about how Manco the rebel's entire life had reached its culmination in that one word. A word that he had spoken calmly and from the depths of his soul: *No*.

Katari and Gabriel had dashed through the empty *cancha*, dodged the soldiers patrolling the fortress's bailey, and reached a path leading into the jungle without exchanging a single word. When he felt that it was safe, under the shelter of night and the trees, Gabriel asked:

'What is it?'

The Master of Stone shook his long black hair.

'Your friend Bartholomew arrived three days ago. He was wise enough not to go to the fortress and to send me two messengers instead. We've hidden him in a *huaca* an hour's walk from here.'

'Bartholomew . . .'

'He's a wise and knowledgeable man,' continued Katari. 'We

spoke about the origins of the earth, of its creation, and also about its strangest creature, Man.'

'Don't tell me that he traveled through the jungle just to have a metaphysical conversation with you!'

'We talked about what was before, and what will be.'

Gabriel had lost his sarcastic tone when he said:

'I know my friend the monk. No matter how deep his friendship for you is, he wouldn't have journeyed through the jungle without good reason.'

'He'll tell you his reason.'

The rain softened the usual sounds that the jungle made at dusk.

'And Anamaya?'

'I had to get you away before Manco's rage turned against you. She will join us soon, along with the dwarf.'

The two men made slow progress. Although it had stopped raining, the jungle was sodden and water dripped on them endlessly, as though the trees and sky themselves were sweating.

They came out into a glade in the center of which a wall built of a few blocks of hastily hewn stone stood around a simple bamboo cabin.

Bartholomew's familiar figure stood in the doorway. The gray-eyed monk gave Gabriel a long embrace. He seemed to be trembling feverishly.

'You're unwell, Brother Bartholomew.'

'Don't worry about me. I feel much better now that you're here. Where is she?'

Bartholomew turned to Katari, who pointed to the jungle.

'She will come with the dwarf as soon as she can.'

'Good,' said Bartholomew. 'I need her.'

A break in the clouds allowed the last of the dusk's light through, and the three men spent a moment looking at the brilliantly coloured butterflies darting around the glade. Monkeys created a hullabaloo in the jungle, and the men could hear two vividly feathered macaws perched in the nearby trees calling to one another.

The monk looked fondly at Gabriel and said:

'You've made great progress since I saw you last. There is no trace of anger in your expression and you no longer seem like a man haunted by the devil.'

'Was it that bad?'

Bartholomew touched Gabriel's forehead with his joined fingers.

'Love has taken a hold of you, my brother. I mean the kind of love that nourishes and kindles one's heart, a love that gives, that shares.'

'That's the love that I know.'

The three of them sat down on tree trunks set out in front of the cabin and conversed quietly in the splendor of the falling night. Gabriel wasn't impatient, but every now and then he glanced at the jungle's edge, watching for any movement in the foliage that might indicate Anamaya's arrival.

There was a sense of peace between them, a feeling shared by three men who had each seen much in their lives but who had managed to avoid the emotional and spiritual ravages that the war had inflicted on the hearts of others.

Anamaya and the dwarf appeared only as night finally fell, when Katari was already lighting a fire.

Bartholomew looked at her with admiration and respect.

'Here you are together,' he said, his gray eyes burning feverishly. 'Seeing you side by side, I see what is noble about each of your peoples, and why your union, brought about by mysterious forces, is more important now than all the destruction it has weathered.'

Anamaya had sat down beside Gabriel. The two young people were holding hands and listening to Bartholomew in silence, both sensing the solemnity of his words, and both wondering what he was leading up to.

'You remember, Gabriel, how I wanted you to carry dispatches describing what is really happening here back to Spain. Well, I learned something a short while ago that I can only interpret as a divine sign.'

A smile creased the monk's weary face, as though he was mocking the depth of his own faith.

'Emperor Charles the Fifth is sending a permanent judge to this country. His name is Vaca de Castro and, as far as I know, he's a just and moral man. Perhaps he's even at sea at this very moment, on his way to Lima. It is an unhoped-for opportunity for us, one that may well never happen again. We wanted to go to Spain, and now Spain is coming to us!'

'How do you know this?'

'I know it, Gabriel. Oh, I can hear the doubt and caution in your voice, and believe me, I share them with you. But there are some signs that cannot mislead: for his crimes, the vile Hernando has been imprisoned in Spain.'

'Yes, but surely not for his crimes against the Indians. Most likely they jailed him for having murdered de Almagro.'

'It doesn't matter. The time of impunity is over. Everywhere, in the Church as much as at Court, voices are denouncing the conquest's excesses, and clamouring for justice for the crimes done to this country's peoples!'

Gabriel sighed.

'One needs a faith like yours to hope that it will come to anything, Bartholomew. For my part—'

'Forget about my faith in God, and forget about my faith in the nobility of the Spanish soul,' interrupted Bartholomew. 'Don't you share my faith in Man? Don't you think that this de Castro must hear, as soon as he arrives, something other than the rants of two sides determined to destroy one another and to pillage as much as possible so long as there remains a single ounce of gold or silver in this land?'

Gabriel raised his hands in a gesture of uncertainty.

'I don't know . . .'

'Heed him!'

Katari had spoken so loudly that he startled Gabriel.

'What do you mean, Master of Stone?'

'I mean that his words are true and just. I mean that we cannot spend our entire lives in the jungle, hunted like animals, fearful of the slightest rustling in the bushes, weakened by humidity and diseases, and always at the mercy of hostile troops. That is the life that Manco has chosen, but it cannot be ours.'

'And Anamaya?' asked Gabriel, turning toward the *Coya Camaquen*.

'She must go with you to meet Vaca de Castro,' said Bartholomew, looking for Katari's nod of agreement. 'She must go with you and bear witness that the Indians are not ignorant beasts but human beings whose history, religion, traditions and way of life deserve our respect and protection.'

'And what if she falls into their hands?' said Gabriel, his voice cracking. 'What if this permanent judge is not a sage or a saint, but another Gonzalo? What if they take her and do to her what they did to Curi Ocllo?'

'It's a necessary risk,' said Anamaya calmly. 'You too might be arrested and imprisoned. Bartholomew and Katari are right. We must try.'

'And the Sacred Double?'

It was Katari's turn to speak:

'If the *Coya Camaquen* agrees, I shall take care of the Sacred Double and prepare him for his voyage.'

Gabriel looked at each of them in turn.

'Apart from Sebastian, you are the three people in this entire country whom I trust more than myself. Why, then, am I plagued by doubts?'

'So are we, Gabriel,' said Bartholomew. 'I'm not talking about the certainty of success, but about the chance, however slim, of founding a nation.'

'Over a hundred moons have come and gone since your arrival,' said Katari quietly, 'and you'd have to be blind not to see that the Strangers are here to stay. You can seize this opportunity to ensure that generations to come will have a peaceful future and not a hateful one born of destruction and looting.'

'What if we fail?'

No one offered a reply. But they could all hear Gabriel's agreement to the plan in the gentleness of his voice.

'I'll go,' he said.

He took Anamaya's hand and held it between his own.

'We shall go, since you consider that it's the path we must travel. I shall ignore the premonition of danger that I feel within myself. You will have to pray for us, my brother.'

Bartholomew grinned.

'You're always in my prayers, whether you like it or not.'

Gabriel turned to Katari.

'And you, Master of Stone, don't abandon us.'

'We shall meet again soon.'

'How shall we know it?' asked Anamaya.

Katari pulled some cords from his *chuspa*, and deftly tied a series of knots in them with his strong fingers. He handed them to Anamaya and said firmly:

'Take this *quipu*. When the time has come, it will direct you to where I am. And the stone key will open up space and time to you. I shall be reunited with you as I am separated from you, I shall bury myself while you raise yourselves up, I shall sink where you rise. But together, we shall be in the eternity of Viracocha's way. Now go.'

As Katari set off back to Vitcos alone, without even a torch, Bartholomew, the dwarf, Anamaya and Gabriel set off into the jungle on their journey of hope and doubt.

CHAPTER 30

Lima, 24 June 1541

S EABIRDS CAME IN FROM THE FOG-LADEN OCEAN AND glided on their big white wings over the newborn city. They wheeled around in the air over the city square and the unfinished cathedral, then headed off toward the verdant hills along the coast, squawking as they went.

Anamaya looked up and watched them. The mild morning breeze caressed her forehead. The strange veil covering her hair fluttered gently against her cheek and lips, and she pushed it away with a surprised gesture.

Everything that she had seen since arriving in Lima had amazed her: the birds, the houses, and the immense ocean, which she had never before laid eyes on.

Gabriel had taken her to the top of the scaffolding around the cathedral, and from there she had seen the entire plan of the city. She saw that the Strangers arranged their houses with as much systematic order as the Incas did their *canchas*. Each was exactly the same size and perfectly square. Their roofs here had no tiles. They were flat and covered with a thick layer of earth, and the houses sat between identical courtyards and perfectly straight streets down which the Strangers came and went all day long, as if that was all they ever did.

Like the cathedral, which still had no bell tower and whose nave had been hastily given a temporary roof of planks and straw, most of the houses were unfinished. Some were nothing more than a few beams and some shingles. Plots here and there with no buildings on them yet served as enclosures for pigs or poultry and sometimes even for those strange things that the Strangers called 'carriages', wooden contraptions consisting of a box set on four wooden circles on which they sat and had themselves pulled along by their horses.

The building across the square from the cathedral was far bigger than any other in Lima. Its walls were evenly covered with a perfectly white roughcast, and wooden balconies and louvred shutters painted blue jutted out from them. The building included two courtyards and a bushy garden the size of the ground floor of a house. This was the home of the Governor, Don Francisco Pizarro.

'Do you remember the letter I sent to Bartholomew to read to you, when I was on my way to join de Almagro in the south?' Gabriel asked Anamaya in a low voice, holding her hands in his. 'Do you remember? It must have been seven, eight years ago now. I think it was also in June. Well, this is where I wrote it, just before nightfall. The sun was already low over the ocean. There were no houses then, only a stand of trees ripe with fruit. There were a few huts in a clearing from which children stared at us, flabbergasted. It had all the elements of paradise that one can imagine.'

He pointed at the spot where the river met the ocean in a whirl of yellow water and then beyond it, toward the opulent orchards and then at the still-empty land beyond them.

'Don Francisco very solemnly declared to me: "It shall be here!" The next day, a few stakes were driven into the ground and everything was decided: the square would be here, the church there, over there the houses and the streets. Nothing could have been simpler! Each plot four hundred and fifty feet square and to contain four houses, and each street forty feet wide. And so it was done: the capital of Peru was born!'

There were notes of both pride and bitterness in Gabriel's voice. Anamaya gently remarked:

'It displays the power of the one who has conquered a nation. Emperor Huayna Capac did the same at Quito after having defeated the northerners. His Powerful Ancestors did the same before him throughout the Empire of the Four Cardinal Directions. But all that's over now. We shall no longer build cities.'

She said this with real sadness, but also with a serenity that made Gabriel feel ill at ease. He felt her shiver, even though the breeze off the ocean was warm.

'Are you cold?' he asked, worried.

'No,' she said, smiling. 'No, it's nothing.'

In truth, it wasn't any feeling of cold that made her shiver but the unnatural silence reigning over Lima that morning. Apart from the cries of the birds, not a single sound rose from the city: it felt as though the day was holding its breath, the better to scream later. Very few people were hurrying through the streets. The wind created little whirlwinds of dust here and there on the empty square.

Anamaya had heard silences like this before. Every time, they had preceded an upheaval. She thought of Emperor Huayna Capac's words despite herself: *'The Strangers, in their triumph, will know misery.'* She noticed the concerned look on Gabriel's face and said, with an amused smile:

'It's only that I'm not used to these clothes!'

Less than a week ago, before they had entered Lima and despite Gabriel's protestations, Bartholomew had forced them to put on Spanish clothes. 'Can you imagine the reaction were Anamaya to go into town all dressed up like an Inca princess? In less than an hour, all those gentlemen would be interrogating her about why she had come! And it wouldn't take Don Francisco's henchmen any longer to begin asking her about the whereabouts of the gold statue. No, dressed in the Spanish manner, with her hair curled and her blue eyes, no one will think that she's an Indian. There are already many well-dressed, young, mixed-blood women in Lima. And the same goes for you, too. You've been forgotten: try to stay that way, at least for a while.'

'These damned clothes,' grumbled Gabriel, unbuttoning the collar of his shirt, which he had become unused to wearing. 'I guess we're going to have to wear these disguises for a while. There was bad news yesterday. Bartholomew heard that the vessel carrying Judge Vaca de Castro was wrecked before even reaching Tumbez.'

'Does that mean that he's not coming?'

'For the moment, it means nothing at all. Except perhaps that this city seems to me even sicker than Bartholomew, and that I'm beginning to regret agreeing to his request.'

Gabriel looked at the houses around the square, then shook his head and said:

'No, that's not right. The city isn't sick: it's just stuck between Pizarro's people and those loyal to de Almagro, now dead. It's stuck in the mire of mutual hatred. I don't like this silence, and I don't like the emptiness in the square. I don't like being here and I like even less having brought you here. And I don't like this disease that is consuming Bartholomew. It could well be contagious, particularly for you. I've heard that vast numbers of Indians are dying from the fevers that we have brought with us.'

'Don't worry, I'm safe,' Anamaya reassured him. 'And if your friend would accept my help, I could cure him.'

'Bah! Bartholomew is as stubborn as a mule. He grows worse with each passing day, yet he accepts no other remedy but his prayers! I've never seen him like this, at once so impassioned and so doubtful about his god – not even when he arrived at Titicaca in rags. Indeed, if he wasn't so consumed by fever, I wouldn't stay here.'

'We must do what we must do,' said Anamaya quietly.

'I'm not so sure that we can do anything at all!'

She was about to answer when a sudden gust lifted the hem of her long Spanish skirt. She cried out in surprise and slapped it down, and as she did so, her shawl slipped away so that her long hair streamed out in the breeze.

Gabriel laughed a tender, teasing laugh. He helped her set herself right, and each time he looked at her, he felt stirred by her beauty. Her innate grace was accentuated by the long, large-pleated silk dress that followed the curve of her waist, and by the cambric camisole she wore beneath a velvet blouse, revealing the curves of her bosom.

'How beautiful you are,' he said, moved. 'Sometimes I feel as though nothing can touch you, that your beauty protects you and me with you.'

Gabriel was about to pull Anamaya to him, but he remembered where he was and refrained. A man was walking quickly across the square. He was tall and Gabriel instantly recognized his gait. Before entering the cathedral's shadow, the man looked over his shoulder, as though he feared that he was being watched. His hat hid his face and his hands were concealed beneath an old, faded cape that hung from his shoulders. But Gabriel knew exactly who he was.

Gabriel grabbed Anamaya by the hand and led her toward the wooden stairs.

'Come,' he said. 'It seems that we have an unexpected visitor.'

'Sebastian de la Cruz!'

The brim of the broad hat tilted up, revealing the dark shadows beneath Sebastian's eyes. His face was marked with more lines than it had been when they had last met. But his eyes still had that familiar twinkle, glowing brightly in his black face. The former slave flung his cape over his shoulder and warmly extended his strong hands toward Gabriel:

'God's blood, it's true, then! You're here!'

They embraced fervently, albeit briefly, and Sebastian's happy, welcoming grin quickly gave way to a furious expression.

'Damn the devil!' he fulminated. 'What has corrupted your mind so that you return to the wolves' den? And, what's more, accompanied by a—'

He stopped short, dumbfounded as he recognized Anamaya.

'Damn my eyes, it's you! Forgive this fool, princess,' he guffawed, bowing gallantly. 'Your disguise is most effective. I had taken you for one of those gold-diggers who are arriving here by the boatload. Indeed, I was asking myself what our dear Gabriel was doing with a woman like that.'

'Bartholomew wants Anamaya to meet this judge, Vaca de Castro, when he arrives,' Gabriel explained, smiling.

'If that's the case, you're going to be waiting for a long time.'

'What do you mean?'

'I mean that the judge won't be here until hell freezes over.'

'Those are hardly appropriate words to speak in this place, Don Sebastian.'

All three turned around at the same time. Sebastian chuckled about having been addressed as 'Don'.

Leaning against the post of the door leading into the sacristy was Bartholomew. His skin was pallid, his forehead glistened with clammy sweat and his eyes were strangely dilated. The scar across his left cheek was swollen and looked as though it had been applied with a branding iron. Anamaya went toward him, but he held up his hand to stop her and protested:

'I am fine, my girl. My appearance is deceiving. It's like this every morning, but the fever abates after a few hours. I must simply be patient: the day will come when God wills that I be cured.'

'You've been saying that since we left the mountains,' said Anamaya gently, 'and yet it seems as though your god cannot hear you. I have some herbs here that will cure you in just a few days, and—'

'Quiet,' interrupted Bartholomew. He took Anamaya's hand and brought it up to his lips, much to Sebastian and Gabriel's surprise.

'Quiet – don't say another word, *Coya Camaquen*. I know what you can do; I've seen you at work. But you are in a house where it's best to not mention those things.'

He crossed himself and uttered a little laugh, which set off a fit of coughing. When he had recovered, he waved at Sebastian and said:

'Let's forget about all that. Don Sebastian has more important things to tell us. What do you know about Judge de Castro?'

'He's dead – drowned.'

'By the blood of Christ! Are you sure?'

'Whether it's the truth or a rumor? It's hard to tell. Don Juan Herrada spent three hours last night assuring us that the sinking of Judge Vaca de Castro's vessel was no act of God. The waves and currents had nothing to do with it, according to him. He claims that the Governor sent a ship to sink the judge's.'

'Does he have proof?' asked Gabriel.

The question made Sebastian smile. He shrugged and said:

'We're beyond needing proof, Gabriel. In any case, there's another rumor going around town as well: that the judge's vessel was damaged beyond repair in Panama, and that it will never reach Peru. Whatever the truth, everyone is convinced that the judge is dead, and as a consequence the Pizarros' tyranny will last as long as the Governor lives.'

'So,' said Bartholomew, running a bony finger along his scar, 'Don Herrada fans flames from the embers, knowing full well what his fire will burn.'

'Do you mean to say that Herrada and his followers are plotting to kill Don Francisco?' exclaimed Gabriel.

'At this late hour, it's more than a plot: it's a commitment,' said Sebastian.

'Be careful, Don Sebastian,' mumbled Bartholomew, opening the door behind him and glancing out. 'Your voice carries far, and the unfinished walls of this church will not hold your words in. Let us go into my cell.'

'May I ask what you're doing here?' Gabriel asked Sebastian as they passed through the sacristy toward Bartholomew's tiny room.

'Oh, playing the fool, like you. Three months ago, I decided that I had had enough of this country, and particularly of its inhabitants.'

Sebastian put his hand on Anamaya's shoulder, walking between them, and clarified:

'Its Spanish inhabitants, I mean. Those whose skin remains white despite the mountain sun. Whether they're part of the Governor's clan or allied with de Almagro's son, I cannot condone what they've done to Peru. I continue to see clearly, despite having become a free and rich "nigger". And what I see is entire boatloads of slaves being unloaded here and each slave sold for half the price of a pig or a mule. So I sold my house in Cuzco, with the intention of moving to Panama. I sold it for a good price, I'll admit, and I've bought myself a lovely boat with some of that glittering gold, big enough to carry all my treasure.'

'Panama?' said Anamaya. 'Where's that?'

'North of here, princess. It's the country where I was born and where we were when we discovered that yours existed. But my plans may shift like the wind. After all, who knows? Perhaps Panama will prove itself to be as nasty a place as Lima, and I too will have to discover my own country!'

Sebastian's laugh sounded a little forced, and his eyes revealed more emotion than he might have wished.

'Why haven't you left yet?' asked Gabriel.

'Ah, as for that, it's a long story. My caravel lies at anchor three cable-lengths from the port. But for the past eight weeks, Don Francisco has forbidden any boat belonging to de Almagro's people to take to the sea. He's worried that they'll sail to meet Judge de Castro. And although I did my utmost to distance myself from Herrada and de Almagro's son, I will forever remain "Almagro's nigger" in the Pizarros' eyes. As for de Almagro's people, they never miss an opportunity to show that I belong to them.'

'What do you mean?'

Sebastian sighed a deep, heart-rending sigh. He watched Anamaya as she left through a little side door, the hem of her dress brushing along the stones. He smiled and murmured to Gabriel:

'One almost regrets that she's not always dressed like that. The fashions of Spain suit her like a glove.'

'Don Sebastian,' interrupted Bartholomew abruptly, pushing him into his tiny study, 'we're safe from indiscreet ears here. Let us talk about fashion some other time. Are you sure that a plan to kill Don Francisco is afoot?'

'Don Herrada is not the only one whipping up dissent. The weapons have been ready for the last two days. Even the moment has been chosen.'

'Where and when?'

'Later, when the Governor crosses the square on his way here.'

'Before Mass?'

'Herrada hopes that the Governor will find his place in hell as soon as possible, despite Don Francisco's daily devotions. He doesn't want to allow him the opportunity to repent at Mass.'

Bartholomew shook his head and sighed, as though the last of his strength was draining from him. He slumped into a high chair and closed his eyes before murmuring:

'What can I do? Don Francisco knows that I had something to do with the judge's coming. And he even holds his brother Hernando's imprisonment against me. Even if I tried to warn him about the plot, he would never listen to me. No doubt he'll even suspect that I'm part of it.'

'Forgive me, Brother Bartholomew,' said Sebastian, 'but there is one person who can warn the Governor – he even has an excellent reason for doing so.'

Sebastian and Bartholomew looked at Gabriel at the same time.

'No!' protested Gabriel, raising his hands in front of him.

'Gabriel . . .'

'No, Bartholomew! Whatever quarrel there is between these murderers, it's no concern of mine. The time when I lent support to Don Francisco, and even justified his actions, is long gone. And what's happened over the past few months, including Curi Ocllo's horrendous death, has done nothing to change my mind.'

Sebastian grabbed Gabriel's open shirt with his right hand and almost shouted:

'Why do you think I'm here, Gabriel? Your soul to the devil! Your name was mentioned in de Almagro's house last night. Herrada and his men know that you're here in the church. Someone must have recognized you. And do you know what they concluded?'

Gabriel said nothing. Sebastian released him and hammered his finger into his chest, emphasizing each word as he said:

'They concluded that Don Francisco felt he was in danger and that he has summoned you to save him! You, his follower from the beginning of the conquest, the one he called "son" for so long. Gabriel de Montelucar y Flores, the "Santiago" of the siege of Cuzco! Don't you realize how terrified they are of you?'

'They're insane.'

'No. They're angry and they're frightened. They see threats and traps everywhere. And not always without reason.'

'What he says is true, Gabriel.'

'Of course it's true, Brother Bartholomew. And what will happen, my dear Gabriel, is that if you don't hurry as fast as your feet will carry you to the Governor and warn him, they will kill you along with him. Unless they decide to kill you first, so that they feel safer.'

The door hinge creaked, startling them all. Her dress rustling, Anamaya entered, carrying a bowl containing a hot, dirty brown liquid. She smiled, handed it to the monk and said:

'Come, drink this. Your god will not hold it against you. There's nothing in it that he didn't make himself.'

'I'm pleased to see that you haven't remained immune to the teachings of Christ.'

Bartholomew smiled waggishly. He was about to push the wooden bowl away, but then changed his mind and, with a shrug, took it.

'Since it means so much to you,' he murmured.

Anamaya turned to Gabriel as Bartholomew drank and said:

'Sebastian is right. You must go and warn the Governor.'

'Anamaya,' protested Gabriel, 'I told you before: the only intelligent thing for us to do is to leave Lima immediately.'

'No. Everything begun must be finished. Only then may we return to the mountains.'

Gabriel scowled gloomily. Sebastian leaned close to him and said in a deep, serious tone:

'Please, my friend, I beg you.'

Gabriel was startled by the solemnity in his voice.

'As I told you,' continued Sebastian, 'they're harrying me to join them. Herrada made it clear that if I didn't join them, sword in hand, then my boat and my plans were finished.'

'Then I shall go to Don Francisco,' said Gabriel.

Gabriel had to insist that the door of the Governor's house should be opened to him. It was only after he had announced his entire name – 'I am Gabriel de Montelucar y Flores!' – and then had waited a little while longer that the heavy studded door creaked open. Two peasant faces appeared on top of bodies dressed in blood-red livery and scrutinized him warily before letting him pass.

'His Lordship the Marquis is waiting for you in the garden,' said the younger of the two pages.

Gabriel walked out into the courtyard and saw a dozen other faces staring at him from the gallery. He recognized some of them, old companions from Cajamarca or more recently arrived courtiers whom he had briefly met in Cuzco. But none of them doffed their hats in greeting, so nor did Gabriel. The heels of his boots clacked against the courtyard's round flagstones, and he followed the page down a corridor. He saw Don Francisco as soon as he passed through the low door leading into the garden.

His shoulders were perhaps a little more stooped, but on the whole his tall figure was still upright beneath the long, black garb he wore draped down to his ankles. He wore a gold-studded belt around his waist from which hung a silver scabbard holding a dagger. His felt hat was as immaculately white as his deerskin boots. He had his back to Gabriel, and he held a copper watering can from which he slowly trickled water onto the base of a young fig tree. Old age had marked his hands with large brown stains, which clearly suffered only slightly from rheumatism. His voice hadn't changed at all, and it remained slightly abrasive but with a note of tenderness, as was evident when, without turning around or even uttering a greeting, he declared:

'This is the first fig tree planted in this country. I water it every day, and even speak to it a little. Did you know that plants like to be spoken to as they grow?'

'Don Francisco,' said Gabriel dryly, 'de Almagro's people have decided to kill you as you make your way to the cathedral later.'

Don Francisco didn't react; he showed no sign that he had even heard Gabriel's words. He kept pouring his trickle of water into the base of the fig tree, creating a little hole in the loose, crumbly earth.

'Governor, did you hear what I just said?' asked Gabriel in a harsh voice. 'Don Herrada has been rousing his troops all night. They have unsheathed their swords.'

The trickle of water ended. Gabriel heard someone opening the louvres of a shutter at one of the windows, and he could sense eyes watching them both, studying their every move.

Don Francisco turned around at last and looked at Gabriel with his faded eyes, his pupils like dagger points. Gabriel searched them in vain for some flash of the truth. Although the Governor still trimmed his beard neatly, it no longer hid the lines that had accumulated on his face. And when he smiled, parting his lips, Gabriel saw only three bad teeth jutting out of gums as pink as a baby's.

'No one calls me "Governor" anymore,' he almost whispered. 'Rather, they call me "My Lord Marquis".'

'God's blood, Don Francisco, this is no time for simpering airs! Two hundred men are bent on killing you!'

'Bullshit!'

'You know very well that it's true! Half the Spaniards in this country hate you and are furious with you, baying for your blood!'

'They've no reason to be furious. It's nothing more than spitefulness and treason.'

'They have very good reasons, Don Francisco,' said Gabriel, raising his voice in irritation. 'As you know very well!'

'What reasons? Haven't I been like a father to everyone? Do you know what I do when I see someone destitute? I invite him to play skittles!'

'Don Francisco—'

'Listen to me, Gabriel! I invite him to play skittles. Ten pesos a game, sometimes more, twice as much if he can afford it. Sometimes, if he's a man with a name, for a gold piece. And then I lose. I take my time, because I like playing, but I lose. I always lose, do you see? That way, the poor man is no longer poor, he keeps his honour, I haven't condescended to him by offering him alms. People speak ill of me, and no one lets me have a moment of peace. I have no other concern than the good of all, and yet people spread lies about me – they twist my words, they betray me!'

'Allow the boats belonging to de Almagro's people to leave, and you'll have peace.'

'Why have you come to tell me these things, my boy? And dressed, I see, as the good Spaniard that you are?'

'I didn't come to Lima to see you, Governor. I came to meet the judge sent by the Crown.'

'Ah?'

'But apparently you drowned him.'

'That's a lie! Another damned lie! I offered to bring him here on one of my galleons, but he preferred his leaky boat. But he will come. He's not drowned at all. What do you want to say to him?'

'That it's time to give the Indians of this country the respect that is due all human beings. I will tell him that they are humans just like us, and that the pope shares this opinion.'

'You know the pope's opinion?'

'Do I know yours? I will tell him how you and your brothers inflicted suffering on hundreds, on thousands of innocent souls.'

'And you're innocent?'

'Oh no, I did too, foolishly following your orders. I followed you blindly until the cries of agony and the horrors that we brought everywhere we went opened my eyes for good.'

'In that case, my friend, you will tell him how you and I had to fight those savages to make this land a Christian one. You will tell him how the Very Blessed Virgin saved us from perdition a thousand times, and that without Her nothing would have been accomplished. You will tell him how, at Cajamarca, we were nothing more than Almighty God's instrument!'

'No, Don Francisco.'

'Well then, you will be a liar, like the rest of them! You, whom God favored above all others. Have you forgotten how He protected you during the siege of Cuzco?'

'I don't know what it was that protected me.'

'You dare to renounce us!' shouted Pizarro all of a sudden, brandishing his watering can about. 'You dare to renounce your God, and to renounce me? Who brought you here? Who gave you a name when you were nothing more than a louse crawling on the surface of the world?'

'You're referring to a story that is no longer mine to tell, Don

Francisco. Those gentlemen over there, leaning at your windows and listening to us, who shower you with compliments every day, will tell it, I'm sure. But I can't play that tune anymore, Don Francisco: my eyes and my heart remember too many things that you never even wanted to prevent, too much suffering that you never tried to check, and some vilenesses that you even caused!'

'So, you too are angry with me, my son?'

'That word means nothing anymore between us, My Lord Marquis. What's more, it is useless. I got used to having no father a long time ago.'

'And yet you worry about me. You don't want me to die – you're prepared to draw your sword to defend me.'

'I didn't say that. I won't fight for you. I came to warn you because your death could very well lead to mine, and I still have much to do before leaving this world.'

'Ha! What could you possibly have to do that's so important?'

Don Francisco's bitter sarcasm took Gabriel by surprise, and his surprise restored his calm. He smiled and stepped away.

'I don't believe that I could explain it to you, My Lord Marquis. It would take a lifetime.'

Don Francisco's face closed like the door of some very old, isolated, and dilapidated cottage. The furrows on his face deepened, and his eyes showed nothing but a haughty contempt.

'I'm going to have Mass performed here, in my room,' he announced in an even voice. 'Then we'll see if Herrada and his bums dare to come for me here! As for you, you can drink some juice from my oranges while I pray. They're the first ever to be picked in this country.'

'I'm not thirsty, Don Francisco.'

The Marquis extended his hand toward Gabriel's shoulder, a gesture that he had made many times before, one that coupled a mark of friendship with his demand for submission. But something new in Gabriel's eyes, an expression of determined calm, caused him to stop in mid-movement.

Don Francisco remained like that, his hand suspended in the air between them, his black eyes desperately peering into his 'son's'. Then he slowly let his hand fall.

'It shall be as you wish,' he grumbled, his voice low.

Gabriel was moved more by this evidence of powerlessness than he had been by all the words that had preceded it.

'Be careful not to die.'

The hint of weakness and of doubt that had appeared on the Marquis's face immediately disappeared. And it was with a straight spine and a firm voice that he declared arrogantly:

'A man like me doesn't die.'

'Long live the King! Long live the King! Death to the tyrant!'

About thirty men emerged from an alley and made their way across the square in front of the cathedral. Anamaya had taken Bartholomew to the top of the scaffolding, and though she was too far away to make out their features, their fervor electrified the increasingly muggy air of Lima.

Again they howled: 'Long live the King! Long live the King! Death to the tyrant!', working up their frenzy and waving their weapons about. They had crossbows, pikes, spears and lances, and even two arquebuses.

'They've gone mad,' murmured Bartholomew, involuntarily tightening his grip on Anamaya's arm. 'Are they trying to provoke a pitched battle?'

Anamaya was scanning the square for Sebastian's giant figure, and she didn't answer the monk right away. But before she had spotted the huge black man, a thunderous clamor shook the scaffolding. Two or three hundred men, most of them on horseback and wearing breastplates or coats of mail and all of them shouting, emerged from the alleys that had been empty just a moment before. Some of them had been concealed in the apparently lifeless houses surrounding the square.

'Sweet Jesus,' exclaimed Bartholomew, his face pale and running with beads of sweat.

'Are they so frightened of the Governor that there have to be so many to kill him?' asked Anamaya.

'Certainly they're frightened of Don Francisco. But they fear Gabriel, the "Santiago of Cuzco", and his magic powers far more.'

Anamaya couldn't help but giggle, surprising Bartholomew.

'That makes you laugh, *Coya Camaquen*?' he murmured anxiously. 'I find you unreasonably calm.'

He was interrupted by the sound of a blank being fired from an arquebus, and he almost shouted as he continued:

'Just look at them! If things continue at this rate, Pizarro will be dead within the hour, and maybe Gabriel as well. That doesn't worry you?'

'Don't worry, Bartholomew, my friend. Gabriel isn't going to die.'

'How can you be so sure?'

Bartholomew looked up angrily. But when his gaze met Anamaya's, he realized instantly that she was right – and also that he could never know from whence came her knowledge and her certainty.

He closed his eyes and crossed himself fervently. Down on the square, the mob rushed Don Francisco Pizarro's house.

'To arms! To arms! They're trying to break down the door! They want to murder the Marquis!'

The page's alarmed cry echoed throughout the enormous building and caused a panic in the courtyard. Gabriel saw the courtiers stumbling over one another up in the gallery, more desperate to flee than to draw their swords. An iron fist grabbed his arm and pulled him back. He turned around and found himself so close to Don Francisco's face that he could count the number of furrows leading away from his eyes into his beard.

'Follow me. Come to my room – you can at least help me put on my breastplate. They'll all have run like hares soon enough, and there won't be many of us left to defend this place.'

And indeed, only three or four men joined Don Francisco in the antechamber at the corner of the building, a room that had the advantage of having only one point of access.

'Stand by the door,' Pizarro ordered two lords, each of whom had a dagger in one hand and a sword in the other.

He took off his long coat and said to his ever-present page:

'My dear Diego, watch what they're doing, and tell me everything.'

As he opened the chest containing his old breastplate wrapped in a cotton sheet, he glanced at Gabriel, who was certain that he saw a smile flash across the old man's face.

'My Lord, my Lord!' cried the page. 'They're in! They've broken down the door, and they're in the outer courtyard!'

'How many?'

'Ten . . . no, fourteen, maybe fifteen. They're rushing about, I can't count them exactly.'

'The poltroons. D'ye hear, Gabriel? Two hundred of them out of the square, and only fifteen who dare to enter. They've balls like peas.'

'My Lord! Lieutenant Velasquez and Secretary Salcedo took fright and jumped through the window to the garden.'

'Ah! Two more with nothing but air between their legs!'

There was mirth in Don Francisco's roar.

'In the name of God, Gabriel, undo these straps while I put on my armor. They don't know what they're in for, trying to murder me!'

'My Lord, Don Herrada and his men are coming up the stairs of the inner courtyard. They're fighting . . . oh, my Lord, Don Hurtado and Don Lozano are wounded!'

'It's happening quickly. Shut the doors to the gallery and post three men behind each of them.'

'Impossible, my Lord. Many of their lordships are hiding under the beds and in the cupboards!'

'The damned cowards! May they eat dust and swallow their own bile! Gabriel, my boy, pull! Pull it tight!'

Gabriel yanked at the straps that joined the front and the back of the breastplate. With growing distaste, but also with a calm that surprised even him, he felt as though he was entombing the clamorous old man in an iron grave. Meanwhile, the sound of fighting drew closer and closer.

'Oh, my Lord, his Lordship Chavez has been killed! They've stuck knives into his neck! My Lord, they're killing everyone!'

'The mongrels! In the neck, ten against one! The whoresons! Shame on them!'

The shouts and curses grew suddenly louder, and the door was forced open so hard that it swung inwards violently and bounced off the wall. Pizarro's loyal page stumbled wordlessly backwards, his throat slashed open, and fell to the ground, never to rise again. For a brief moment, everybody was frozen, wide-eyed and holding their breath. Then the cry 'Death to the tyrant!' reverberated through the room.

Gabriel instinctively jumped to the side, and although he had promised himself to leave it in its scabbard, his blade was now bare. The room descended into chaos. There was a whirlwind frenzy of sword striking sword, of men screaming ferociously, their stinking breaths mingling in the air. In the chaos, no one paid Gabriel much heed as Don Francisco defended himself like a demon disguised as a man. He waved a lance about with his left hand as his right whipped his sword through the air, parrying blows and slicing through the enemy. He showed no sign of his age, no sign of weakness. Even his beard seemed to be made of metal sharp enough to cut. He furiously forced back the conspirators, who seemed to be weakening.

'Death to the tyrant!' screamed Don Herrada, pale-faced and shoving his men ahead of him.

'Traitors! Buffoons! Your souls to the devil!' answered Don Francisco.

A second wave of conspirators rushed into the room. Gabriel saw Sebastian's tall figure enter with them, awkward and stiff in the confusion.

'Sebastian!' he shouted. 'Don't stay there! Get out of the way – let them fight!'

Sebastian deflected Pizarro's lance with an awkward flourish, but one of the Governor's men struck his arm. Grimacing with pain, blood already spurting through the gash in his sleeve, he turned to Gabriel, who moved toward him. But Don Herrada, as though he had guessed Sebastian's intention, used both his hands to shove Sebastian forward onto Don Francisco's deadly sword.

'Sebastian!'

Gabriel whipped his sword through the air in an attempt to deflect Don Francisco's. But the Governor had stabbed with all his might. His sword, a veteran of so many battles, found the gap at the bottom of Sebastian's coat of mail. It pierced Sebastian's flesh so easily that Don Francisco, carried along by the momentum of his thrust, stumbled forward into the African giant's chest as he let out a long, quiet groan.

And then everything happened at once. As Sebastian collapsed, Don Francisco's sword still embedded in his side, the Governor froze with surprise. And in that instant, ten daggers plunged simultaneously into him, with ten voices crying as one:

'Kill him! Kill him! Death to the tyrant!'

Gabriel grabbed Sebastian's shoulder and with great difficulty managed to drag him back. As Gabriel pulled the blade out of his friend's guts, Don Francisco collapsed onto the floor not two paces away, his toothless mouth agape in a silent cry. Blood streamed from his mouth as he gasped:

'Confession! I beg you, let me confess! For mercy's sake, let me kiss the image of the Very Blessed Virgin one last time!'

Gabriel felt Sebastian's body convulse in agony in his arms.

'Hold on!' he begged, pressing his hand over his friend's gaping wound and noticing without feeling it that his own hand had slipped on the blade, leaving a large gash across his palm. 'Hold on – don't die, Sebastian. Anamaya will fix you.'

'Let it be, Gabriel. It's better this way.'

Sebastian placed his hands on his friend's, smiled, and looked over at the Governor's twisted face. In response to Don Francisco's final plea, one of his murderers had smashed a jug into his face, ripping his mouth apart and silencing his prayers.

'He's already dead,' breathed Sebastian, 'and soon I shall no longer be a slave.'

'Hold on, hold on.'

Gabriel felt his tears stream down his cheeks and mingle with his sweat as the words came out of his mouth.

'I'm going to ask you yet another favor, Sebastian.'

'Ha! I know you, your grace. You want to win a little more time . . .'

'I promise you, I need you!'

'You've always tended to sob like a woman at farewells, Gabriel. Shut up and hold my hand.'

And as his friend closed his eyes and boarded the vessel that would carry him to his final and absolute freedom, Gabriel never once let go of his hand.

A clinging, muggy fog rolled in from the ocean and blanketed the meandering coastline of ocher rock. The haze repelled the assaults of the merciless sun that scorched the immense desert to the north of Lima.

It took only three hours' ride on horses and mules for the green opulence of Lima to disappear behind them, along with the madness that had reigned over the city since Don Francisco's death. The cries of hatred had given way to demented dances, farandoles of revengeful unleashed emotion. The old Governor's slashed body had been paraded through the great square like an old rag, as though it was some tattered banner taken from the enemy on which to wipe old grudges and fears engendered by too many years of lawless living.

As the Pizarros' palaces were looted amid a cacophony of raucous yells and sinister laughter, Bartholomew pressed Gabriel to leave town before Don Herrada came after him.

'I must bury Sebastian first,' Gabriel had protested, his eyes completely bloodshot.

'It's impossible, they won't give you the opportunity. You're the last remaining person who frightens them. Don't think that they're going to forget about you just like that.'

Then Anamaya had suggested that they leave and take the former slave's body with them.

'Why not?' Bartholomew had murmured, shrugging his shoulders. 'I'll consecrate a plot to bury him in, and he won't be any less at peace there than he would be here.'

And now they were at that place and had dug a grave between two stones standing like two giant, welcoming arms. From two pieces of driftwood they had erected a cross as tall as a man, and its shadow shrouded the rectangle of dusty earth. Bartholomew was on his knees, murmuring a prayer, but Gabriel didn't join him.

With his uninjured hand, he held Anamaya's, and he let the memories come back to him like a flight of dark-feathered. birds. He remembered the first time that his friend had smiled at him, at the inn called the Bottomless Jug in Seville, and he remembered his first words: 'We've discovered a new country.' He remembered Sebastian repeating: 'Never forget, my friend, that I'm black and a slave. Even if things look like they've changed, I'll never be anything else.' He remembered Sebastian tightening the garrote that had killed Atahualpa. He remembered Sebastian saving his life, protecting him, mocking him, unfailingly faithful until the very last.

'He will rest well here,' murmured Bartholomew as he stood up and stared at Anamaya as though he didn't dare look into Gabriel's eyes. 'This was another of your good ideas, princess.'

'Yes,' agreed Gabriel, his face twisted with bitterness. 'For a man who lived his life like another's shadow, he's definitely on his own here. No doubt Herrada and his people have already seized his boat. He will have vanished from their minds in only a few days, as though he had never existed.'

His lips quivered with rage. Bartholomew looked at him with his gray eyes.

'I'll never forget that it was I who baptized him,' he murmured.

'Baptized? Sebastian?' said Gabriel, astonished.

'Yes. He asked me to baptize him shortly before I left Cuzco. But I promise you, I didn't bother examining his faith too closely. Let's just say that he wanted to put his mind at rest.'

Bartholomew wrapped his hand with the joined fingers around Gabriel and Anamaya's.

'I baptized him with as much love as I married you two.'

Gabriel was startled.

'I don't remember any marriage ceremony, Brother Bartholomew.'

'Be at ease, my friend. Wasn't I the first person to urge you to go to her? And didn't I come to fetch you both in the heart of the jungle? I married you privately that day, in my heart, although I do believe that my friend Katari assisted me during the rite. There have been times when words have stood between us, Gabriel, but I don't want to leave you without first having given you my friendship and a sign of divine as well as human love. Will you agree? Will you both agree?'

'Thank you,' said Anamaya, and Gabriel nodded his head.

'No, *Coya Camaquen*, it is for me to thank you. And for much more than you can imagine. I know that, if it had not been for you, the shame and suffering in this land would be far greater than it is. I shall never forget you. And when I speak to Judge de Castro, and when I go to Toledo and plead your case, and that of all Peru, it is your face that I shall see in my mind.'

They shared a moment of silence together, joined as much by their shared emotion as by the touch of their three hands. The heat of the desert and the crash of the surf on the nearby coast enveloped them in a feeling of solitude as immense as the sense of peace they shared. Gabriel was surprised to feel his sadness ebbing away, as though the vastness surrounding him was absorbing him and revealing to him the true beginning of his life.

Bartholomew drew his hand away first. He ran his joined fingers along the scar on his face, a gesture that had become automatic to him whenever he was embarrassed by emotion. He laughed and said:

'As you can see, my fever has been lifted. We'll never know whether God answered my prayers or whether it was the princess's brew. But it doesn't matter. Know that I intend to live for a long while yet!'

And with that Bartholomew clambered onto his mule and headed north. Anamaya and Gabriel stood enfolded in each other's arms, watching him go. She said:

'Don't you think it's strange that he too talks about a sign from his god?'

Gabriel knew to what she was referring. The Emperor Huayna Capac's words were running through his mind as well:

War visits the Sons of the Sun and war visits the Strangers; it is the sign.

The brother's blood and the friend's blood are shed far more than the enemy's: it is the sign.

The Stranger who worships a woman rather than his Ancestors is killed: it is the sign.

Yes, each thing had now reached its end.

'Come,' murmured Anamaya. 'It is time to go to the mountains and free the Sacred Double from our presence.'

'*Never doubt me. Remain in my breath, and trust the Puma,*' replied Gabriel, looking one last time at Sebastian's grave.

CHAPTER 31

Machu Picchu – Caral, 1542

THEY HAD SAID LITTLE TO EACH OTHER SINCE LEAVING Lima.

Each was lost in their own thoughts, reliving the chaos, the passions, and the amazing events that had happened in their lives. Gabriel would stare at the stone ribbon of the Inca royal road stretching ahead of him and imagine that he was bobbing on a choppy sea; Anamaya would gaze at the mountain peaks and occasionally stretch her arms to remind herself that she was only a human being. Any pride that they might have harbored had disappeared: the *Coya Camaquen* and the white knight of Santiago were now only a woman and a man traveling along a road, accompanied by a few porters. Their love required no words: it lived in their gestures and glances.

They had stayed dressed in their Spanish clothes. Gabriel looked at his wounded hand by the morning light. It was slowly cicatrizing, and a strip of young skin, as smooth as a child's, had formed next to his hardened adult skin. He thought about Sebastian. The giant African's death had torn the fabric of Gabriel's soul, and like the wound on his hand, he knew that it would never fully heal. It was strange to be alive after Sebastian had died, thought Gabriel. It had taken so many deaths for him to realize such a simple thing.

They had reached the Apurimac valley, and Gabriel turned every now and then to look at the perfect triangle of a mountain rising over the steep-sided valley up which they were traveling.

They were a day away from Rimac Tambo.

Constant reminders of battles haunted Gabriel throughout the journey: a rushing river here, a mass of fallen rocks there. Beyond them was the unknown.

Yet he didn't feel any need to ask where they were heading.

He knew.

He knew that, when they reached the *tambo*, the porters would leave them and they would stay there alone.

He knew that then they would take off their Spanish clothes, never to wear them again, and that he would once again put on his *unku* and she her *añaco* of fine white wool.

He knew that she would look to the north and show him where the comet had appeared to her; that they would then enter the thick jungle, taking the road down which the sage Villa Oma had first led her.

She would say: 'This is the place.'

Night was coming, and a thick fog rose up and blanketed them so that they were almost invisible to each other. Gabriel couldn't help but imagine her disappearing in the fog, and his fingers tensed involuntarily. He swung around like a drunkard, only stopping when she took him by the hand. He stood still, his heart pounding. She took his wounded hand and brought it to her soft lips.

Katari felt the thousands of drops of water brought by the sea wind gather on his forehead.

Everything receded from sight.

The sky, the sea and the earth were all shrouded in the same mother-of-pearl whiteness. He had to touch his skin to be sure of its texture, to be sure of his own physical existence. His other senses had been all but annihilated, as though the three Worlds had merged into one, as though all the elements had been concentrated into one.

Yet he continued walking toward the north, guided only by the light within him.

He had walked every day since leaving Vilcabamba and Manco's vacant stare. The Inca hadn't even noticed him leave, and hadn't paid any attention to the preparations that had been made for the Sacred Double's voyage. Manco only interrupted his solitude by giving the occasional brief order, and the only sign of life he showed was in the middle of the night, between the legs of one or other of his concubines. What had once been gestures of respect by members of his court had been reduced to signals of fear. He woke every morning screaming at the top of his voice, and he ordered all his soothsayers to his bedside to interpret the dreams and visions that terrified him and twisted his features. His lips had been trembling uncontrollably when Katari had taken his leave of him, as though the Inca had been trying to say something to him but the effort was too great and he had found it impossible. Oblivion was consuming Manco from within.

Katari had entrusted the Sacred Double to his Kolla kinsmen, who obeyed his commands without demanding any explanations and who, since boyhood, had maintained an inflexible tradition of saying very little. They would escort the statue's palanquin through the jungle, making as little noise as an anaconda. They would take it where it was to go, in keeping with Huayna Capac's words, to meet with Anamaya and the Puma, and so to its eternal resting place.

Katari had preferred to leave and travel on his own.

The mere presence of another human being would have disturbed his thoughts, and perhaps would even have led him astray. For almost a month, he had lived with only the sounds of nature, had breathed only the perfume of orchids, their leaves dripping dew, and had conversed only with birds.

He had slept very little, but he always had the same dream in which he knew exactly where he was, despite never having been there before. He had woken happy and full of a certainty that made him leap to his feet and push on ever faster. His strong legs had led him through many landscapes, from heat to cold and back to heat.

He had left the jungle for the undulating plateaus of the *puna*, where the hills receded to the vanishing point of the horizon. He had gazed upon the yellow tufts of *ichu* growing under the pure blue sky. Whenever he had seen a dust cloud, he had known that it wasn't men who had kicked it up but a herd of vicuñas, the ground trembling beneath their collective tread.

Heading down toward the coast, Katari had crossed stony deserts, occasionally intersected by streams on the luxuriant green banks of which sat almost completely naked Indians, perfectly immobile, who watched him approach without uttering a word.

As he had approached the sea, he saw an increasing amount of fog banked across the sky, filling the air with dampness and moistening his skin. Now it was so thick that it surrounded him entirely, and though it obscused his vision he could see everything. It made it seem that the atmosphere was made of wool, and that it absorbed all sounds. But he could hear everything. The fog brought with it the odor of the sea, but he could smell scents from much further away.

'You have arrived,' Katari whispered to Anamaya and Gabriel. 'You are far off, yet you are very close to me. We are together.'

The fog lifted as Anamaya and Gabriel journeyed into the mountains, leaving the Apurimac behind them. They had walked throughout the night and now, in the cool dawn, she was in his arms. He surrendered to the blue in her eyes – the blue of the sky, the blue of the night, the blue of the sea, and the blue of the lake into which he had dived to find her again.

When they had passed the stone columns rising up toward the sky, Anamaya had passed her hands over Gabriel's eyes, making him close them. As they continued climbing the stairs suspended between sky and earth, he was overcome by a profound apprehension. Then Anamaya squeezed his hand, signaling that he could now open his eyes.

The sight that greeted him was more beautiful and more powerful than anything that he could have imagined. It was as though, here in this secret place, a covenant had been struck between Man, the sky, the mountains and the river to build a temple in which to glorify the gods on nature's, rather than Man's, scale.

'Picchu,' murmured Anamaya.

Gabriel's eyes shone, and his lungs were filled with an exalted, serene and altogether other-worldly air. He knew that he was where he was meant to be, that he had reached the end of his pilgrimage. He let his gaze slide over the stepped terraces, over the houses and temples, he let it follow the murmuring water, the smoke spiraling in gray columns from the *ichu* roofs, beyond which he could see a vast square. But his gaze was repeatedly drawn to the mountain looming over the place. His heart thudded as he recognized its shape as the same as that of the rock with four niches in Ollantaytambo, and he saw in its stone the form of a puma coiled around itself, looking down over the city, dozing yet still terrifying and watchful.

There were so many questions to ask yet no answers to be had: everything was there.

Anamaya stood at his side.

'I made a promise,' she murmured. 'I promised that I would never reveal the secret, that I would never pass through this door with a Stranger.'

'Isn't that what you're doing now?'

'You're not a Stranger. You are the Puma. The secret belongs to you. You are home.'

Gabriel felt happy and free, and the young child asleep within him would have rushed down the terraces, would have darted through the narrow alleyways that came out onto the vertiginous slopes beneath which shimmered the silver ribbon of the river. But the place radiated such solemn dignity that he contained his excitement and stilled his soul.

Anamaya descended the steps that led to the monumental door through which, many years before, she had watched Villa Oma disappear. The same heavy wooden palisade was in place, securely sealing the access to Picchu's centre. She placed her hands on it and it immediately swung open, revealing a street lined with low-roofed houses. Three impassive guards bearing spears welcomed them, their faces completely neutral, and wordlessly led them to a huge house with carefully roughcast walls and a steep-sloped gabled roof. Two trapezoid windows offered a view over the entire valley.

An old man sitting on a *tiana* greeted them. His long hair was as white as the snows of Salcantay.

'Many years have passed, Huilloc Topac,' said Anamaya slowly. 'But you're still the guardian of this place.'

The snow-haired Indian's eyes were covered in a film the color of mother-of-pearl, like those of a blind man. Yet when he turned to face them, Gabriel felt as though the old custodian was looking into his very soul. The guardian said simply:

'I've been waiting for you.'

Set in the middle of an immense cradle of hills entirely bathed in a gray light, the six mounds formed an almost perfect circle. The sea was many days' walk behind Katari now, and yet he could still smell its scents. A river snaked along at the bottom of the slope, both its banks crowded with vegetation.

Katari's heart beat hard.

To the uninitiated eye, the mounds were nothing more than piles of dust and dirt that stood out only because they were of a darker tint than the rocks and stones surrounding them. For the Master of Stone, on the other hand, who had traveled from far further afield than the dimensions of his own lifetime, this was the end of the road.

Here, time ended and began.

Katari slowed his pace and let the wind sound in his ears as though they were seashells; a trumpet echoed throughout his body, a horn from before the birth of time that told Katari the legend of what had been and what was to come.

This was where it had all begun. It had even started well before the time when Viracocha had emerged from Lake Titicaca, long before he had headed north and waded into the Great Sea at Tumbez, now desecrated for all time by the coming of the Strangers.

It was here that the monolithic *huaca*, the *Stone of Origin*, lay, marking Man's link to the Andes.

The stones had told him this, and the ancient *quipus* saved from the rape of Cuzco had confirmed it.

Katari drew the *quipus* from his bundle and ran his fingers along the knots on the cords. With his eyes closed he chanted a wordless invocation. A very ancient *amauta* had given him the key. The *quipus* were the memory of the Andes, and he knew how to interpret them. He could smell the scent of the river mixing with that of the sea in his nostrils. His long black hair blew across his face. He headed unhesitatingly for the highest of the mounds.

Its shape became clearer as he approached, and he could see the regular staging of terraces hidden beneath the pile of earth. He was standing in front of a pyramid.

His *quipus* still in his hand, Katari didn't waste any time looking for an entrance beneath the pile of stones. He slowly walked around the pyramid, letting himself be inspired by its presence and that of the cults of past generations who had practiced their rites here.

When he was at the base of a ramp that he could make out beneath the mass of earth, he saw that he was within a vast circle.

His face lit up.

'*Urku Pacha*,' he whispered. 'The passage to the Under World. It is here. Come.'

Katari sat down in the center of the circle and spread his *quipus* out in front of him. Then he lay down on the ground and spread his arms and legs. A rumble from the heart of the earth rose up around him.

Anamaya and Gabriel had spent the entire previous day and night with Huilloc Topac. The old man hadn't wanted to know anything about the wars or what was happening in the outside world. He displayed none of the contemptuous hostility that Anamaya remembered from their first meeting. He was now as smooth and tranquil as a stone polished by centuries of rain.

At dawn, just as first light was skimming over the uppermost terraces, he had led them silently through a series of steep alleyways until they reached a stone terrace with a cave entrance at one end. Dominating it was the statue of a condor, its beak plunging into the earth.

Huilloc Topac set out a few coca leaves, and Gabriel felt oddly in harmony with the old guardian as he helped him light a fire and pour *chicha*.

'Soon,' said Huilloc Topac, his eyes rolling back, his head turning slowly from side to side as he slipped into a visionary trance.

They left him and wandered freely through the city. They encountered young girls and priests, goldsmiths and weaver women. They saw workers already toiling in the corn terraces off in the distance. A heavy black stillness had fallen over the city, the calm before the storm.

They spoke to one another only occasionally, saying very little, sometimes only a word or two.

At dusk, they returned to the house overlooking the valley and watched the evening fall.

Suddenly a voice rose up and reached them, and soon the entire valley was loud with song. The music's beauty was tragic and mysterious, a penetrating, monotone melody in which human voices, trumpets and drums all merged into one haunting cadence.

Anamaya and Gabriel rose and followed it to its source.

The entire population of Picchu had gathered out on the square, below the temple with the five niches. They all wore white *unkus* and *añacos*, and those lining the way to the center of the square held torches. The song grew louder, all the singers' chests rising and falling – a harmony that echoed endlessly across the valley. Gabriel and Anamaya drew nearer.

He had arrived.

The Sacred Double was there, waiting for them, the sun setting behind him.

The people of Picchu bowed their heads. Some had even prostrated themselves on the ground to show their reverence.

Anamaya approached the Sacred Double on her own. When she touched his head, the song ended instantly, and the only sounds to be heard throughout the entire valley were those of the wind and the Willkamayo's rumble from below. Then a prayer arose:

Nothing exists in vain, O Viracocha!
Everyone leaves from the shores of Titicaca.
Everyone arrives at the buried pyramids.
Everyone returns to the place that you have accorded them!

The people prayed slowly. When they had finished, Anamaya spread the *quipus* out in front of her and ran her fingers along the knots as Katari's spirit passed through her. To Gabriel, she appeared more beautiful, more luminous than ever as she straightened and said:

'A long time ago, the Sapa Inca Huayna Capac confided in an inexperienced young girl from the forest. Since then, many have fought to possess the secrets, many believed that they could find them in war and endless destruction. That time is now over. There is but one secret: that the Sacred Double must now find his home so that the eternal soul of our mountains and the unity of all the worlds – this one, the Other World, and the Under World – are conserved for the rest of time, which is itself the soul of our people.'

They began chanting again when Anamaya fell silent. The people of Picchu now moved their bodies in a slow, undulating dance, a solemn, somehow *trusting* ritual. The bearers raised the Sacred Double onto its palanquin and Anamaya led them through the three levels of terraces below the square, where the throng remained, chanting and swaying. They went to a small, steep-sided platform, one edge of which fell away into the Willkamayo ravine and where tunnels driven through three rocks embedded in the sheer hillside seemed to plunge into the very bowels of the earth.

'*Urku Pacha,*' said Anamaya, taking the stone key that had been given to her by Katari. 'This is the place.'

The sun's last rays linked themselves to the *Intihuatana* and lingered there for a moment as the Sacred Double disappeared into the central tunnel.

The chant stopped once more. Now the entire earth trembled as though everyone in the world was stamping their feet, or as if ten thousand drums were being beaten beneath them.

Seeing that the sun was about to slip behind the mountains, Katari sat down and prepared for the last throw of the stone-that-stops-time.

He saw a ray of light hitch itself to the top of the pyramid before sliding down its side like a barely slowed-down bolt of lightning. It landed at his feet, at the spot where the portal of the underground temple opened.

'This is the place,' Katari repeated, and took out his bronze key.

A muffled hammering sound came from below the ground, which began to tremble. He felt its vibrations penetrate his feet and move up his legs, as though a thousand armies were on the march and converging on him. The age-old hardened detritus that covered the *Stone of Origin* at the top of the pyramid cracked, then crumbled away. The wind from the ocean carried away its dust. As the bare point of the pyramid emerged, drops of rain exploded against its granite skin.

Katari raised his face and offered it to the downpour.

The sun had disappeared behind the mountains, and Gabriel had joined Anamaya on the terrace at the ravine's edge.

The people of Picchu slowly walked away and were swallowed by the night. They walked in long, silent columns, leaving the city forever. They left toward the Four Cardinal Directions, carrying torches, and they appeared from afar like enormous snakes of fire slipping down the mountainside. Stars were beginning to appear in the sky.

They had spent years building the secret city of Picchu so that it would be a final resting place worthy of the Sacred Double. His gold entrails contained the entire history and power of the Incas, the past and the future of the Andes, the memory of the glories that they had created and the tests that they had endured. Did those leaving now know it? *Most probably not*, thought Anamaya, *yet they're still proud of the work that they accomplished.* They left without a word, and without looking back: what had to be said had been said, what had to be done had been done.

Anamaya and Gabriel watched Huilloc Topac leave with them, his long, snow-white hair fluttering on the night breeze the last thing visible as the people of Picchu walked into the darkness. Then he too was gone.

Nothing remained but silence.

The air was heavy, and they felt a dampness suddenly against the skin of their faces. They looked up and saw storm clouds, blacker than the night that they were traveling through, shut out the sky. It began to rain. They could make out the silhouettes of the mountains by the pale, silent flashes streaking through the sky. The clouds and lightning bursts very quickly surrounded Machu Picchu like a pack of wild animals, fangs gleaming through the dark. The thunderbolts struck here and there with ear-splitting crashes.

Anamaya instinctively huddled against Gabriel, whose breathing had quickened. She reached for his hand and held it against her belly. As though attracted by her gesture, a thunderbolt landed very close to them, on the highest of the terraces. They trembled together, their eyes closed, expecting a roar of thunder. With a sound like that of dead wood cracking, all the flames in the sky converged into one dazzling sphere. It hurtled down the slope, spitting sparks of molten gold, and exploded into a multitude of blazing rivers that flowed into the slightest cracks in the stone. An acrid, sulfurous odor filled the water-laden air. Only then did the thunder begin rolling from peak to peak and into the depths of the valleys, so intense that it echoed in Anamaya and Gabriel's chest cavities. It fell like sky-fury from above and rose like earth-wrath from below, shaking the entire world.

They weren't frightened.

The storm ended. A fresh wind came up and blew away the clouds, clearing the sky.

Once again the wind rustled through the leaves.

The night was so absolute that it seemed as if the world consisted of nothing but sky.

When the rain ended, Katari traveled through the stars. From the horizon, he followed the way of the *Mayo*, the celestial Sacred River, and when he stopped in front of the hazy cloud of the *Llama*, he smiled. The Powerful Ancestors of the Other World were thanking him for what he had accomplished.

The cloud parted and he saw clearly the *llamacñawin*, the llama's eyes. The two stars twinkled softly. Theirs was a regular, slow, harmonious pulsation – the eternal couple sharing the beat of one heart.

'You have arrived,' Katari murmured within himself, 'and I am with you. Time is unified. We have come from the past and we shall be here again in the future. All is well.'

Gabriel and Anamaya spent the entire night wandering through the constellations.

Anamaya called the Pleiades *Collca*, and said that, together, they were the Celestial Mother of all the other stars. She pointed at the three stars of Orion's belt and whispered in Gabriel's ear:

'The Condor, the Vulture, and the Falcon.'

He flew with her and discovered, outlined by stars, the shapes of the Bird, the Bear, the Snake, and, finally, the Puma.

By the half-light of dawn, Anamaya pointed out Venus to him, calling it *Chasca Cuyllor*.

The world had been swallowed up, and now the world was reborn.

Like a snake, time had coiled up, and time was now unfurling itself.

They kissed for a long time.

Then they climbed back up the terraces and made their way

through the city's alleys to the steps leading out of it. Anamaya led Gabriel up the steep and slippery slope through the jungle to the summit of Machu Picchu where, years before, she had held the hand of a little girl who was meant to be sacrificed, but wasn't.

They climbed through the lush vegetation, their eyes dazzled by the sun of the new day. They passed through the stone doors and looked up, feeling as though the vault of the sky was within reach of their hands.

The wind played with the clouds and fog, and they walked on fearlessly to the rock at the peak. Still hand in hand, they stretched out their arms as though they were wings, as though they were about to launch themselves into the void.

The wind strengthened. The blue on the horizon grew deeper. They still held each other, two bird-people filled with love, facing the rising sun.

Down below there was nothing but rocks and, already, ghosts.

'We're alone!' Gabriel shouted to the wind.

Quietly, Anamaya replied:

'We're together.'

A ROUND 1520, A DECADE BEFORE PERU WAS DISCOV-
ered by Francisco Pizarro, the Inca Empire faced invasion
along its eastern borders by hordes of Tupinambas. Leading
these Indians from Brazil was a European called Alejo Garcia. The
Sons of the Sun managed to check the invaders, who nevertheless
established themselves at the base of the Cordillera and came to be
known as Chiriguanos.

A legend tells that Alejo Garcia, a Portuguese man of Flemish
descent, captured an Inca princess and took her as his companion
before disappearing into the east. Garcia had eyes as blue as
turquoise.

After having first rescued his son Titu Cusi, who had been captured
by the Spanish, Manco managed to survive for a few more years in
his refuge at Vilcabamba. He was killed at Vitcos in 1544 by seven
men loyal to de Almagro whom he had received as friends. The men
were hoping that their cowardly murder would earn them a pardon
from Gonzalo Pizarro.

Along with the most important members of his family, Paullu was
baptized as 'Cristoball' in 1543. In 1545, a title was conferred
on him, and he became a hidalgo. During those dark times,

he was one of the few main players to die a natural death, in 1549.

The dwarf, Chimbo Sancto, most probably spent his old age on his land in the Yucay valley. Of his many children, only two daughters inherited his dwarfism. But all trace of them has been lost in the shadows of the past.

Hernando Pizarro spent twenty years in captivity in Spain. From his prison in the de la Mota castle, in Medina del Campo, he carefully and tenaciously managed the Pizarro clan's immense and ultimately useless fortune, a position he obtained thanks mainly to his marriage to his brother Francisco's daughter. When he was released in 1561, he built a palace in his native Trujillo. He died there in 1578, almost completely blind, having reached the ripe old age of seventy-one – something of an achievement during that era.

Gonzalo Pizarro never changed his ways, and life appeared to reward his undiminished ambition. In 1544, he declared himself Governor of Peru, in open rebellion against the Spanish Crown. He spread terror among his enemies for four more years, especially through the armed forces of his lieutenant Francisco de Carbajal, nicknamed 'the Demon of the Andes'. In 1548, Gonzalo was finally defeated by royal troops and was beheaded on the battlefield.

Manco's successors resisted from their base at Vilcabamba until 1572. Throughout that time, periods of guerrilla war alternated with peace negotiations. In 1572, Tupac Amaru, the last legitimate Sapa Inca, was captured in his jungle refuge, taken to Cuzco, and beheaded on the square of the Inca Empire's former capital, by order of the Viceroy, Francisco de Toledo.

Tupac Amaru's head was nailed to the pillory. But instead of putrefying, it grew more handsome every day, and became the object of growing veneration. To this day, a myth predicts that the Inca will return when his head is once more joined to his mutilated body.

GLOSSARY

Acllahuasi   – House of the Chosen Women (*acllas*).
Amauta   – Sage, learned man
Añaco   – A long, straight tunic reaching to the ankles, worn by women.
Apu   – Quechua word meaning 'Lord' or 'Governor'; also used as a title preceding the names of sacred mountains.
Ayllos   – A throwing weapon similar to a bola; it consists of three leather strips ballasted with rocks, designed to entangle the legs of a running quarry.
Balsa   – A wooden raft made of balsa wood.
Borla (Spanish) or *mascapaicha (Quechua)* – Along with the *llautu* and the feathered *curiguingue*, this woolen fringe makes up the royal headpiece of the Sapa Inca.
Cancha   – An open inner courtyard; also, a collection of three or four buildings around such a courtyard, forming a single living area.
Chaquiras   – small pearls from pink shells (*mullus*), which are made into necklaces or woven into ceremonial costumes.
Chaski   – Runners who carry messages by relay.
Chicha   – Ceremonial beverage; a fermented beer, generally made from maize.
Chuño   – Naturally dehydrated potatoes that keep for months.

Chuspa   – Small woven pouch decorated with religious
              motifs and used to carry coca leaves.

Collcas   – Circular or rectangular buildings made up of
              a single room and used as warehouses to store
              foodstuffs, weavings, weapons, and luxuries.

Coya   – Title accorded to the Inca's principal wife.

Cumbi   – The finest quality of woven fabric, usually
              made from vicuña wool.

Curaca   – Local chief or official.

Curiguingue – Small falcon, the black and white feathers of
              which were used to decorate the Sapa Inca's
              headpiece.

Guanaco   – From the Quechua *huanaco*, an undomesticated
              Andean member of the *Camelidae* family, related
              to the llama.

Hatunruna   – Quechua word meaning 'peasant'.

Huaca   – Quechua word meaning 'sacred'. By extension,
              any location or sanctuary in which a divinity
              is kept.

Huara   – Shorts. Boys were given a pair of these during
              the initiation rite called the *huarachiku*.

Ichu   – A type of wild grass that grows at high
              altitudes and is used mainly to thatch roofs.

Inti Raymi – One of the major festivals of the Inca calendar;
              occurs during the winter solstice.

Kallanka   – Long building with doors that generally give
              onto the square of an administrative center.

Llautu   – Long woolen plaits wrapped several times
              around the wearer's head to form a headpiece.

Manta   – Spanish word meaning 'blanket', but used to
              denote the cape worn by Inca men (*llacolla*) and
              women (*lliclla*)

Mascapaicha – See *borla*.

Mullus   – Shells from the Pacific coast, usually of a red
              or pink colour. They were widely used during
              Inca religious rites, either in their natural state
              or after having been worked.

Pachacuti — A great upheaval signaling the beginning of a new era.

Panaca — Lineage from an Inca sovereign.

Papas — Potatoes

Plateros — Spanish word denoting those metalworkers who specialized in precious metals.

Pututu — Large seashell, used as a trumpet.

Quinua — An Andean cereal rich in protein.

Quipu — A device of coloured strings in which knots were tied. The knots served as a mnemonic system for keeping records.

Sapa Inca — Literally, 'Unique Lord'. The title of the Inca sovereign.

Tambo — Inns set at regular intervals along the Empire's roads. In such places the traveler could find food and shelter, as well as fresh clothes, all provided by the State.

Tiana — A small bench or stool reserved exclusively for the Inca and for *Curacas*, and which was a symbol of power.

Tocapu — A geometric motif with symbolic meanings used to decorate Inca weavings.

Tumi — A ceremonial knife, the bronze blade of which is set at a ninety-degree angle to the handle.

Tupu — A long needle made of gold, silver, bronze or copper, used to clasp a cape, or *manta*, together.

Unku — A sleeveless, knee-length tunic worn by men.

Ushnu — A small pyramid set on the square of an Inca settlement and reserved for the use of those in power.

Viscacha — A rodent of the genus *Marmota*, with a tail similar to a squirrel's, that lives in scree.

**POCKET
BOOKS**

RAMSES
Christian Jacq

The internationally bestselling series

Whenever the grandeur of Ancient Egypt is evoked, there is one name which comes immediately to mind – Ramses II, the pharaoh who reigned for more than sixty years.

Christian Jacq brings us the fictional biography of Egypt's greatest pharaoh – Ramses, the miracle worker, The Son of the Light.

Praise for *Ramses*

'Funny and exciting, full of drama, romance and intrigue and extremely hard to put down' *Daily Mail*

'Historical fact combines potently with a vivid imagination' *Literary Review*

'The perfect epic . . .mixing adventure and mysticism with romance and sex' *Daily Telegraph*

**POCKET
BOOKS**

THE QUEEN OF FREEDOM
trilogy
Christian Jacq

The internationally bestselling series

Egypt is a shadow of its former self. An army of bar-
barians, mounted on horse-drawn chariots, has swept
through the Empire, destroying everything in its path.
Known as the Hyksos, the 'leaders from foreign lands',
they have reduced the land of the pharaohs to slavery.

Only one city resists: Thebes, where the widow of the
last pharaoh, Teti the Small, still reigns. But Teti knows
it's only a matter of time before her men succumb
to the barbarities of the cruel Hyksos. She has an
18-year-old daughter, however: Ahotep. Fierce, beautiful
and courageous, Ahotep will never accept defeat. And so
she decides to re-ignite the flame of Egyptian resistance.
All by herself.

**Book One – The Empire of Darkness
Book Two – The War of the Crowns
Book Three – The Flaming Sword**

**POCKET
BOOKS**

This book and other Pocket titles are available from your book shop or can be ordered direct from the publisher.

The Incas Trilogy:

0 7434 1604 X	**The Puma's Shadow**	A.B. Daniel	£6.99
0 7434 1605 8	**The Gold of Cuzco**	A.B. Daniel	£6.99
0 7434 1606 6	**The Light of Machu Picchu**	A.B. Daniel	£6.99

The Ramses Series:

0 671 01020 4	**The Son of the Light**	Christian Jacq	£5.99
0 671 01021 2	**The Temple of a Million Years**	Christian Jacq	£5.99
0 671 01022 0	**The Battle of Kadesh**	Christian Jacq	£5.99
0 671 01023 9	**The Lady of Abu Simbel**	Christian Jacq	£5.99
0 671 01024 7	**Under the Western Acacia**	Christian Jacq	£5.99

The Queen of Freedom Trilogy:

0 7434 4956 8	**The Empire of Darkness**	Christian Jacq	£6.99
0 7434 4957 6	**The War of the Crowns**	Christian Jacq	£6.99
0 7434 4958 4	**The Flaming Sword**	Christian Jacq	£6.99

Please send cheque or postal order for the value of the book, free postage and packing within the UK; OVERSEAS including Republic of Ireland £1 per book.

**OR: Please debit this amount from my
VISA/ACCESS/MASTERCARD** ....
CARD NO: ....
EXPIRY DATE ....
AMOUNT £ ....
NAME ....
ADDRESS ....
SIGNATURE ....

Send orders to: SIMON & SCHUSTER CASH SALES
PO Box 29, Douglas, Isle of Man, IM99 1BQ
Tel: 01624 675 137, Fax: 01624 670923
www.bookpost.co.uk
Please allow 14 days for delivery. Prices and availability subject to change Without notice